LIFE'S WHAT YOU MAKE IT

SIÂN O'GORMAN

Boldwood

First published in Great Britain in 2021 by Boldwood Books Ltd.

Copyright © Siân O'Gorman, 2021

Cover Design by Head Design Ltd

Cover photography: Shutterstock

A CIP catalogue record for this book is available from the British Library.

Paperback ISBN 978-1-80048-377-4

Large Print ISBN 978-1-80048-378-1

Ebook ISBN 978-1-80048-379-8

Kindle ISBN 978-1-80048-380-4

Audio CD ISBN 978-1-80048-372-9

MP3 CD ISBN 978-1-80048-373-6

Digital audio download ISBN 978-1-80048-376-7

Boldwood Books Ltd
23 Bowerdean Street
London SW6 3TN
www.boldwoodbooks.com

For my wonderful friends Jenny and Arantza...

Give me my robe. Put on my crown.
I long to be immortal

— CLEOPATRA

And everything went from wrong to right...
Then there was you

— KYLIE MINOGUE

work and that, by 7.32 a.m., I was always on the escalator, rising up from the underground, before the thirteen-minute trot to my office.

'Hi, Mum, how are you? Everything okay?'

'I am...' She hesitated.

'Mum...?'

'I am...' She stopped again. 'I am fine... absolutely fine. It's just we've been in A & E all evening... we got home back at midnight...'

'A & E?' I was so worried that I didn't ask who the 'we' was.

'It happened the other night in Pilates,' she said. 'I reached down to pick up the ball and I felt my knee go.'

My speed walk through the station stopped mid-concourse, making a man in pinstripes swerve and swear at me under his breath. It didn't make sense. My mother was fitter than me, this walk from tube to desk was the only exercise I did. She was fifty-seven and power walked her way up and down the seafront every evening, as well as the twice-weekly Pilates classes. 'But you are brilliant at Pilates,' I said. 'Didn't your teacher say you have the body of a twenty-five-year-old?' I'd moved myself to the side of the newsagents' kiosk, where I would buy my *Irish Times* to keep when I was feeling homesick – which was increasingly more frequent these days.

Mum gave a laugh. 'She said my hips were the hips of a younger woman,' she explained. 'I don't think she said twenty-five-year-old. My hip flexors have stopped flexing and I'm on crutches. It's not the worst in the world and within a few weeks, with enough rest, I should be back on my feet. The only thing is the shop...'

Mum ran her own boutique in Sandycove, the eponymously named Nell's. She'd opened it when I was just a toddler and had weathered two recessions and a handful of downturns, but was just as successful as ever. And even when a rival boutique, Nouveau You, opened ten years ago, Nell's was definitely the more popular.

'Jessica can't manage the shop on her own,' Mum continued. 'I'll have to try and find someone for the four weeks. I'll call the agency later.'

'Oh, Mum.' I couldn't imagine Mum on crutches – this was the woman who had only ever been a blur when I was growing up, coming home from the shop to make dinner for her second shift and all the business admin she had to do. I used to imagine she slept standing up, like a horse. I tried to think how I could help, stuck here hundreds of miles away in London. 'What about your Saturday girl?'

'Cara? She's got her Leaving Cert in a week's time. I can't ask her. So... it's just a bit of a hassle, that's all.'

I really wished I was there to look after her. Maybe I could fly in this weekend? Just for Saturday night.

'Please don't worry,' said Mum. 'It's only four weeks on crutches, and I've been ordered to rest, leg up... read a few books. Watch daytime television, said the doctor.' Mum gave another laugh. 'He said I could take up crochet or knitting. Told me it was very popular these days. So I told him that I was only fifty-seven and the day I start knitting is the day I stop dyeing my hair.'

'But you'll go mad,' I said. 'Four weeks of daytime television. Who will look after you?'

'I can hobble around,' she said. 'Enough to make cups of tea, and I can get things delivered and, anyway, I have Henry.' She paused for emphasis. 'He was with me in the hospital and has volunteered to help.'

Mum had never had a boyfriend that I'd known of. She'd

always said she was too busy with me and the shop. 'And Henry is...?'

'Henry is my very good *friend*,' she said. 'We've become very close. He's really looking forward to meeting you.' She paused again for dramatic effect. 'We've been seeing each other since Christmas and... well, it's going very well indeed.'

'That's lovely,' I said. 'Tell him I'm looking forward to meeting him. Very much. Who is he, what does he do?' I really would have to fly over to vet him... maybe Maribelle might be in a good mood today and I could leave early next Friday?

'Henry took over the hardware shop from Mr Abrahamson. Henry's retired from engineering and needed something to do. He's like that, always busy. He's been a bit of an inspiration, actually,' she went on, 'taking on a business when he's never run one before. And he's trying to grow Ireland's largest onion.' She laughed. 'Not that he's ever even grown a normal-sized one before, but he's read a book from the library on what you need, gallons of horse manure apparently, and he wants to win a prize at the Dún Laoghaire show in September.'

If anyone deserved a bit of love Mum did and considering I would not win any awards for daughter of the year with my generally neglectful behaviour, I was happy she had someone. And surely anyone who grew outsized vegetables could only be a good person.

But I felt that longing for home, that wish to be there. Even if she had Henry and his onions, I wanted to be there too. I restarted my speed walk to the office. Being late for Maribelle was never a good start to the day.

'So you're sure you're all right?' I said, knowing that going over probably wouldn't happen this weekend, not with the presentation I had to help Maribelle prepare for on Monday. I passed the only tree I saw on my morning commute, a large and beautiful cherry tree, it was in the middle of the square outside the station and blossomed luxuriantly in the spring and now, in late May, all the beautiful leaves which I'd seen grow from unfurled bud to acid green were in full, fresh leaf. Apart from my morning coffee, it was the only organic thing I saw all day. If that tree was still going in all that smog and fumes and indifference from the other commuters, I used to tell myself, then so could I.

'I'm fine,' Mum said. 'Don't worry... Brushing my teeth this morning took a little longer than normal, but it's only a few weeks... I'm getting the hang of the crutches. I've been practising all morning. Anyway, how is Jeremy?' She and Jeremy were yet to meet.

'Jeremy is...' How was Jeremy? Just the night before, Roberto had described him as a 'wounded boy, shrouded in a Barbour jacket of privilege'. But I felt a little sorry for him, especially after meeting his family last New Year's Eve and seeing how he was treated. I hadn't actually seen him for a week as he'd been at a wedding the previous weekend and we'd both been busy with work. 'Jeremy is fine,' I said. 'I think. Sends his love.'

Jeremy wasn't the type to send his love, but Mum didn't know that. 'Well, isn't that lovely,' she said. 'Say we're all really looking forward to welcoming him to Ireland.'

I really couldn't imagine Jeremy in his camel chinos striding around Sandycove's main street and speaking in his rather loud, bossy, posh voice. He'd stand out like a sore thumb.

'And you'll have to bring that dote Roberto as well,' said Mum. 'He probably needs a bit of time off as well, the little pet.'

'I don't think we'll get *him* over,' I replied. 'You know how he says he can't breathe in Ireland and starts to feel light-headed as though he's having a panic attack. He says he's done with Ireland.'

Mum laughed, as she always did when I told her something Roberto had said. The two of them were as thick as thieves every time she came to London, walking arm in arm around Covent Garden together, Roberto showing her all his favourite shops and deciding what West End show we would go to. 'He's a ticket, that one. Anyway, there's the doorbell. It'll be Henry with some supplies. I'll call you later.'

'Okay...' I had reached my building. If you dislocated your neck and looked skywards, straight up the gleaming glass, my office was up there somewhere on the seventeenth floor. I had to go in, any later and it would put Maribelle in a bad mood and that wasn't good for anyone.

In the lift, among the jostle of the other PAs, behind some of the other equity managers who, like Maribelle, were overpaid and overindulged, we ascended to our offices where we would spend the next twelve hours.

I thought of Mum at home in Sandycove. The end of May, the most beautiful month in Ireland, and I remembered the way the sun sprinkled itself on the sea, the harbour full of walkers and swimmers all day long, people in the sea as the sun retreated for the day, or the village itself with its small, bright, colourful shops and the hanging baskets and cherry trees, and Mum's boutique right in the middle. I wished I was there, even just for a few hours, to hug Mum, and go for a walk with Bronagh. To just be home.

The doors opened on the seventeenth floor. It was 7.45 a.m. exactly and dreams of Sandycove would have to be put on hold as I had to get on with surviving Maribelle. I hung up my coat and sat down at my desk and switched on my computer. My screen saver was a selfie of me and Bronagh, taken last summer sitting on the harbour wall at the little beach in Sandycove. Every time I looked at that picture of the sun shining, the two of us laughing, arms around each other, seagulls flying above us, the pang for home got worse. I should change it, I thought. Replace it with something that doesn't make me homesick, something that doesn't make me think of all the things I am missing and missing out on. I clicked on my screen and up came the standard image of a scorched red-earth mountain, as far from Sandycove as you could get.

Roberto: Have a good day Princess Liv.

Me: You too Prince Roberto. My tree was looking gorgeous.

Roberto: Just like you! Love you!

Me: You too. See you later.

Roberto: Bring home bouteille de vin, please. Tis Friday! And les chips. Mercy buckets!

Sandycove is a village just outside Dublin, but the kind of place where people visit for a day trip for an ice cream or a walk along the pier in Dún Laoghaire and down to the Martello Tower. Or, on rare sunny days, to go for a swim at the Forty Foot, stripping off and stepping into the freezing water and trying not to scream too loudly. Bronagh had taken up sea swimming years ago and had transformed herself into a hardy type who swam throughout the year. She would send me photographs of herself surrounded by a bunch of towel-clad, blue-tinged fellow swimmers.

I had thought I'd spend the rest of my life in Sandycove. My dream was never to go to London, and from the age of sixteen to twenty-two, I ran my little skincare company, Seasalt. It was all home-made creams and balms, oils and soaps. And I had *loved* it. It had all begun when I was sixteen and my eczema had become unbearable, I started experimenting with different oils, desperate to find something to help. And it grew from there. When I met a wonderful local woman with a magnificent garden, I began making my own floral-scented oils and flower essences which led to a market stall on Sunday mornings in Dún Laoghaire. By the time I was twenty-two, Brown Thomas – a huge department store in Dublin's city centre – had agreed to take my range on a three-month trial. But when my lovely woman suddenly retired to look after her husband, and the price of packaging shot up, the business started to unravel. I couldn't fix any of it, and even though Mum tried to advise, I refused to listen, believing that there was nothing that could be done and that I just wasn't cut out for business. I remember phoning Brown Thomas and having to explain that the business was now closed and that I wouldn't be able to fulfil their order. It was all gone and all I was left with was the lingering feeling of failure.

I was at an age when I wouldn't take advice from anyone, especially Mum. And I felt the lingering resentment that had been growing over the years come to the fore. I loved her, but I was also feeling angry. It had always been just the two of us – no dad, no siblings, no grandparents – but Mum would never tell me anything about my father or her story. Everything was brushed away, my questions left unanswered, and even by the age of twenty-two, Mum still didn't trust me enough. Who was he? It was a simple question. She knew the answer and she wasn't telling me. It was the one thing that had created a wedge between us and I wanted to be the person for whom it didn't matter, who could go about my life not knowing, but it was the one thing I needed to know. It had been bubbling up below the surface, and it wouldn't go away.

So I went to London for the summer, but stayed ten years. Now, I still would give anything to know my story, my history, but I had slowly come to the realisation that there must have been a reason why Mum hadn't told me.

London life wasn't all awful. I had Roberto for one, and if I wasn't working on a Saturday morning, we would head off to Portobello Market and return home on the Tube with far-too-large pieces of woodworm-riddled furniture with which to further clutter the flat. Or there were the picnics on Primrose Hill or the trips to Kew Gardens. Or we'd embark on what Roberto would call Arty Farty days and we would head off to a museum where he'd insist on reading every leaflet, listening over-intently to the audio guide and studying the labels on each artwork.

'My mind is a garden,' he'd said. 'It is not a wasteland. It needs cultivation.'

'So where does *OK!* magazine fit in with that?' I'd asked.

'One needs a broad range of influences,' he'd replied, loftily.

Of course, on Saturday evenings he would be working at the club, transforming himself into his drag alter ego Miss Minogue, his tribute to his favourite person (after me, he said), the one and only Kylie. His job was all about fun and entertainment – although he moaned about the make-up which he claimed gave him spots – but I hated every second of mine. Managing Maribelle was all-consuming and all-encompassing with tantrums, meltdowns and hissy fits, the 2 a.m. phone calls, the shoe throwing (navy Manolo Blahniks) and the vodka-induced rages.

Over the years, Roberto tried to disentangle me from Maribelle, but even he was giving up. 'You might be a lost case by now,' he'd said. 'I don't know if you could function with a *normal* job.'

'Says the man who performs as a Kylie Minogue tribute act.'

'You need to get out of there,' he'd continued. 'Before she brains you.' He gave me a hard stare, the effect of which was somehow lessened by the sprinkling of shimmer clinging to his cheekbones. 'With one of her overpriced, under-styled shoes. You're co-dependent,' he went on, warming to his theme. 'It's not healthy.' He gave me another hard stare. 'Where's your crown, Liv? You had better find it and put it on! You can't work for a sociopath all your life.'

All I could do was agree. And yet I was still here. But life for Roberto was always more adventurous than me. Last year, he had a wild and passionate fling with a sexy Spaniard. Felipe was on a round-the-world gap-year trip, his time in London radically extended because of Roberto. For months, Felipe became our flat-mate, making the bathroom permanently inaccessible as he spent hours bathing and showering, and replenishing food supplies became quite a struggle as he soon discovered the delights of cereal and toast with Irish butter. Felipe was five foot one with the appetite of an elephant. But then came the bombshell. He announced, 'I have to go to Buenos Aires!'

'Buenos Aires?' Roberto was shocked into silence.

'And Christchurch and Singapore and... back to London?'

Roberto took it as a very personal rejection and told Felipe never to bother contacting him through any means ever again. But not one to let anything break his stride, not even heartbreak, the night Felipe left, Roberto took to the stage as Miss Minogue, putting in the kind of performance you wish Kylie herself had witnessed. It only made me love Roberto more, and I wished I had half his strength. And he was right, when it came to wearing crowns and knowing your worth, he was born in a tiara. I hadn't quite located mine.

* * *

I looked at the clock: 7.59 a.m. No sign of Maribelle. Maybe I had forgotten about a breakfast meeting? But I knew I hadn't as one thing that helped me survive this job – and *her* – was being super-organised, always checking and double-checking every appointment in her schedule. Keeping away the constant threat was part of my job. Except... she wasn't here.

I started to worry. Despite everything, Maribelle was always at her desk at 7.45 a.m. every morning. She'd never missed a day, even when we'd arrived back from New York that time and she'd nearly got us thrown off the flight, or the evening after her divorce hearing from Doug – she'd rung me crying, but had turned up the next morning in brisk mode as though nothing had happened. So where was she this morning?

My phone rang and I grabbed at it. 'Hello?'

'Hello.' It was an exceptionally posh woman's voice. 'Is that Olivia?'

'It is,' I said, sitting at my desk in my little corner outside my boss Maribelle's office which was the size of the entire flat I shared with Roberto in Hackney.

'I hope you don't mind me calling you so early. I took your number from Jeremy's phone...'

'Who is this, please?'

'I'm Cassandra. Jeremy and I are old, old friends,' she said. 'I'm sure he's told you about me.' Cassandra was Jeremy's ex-girl-friend who had finished with him the year after she'd met some hedge fund manager and decided that Jeremy, being a mere investment banker, wasn't quite enough.

'No... not a word.' He'd claimed to be over her, but he hadn't actually stopped going on about her – the things they'd done, the Barry Manilow song she used to sing as her party piece, the fact that she once parked on the double yellows outside Harrods because she needed some kind of special cheese for a dinner party, the trip to Tuscany where she'd roasted an entire hog she'd bought in a market and the fact that she once spoke perfect Portuguese to José Mourinho when they met him in a pub one evening. 'She sounds,' Roberto had said, when I confessed I was feeling a little put out by the mentions, 'utterly tiresome. Like Princess Margaret crossed with Violet Elizabeth Bott.'

'We used to live together in Fulham?' said Cassandra, sounding slightly irritated and surprised. 'For five years?'

'No, sorry.'

'Well, I suppose it doesn't matter, but the reason I'm calling is because I'm a girl's girl and I thought you should know that Jeremy and I *met up* last night... in fact, I'm still here in his flat. He's just in the shower. We met at the wedding and... well, he never mentioned you until this morning.'

'Okay...' I tried to take it all in.

'If I'd known about you,' went on Cassandra, 'then obviously we wouldn't have...' She paused. '*Done* anything.'

Oh God.

'I love your accent,' she said. 'I just love the Irish. They are so friendly!'

I really didn't feel like being friendly. How long would it be before I could end this awful conversation and then dwell on what she had said?

'Do you know the Fitzgeralds?' she went on. 'The Glin Castle Fitzgeralds? I was there for a wedding last year.'

'No,' I said. 'I don't.'

'Oh...' she trilled. 'That's a shame. They are such absolutely lovely, lovely, *lovely* people. So down to earth.' Cassandra pronounced the word 'earth' as though she was regurgitating air.

'Okay then, thanks...'

'I thought you should know,' she said. 'Being a girl's girl...'

'Yes, thanks for letting me know.' I put the phone done.

Firmly. I had stayed with Jeremy for months because I felt sorry for him and then he went and did this.

I dialled Roberto, he'd know what to do.

'Liv?' The sound of the TV was turned down. 'Just muting *Good Morning Britain*. Susanna is wearing what can only be described as mother of the bride of Frankenstein…'

I wished I was back in the flat right now. 'Jeremy and his ex-girlfriend slept together last night.'

'How do you know?' I could imagine him narrowing his eyes in that way he did when he was feeling particularly overprotective of me.

'She called *me*. She got my number from Jeremy's phone… what's my next move?'

Roberto thought for a moment. 'Right, you call Jeremy and tell him what you think of him,' he said. 'You, in no uncertain terms, tell him what you would like to do to the softer, more delicate parts of his body. You eviscerate him. Got it?'

'Maybe I will just tell him that I don't want to go out with him any more?'

'Where are we?' said Roberto. 'Junior school? No, this is your chance for a "scene". You've earned one.' He sounded almost delighted.

'A scene?'

'Yes! Where you get to be all dramatic and you can shout and stomp around and say terrible things… I'm quite jealous, actually. My last scene was the night before Felipe left.' His voice wobbled, which was my cue to bolster him. Roberto had ordered me to stop him from dwelling on Felipe under any circumstances. He was going to get over this heartbreak in express time.

'Don't think about him!' I said quickly. 'Snap out of it!'

'Thanks,' he said, his voice back to normal. 'So, back to Jeremy the worm. Call him and dump him. Make that scene! Add

a few bon mots, a few pithy remarks. But, most importantly, Liv,
you're rid of the lame duck. Run free, my pretty one! Run for the
wind!'

* * *

The scene with Jeremy – which I knew would never be up to
Roberto's standards – would have to wait, however, because it was
getting on for 8.45 a.m. and there was still no sign of Maribelle. I
began repeatedly calling her mobile.

By 9.15 a.m. I had gone to the drastic length of calling her ex-
husband. After working for Maribelle for eight years, there was
no way I would call us friends, or even friendly, and she remained
unknowable and often unlikable, but I had been involved in her
life in an intimate way. I'd organised her fiftieth birthday in Posi-
tano, I looked after the buying of presents for her son, Sasha, and
organised getting him to and from school, and it was me who'd
filed all her divorce papers last year.

'Ah, Olivia,' Doug said, sounding wearier than usual. 'I
thought that perhaps HR might have called you by now. But then
I seem to spend my life thinking people are doing what they
ought and then being bitterly disappointed.' He sighed heavily.
'Well, suffice to say, Maribelle was stopped by the police while
driving under the influence last night. And as it is the third such
auspicious event this year... and where are we? The end of May?
Well, it's not bad-going. Impressive really. She's obviously determined to make it a record year. Except this time, Sasha was in the
car.'

'Oh my God.'

'Exactly.'

'So, where is she?'

'Still at Her Majesty's pleasure, or rather the cells of Marylebone police station,' he said. 'I've been asked to go and pick her up.' He let out another sigh. 'Anyway, I believe your esteemed workplace has decided that Maribelle goes to a rehabilitation centre. It seems she's too valuable an equities strategist just to fire. When there's money to be made, it's amazing how solutions and sticking plasters can be found.' He paused. 'So, there you have it.'

I'd known about Maribelle's drinking for years, but now it was public, my heart went out to her. The fact that her bosses, the board who ran this equities company, knew her deepest and darkest would be awful for her. Worrying about Maribelle had displaced the scene with Jeremy and Cassandra. They were welcome to each other, I thought. Roberto was right, I was free as a bird. Unlike Maribelle.

* * *

At 11 a.m., Valerie from HR called me. 'Olivia? I take it you've heard? Now, we want to keep it quiet, obviously. We can't let any competitors know that one of our finest has something of a problem. Hush-hush, you know how it is. We're saying there's been a bereavement and she is taking time out to be at her mother's side. Does she have a mother? No one seems to know. Do you?'

'Um... she must do,' I said. 'Or at least one somewhere along the way.'

'Anyway,' went on Valerie, 'it's five weeks in an exceedingly swish clinic. Can you use the word swish when referring to rehab? Anyway, it looks lovely on the website. The Cotswolds, obviously. More like a spa really. I wouldn't mind checking myself in!' She gave a little laugh. 'I'll have to hit the cooking sherry, won't I?' Her voice turned serious again. 'No, it's very sad, that's what it is. Did you know about the... vodka?'

'I'm not sure.' *Of course* I knew about the vodka, but I'd been covering for Maribelle for years, watching her jealously guard her 'water' bottle in the same way Gollum minded the ring.

'Or the Tia Maria in her coffees?'

'Really?' Now, *this* I wasn't aware of. It sounded like something Roberto would insist we drank on Christmas morning.

'And the car accident last year?'

'She had cut her face...'

'Under the influence, I'm afraid. There were rumours, obviously. But she is such a talented woman – an equities strategic genius, really. The general consensus, according to our grapevine, was that Maribelle would conquer her demons herself. But... obviously not.'

I wondered what it meant for me, while Maribelle was baring her soul in this Cotswolds rehab, would I be twiddling my thumbs? Or would I be redeployed to one of the other strategists? Which maybe wouldn't be a bad thing... it might be quite nice to work for someone who was easier than Maribelle. I felt a pang of guilt for being so disloyal. Maribelle may have won awards for being a truly awful person to work for. But she was *my* truly awful person to work for. And there she was in rehab. On her own. Probably scared and lonely, *sans* mobile phone, her only comfort a towelling dressing gown.

'So,' went on Valerie, 'suffice to say, you have a month off, longer if you want to tag on some holiday leave? If that's all right with you? Obviously, full pay. Take time to rest and recoup. Mr Edwards is aware of Maribelle's slightly more eccentric managerial style and says we won't redeploy you, but we will see you back here when Maribelle is released from her... confinement.'

My silence in return for time off. 'Full pay?' I checked. 'A month off?'

'Mr Edwards does, however, hope that not a word will be breathed to anyone in the industry.'

'I promise...'

Breathe a word? I could barely *breathe* with excitement. I could already feel a weight being lifted off my shoulders. I was free. Well, five whole weeks of free, but still free. It was like that feeling on the last day of summer term when you had weeks and weeks stretching into the future.

'That sounds fine, Valerie,' I said, actually punching the air. And I knew exactly where I was going.

3

Me: Cassandra called me and told me what happened.

Jeremy: Don't believe a word she says. Cassandra is a well-known liar and fantasist.

Me: I believe her though.

Jeremy: Well, you shouldn't.

Me: …

Jeremy: Do you want to meet? I can come and see you after work? Grapeshots at 6?

Me: Meeting Jeremy after work.

Roberto: Can I be in the audience?

Me: It's not going to take long. Will be home later.

Roberto: I'll have the vino ready. BREAK A LEG LIV! LOVE YOU!

Me: Love you too!

Roberto would have been disappointed with the scene between Jeremy and me. It lacked all drama when Jeremy realised there was no wriggling out of this. He blamed it on Cassandra. 'It's all her fault,' he said. 'She's needy and vulnerable and I felt sorry for her. But it's over and it won't happen again.'

Jeremy was a handsome man, blond hair and a gym-honed physique but with a soft and squidgy face, resembling the boarding-school tapioca pudding on which he'd been raised. Once, it had made him endearing, but this evening he looked like an angry teddy bear. I wondered what I'd ever seen in him. I had felt sorry for him when he'd told me about his school days and then my empathy was even further magnified once I'd met his awful parents. But feeling sorry for someone was no reason to be in a relationship. Cassandra, I thought, had done me a favour. Without her, I might have wasted more months with Jeremy. I was already tasting freedom. Sitting in this dark bar with the summer evening stretching ahead, I thought of Sandycove and what it would be like right now. There was a pub that Bronagh and I used to go to, The Island, which had a small courtyard at the back, and on summer evenings the whole village would seem to be there, fresh from swims, their hair still wet, noise and laughter in the air.

'Can't we just forget about it?' said Jeremy, turning his tapioca mouth into a little pleading smile. 'We're good together. We complement each other. I'm a leader, you're the follower.' He was looking increasingly confident.

'Follower?' This conversation wasn't going quite the way I had imagined. Roberto had sent me off with the kind of instructions some barbarian might have imparted to his second-in-command, but this was less West End show and more end-of-the-pier summer special.

'You can't have two leaders or two followers,' went on Jeremy, in his smooth public-school drawl, 'didn't you know?' He looked at me fondly, as though I was slow on the uptake. 'We suit each other. Follower, leader. Leader, follower.' He pointed from him to me and back again.

'Can we get back to Cassandra?'

'Do we have to?' he whined.

'No, we don't *have* to,' I said. 'But...' I thought of Roberto. And I thought of Ireland. 'I've got some time off. A month... and I'm going home.'

'Home?' He looked confused. 'As in Hackney?'

'No, home as in Dublin,' I said. 'Sandycove. My mother has had a Pilates-related accident and she needs some help in the shop.' And that was it, my subconscious had organised everything. I felt an excitement I hadn't felt in years. Four weeks at home, looking after my mum, working in Nell's, making up for being a less than dutiful daughter, and making amends for being a little difficult and resentful over the years.

'Her *shop*?'

I'd told him about it many times. 'Her clothes boutique, Nell's...'

'And you're going to what?' He looked confused.

'I'm going to work there. I can make sure she's all right and do whatever she needs.'

'Doesn't she have someone else who can do that?'

'She does, actually,' I said. 'But I want to help as well... and...'

Jeremy was looking totally put out, as though this was all about him. 'But what,' he said, 'about your job? Your *proper* job. Here in London.'

'I'm on sabbatical,' I said. 'Time off for good behaviour.'

'Ah! I see. You're punishing me. You're doing all this just to teach me a lesson. I've said I'm sorry! How many times do I have to say it? It's because I went to boarding school,' he said. 'I've told you I'm trying to learn how to be more emotionally available.'

I stood up, thinking how exhausting scenes were. I didn't know how Roberto managed all of his. 'I'm going to Ireland,' I said. 'I'm going tomorrow morning and... well... goodbye. Say hi to Cassandra.'

'Be like that, then!' he shouted, making me realise that I didn't need time to think about it and I would be like that, then. He grabbed my hand.

'Jeremy,' I said. 'I think it's best if we just go our separate ways.'

'What, now or forever?'

'Forever.'

'Are we still friends? Can I still text you?'

'I don't think so...'

'God, you're cold as ice.' He scowled, his pudding face souring. 'All I want is to be able to text an old friend.'

'Well, okay then.' I really just wanted to get out of there and, anyway, I didn't have to answer any of his messages even if he did contact me.

He stood up. 'I'm going to the gym. There's an eighties aerobics session starting in fifteen minutes. Enjoy your trip to Ireland.'

'Thanks.'

'And I'll text you!' And off he went.

Roberto was waiting up for me, dressed in his long silk dressing gown, in which he liked to waft and swirl around when he was feeling extra dramatic, which was every evening. He poured me a large glass of red wine.

'What did you say? Did you slap him across the face with your gloves? Did you throw a glass of wine in his face? Did you slam the door on your way out?'

'None of the above,' I said, sitting down on the sofa, Roberto on the armchair beside me. 'Sorry to disappoint you. I told him it was over.'

'Right...' He had his hands together, forefingers against his lips, as though he was Sherlock Holmes ruminating on a tricky case.

'Except I feel guilty.'

'Guilty!' He threw his hands up in the air in exasperation. 'Why, for God's sake?'

'He's a tortured soul, he went to boarding school when he was eight, he just seems a bit... lost.'

'Lost?' Roberto snorted. 'Get him a Garmin and let him find his way back to being a mature adult. Anyway, you were too nice to him for too long. I never understood it.'

'It's his background,' I tried to explain. 'He can't help it. He's confused and finding it hard to deal with the legacy of parental neglect.'

'I told you,' said Roberto, 'you're co-dependent. You can't break away from Maribelle and it's why you put up with crap from Jeremy. Neither of them deserves you. Your problem is you don't think you deserve better. You are in the victim zone.'

'Victim?' I said, drinking my wine. 'That's a bit harsh!'

'I used to be like you,' he continued. 'When I was ordinary Robert of Ballymun Towers, Dublin. A fully paid-up resident of the victim zone. Teased, slagged off, shouted obscenities at. And then I decided that I was a queen and that I would wear my crown.'

'Good for you,' I said.

'And did I crumble when Felipe left me?' he asked. 'Did I lay down and die?'

'Felipe continued travelling,' I reminded him. 'His round-the-world ticket was about to expire.'

'You're missing the point,' Roberto tutted. 'The point is I know my worth. It's about time you knew yours.'

I drained my glass of red wine. He was right. As always.

Roberto did know his worth and he wouldn't have gone out with someone like Jeremy just because he felt sorry for him. And then he definitely wouldn't have experienced the humiliation of a boyfriend sleeping with his ex.

'At least,' said Roberto, softening, 'you are free of them both. Jeremy *and* Maribelle.'

'She'll only be gone for a month, though,' I said.

'But *still*. It's enough time for life evaluation and strategy-forming. It was on a ferry around the Dodecanese that I had my biggest brainwave ever. It came to me like a vision, to channel my love for Kylie and my love for performing. Mam had me tap dancing from the age of three and I was in all the local talent shows in Ballymun and obviously was hated by all the other boys. But little did they know that a little trip around the Greek islands could produce a superstar.' He flicked his robe like a flamenco dancer.

I laughed. Roberto did like to romanticise his own life somewhat.

'Maybe we could go away together,' he said. 'What about Australia? We could do a pilgrimage to the great Kylie sights. The *Neighbours* set, the first place she performed "The Loco-Motion", her childhood home?'

'I'm going to go to *my* childhood home,' I said.

But Roberto was looking horrified. 'Home?' he said. 'As in Dublin? Like, why would you want to go there? We *know* Dublin. We both grew up there.'

'You can come with me if you like. You know how much Mum loves you. Anyway, she needs someone to work in her shop for a few weeks. She's on crutches.'

'Oh my God. Is she okay?'

'She was doing Pilates...'

'That thing is dangerous,' he said. 'How many times have I said it! All that twitching and flexing. It's not serious, is it?'

I shook my head. 'Not that I can tell. It's a few weeks of sitting around watching daytime television...'

'The dream!'

'You can come and see me,' I said. 'It's only an hour's flight.' Roberto never went home. His mother and his sisters came to London twice a year for shopping trips, but he always said he wasn't ready to go back.

'Maybe,' he said, unenthusiastically. 'How long will you be gone?'

'A month,' I said. 'I'll be back before you know it.'

'When are you going?'

'Tomorrow morning.'

'You'll miss London,' he predicted. 'It's not as if *anything* ever happens *there*.'

'I really want to go,' I said. 'For Mum.' *And for me*, I was thinking.

'It's just that I'll miss you, that's all.'

'I'll miss you too,' I said.

Roberto paused, as though he was King Solomon. 'Right,' he finally pronounced, 'you can go. I'll allow it, as long as you promise me one thing...'

'What?'

'That you go and get the life you deserve? And you find that crown and wear it with pride. Okay?'

'I promise,' I said.

'Once more with feeling,' he ordered.

'I promise you, Roberto Donoghue, that I will find my crown and wear it.'

He nodded, satisfied. 'It's your time, Liv,' he said. 'Go forth and be fabulous!'

4

Roberto: Are you at the airport yet? Will you be buying a giant Toblerone? Asking for a friend.
Me: Have bought some v posh Fortnum and Mason biscuits for Mum. No Toblerone. Yet! Will buy you one when I come home.
Roberto: <excited>
Roberto: I will obviously be more excited to see you than the Toblerone, I should make that clear... but still... am already dreaming.
Me: I will buy two! Or three...
Roberto: Have a good time. Give my love to Nell. And Bronagh. Tell them to come to London soon. Love you!
Me: Just about to board! Speak soon! xxxx

I'd forgotten just how much I missed home until the grey of the sea below the plane as we began our descent gave way to the patchwork green of Ireland, the country taking shape like a jigsaw. And there it was, first the islands off the coast and then the cliffs, the fields, the golf courses, the houses, roads, tiny cars. And I did what I always did, looked left, across the bay to Dún

Laoghaire where the two piers stretched out into the sea as
though hugging the boats within them.

Just beyond, of course, was Sandycove. I squinted, looking for
my other landmarks, the Martello Tower and beside it the Forty
Foot swimming place. I wondered if Bronagh was there now,
having a Saturday afternoon swim. Down there was the life I left
behind, what once had been my whole world.

* * *

Our house was a small, two-bedroomed brick terrace, with a neat
front garden and – Mum's pride and joy – a monkey puzzle tree.
This was home to me, just the sight of the front door and the
crazy little tree or the small wooden gate at the front was enough
to make pent-up London air leak out of me like a slow puncture
as I wheeled my case up the road.

From the front window, I saw Mum's face disappearing and, a
moment later, the door opening and there she was. We clung to
each other, wordlessly, me breathing in her Jo Malone Red Roses
which she'd been wearing for the last decade since I bought it for
her one Christmas. Her two crutches were propped up against
the door, as she pulled back to study me.

'You look beautiful,' she said, pushing back my hair behind
my ear and leaning on one crutch. 'Your hair is so long. But you
look tired... have you been sleeping? If anyone deserves a little
time off, it's you. After all you put up with.' Mum was her usual
impeccably dressed self, even with the crutches. She had a pair of
black joggers on with her Chanel jacket and pristine white
trainers.

'I'm fine,' I said. 'Honestly. *You're* the invalid!'

'Invalid!' She picked up her crutches. 'Well, temporary

invalid,' she admitted. 'But are you sure you want to work in the shop? You look exhausted.'

'Can you stop going on about how exhausted I look?' I said. 'I'm fine. I want to be here.'

She smiled. 'We'll just see how it goes, shall we?'

'It's going to be like a holiday. Anything is better than working for Maribelle. Anyway, how are you finding the crutches?' I said, going inside and putting my case on the floor, and looking around the pink-painted hall, the large art deco mirror on the wall, the row of coat hooks, the cream-carpeted stairs, the framed photograph of me as a baby, the one of us when we were on holiday in Kerry when I was little, another of the two of us standing outside Nell's when Mum was given the Retailer of the Year award about ten years ago, our arms around each other, both grinning for the camera.

'Oh, it's not too bad,' said Mum. 'Nothing serious, I can still drive but...' She was back on both crutches and lifted one up. 'They are a little cumbersome, I've got to admit it.'

'We'll have to get you roller skates,' I said. 'I could pull you around.'

Mum laughed. 'Come on, I'll put the kettle on. We'll sit outside, it's such a glorious afternoon. We'll make the most of it.'

She moved clunkily but surprisingly swiftly into the kitchen, where double doors led out to our small garden.

'I'll make the tea. You sit down.'

Mum pulled herself onto the stool, leaning her crutches beside her.

'Roberto sends his love and says stay off the Pilates. Says it's a dangerous sport.'

Mum laughed. 'He's a tonic, that one,' she said. 'Tell him I won't be giving it up. It's not the Pilates that did this, it was me. By the way, have you heard from Maribelle? How is she getting on?'

'No, no news. I have tried to call her a couple of times, but her phone is off. Which is to be expected. They probably take everything away from you on day one.' It was strange not being at Maribelle's beck and call, as though she had just disappeared off the face of the earth. 'I've googled the place and there's twice-daily meditation, counselling, forest walks and yoga. She wouldn't possibly have time to call me even if she could.'

I boiled the kettle and filled the teapot on the tray, making sure that Mum had her china teacup and saucer and a mug for me.

'She might improve when she is released,' said Mum, manoeuvring herself off the stool and swinging herself on the crutches over to the double doors and to the patio.

We sat looking out at the grass and the apple trees as the sun shone. Even the air felt different, lighter, breezier, more ozoney than London. I closed my eyes for a moment and felt my body decompressing.

'There's a chance she might actually be a nice person to work for...'

I raised my eyebrows sceptically.

'Well,' Mum went on, taking a biscuit, 'you never know. Leopards have been known to change their spots. Look at Hugh Grant. He managed to become quite a good actor. Or there's Elton John, he stopped having all those tantrums. And Andy Murray turned out to be quite charming.'

'We'll have to see.'

'And Jeremy?' she said, carefully. 'He's well? Are you and he...?'

'We're not seeing each other any more,' I said. Best of all, I thought, I would never have to spend New Year with his family, trying to pretend his father wasn't looking at my breasts or saying how he used to have an Irish girlfriend and that I reminded him of her.

Mum's eyebrows raised. 'Really? But I thought you and he were getting on fine.'

'Not really.'

Mum nodded, not wanting to pry any further. 'How are you?' she said, gently.

'A bit hurt,' I admitted. 'But I'll be fine.' I smiled at her. '*Really.* Anyway, I'm really looking forward to starting in Nell's on Monday.'

'Jessica will be there, she'll look after you. I couldn't do any of it without her. She's a born salesperson. And so stylish.'

'I'll assist her, then.'

'Why don't we go to the shop tomorrow morning, and I could go through a few things – the till, the accounts, the keys, all that?' She took my hand. 'I was thinking,' she said, casually, 'that you might think about Seasalt again?'

I felt my whole body tense up. Why was Mum bringing *that* up? Seasalt was my great embarrassment and my huge failure.

'That was years ago.' I looked away.

'You were so good at it,' she persisted. 'The market stall, your lovely products...'

'But I wasn't any good at it,' I said, annoyed. 'If I was, I would still be running it.'

'I've said it before and I'll say it again,' she replied, 'you lost confidence, and the more you thought about, the less confidence you had.'

'It's hard to be confident when you don't know who your father is,' I said, immediately regretting it.

For a second, Mum's face crumpled, as though I'd landed a punch.

'I'm sorry...' She didn't have to tell me. I had thought I wasn't that selfish person any more. Obviously, I was wrong.

'It's okay.'

'No, I am, really.'

'You shouldn't be. It's my fault. It's just... it's hard to talk about. I'm trying to talk about it,' she said. 'I... I really am.' She smiled at me.

'Thank you,' I said. 'I would really love that.'

And Mum suddenly hugged me again, this time her crutches falling to the ground. 'I really wish I could,' she said. The expression on her face was one of such helpless sadness.

The doorbell rang but neither of us moved. 'Mum...' We'd never talked about it before. She'd brushed me away any time I'd asked, hinted, nagged about it.

The doorbell rang again.

'It's Henry,' she said. 'He's brought some supplies and he really wants to meet you.'

I stood up. 'Well, I'd better let him in.' I turned at the kitchen door. 'Tell me when you're ready, all right? But please tell me.' I paused. 'If you can.'

She nodded. 'I will. I promise.'

* * *

Henry was a large man, with a giant handlebar moustache, behind which were bright, beady eyes like black diamonds, his whole being exuding joie de vivre. He wore long, baggy cargo shorts, an open-necked check shirt. A cloth tote bag was on the ground next to him.

'Aha!' he said, taking my hand in his two giant paws. 'Well, I think I might be right in presuming that you are Olivia, the daughter of the beautiful Nell. I hope you don't mind me calling in on your first evening home, but I have a few supplies for your mother. A new thriller she was looking for. The body count is particularly high in this one. Two on the first page. She'll love that. And I've bought some cheese from James's Deli – she is partial to Cashel Blue, as you know. And some posh crackers. And a couple of mini bottles of wine, just in case the cellar is worryingly low.' He beamed at me.

'It's really lovely to meet you,' I said, meaning it.

'You look just like her,' he said. 'The same blue eyes. The same smile. Well, it's a great pleasure to meet you too, Olivia. Your mother doesn't stop talking about you and how much she was longing for you to come home.'

Had she been? Mum never gave the slightest impression that she was lonely or that she was even missing me. Mum, always so self-reliant, was the kind of person who said 'don't worry about me' with such conviction you believed her.

'And now you're home,' he went on, still holding my hand. 'Back where you belong.'

I found myself smiling at him. 'It's lovely to be back. For the next month, anyway.' I felt obliged to remind him that I was going back to my actual life in London. 'Would you like to come in?' I said. 'Mum's in the garden.'

'I won't take up more than a few minutes. Drop the provisions and be on my way.'

He followed me to the garden.

'Isn't it a beautiful evening? Normally, Nell and I go for a walk around this time, up to Dún Laoghaire and down the pier. Stopping for an ice cream at the FroRo van. But now your mother is temporarily incapacitated, those delights will have to wait. Ah, there she is...'

He and Mum smiled at each other, a smile of recognition and connection. And of just being happy to see someone.

'I come with essentials,' he said, putting down the bag and heading over to Mum's chair. 'Don't get up. The more you rest, the sooner we get you back walking the pier.' He kissed her on the lips.

'It's a few weeks,' she said, smiling at him. 'Hopefully sooner rather than later.'

'I've bought you a book on car maintenance, a bottle of sarsaparilla – good for invalids, apparently – and some prunes. Perfect for constipation.' He winked at me, as Mum giggled. 'Don't tell me I'm not good with the sick and the infirm. I should be given my Red Cross Order of Malta for services to medicine.'

'You're a veritable Florence Nightingale,' said Mum.

'Florence from *The Magic Roundabout*, more like,' said Henry, as Mum laughed again. 'Or I like to think of myself as the Mr Bean of healthcare. Always there when not needed and not to be found at times of need.' He winked at us again. 'Now, shall we crack open the sarsaparilla...?'

'Or what about a cup of tea, Henry?' I asked.

'No tea, thank you, Olivia,' he said. 'I'll only stay for a moment because I have other highly important missions this evening. Hopefully, this will not be a mission impossible. My neighbour Maureen has had a rather large delivery of flat-pack furniture and so, being a man with the all-important Allen key, she's asked me to give her a hand. And after her, I will be in the greenhouse checking on my onions.' He perched on the edge of the chair beside Mum. 'Did your mother tell you about my gardening experiment? She did? Well, every night I put the onions to bed, and every morning I wake them up. They take more time than a toddler. Well, not that I ever had a toddler, not being blessed in that way, but I can only imagine that these onions are just as much work, if not more.' He winked again at me, as Mum laughed again. 'They need feeding and straw to rest on and making sure the light's not too bright and that the temperature is just right.' He stood up. 'So, Nell, Olivia, I must take my Allen key and go. Nell...' He took one of her hands in his. 'Goodbye. Let me know what you think of the new Val McDermid. And, Olivia,' he shook my hand again, 'a pleasure to meet you finally. The apple of your mother's eye. And a chip off the old block. I'll see myself out and look forward to seeing you again soon.'

As soon as we heard the door close, I said, 'What a gorgeous man.'

'He's brought a great deal of happiness into my life,' Mum said. Her smile was one I hadn't seen for a very long time. She seemed brighter and happier than I could remember. 'I never thought I could ever...' She stopped.

'Ever what?'

'Feel like that again. Now,' she said, changing the subject abruptly, 'would you like some more tea before you go and meet Bronagh?'

'No, I'd better start getting ready,' I said. 'I don't think it's a late one because she's going out later. She didn't expect me home.'

5

Roberto: How is it? It's awful, isn't it? You don't have to tell me. All the adrenaline has leached from your body and you are now a comatose shell… a body with no soul. How much are you missing London? Too much to quantify?

Me: Missing you but not London. Not yet, anyway. I've only been here precisely six hours. Don't worry, I'll be bored soon. Off to meet Bronagh for a drink later. What are you doing?

Roberto: Watching Murder She Wrote. Eating cereal.

Me: Try to include a few vegetables. Or an apple.

Roberto: Vegetables? Never! The very idea. Am going to spend the next month you are away mainlining highly refined carbohydrates. You will return to my nutrient-deficient shell and feel v guilty.

Me: I am ordering you a weekly organic vegetable box. Eat that daikon.

Roberto: Love you. Give Bronagh my most ardent love. Tell her not to keep you though.

The village of Sandycove is a long curving line of shops, pubs and cafés with a church at one end and, in the middle, a crossroads, one way leading to the sea and the harbour and the other way leading up to Sandycove Avenue, one of my favourite roads in the whole village, especially when it blossoms with pink in spring.

It was a bustling place but not *Hackney*-busy. Here there was a sense of people quietly and quickly getting on with their lives, or sitting with a coffee outside, or walking dogs, or doing the shopping. I was sure that in a few days I'd be dying to get back to London, bored senseless and desperate to see different faces, rather than the same ones you saw all the time. But... I'd actually forgotten how much I liked it.

It was a Saturday evening and the village was looking its very best. There were more hanging baskets than ever, spilling over with purple lobelia and orange nasturtiums and the shops were painted in bright colours, their names above in curlicued gold. There was Bernard Murphy the butchers, Adrian's newsagents, Janet's bakery, The Island pub, Betty Boyle's boutique Nouveau You... and, of course, Nell's, Mum's shop. As I walked past, I looked inside, where a young woman – long blonde hair, wearing a fuchsia-pink trouser suit and smiling broadly – was serving a customer. Had to be Jessica.

But there we so many new shops as well: a lovely flower shop called The Garden, a hipster café Albatross and, just as I crossed over, there was a cool-looking deli called James's. I had seen it before, but I'd never taken the time to look inside properly. I peered in through the glass to see a long oak counter running the full length of the shop, floor-to-ceiling shelves, glass jars of spices and tins of Italian tomatoes and packets of pasta. There were shelves full of wine and a large cheese-and-cold-meat cabinet at one end of the shop.

Someone was closing up for the day as I peered in, a black Labrador stretched across the doorway while the man fiddled with the lock. He stood up, smiling with recognition.

'Olivia?'

'James!' We'd been in youth orchestra together, years ago, just a couple of chairs away – him bassoon, me clarinet. But he now had a full beard, shaggy hair and was wearing a pristine checked shirt tucked into jeans, like an Appalachian going to a wedding. 'How are you? It's so great to see you!'

'You too, Olivia,' he said. 'I heard you were coming back.'

'I'm not exactly *back*,' I replied. 'I'm only here for a few weeks to help Mum out while she's on crutches.'

'Ah, right. Well, welcome home for a bit, anyway.'

I looked up at the shop. 'This must be yours?'

He nodded. 'Opened last summer and we're doing well. I had my own food truck for years, festivals and events. Did a few weddings, parties, corporate things, and then I managed to get a bank loan and open a shop.'

'It's a big move,' I said, impressed.

'Well, I was ready to settle down... and Sammy here had had enough of travelling, hadn't you, boy?'

'Hello, Sammy,' I said, giving the dog a stroke. 'He's beautiful.'

'He is,' James agreed. 'But he's slowing down, the poor thing.' He leaned and stroked the top of the dog's head, who stared up at him lovingly. 'Don't know what I'd do without him.'

'So the shop's going well?'

'It's going really well,' he replied. 'I make a different dish of the day every day. It was paella today... you should come pop in.' He paused. 'By the way, it's you I need to thank for this...' He waved towards the shop behind him. 'I always admired you doing your market stall. You used to talk about it at orchestra. I remember thinking I really wanted to run my own business. The year you left for London... when was that?'

'Ten years ago...' Was *everyone* going to mention or allude to Seasalt? Would I have to hold up a sign?

Please don't mention Seasalt! It's over and done with!

'Right, well, that year I got the food truck, making my lasagnes and my chillies. Did it for a few years. Without doing that I wouldn't have had the confidence to go to the bank, and all *this* wouldn't have happened.'

There was a shout behind us. 'Olivia!' Bronagh was running towards us, waving. 'OLIVIA!'

'BRONAGH!' I laughed, holding my arms open and she ran into them.

'Oh my God,' she said, hugging me. 'It's so good to see you!' She stood back as we both grinned at each other. 'Looking fabulous.'

'So are you!'

Bronagh was tall, with black-framed glasses and shoulder-length hair which was pushed to one side. She had a towel under her arm, her hair still wet. She only wore navy, black or white and on first impressions she was terrifyingly put together and assured and successful – but she'd been like that since she was thirteen when we met for the first time in Mrs Madden's French class. She now ran her own architecture practice which was between the new flower shop and Albatross café.

'I can't believe you're home for a MONTH,' she said. 'It's amazing.' She smiled at James. 'Isn't it great?' she said, laughing.

'Yes, Bronagh,' he humoured her. 'It's great.'

'Been swimming?' I said to her.

'Of course!' She grinned at me. 'Can't get enough of it. It's the only way to get my body to feel *anything* these days. Even cold. Come on, let's go and have that drink. We can sit in the courtyard. It's such a beautiful evening. God, I love June.'

'Bye, James, great to catch up,' I said.

'You too, Olivia. I'll see you here for my paella...'

'It's incredible,' said Bronagh to me. 'He's a culinary genius.'

'Or my chickpea stew... that's Monday.'

'Deceptively delicious,' said Bronagh, slipping her arm through mine. 'Bye, James, see you later.'

And we began to walk to The Island, the pub we'd been going to since we were teenagers.

'Finally,' she went on, 'we can go for proper drinks again. I'm sorry I'm meeting Paul later, but it was all arranged before you told me you were coming home. Now, were you serious when you said that you *won't* be working and won't be worrying about calls from London?'

'I promise,' I said. 'I'm entirely focused on being here for the next few weeks. Obviously, I'll be working in the shop during the day, but my evenings and weekends are totally free.'

'Okay, so I am thinking drinks in The Island. Walks on the seafront. Yoga on Saturday mornings. I've got it all planned out.'

'How is work?' I asked. 'How is the wonderful world of architecture? Still having meetings with men with pointy beards and yellow spectacles?'

She laughed. 'I think you are referring to Hans,' she said. 'And yes, last time I spoke to him on Zoom his beard was still pointy, but, in a major plot twist, his glasses were green. But we're busy. Two university libraries on the go, one in Berlin and another in Limerick. And then there is the Ballinasloe community centre and the ecolodge on the Faroe Islands. But they are still only in discussion stage.'

We were standing right outside The Island. 'Shall we go in?' she said. 'I've been dying for a drink all day.'

* * *

The pub hadn't changed at all, still the same decor, with glass buoys and lobster nets and old front pages framed showing great sea disasters of old. The only thing that was new was the fact that a group of women in one corner were drinking cocktails.

'Cocktails?' I said. 'Since when did The Island get fancy?'

'Since they got new staff,' Bronagh said. 'Matt's the new barman and he came back from Toronto with all these new ideas. They even do tapas here on a Friday night. You go and sit in the garden and I'll bring the drinks out. I'll get two margaritas... all right with you?'

'If you're twisting my arm. Go on then.'

The garden was a small courtyard with four long tables and benches, there were ferns and banana plants and acer trees in pots, giving a jungle feeling to it all. Above, the sun was still shining. I could hear the birds singing and, as I went to sit down, I felt that feeling as though I was on holiday. A proper holiday, not just visiting home, like I was truly on a break. Irish weather is, as everyone knows, a heady mix of horizontal rain, bleak and buffeting winds and short patches of sun. July and August are as unpredictable as the winning lottery ticket; you could easily have months of torrential rain as much as you could have blazing sunshine. But May and June rarely let you down and are the only times when the weather can be relied upon to deliver.

Going to sit down, I edged past a man sitting with his back to me, a cup of coffee and *The Irish Times* laid out in front of him and a teeny-tiny Yorkshire terrier asleep on the bench. Sandycove was no magnet for handsome men, but this one was striking, like a young Daniel Day-Lewis. Not, of course, that I was interested. I was, however, a sucker for a sweet dog and as I slid past, just as my hand hovered near his head ready to pet him and coo over his cuteness, the dog's eyes shot open and he suddenly transformed into a snarling, miniature wolf.

'Oh my God!' I shouted, snatching my hand away, nanoseconds before those horrible jaws clamped down.

'I'm so sorry.' The man stood up, the dog in his arms – now looking as though butter wouldn't melt. 'Are you all right?'

The man was taller than I'd thought so I had to angle my head to forty-five degrees to look into those brown eyes. He looked around my age, maybe slightly older, and was wearing jeans and a blue shirt, sleeves rolled up.

'It was my fault,' I said, relieved to have an untouched, intact hand. 'He was asleep and I woke him up. I'm the same in the mornings.'

'Pablo needs to learn better manners,' he said.

'No, I do,' I replied, prolonging the conversation. 'I invaded his personal space. There he was, having a nice dream, and I disturbed his slumbers.' I tried to laugh, thinking he would laugh as well, but he was already sitting back down again, as though finished with our conversation. The dog had hopped back onto the bench and had settled down again.

Bronagh came towards me, carrying two margaritas. 'I was just thinking, finally, someone sane to talk to.'

'Sane-*ish*,' I said.

'Oh, we don't want *perfectly* sane,' she said, sitting down. I was aware that the man had looked up briefly and seemed to be listening. 'Perfectly sane is boring. Sane-ish is all I require.' She grinned at me, and then looked over at the man. 'Oh, hi Will,' she said. 'Good day?'

He nodded. 'I was on a few calls,' he said. 'You?'

'Grand. Been swimming lately?'

'Yesterday,' he said. 'And it was *cold*... I mean, it's June and the water still isn't warm. But Dermot is insisting on going again. I'm heading down there now.' He got to his feet, picking up his paper and bag. 'Come on, Pablo,' he said, as the dog hopped off the bench to the ground and they left.

'Who is *he*?' I asked.

'A handsome devil,' she said, 'that is who he is. Every straight woman or gay man in the village is after him.'

'Mr Handsome Devil, Sandycove.'

'Well, he's actually Will Butler. *Dr* Butler. He's just opened up a surgery in the old chemist's. Remember Dermot Butler, a year ahead of us in the boys' school? It's his older brother. I think he was the studious type, he was too busy reading books to be out and about. Why... do you *like* him? Being of sane-ish mind, I assume you do.'

'No, just curious.' He was too aloof for me and, after Jeremy, I was done with complicated men. However handsome they were. 'Anyway, he's the owner of an evil dog. What's that saying, judge me not by what I say, but by what my dog does?'

Bronagh laughed. 'But dogs can be tamed. Even vicious lapdogs. Never judge a dog by its snarl.' She held up her glass. 'Anyway, welcome home.' She held up her glass. 'I am so glad to see you.'

'Me too,' I said.

'Here's to Maribelle,' she went on. 'And to thank her for giving you this extended holiday!'

I had an image of Maribelle in a white dressing gown, drinking carrot juice, desperate to get back to London, and I hoped she was doing okay. 'To Maribelle! So, how is Postman Paul? When will I finally get to meet him?' Bronagh and Paul had been going out with each other for the last few months.

'Probably never,' she said, shrugging. 'We're just two mismatched people spending a minuscule amount of time together keeping the cold hand of loneliness from knocking on the door. It's not going to last much longer, nice as he is.'

'But nice is good, isn't it?' If I was ever going to get involved with any male ever again, then nice was going to be top of my list. 'What's wrong with nice?'

'Nothing,' agreed Bronagh. 'I like nice. But Paul is so *nice* he wants me to share his *Star Wars* obsession. He knows every character and every storyline and God knows what else. And, at first, I thought, yes great. It's good to be interested in different things. I mean, he thinks buildings are just buildings.'

'They're *not*?'

'No, they're not. They are everything...' She laughed again. 'Please don't let me start talking about buildings. I realise that we building enthusiasts are not easily understood by the general population.'

'Opposites attract,' I reminded her.

'But I think we're like two magnets repelling each other. I just have to find the right moment and tell him.'

'Talking of which,' I said. 'Jeremy and I are over. He got together with his ex-girlfriend Cassandra and she very kindly called to tell me.'

'Really?' She shook her head. 'What an idiot.'

'Cassandra or Jeremy?'

'Both.'

'But it's fine,' I said. 'I'm fine. He had a few eccentricities that I am quite glad to be rid of.'

'Like what?'

'He didn't own a single pair of jeans.'

Bronagh froze in motion, her margarita millimetres from her lips. 'Didn't own a single pair of jeans? What kind of monster was he?'

'And he ironed his socks, and he had never eaten baked beans... not even as a child.'

Bronagh's face was grave at the mention of these heinous crimes.

'It gets worse,' I said. 'He hates fish. Doesn't consider it food. And, as far as I can tell, he's only ever read two books in his life. One of which was *The Tao Of Pooh* and the other the theory driving test book.'

She looked shocked. 'How could you...?'

'I know.'

We looked at each other with a muted horror. Bronagh was making me feel better already, as she always did. But even as I spoke, London and Jeremy and the office already seemed so far away. It was as though I had moved on, just by moving away.

Bronagh held up her glass again. 'Here's to lucky escapes.'

'To lucky escapes,' I echoed. 'I don't know why I put up with it six whole months,' I said. 'I have decided to work on my spinster habits. Must take up knitting.'

'And witchcraft,' said Bronagh. 'Isn't that what single women are meant to do? I am going to buy myself a black cloak and sweep through the village uttering curses at everyone, terrifying all the men. Luckily, I already have Mies van der Rohe as my familiar.' Mies was her small, black, aged cat, named after Bronagh's favourite architect. I smiled at her, thinking how much I'd missed our chats; phone calls and FaceTime weren't the same. 'By the way,' she said, 'would you like to come to my parents' anniversary party next Saturday?' She released a long sigh of despair. 'I'm dreading it and it would be nice to see a friendly face. Moral support, that kind of thing.'

Family events were always a trial for Bronagh. Even though she did all the organising and arranging, she hated them, usually because her mother always said something horrible to her, no one ever appreciated her efforts and she was left with the impression that she was surplus to the requirements of the family.

Bronagh was the youngest, her three older brothers – 'the boys' – were adored by her mother, and Bronagh had always been ignored.

'I'd love to come,' I said immediately, taking another sip. 'Count me in. So, how *are* the boys?'

'Fine, as far as I know. Chris's new theory is that body odour is a capitalist concept. Apparently, we all wash too much and are depleting our natural oils.' She paused. 'It's funny, because even though Mum has a Lady Macbeth-esque obsession with washing her hands and dousing herself in Shalimar, she doesn't seem to be able to smell her three sons.' She shrugged. 'And none of them smell particularly sweetly. Chris is still in his tribute band, Mark is a rickshaw driver in Dublin city centre, which Mum refers to as a "boutique travel experience", and Alan works in a Tex-Mex restaurant, which Mum is convinced is on the verge of winning a Michelin star.'

'Didn't Alan have such a nose-picking problem that the doctor told him he was in danger of it falling off? That's not going to go down well with the hygiene inspectors.'

Bronagh laughed. 'He did wear away part of his septum, that's true. But in his defence, I think he has managed to reduce his nose-picking to less critical levels. In public, anyway. So how's your mum? How is she getting on with the crutches?'

I thought of how she'd looked earlier when I'd asked her about my father. I loved her with every part of me, but this had lingered for too long. I knew I had to get over it and just leave it be. But I wished I knew and then perhaps I could help Mum. I put down my empty glass.

'What's wrong?' said Bronagh. She'd known for years how I'd struggled with Mum's silence.

'Mum still won't tell me...'

'He could be a murderer,' suggested Bronagh. 'Or someone

famous. You really should be put out of your misery. You need to know if you are the love child of Keanu Reeves.'

I laughed. 'But she looked so sad,' I said. 'Before, she used to brush me aside, and for the first time she didn't. I felt she might tell me.'

'Really?'

'Henry turned up… and she couldn't.'

'Maybe she's ready. Finally.'

'Maybe.'

Bronagh smiled at me. 'Hopefully. You deserve to know.'

'I don't want to force her.'

'What do you think of Henry?'

'Well, he arrived with a bag full of wine and some chocolate. So I think he's very nice.'

'They do look very happy,' said Bronagh. 'I see them walking by the harbour every evening, arm in arm. They always seem to be laughing.'

I nodded. 'She did of lot of that earlier when he was there. Despite the dodgy hip flexors. Now, another margarita? I will go and order another two of these glasses of utter deliciousness!'

6

Roberto: Just invented a new breakfast. Or dinner. Rice Crispies
served with chocolate milk. It's like cheap Coco Pops.

Me: Please eat a vegetable. Any one. There's lots to choose from.

Roberto: I did. I had some last night. Chips from the chip shop. Had
them in bread.

Me: Please learn to cook!

Roberto: I can't. That part of my brain was removed at birth. I'll just
have to keep eating chips until you come home.

Me: This is blackmail.

Roberto: If it makes you feel better I promise to buy and eat a tin of
soup.

Me: Please heat it up.

Roberto: With a side order of chips.

It was Monday morning, and my first day working in Nell's. The
previous day, Mum and I had gone in and she'd shown me where
everything was and how everything worked. I hadn't been into
the shop for years as my visits home had all been so fleeting, but
it was looking good. Wooden floors, a modern-looking green

chaise longue at the back, beside the two changing rooms. There was the till and packing area to the left, shelves and rails around the back and the right wall. The front was taken up by the large shop window with three headless mannequins. 'Did they displease you?' I'd asked. 'Did they do something wrong?'

Mum had laughed. 'That's what happens to sales assistants who get things wrong,' she teased.

'But what if I do?' I'd said. 'What if I charge too much or too little or give the wrong change?'

'Everything is scannable and anyway no one pays in cash any more,' she'd replied, while I made notes, desperate not to get things wrong. 'And if you're not sure, just ask Jessica.' There was a tall stool behind the till, and Mum propped herself up. 'But are you sure you want to do this? It just seems wrong when you need a break more than anyone? I shouldn't have agreed to you helping in the shop.'

'But it's going to be fun,' I'd said, hoping it was. 'I just need to perfect my selling. Which technique do you prefer – the hover and pounce or benign neglect?'

'Neither,' Mum had laughed. 'I just try and be welcoming, no pressure to buy, and create as nice an atmosphere as possible.'

'So, I don't have to make my targets, or try and drive my commission up?'

'As I said, no pressure. Betty in Nouveau You does have sales targets for her staff. I've never bothered.'

Nouveau You opened in the village long after Mum had been established, but even though they could and should have been rivals, I had never heard Mum say a single disparaging thing about Betty. Her shop was, I thought, far inferior, catering for the frou-frou golf society dinner crowd. Mum always said competition was good for business.

And now it was Monday morning, for the first time I was

regretting volunteering. Nerves and feelings of general inade-
quacy clung to my insides. One reason, I thought, why people
stayed in toxic, unsatisfying jobs, was because it was preferable to
having to do anything new. Being home was wonderful in so
many ways and yet... there were all those confusing feelings. I
loved being here and being with Mum, but I kept having to
remind myself that my need to know my origin story was irrele-
vant. Making sure Mum was okay was the only important thing. It
didn't matter where I came from or what had happened. Mum
had loved me and looked after me better than most parents I
knew – and certainly better than Bronagh's. That was all that
mattered, wasn't it?

Mum gave me a once-over. 'You look beautiful.'

'I don't,' I said, immediately. I had agonised over my wardrobe
this morning, finally choosing jeans and a floral shirt. After
working for eight years in London, where personality was a curse
and anything other than navy was viewed with suspicion, my
sense of style was totally gone. 'I look awful.'

'Awful! Don't say such a thing, if you can't be nice to yourself,
how do you expect anyone else to be nice to you?'

'But you're only saying I look nice because you don't want me
to have a crisis of confidence or meltdown which might preclude
me from going to the shop. I know I look awful and not stylish
like you. I didn't inherit your style gene.'

She came over and gave me a hug. 'You do look nice, you
always do. You're my beautiful daughter who would look nice in a
paper bag.'

'But I don't really look *nice*, though,' I continued. 'Not to *your*
standards. Be honest.'

'I think you are gorgeous,' she insisted. 'You always are.'

But I did feel really rather frumpy, like someone in the wrong
clothes or the wrong life. In London, looking 'city-smart' – suits

and boring shirts and flat shoes – was a no-brainer and didn't require a personality. Over the years, I had forgotten what I actually liked to wear and what suited me.

Mum went and sat down on the small sofa in the kitchen, in front of the portable television. I brought her over a cup of tea.

'Do you need anything before I go?' I asked. 'Have you got the remote control? A rug for your knees, your phone?'

'Olivia, I am not an elderly woman,' said Mum. 'I *may* watch some TV. Henry was suggesting a series I might like... but I won't be sitting down *all* day. I have strained my hip. Not broken it.'

'I know,' I said. 'But I am meant to be looking after you.'

'And I am looking after you,' she said. 'It's a mutual thing. Now, call me if you need anything, but Jessica is fabulous, you will love her. And Cara, my Saturday girl, might drop in this week. Her exams are starting today, so she may or may not have time. She's a lovely young woman, I'm very fond of her. I know you will be too.'

The village was busy with the usual Monday morning bustle and I called into Albatross, the café, for a coffee which I hoped would quell my nerves. It was a lovely café with Formica tables and wooden benches with velvet cushions. On the wall, behind the counter, was a large orange *Vertigo* poster. A small queue of people hovered in front of the counter, while a small woman, with a head of black curly hair, tonged croissants into paper bags, handed over flat whites and swiped cards in a whirl of motion.

As the queue shuffled up, I became aware that the woman in front of me was Betty Boyle, the owner of the *other* village boutique, Nouveau You. I kept my head down.

'I can't *abide* people who complain about their health,' Betty was saying to the person ahead of her. 'You see,' she went on, 'there are people who are well and there are people who just aren't. And never will be. You know the type, the snifflers and the coughers, the ones always putting their backs out or twisting something or coming down with some deficiency or allergy or *condition*. You must get those in your surgery a great deal, Dr Butler?'

Dr Butler? I glanced up to see that it was indeed the handsome man from The Island. His little dog with the huge teeth was standing quite benignly at his feet.

'I call them the Waiting Room Wasters!' Betty gave a cackle. 'Now, you must be in good health being a medical man. Anyway, it's wonderful to have another doctor in the village. Dr Smyth is always so busy. *Not* that I have need of you, you won't be seeing me much knocking at your door complaining of something or other.' She laughed again. 'There is literally nothing I suffer from.' Betty then lowered her voice, but I could still hear every word. 'Of course,' she said, 'my Jennifer-Louise will be in and out of the surgery. When she has the *baby*. Scans and weighing and whatnot. Not that we went in for that nonsense when I was with child.' She gradually came to a halt.

Jennifer-Louise was Betty's daughter, a couple of years younger than me at school, and now, as I'd just learned, pregnant.

'Your turn!' Betty shouted to Dr Butler, giving him a shove. 'Quick, quick,' she laughed. 'And you a doctor. You need to be off on your rounds. Not that I have need of you...' She raised her voice and spoke to the room. 'Being in the *prime* of life.' She looked around to see who was listening in and her gaze fell upon me. 'Olivia!' she said, kissing the air near my cheeks. 'Your dear, dear, *dear* mother said you were coming home. Do you know, I think she's been so lonely without you? I really do! She wasn't blessed as I have been with a daughter who chose to stay close to home.'

Dr Butler turned around and gave me a look which I couldn't quite decipher, but Betty was scrutinising my face, like a beautician before a facial. 'Still pale, I see,' she said. 'Your mother used to be so worried about you. Probably still is. "Betty," she used to say, "my Olivia is so ghostly, and your Jennifer-Louise is so healthy... what *do* you feed her?"'

Betty was one of the downsides to small-town life.

Dr Butler nodded at me, still inscrutable. Did he look apologetic, as though he was sorry for me to be under Betty's microscope? Or was he just hoping to escape unscathed, glad that I was being held captive by her questions?

'Didn't you used to have eczema? Didn't you have it all over your body? Weren't you *riddled* with it?' she continued.

Faces turned around to look at me, the person riddled with eczema.

'I wouldn't have described it quite like that, Betty,' I said, feeling duty-bound, for the sake of my reputation and dignity, to let everyone in the café know – including Dr Butler (*especially* Dr Butler!) – that all was well with my skin. 'It's fine now. I make my own cream. It's very effective. I haven't had a flare-up in years.'

'You make your own cream?' Betty was looking at me as though I had just announced I was holidaying on Mars. 'How on earth...? Oh, yes, your *stall*...' Her nose wrinkled. 'I would say over-the-counter might be better. Or I am sure Dr Butler might be able to prescribe something a little more medically sound. Have you met Dr Butler yet? Dr Butler?' She tapped him on the shoulder.

He turned around. Again, that inscrutable look. What did I detect? Pity? Did he pity my terrible skin condition? Or was it pity that I was locked in this awful conversation? The coffee in Albatross had better be worth it. I couldn't go through this every morning.

'Olivia is just back from London. How long are you staying, Olivia?'

'A few weeks,' I said.

'Olivia makes her own...' Betty began, but Dr Butler cut her off, having just received his coffee from the woman behind the counter.

'I'm so sorry,' he said, 'I can't stop. I have to open the surgery.'

'Of course!' said Betty. 'No rest for the wicked. Not that you look the wicked type, of course. Remind me to invite you to my annual showcase... it's quite the fixture in the Sandycove calendar. But, before that, we have the midsummer festival, which my Jennifer-Louise organised wonderfully well last year. Of course, now she is...' Her voice dropped again. 'Well, suffice to say, we'll have to ask someone else to take over the reins. Someone with a little time on her hands.'

Her eyes alighted on me as Dr Butler made good his escape.

'*So* good-looking,' said Betty, as soon as he was out of the door. 'Like an Errol Flynn. Must take after his mother, she was a beauty in the village. His father...' She paused. 'Not so much.'

'Morning, Betty,' said the woman behind the counter. 'Your usual?'

'Yes, please, Alison,' said Betty, turning back to me. 'Green tea in the morning is excellent for the complexion. You should try it.'

Finally, she had her tea in one hand. 'Bye, Olivia. Bye, Alison, and the apricot is beautiful on you. Wasn't I right? Ciao-ciao! Give my love to that man of yours. Tell James we had his lamb stew and it was delicious.' And she was gone.

The woman behind the counter looked up. She held out her hand across the counter. 'I'm Alison. Your mum told me to look out for you. I could have spotted you a mile off. You look exactly the same.' She smiled. 'So what would you like? On the house.'

'No... I couldn't...'

'I'd really like to,' she said. 'It's a welcome-home present. Coffee?'

'Thank you! Cappuccino then would be lovely,' I said.

She nodded and poured one into a cup. 'Say hi to Jessica,' said Alison. 'Tell her I've got more of the matcha she likes. Delivery last night.' She smiled at me. 'And see you around.'

7

'Morning!' Jessica called through the glass of the door of Nell's. 'Just be a sec!' She reached to open the high bolt and then the main lock and pulled open the door, standing to one side to let me in. 'Lovely to meet you,' she said, as we shook hands. 'I can't believe we haven't met before, but I suppose I've only been here a year.' She laughed.

She was slim, petite, with small features and perfectly turned out in skinny jeans and a floral shirt with a small frill around the neck and cuffs, her blonde, glossy hair cascading around her shoulders. I felt the frumpiness of what I was wearing even more acutely.

'Well, Mum says she couldn't do without you,' I said.

Jessica threw me a look, which seemed almost grateful, and I realised that she had been nervous to meet me too.

'Would you like to hang up your bag and jacket?' she asked. 'You probably know the shop so well... did you work here when you were younger?'

I followed her through the shop and into the back, to the kitchenette and office. 'Not really,' I said. 'I helped out but didn't work in the shop with customers. I had my own... my own *thing* from when I was sixteen.'

Jessica had been filling the kettle while I sat at the small yellow table. 'What was that?' She turned to look at me.

'I used to make my own skincare,' I explained, wishing I hadn't brought it up.

'Skincare?' Jessica looked impressed.

'It was nothing, really,' I said. 'I made balms and oils and things like that. It's not rocket science... I mean, I suppose it's *science...*' I gave a weak little laugh and sipped at my coffee.

'What kind of skincare?' Jessica was stirring her pot of tea and brought everything to the table and sat in the slightly rickety chair, across from mine.

'Oh, you know...' This was so long ago that I had to think. 'I still make my own eczema cream just for me, but I used to make huge batches of it. And face oils and rose moisturiser and lip balms...'

'Sounds amazing,' she said. 'And you used to sell them?'

'Mum stocked them here,' I replied. 'And I had a market stall and there were a few other stockists. Nothing very successful and, anyway, it's gone now.'

But Jessica seemed impressed. 'Oh wow... that's amazing. Your mam didn't mention that. She said you were a personal assistant in London.'

'Yes, that's what I do now,' I said, drinking my coffee. 'It's a very busy... it's a really... I suppose you could say it's...' I paused. 'It's actually a really horrible job. I suppose I hate it.' I'd never said it out loud before, I'd never expressed it to anyone, not even Roberto. But I actually dreaded going to work every day, waking up with that sinking feeling and going to bed feeling drained emotionally and intellectually. At the weekends, I could barely drag myself out of bed. Going out with Jeremy was, I think, an attempt to try and have a normal social life.

'You *hate* it?'

I nodded. 'But I don't know why I'm telling you this,' I said. 'I just couldn't lie and say it was amazing.'

'I've had some not very nice jobs,' Jessica said. 'This is the best I've had. I'm just lucky that my husband lets me work... well, not that Damien *lets* me work, more like he doesn't have a problem with me working. You know, I have two children and I could be at home...' She seemed to be getting flustered, but she looked at me and smiled.

'Well, you're lucky,' I said, 'to have a job you love and you're good at.'

She nodded. 'I do feel lucky,' she said. 'Every time I come in through that door, I feel really blessed. And your mam has taught me so much. Including drinking out of a china cup. I can't go back now!' She held up her cup. 'Damien says I've got notions. I've tried to show him that it tastes nicer... well, not nicer, but it's a nicer experience. And I bought my own mam a gorgeous Wedgwood cup and saucer for her birthday. But she's put it straight in her glass cabinet. Refuses to use it and says she would prefer to admire it than watch it break.'

I laughed, already really liking her. 'How old are your children?'

'Ellie-Mae is nine and Frankie is seven. My mam says she's never seen kids with such energy. She picks them up every day from their after-school club and I collect them from hers. She's only two streets away, we're on Seapoint Crescent, number twenty-five, at the top of the cul-de-sac. Do you know it?'

'I think so,' I said.

'Sorry for talking so much. Damien says I could talk for Ireland, or if I was on the *Titanic*, I'd still be talking as we went under.' She gave another little laugh, pulling at her long hair. 'I'm trying to get better, let others speak and not hog the airspace, as he calls it.' She smiled. 'Mam's the same. The Mighty Mouthers, Damien calls us. Not to Mam's face, because she wouldn't be pleased.' She laughed again and took a quick sip of her tea.

'Mum says you are an amazing salesperson,' I said.

'Did she?' Jessica savoured the compliment. 'I do want the customer to feel amazing. Feeling is so much better than looking, do you know what I mean? It's nice to look nice, isn't it? But *feeling* nice is the bee's knees.' She looked at the clock on the wall. 'I'm going on again,' she said. 'It's twenty-nine minutes past. Time to unlock the door!'

* * *

All morning, Jessica was brilliant in the shop. She could size up customers, sussing them out at a glance, knowing instinctively who was up for full-beam attention or those who needed a lighter touch. Luckily, she was so good that I didn't have much to do and for the first couple of hours I folded jumpers and rearranged the clothes – anything to keep busy and not have too much face-to-face with the customers.

However, one entered the shop when Jessica was busy with someone else.

'Hello,' I said, trying to look friendly and approachable, hoping she was the 'just looking' kind. 'If you need anything, I'm right here.'

'I need a few pieces,' she said. 'I have in my mind a little bit Princess Caroline of Monaco, a little bit Helen Mirren, some Gwyneth Paltrow. You, know, fresh-faced, healthy. Definitely *not* Camilla Parker Bowles and *nothing* like Mary Robinson. I always think she overdoes the polo necks...'

'Okay... right...' Jessica was still mid-customer.

'And I'm a true, golden, warm spring...'

'A what?'

'Golden spring,' she repeated, irritated. 'My God. I couldn't have been clearer about what I am looking for if I had written it out. Helen Mirren, yes. Camilla, no. Warm spring.'

'What colours do you like?'

'I told you,' she said, losing patience. 'Golden, warm spring.'

'So gold?'

'No! *Not* gold. Colours that suit those with warm spring tones. Pinks and light blues or whatever. You're meant to be the expert.'

Thankfully, Jessica was saying her final goodbyes to her customer and spotted that I was in difficulty. She came over to us, to both my and the customer's relief.

'Sandra!' Jessica greeted her, smiling. 'How are you? You are looking lovely. Are you here for anything specific?'

'Helen Mirren, subtle pizzazz,' said Sandra.

'Got it.' Jessica quickly turned around and plucked around eight items from the rails. 'These might work?'

Sandra's face turned from furrowed to almost pleased. 'Yes,' she said, slowly, 'yes... they *might*. Let me try them on.'

She disappeared into the changing room and emerged intermittently in different outfits and Jessica would pull at them or slip a belt around a dress or a jacket. Sandra's sour face slowly became less curdled, and a possible smile threatened to materialise.

'I'll take them all,' she said, and I helped carry everything to the till, and as Jessica rang the items through, I folded them, wrapped them in tissue and popped them all into Nell's paper bags.

'So where,' Jessica was saying to Sandra, 'is Stephanie?'

Sandra's face flickered with pain. 'Oh, she's had a terrible time!' She clutched at her throat. 'She had a haircut which made her look like she had been shaved on some awful stag weekend. She was too embarrassed to even go out of the house. But then she overdosed after eating an entire bar of Dairy Milk. Tom...' She threw her eyes to heaven. '...had left a bar in his golf bag. Which, of course, he had left in the hall just so I could trip over it. And so, poor Stephanie threw up in bed.'

'Oh, that's terrible,' said Jessica, handing her the bags. 'The poor little thing.' She walked Sandra to the door. 'Bye, Sandra, love to little Stephanie.'

'Who is Stephanie?' I said, when she had gone. 'Her daughter?'

Jessica laughed. 'Oh no! Her chihuahua. The love of her life. Without Stephanie, she would be even more grumpy. But that's customers for you,' she went on, rehanging the dresses. 'They are all different. You just need to know *how* they are different.'

I could see exactly what Mum meant when she said Jessica was amazing. I made a note to ask her to style me when we had a quiet moment over the next few weeks.

8

There was a small gathering of locals in James's Deli when I popped in to buy a sandwich at lunchtime. James, dressed in a navy apron, looked over from behind the counter and gave me a wave. 'Hi, Olivia,' he said. 'How's it going?'

'Olivia!' said Mrs O'Keefe, from the grocers, 'welcome home, love. Your mam said you were coming.'

'Thank you, Mrs O'Keefe,' I said. 'Good to be home.'

Bernard Murphy the butcher stood with his basket and a pile of paper-wrapped packages on the end of the counter, his sausagey hands resting proprietorially on them, his chest puffed like a toddler who has been successfully to the toilet for the first time. 'Well,' he said, 'as chairperson of the Sandycove Shopkeepers Association, I too join in welcoming you home, Olivia.'

'Thanks, everyone,' I said.

'But, Olivia, as someone who has newly re-entered the village, what do you think about the parking situation?'

'Uh... I think there probably aren't enough spaces.' I assumed that was the right answer, but Bernard held up a finger.

'I think we have enough spaces,' he said. 'But I think there should be one outside my butcher's shop. Just for me. You never know when I might need to go somewhere. Last week, I was called to an emergency at the town hall. There was a planning-permission crisis and they needed the benefit of my experience of being a Sandycover born and bred.'

Mrs O'Keefe nodded enthusiastically. 'Parking is a nightmare in the village these days, with all those big cars that people like to drive. But you should walk more, Bernard. Get your heart rate up.'

'My heart is at the rate of a twenty-year-old. Dr Butler ran a few tests. Said I had the physique of a much younger man.'

Mrs O'Keefe looked impressed.

'He asked me for a few tips,' Bernard went on, 'keeping fit and all that. I was very good at the old aerobics once upon a time. And so I was very happy to give him the benefit of my wisdom.'

'What can I get you, Olivia?' asked James.

'I'm not sure,' I replied. 'What would you recommend? I'm buying for Jessica as well.'

'Well,' said James. 'She likes the chicken and green-grape wrap with crème fraîche dressing ... which is good... but today's special is goat's cheese and apple on sourdough.'

'I'll take one of each,' I said. 'And some of those tomatoes... and... some of the salami... and the pasta.' I wanted to cook dinner for Mum tonight.

'Coming up,' James said, taking his bread knife and starting to slice the loaf.

'Such a handsome man,' said Mrs O'Keefe, slyly, eyeing Bernard. 'I was saying to some of the other ladies in the village, that it's a long time since we had someone with those looks around here.'

'Who are you talking about?' spluttered Bernard.

'Dr Butler!' said Mrs O'Keefe. 'You were just talking about

him. He's like Laurence Olivier in *Wuthering Heights*. Magnificent man.' She stared off momentarily into the middle distance.

'He does have a fine head of hair,' Bernard agreed. 'My father always said that you should never trust a bald man and as you can see...' He whisked off his straw boater to reveal a thick thatch of white hair. 'You could trust me with your life!' He laughed heartily. 'It's the way I tell 'em,' he said, laughing even harder.

'Luxuriant,' enthused Mrs O'Keefe. 'Your hair. It has the quality of a shagpile carpet. Do you remember those, Olivia? Too young, perhaps?'

'I think I know what you are talking about,' I said.

'You should ask Dr Butler,' said Bernard. 'He's the fount of all knowledge, it seems.'

'Maybe I will,' said Mrs O'Keefe. 'You went to school with Dr Butler and Dermot, didn't you, James?'

James nodded as he wrapped the sandwiches in white paper. 'They were both *very* well behaved. Both favourites of the teachers. I remember Mr Malone telling us in assembly that we should all be a little less like the scruffy little eejits he thought we were and a lot more like the Butler boys.'

'Well,' said Bernard, 'they had to be paragons because their father was the maths master. A difficult man, I recall. One Christmas, his turkey order had been mixed up and I had delivered him a goose instead. He didn't take it well at all and quite lost his temper. On Christmas Eve, would you believe?'

The door of the shop opened, and Dr Butler entered, stepping over Sammy the Labrador while Dr Butler's Yorkie snuffled around Sammy.

Dr Butler gave everyone a general quick smile. 'How's it going?' he said to the room, and then nodding at me.

'Ah!' Bernard boomed. 'Dr Butler! Talk of the devil! We were just remembering your wonderful father. A fine man, he was.

Your mother would come in and buy the finest steak for him. Said he would eat it raw... now, that can't have been true, can it, Dr Butler?'

'He did like steak tartare,' Dr Butler admitted. 'He was a man of rare tastes.'

'Literally!' said Bernard, with a chortle. 'And are you a man who likes a steak tartare?'

Dr Butler shook his head. 'I'm nothing like him,' he replied, smiling politely. 'At least I hope not.'

'I do a very nice steak,' mused Mrs O'Keefe. 'But they have to be from Bernard. *His* are the finest for miles.' She flashed him a smile which he ignored. 'I do also remember that your father had a brain like a computer. A walking calculator! And the words he would come out with... Oh sweet mother of divine Jesus! Big ones, none I'd ever heard before or since. He was like that, being a teacher. And so handsome. Not unlike yourself. He used brilliantine on his hair, always made me think of James Mason.'

'I can't really remember much about him, to be honest,' said Dr Butler, curtly. 'I'm just here for lunch. What's today, James?'

'Fish pie,' said James. 'Does that work for you?'

'Sounds great,' replied Dr Butler. 'Anyway, how's the old fella doing?' He bent down to stroke Sammy.

'Ah, no change, still very slow, you know how it is.' James handed a paper bag to Dr Butler and swiped his card.

'He's a great boy,' said Dr Butler, standing up. 'I'd better be getting back. See you all...' He left the shop, Pablo at his feet.

'Well!' said Mrs O'Keefe. 'What a handsome young man!'

'So you've said,' replied Bernard. 'Repeatedly. Ad nauseous. Is it James Mason or Laurence Olivier or bloody Muffin the Mule? Anyway, I have to get on with delivering my sausages... I'll be off.'

James handed me my sandwiches and a bag of shopping and I passed over my card. 'Thanks, James,' I said.

'Let me know what you think of the sandwiches,' he said.

'Bye, Olivia,' said Mrs O'Keefe. 'Say hello to your mam and tell her if she needs anything dropping over, to give me a call.'

'Thanks, Mrs O'Keefe.'

As I walked back to Nell's, I realised I already felt sucked into all the little happenings and gossip of the village. London was truly a world away.

* * *

Later, while Mum was in the front room watching the news, I was rooting in the kitchen cupboard and spotted my old orange enamel saucepan. It was right at the back, a little bit battered, the wooden handle slightly charred from a few accidents over the years. It was the one I used when I first began experimenting with beeswax and oils, melting them on the hob, stirring in rose oil and lavender, filling the room with intoxicating scents.

If I closed my eyes, I could still smell them now. There was my lemon and almond soap or my orange and lavender body balm. I would cut slabs of soap up and wrap them in paper or pour my bath oil into bottles. It was a really happy time at the beginning, when it was simple and fun. I would dream up new combinations, thrilled when I loved them and dying to bring them to the market the following week to see what my customers thought. I never did get that chance to do something with seaweed... a salt scrub... a silky seaweed body oil, a hand cream.... I didn't think about it very often, but being home and finding my lovely old orange saucepan brought it all back. Some people were cut out for business, but when things became tricky, I had been out of my depth.

'Something smells good,' said Mum, coming in.

'Just pasta and tomato sauce,' I said. 'Roberto's favourite. He says it's the only meal he could eat every night.'

'I hope he's okay with you being away,' said Mum.

'He's not great at feeding himself,' I admitted. 'His favourite meal is breakfast, and when he's on his own, he eats it three times a day. Cereal, tea and toast, a rasher sandwich.' I gave her a bowl of pasta. 'More parmesan?'

'Yes, please. So, how was the shop today? Did you enjoy yourself?'

'It was...' The day had been better than I could have imagined. Yes, there was that awful feeling of not being very good at something, but I had kept myself busy, tidying up and rearranging the clothes. And I absolutely loved Jessica. And eating one of James's amazing sandwiches every day wouldn't be a hardship. 'You have to be half-counsellor,' I said, 'half-mind-reader when you work in a shop. I had no idea it was such an art.'

Mum laughed, taking a bite to eat. 'I wouldn't elevate it quite that high,' she said. 'But I admit it's not quite just standing around and waiting for someone to buy something. You have to have a light touch, and, more than anything, you want your customer to leave having had a nice experience, whether they have bought their dream outfit or have spent three minutes having a browse. Olivia,' she said. 'This is delicious. I can see why it's Roberto's favourite.'

'Glad you like it. I can cook every night, if you like. By the way, Mum,' I said, 'why is the fridge full of mini bottles of wine? It looks like a hotel minibar in there.'

'I find a whole bottle is far too much for me,' she said, 'and one is perfect with some left over for another evening. Henry isn't a big drinker, so I like to just have one. Why don't you pass one out – a red, I think – and we'll split it between us.'

I did as I was told. Mum held up her glass. 'You see, perfect for two,' she said, smiling. 'Cheers!'

9

Roberto: Are you still there?

Me: Yes.

Roberto: Just wondering.

Me: Are you?

Roberto: Am I what?

Me: Still there?

Roberto: Just about. I have no one to watch Call My Agent with.

Me: I'm sorry.

Roberto: Come back so we can watch the last series.

Me: I've only been gone two days.

Roberto: Feels like a year.

First thing the following morning, Betty Boyle from Nouveau You entered the shop.

'Olivia, Jessica, good morning. All well?' She didn't wait for us to respond and turned to me. 'So lovely to see you, Olivia, back in your mother's shop. Just like my Jennifer-Louise has followed in my footsteps, carrying on the family business.'

'I am just visiting, really,' I said, but Betty wasn't listening.

'Now, I have a little news,' she said. 'It's been very hard to keep this secret. I'm good at keeping secrets, but this one has been particularly hard.' There was a smudge of pink lipstick on her teeth when she smiled. 'Well, my Jennifer-Louise is pregnant! Yes, I am going to be a grandmother! I know! Isn't it simply the most wonderful news you have ever heard? She and Graham are over the moon.'

'That's fantastic,' I said.

'Brilliant,' said Jessica. 'Jennifer-Louise must be...'

But Betty had started up again. 'As you may know, she and Graham are living above the shop at the moment, in the little bijou pied-á-terre, but, of course, Jennifer-Louise is going to have to be careful and reduce her hours working with me in Nouveau You and *all* her other commitments. And she has so many! Such a busy girl and so very much *in demand*. Which brings me to my little visit to you this morning. Obviously, due to her condition, my Jennifer-Louise has not been able to organise the midsummer festival. It's only three weeks away, and she's been so beset with anxiety and feeling unwell, the poor girl, she hasn't been able to pull *anything* together.'

Was she asking me? Did she think that I would...? No, surely not.

'Now, it's *such* a lovely occasion,' went on Betty. 'Just a gathering of the villagers and an adorable recital from the children from the local ballet school. Everyone said what a wonderful job Jennifer-Louise did last year. No one minded the rain or the fact that a member of the tin whistle orchestra from St Joseph's primary went missing a moment before they were about to start "Hot Cross Buns"... which, *entre nous*, wasn't a bad thing, I can tell you, as one of my migraines began to rumble. Jennifer-Louise was so looking forward to repeating her success this year, but as a leading member of the Sandycove Village Council, it falls to me to find someone to fill Jennifer-Louise's large shoes. *Not*, of course, that she has large feet. She's on the dainty side, a petite size five... four and a half in sandals, just like me. Anyway, we need someone who doesn't have a great deal going on, and we... well, I thought of you.'

Wait a minute. She *was* asking me to take over the organising of this festival in *three* weeks.

'I don't think...' I began. 'I am meant to be... I can't...'

I tried to protest, but Betty held up a hand as her strident tones beat my vocal cords into submission. 'All you have to do is make a few phone calls,' she said. 'It's *so* simple. And it's not like you have any other commitments? Your mother said you were hoping to rest as much as possible.' She smiled again. 'So, yes? I can tell the Sandycove Village Council that everything is a-go?'

'Okay,' I said, defeated.

'That's super,' said Betty, handing over a file. 'Voila! The dossier. Now, ladies, I'd better return to the shop. We have a wedding party coming in, and you know how much my expertise and light touch is valued when it comes to anxious brides and flustered MOBs. I'll close the door on my way out. Ciao-ciao!'

Jessica and I looked at each other.

'What just happened?' I asked.

Jessica laughed. 'It won't be too much work,' she said. 'Last year's was pretty simple, actually. Just the tin whistle orchestra from school and the ballet group. My two were in it. Both go to Miss Rachel's ballet school. Frankie loves it more than Ellie-Mae. It was quite a struggle getting Damien to allow Frankie to do ballet. We had a lot of tears.' She paused. 'From Frankie,' she said, hastily, 'but eventually Damien relented. Says he can do it for another year and then we'll see.'

'Why didn't he want him to do ballet?'

'He's a little traditional,' explained Jessica. 'Men are men, that kind of thing. Thinks if he brings his plate from the table to the kitchen counter, then he is amazing.' She gave a laugh. 'He's a hard worker,' she said. 'Likes to provide. He just needs a little softening up sometimes. But he'd charm the birds off the trees, that's what Mam says. I think he looks like a Disney prince.'

But then, before Jessica said anything more, a customer waved to her and she dashed across the floor.

'Morning!' I heard her say. 'The puffed sleeves? Oh yes, so beautiful. One hundred per cent silk... I know! The colour! You sit there on the chaise longue and I will bring them over to you!'

So, I thought, my time here in Sandycove was going to be slightly busier than I had planned. I flicked through the dossier, realising it was less dossier and really just one sheet of A4 with a few scribbled phone numbers. But I was, after all, a PA and could pull things together at a moment's notice. Again, the tentacles of village life were pulling me in. At this rate I would never leave.

* * *

Bronagh and I sat on a bench eating an ice cream from a van on Dún Laoghaire pier. The setting sun bathed the world in a pink glow, seagulls circled ahead hoping for flotsam from the chip van. People walked past us, in the middle of their evening constitutional, soaking up every last ray, like a squirrel might eat too many nuts before hibernation.

'Well, this is nice,' I said.

'It's very nice.' Bronagh nibbled at the flake in her ice cream. 'I feel like I'm on holiday.'

'So do I,' I agreed. 'Even though I am technically meant to be on holiday which isn't a holiday but still feels like a holiday.'

'You lost me at holiday,' she said.

'Did you ever think that you'd stay in Sandycove?' I asked. 'Was that always your plan?'

'I thought I'd be in New York or Berlin,' she replied. 'That was the idea. But I realised that I liked living here too much.'

'I was the opposite,' I said. 'I always thought I'd stay. But I was the one who left.'

'Proves you can't ever make plans,' she said. 'You never know what's going to happen.'

'Which brings me to the midsummer festival... you sure you don't mind helping me organise it?'

'No, it's fine,' she said. 'If it is just a case of a few phone calls, then of course I can. But do you think we could have fireworks? You know how much I love fireworks.'

'I'll make a few calls.' I'd already booked the church car park, the lighting rig, the stage and seating. The rest Bronagh and I were going to split between us.

'I can't believe I am going to be responsible for inflicting that infernal tin whistle orchestra on the village,' Bronagh went on. 'For months after last year's festival, all I could hear was high-pitched, tuneless renditions of old Irish songs. The whole village had collective hearing loss for about a week afterwards.'

'Mum says Henry is in the Sandycove Ukulele Orchestra. What do you think? Should we ask them?'

'Why not? They have to be better than the tin whistle orchestra.'

'And apparently last year there was Miss Rachel's ballet school.'

'I think the word "ballet" is used very loosely,' said Bronagh. 'But, like the tin whistle orchestra, if there's children involved, then quality control is abandoned.'

'They could be *Midsummer Night's Dream* fairies,' I said, starting to enjoy myself. 'What else?'

'A bonfire?' suggested Bronagh.

'And food... and fireworks... and... a DJ... we need to dance.' The thought of the whole village dancing together in some outdoor rave (admittedly, a very sedate rave) suddenly sounded very appealing.

'I love it,' said Bronagh.

'And food trucks,' I said. 'I mean, we don't want everyone getting *too* drunk, we need it to be civilised. So, we could start with the children's events and then segue into a very nice, grown-up disco...'

'What do you want me to do?'

'We'll make lists and we'll tick things off and report back.'

We began walking home. It was nearly 9 p.m. and there was that slow slide into night, the light clinging on for as long as possible. Behind us on the street, we heard the honking of a car horn. I looked around. It was Henry.

'Girls, would you like a lift?' he said.

'No, it's all...' I said, just as Bronagh said, 'That would be lovely.' She was already opening the door of the Morris Minor.

'Thank you, Henry,' I said, scrambling into the back of the car. 'This is my friend, Bronagh Kelly.'

'Bronagh, a privilege,' he said, crunching the car into first gear.

'These are my favourite cars in the world,' Bronagh replied. 'I hate new cars.'

'So do I,' said Henry. 'All that shiny metal and awful bars and the fact that you have to be bigger than everything else on the road. Give me something small and nippy and as old as me, and I am as happy as a clam. I brought this to France last year, was convinced it was going to break down, but not a single problem.' He patted the steering wheel. 'He's a great little guy is Pierre.'

Bronagh laughed. 'I love Pierre too.'

We drove along the seafront and down to the harbour where Bronagh's cottage was and dropped her off. Henry then drove back to Mum's house.

'Thank you, Henry,' I said, at the car door.

'Not a problem,' he replied. 'Tell your mother that I'll be round first thing in the morning.'

It felt like being driven around and dropped off by a parent – someone's dad – as Henry gave the horn another honk – softer this time – and off he went, into the night.

10

Roberto: Have decided I can't watch television without you. Sewing
Bee isn't the same on my own.

Me: But you always talk over everything we watch.

Roberto: So?

Me: So, it means I don't really get to watch it.

Roberto: But I have no one to talk about it to. It's like all the pleasure
has been removed if I can't give a running commentary.

Me: I only like TV with you as well.

Roberto: Am taping everything so we have a televisual cache for when
you get home.

Me: Can't wait.

Roberto: Off to Oxfam for bargains tomorrow.

The first week in the shop flew by and I was starting to get the
hang of things and wasn't as scared when customers came in,
although I still left the heavy lifting to Jessica. She and I spent
most the time talking, and I made sure I was there early enough
in the morning so we could have a cup of tea together before
opening time. More than anything, I was loving my walks to work

– it slightly beat my daily commute in London – where I was sere-naded all the way by birds. I hadn't noticed birds for years. Obvi-ously, I knew they existed but hearing them singing while I walked to work was a soundscape of such utter loveliness that I listened intently to them all the way.

And there was also the sight of the sea every day, that great expanse of shifting colour and light, the endless roll of the waves, the shimmering turquoise, the patches of grey, the sun rising over the bay. The air, the incredible air, filled with ozone and oxygen, my lungs clearing themselves out for the first time in years. I'd spent enough time being cooped up in offices, sitting behind a desk, breathing the stale carbon dioxide expelled by other office workers, being squashed on the Tube, eating three meals a day at my desk.

By Friday, I was making big plans. I was going to start running, I thought. Just a little bit, before going to Nell's. But I really wanted to move and get out into the fresh air and hear those birds and run down by the sea and feel the salty air on my face.

Later on Friday, a girl came into the shop. She was around seventeen or eighteen, dressed in black jeans and a checked man's shirt, with a blue wash in the ends of her long hair. Her skin was pale and slightly spotty. She smiled shyly. 'Hi,' she said. 'I'm…'

'Cara?' I held out my hand. 'I'm Olivia. Lovely to meet you.'

'You too,' she said. 'Your mum said to pop in and say hello when I was picking up my pay.'

'I'll get it!' called Jessica, nipping into the back office.

'Aren't you doing your exams at the moment?' I asked. 'How long have you got to go?'

'We've done one week, and then another two,' said Cara, looking even paler at the thought.

'Are you doing okay? Are you sleeping?'

Cara pulled on her hair. 'Not really,' she said. 'But I keep telling myself it will be over at some point and then I can go back to being generally anxious, as opposed to specifically anxious. It's like the exams absorb everything, it's like there's no life or world beyond them.' She gave a half-smile. 'It will be nice to remember all the other awful things as well.'

Jessica came back with a small brown envelope and put her arm around Cara's shoulders. 'Cara's our resident brainbox,' she told me. 'She's off to college in New York to do something about Russia.'

'I'm not going, though,' Cara said, quickly. 'I'm staying in Dublin. If I get the results.'

'You can't miss out on *New York*!' said Jessica. 'What I'd give to be eighteen again and have a chance to go to New York! What's the course called again?'

'Russian Literature, Life and Thought,' said Cara, squirming. 'And... well, it looks like a good course and you can't do it anywhere else, except... I want to stay in Dublin.'

'Cara got a full scholarship,' Jessica said. 'Everything's paid for.'

'Not flights, though,' said Cara.

'No... but you can get great deals these days,' replied Jessica. 'She had to write an essay about herself. Nell made her bring it in to show us. It was so beautiful. It was about Cara and her nan – Shirley. Made me cry, but everything does these days.' She smiled at Cara, who looked away, embarrassed.

Obviously, going to New York, even with a full scholarship, was going to be expensive, I thought.

'I shouldn't have applied,' Cara said to me. 'It was stupid. I only did it because my English teacher told me I should and I got a bit carried away. She said the course was ideal as it's the only one which places the Russian novel in its cultural and political context...'

'That's Cara's passion,' explained Jessica. 'Isn't it?'

Cara nodded, brightening up a little. 'I had to write about the importance of Russian literature on twentieth-century civilisation.'

'I wouldn't know where to begin!' said Jessica. 'What did you write about again?'

'How Russian literary heroines shaped an idea of powerful women which directly impacted on film and even fashion, politics,' replied Cara. 'They had an influence that went beyond the parameters of the pages of their worlds and I gave real-world examples of this direct influence.'

Jessica and I looked at each other, impressed.

How incredibly lucky Cara was to have a passion, I thought. Anyone with something – anything – that made them excited was fortunate. And for some reason, I thought of Seasalt, my little company. Passion should always be taken seriously, and self-doubt or lack of self-belief shouldn't ever be allowed to jimmy itself in or you might lose it forever.

'I'd better go and keep revising,' said Cara. 'And I've got a waitressing event on tomorrow night, so I'll get more work done tonight.' She turned to me. 'See you, Olivia. Hope you have a good time at home.'

'I will,' I said, 'and good luck with the exams.'

'See you, Cara,' said Jessica, giving her a hug. 'Give my love to Shirley.'

'Will do.' Cara slung her heavy school bag over her shoulder and gave us a wave as she left the shop.

Jessica looked at the clock. 'Six p.m.!' she said. 'I'd better go! Damien will be here.'

On cue, a large black Range Rover pulled up outside, like it had all week, and within moments, Jessica was pulling on her jacket and slipping her handbag across her shoulder.

'See you, Olivia!' she called, breaking into a run.

* * *

At closing, as I was locking the front door of the shop, I stood up and lost my balance, staggering backwards and hitting an immovable object. A *human* immovable object. And then – still stunned – stepped backwards onto a dog, who emitted a yowl so loud that you could have heard it in Dún Laoghaire.

'Oh my God! I'm so sorry!' As my eyes focused, I realised that the person was Dr Butler. 'I didn't see you and I...'

We both turned to look at the dog – the little Yorkie – who was lying, motionless, on the pavement, his tiny body a scrap of fur. Dead. And I had killed him.

'I'm so sorry,' I gushed. 'I don't know what to say. He's so tiny. Like a kind of scruffy mouse. I mean...' *Now* I was victim-blaming the dog. It was his fault for being small?

But Dr Butler actually smiled. 'My little friend Pablo is a fan of amateur dramatics,' he said. 'He likes a bit of limelight.' He looked down at Pablo. 'Come on, little guy,' he said, 'that's enough of that. Up you get. Stop your ham acting.'

Pablo lifted his head, fixing one eye on his owner.

'Come on,' said Dr Butler, sternly. 'Very good, round of applause. Standing ovation. Now, no more drama.'

With that, Pablo jumped up and gazed around him nonchalantly, as though nothing at all had happened and he was back to being a normal dog.

'I've had him since he was a puppy,' explained Dr Butler. 'He was like this from the very beginning. Always acting the maggot. And the amount of times I've stepped on him. He's too small, that's his problem. Or I'm too tall. Whichever it is.' He straightened up his tweed jacket, which I noticed was a little frayed at the cuffs, the kind of coat that had been well-worn and well-loved.

'And I'm too clumsy,' I said, thinking how much friendlier he was today. Perhaps Dr Butler was shy and took his time with people?

'No, he's too small... he's the size of my shoe,' he said. 'I should have got a bigger dog, one that wouldn't be in peril of being squashed all the time. Except I love him.' He smiled at me and I found myself smiling back.

'Thank you, Dr Butler... I mean, not *thank you*, but thank you for not minding me stepping on your dog... I mean...' I was babbling and being an idiot and I wasn't quite sure why. But Dr Butler was looking at me with those brown eyes. 'Well, thank you...' I said again. 'For... you know...'

He smiled. 'You're welcome... and thank you for... you know...'

'You're welcome.' I smiled back.

'Any by the way, I'm Will... not Dr Butler. I mean, I am, but I don't know why people call me that.'

'Because it's your name?'

He laughed. 'Anyway, I'm Will.'

'And I'm Olivia. Or Liv. If we're doing abbreviations.' His dark eyes were really quite *unnecessarily* intense, I thought, making me lose my train of thought.

'Who calls you Liv?'

'Just my best friends,' I said. 'Everyone else calls me Olivia. My ex-boyfriend called me Olive Oil once... which didn't go down well.'

He laughed again. 'Goodbye, Olivia,' he said. 'Liv.'

'Goodbye, Will.'

And with Pablo at his heels, Will began walking away and I

stood on the main street in my old village, on a Friday evening with cars driving past, people talking in twos and threes, Bernard Murphy reeling in the striped awning of the butchers, people leaving the off-licence with bottles in twisted wraps of paper, Betty locking the door of Nouveau You and waving to Mrs O'Keefe who was carrying in her boxes of fruit and vegetables. James was pulling down the blinds of the deli, while across the road, in Albatross, Alison was sweeping the floor of the café.

I was so very glad to be home. I grew up here, but I was always looking beyond it, taking it for granted, never appreciating how beautiful it was. And there was Will, who suddenly picked Pablo up and kissed the tiny dog on the top of his nose. And the two of them walked down the street, away from me.

11

Mum and Henry were watching television together in the living room.

'Hello, darling,' said Mum. 'Good day?'

'Great, thank you.' Mum paused *Gardener's World*.

'No lift needed this evening?' said Henry, smiling. 'Any time you do, give me a call. I like to be useful.'

'Thanks, Henry.'

'Cup of tea?' said Mum, going to stand up. 'I think I can put weight on my leg. Look.' She stood gingerly on both legs, her right hip was the one in trouble and for a moment she was perfectly upright. 'Starting to hurt a bit,' she said, taking her crutch again and sitting down.

'I'll make the tea... would you both like one?'

Mum nodded. 'That would be lovely,' she said.

'Why don't I make it?' said Henry, standing. 'I've had an exceptionally easy day. You two are hard-working women. It's about time you both had a rest.'

'Thank you, Henry,' I said, sitting on the other armchair as he left the room. 'How was your day, Mum?'

'I didn't do much,' she replied. 'Just thought about things, made cups of tea, thought about other things. It's been quite cathartic. I don't think I've had this chance to be just be... what's the word?'

'Quiet?' I suggested.

'Still,' she said. 'It's... it's been interesting.' She smiled at me. 'How was your day in the shop?'

'I met Cara today. She was telling me about New York. She wants to go and doesn't want to go.'

Mum nodded, obviously knowing it all. 'She has commitments here,' she said. 'And New York's an expensive place to live. She's got to think about it very carefully.'

Henry came back into the room with a tray of tea. 'I worked in the kitchens of the Waldorf Astoria for a whole summer once,' said Henry. 'I was nineteen years of age, a first year in engineering and got a working visa. Let's just say, I didn't see many sights while I was there. All I saw were the gloomy kitchens, potato peelings and the giant washing-up sink. I came back to Dublin in September a stone lighter and blinking in the sunlight.' He set the tray down and stood up. 'I won't stay, Nell. I think I will go home and do some what I call onion-ing.' He smiled at me. 'We are at a crucial stage in their development. One wrong move, their growth might be inhibited. And I can say goodbye to first place at the Dún Laoghaire Summer Fair.'

Mum laughed. 'You've become obsessed,' she said. 'I dread to think what will happen if you don't win.'

'I will be a shell of my former self,' he replied. 'I will be a broken man.' He clutched his face, looking devastated, making Mum laugh again. 'Anyway, I'll be off.' He waved to me and then gave Mum a special smile. 'I'll be round tomorrow. Sleep well... I'll let myself out! Don't move, lovely O'Neill ladies. Stay right where you are. Call me at any time, day or night, if anything is needed.'

'Thanks, Henry,' I said.

We heard the front door close.

'He's so nice,' I said.

'I think so,' Mum agreed, turning the television off. 'Will you pass me over my handbag?' Her bag was hanging on the hooks in the hall, by the front door. I brought it into the sitting room. 'I have something for you. Henry drove me into Dún Laoghaire and I picked it up earlier.' She placed a tissue-wrapped package onto my hand. 'I should have given it to you a long time ago.'

I unwrapped the tissue… it was Mum's old locket, the one I used to play with when I was a child while going through all her jewellery, trying on broaches and bangles and bracelets and then slipping this very locket around my neck. But even though I knew lockets should be openable, this wasn't. It was stuck shut.

'Is it fixed?'

Mum nodded. 'The clasp was broken,' she said. 'It was easy to fix in the end. I just didn't do it. My mother's photograph was in there.' She looked at me. 'It made me too sad.'

I still hadn't opened it, just sat with it in my hand, looking at the filigree on the outside, the tiny clasp, the silvery ripple of the chain. 'Why did it make you sad?'

Mum shook her head as though she didn't know. 'I suppose I still miss her every day. Silly really, after all these years. But I was hoping it would fade a little, which would make it easier… but people don't fade away. I can still hear her voice in my ear. Instead, you just get used to the space in your life where someone you loved once was.'

'When did she die?'

'You were a week old…' She looked at me. 'There was me with a tiny baby, I'd been banished from the family home and my mother was dying... it was quite the drama...' She gave a rueful smile.

'Wait... banished from the family home?'

She nodded. 'It's a long story, but lately, I've been doing a lot of thinking and reassessing. When Mam died, it was really hard... for a long time. Really hard. *You* kept me going. But there was so much I wished had been different.'

I nodded, understanding some of what she was saying. She had never talked about my grandmother or even my grandfather. I had the impression he'd been a bit of a bully. But I knew she loved her mother because of things she said. If a song came on the radio, she might say, 'This was Mam's favourite,' and she'd sing along to herself, lost in thought.

I looked again at the silver locket. 'It's beautiful...'

'Open it,' Mum said.

I put one nail into the clasp and gently prised it open. Inside, were two tiny photographs, one on either side of the tiny, shell-like locket. One photograph was a woman with a short bob, looking to the side, her mouth not quite smiling, and then on the other side was the same woman holding a baby.

Mum wiped away a tear. 'That's Mam,' she said. 'And that's her with me. She's beautiful, isn't she?'

We both squinted intently at the face of this long-lost woman.

I felt suddenly overwhelmed. This was my *grandmother*. A woman I knew so little about and yet meant everything to Mum. And she was my family. Until now, I hadn't realised that it was possible to miss someone you had never known.

'Do you want to put it on?' said Mum, reaching for it.

'No, it's yours,' I said. 'It's your *mother*. You have to keep it.'

'She's your *grandmother*,' said Mum. 'I've kept her from you all these years. I could have told you everything. And I didn't. She was the most wonderful person I knew. Until you came along. So loving, so kind. She did everything for me and wanted so much for me, but I... I kind of ruined everything.'

'What do you mean?'

Mum inhaled a huge gulp of air, as though hoping it would sustain her for some time. 'When Mam was dying, I was in love. While my own mother was getting weaker and weaker, I was too busy having fun with your father... I've never forgiven myself for that.' She looked at me, searching for my reaction.

'My father?' I repeated.

'Oh God. I was so in love. I was twenty-five and thought I knew everything.' She stopped. 'I know I should have told you about this earlier... from day one... but it was easier not to. I convinced myself that I didn't need to tell you. He wasn't in our lives, so why bother? My heart was broken... how would I explain that to you? It made me sound like this silly woman, someone who can't cope...'

'I would never think you couldn't cope,' I said. I looked at the photograph of my grandmother once more. 'She looks really beautiful. She looks like you.'

'She looks like *you*,' she said, smiling. 'And she would have loved you.' Mum had tears in her eyes. 'Here, let me put it on you.'

I turned a little and lifted up my hair as Mum put it around my neck and fiddled with the clasp.

'There,' she said. 'It suits you.'

I placed my hand on the locket, feeling its lightness against my throat. 'I love it,' I said. 'Thank you.'

'Thank you for coming home... To help me when you could have gone anywhere.' She paused. 'I should have told you the story long ago. Because it's actually your story.'

'Go on...' I had to keep her focused. In a moment, she could shut down again, and I would be left with half a story.

Mum took my hand. 'My father was a hard man, a stickler for everything being perfect. Mam and I were always scared the house wouldn't be neat enough or the dinner hot enough or his glass of beer cold enough. When it was just the two of us, Mam and I would listen to the radio and sing along to the music, but as soon as he'd come in, we'd switch it off. He wasn't a bad man, just a man of his time.'

'And your mother?'

'This lovely, sweet woman, so kind. She'd have done anything for me. I was the apple of her eye...' Mum's voice wobbled and she squeezed my hand. 'And then she was dying and I was too busy having fun that year... you see, I'd met Joe...'

'Joe?'

'Your father. Joseph Delaney. What can I say? The most handsome man I ever saw. We met in The Island one night and I was with my friends, a big group of us, and he and his friends came over. We chatted all night. He was from Cork and was working in Dún Laoghaire for the summer. That night, I remember walking home on my own thinking I'd fallen in love. Every song I'd ever heard was about me and how I felt about Joseph Delaney.'

Joseph Delaney. My father. I didn't dare to breathe just in case Mum stopped talking.

'He was tall and skinny and he used to wear this leather jacket... his pride and joy.' She smiled. 'And *such* a funny man, he'd have me in stitches. We went all over together. Down to music weekends in Lisdoonvarna, to the Glastonbury Festival, all the way on the back of his motorbike. He used to wear an old silk scarf that belonged to his grandfather. And he had sideburns.' She laughed. 'But the way he'd look at me, like I was the most important person in the world, as though everything I said was pure gold, which I can tell you, it wasn't. And after having a father like mine who thought everything that came out of my mouth was pure rubbish or pure insolence, Joe was different.'

'So... what happened?'

'He left. Never saw him again. He went to Boston to find work with his cousin, and he promised he would write every day, the usual story. I wrote, but nothing from him, not a word, as though he had dropped off the side of the world.' She shook her head. 'I can't explain what that was like. I didn't know his family in Cork or where they were. I had the address in Boston but when I called the operator and was put through, they said they didn't know him.' Mum shook her head. 'I called every day. You see, I was pregnant with you... months along. God, I was desperate. No answer. Nothing. I told Mam and she was as distraught as I was. But by this stage she was weeks from being admitted to St Michael's, and she never got out of there. As soon as Dad knew I was pregnant, he hit the roof. He'd been delighted when Joe had gone, thinking he'd got rid of him, but then there I was, pregnant, unmarried and only twenty-five. He said he wanted nothing more to do with me. And... well, it was awful. I can still remember Dad raging at me, and Mam so pale. Dad never liked Joe, but I always thought he would accept him. You see, Joe had no career to speak of, he was lower class than us... those kinds of things were important to Dad. I mean, Dad worked in the printers in Glenageary, but it was a desk job, he didn't get his fingers dirty. And Joe was a builder... well, he was at that time.'

'Where did you go?'

'A house in Waterson's Street...'

'But I thought Waterson's was your home... where you had grown up.'

'I was just being...'

'Economical with the truth?'

She nodded. 'Yes, sorry. Waterson's was where I stayed while I was pregnant and while Mam was dying. It's was Betty's family home. She and I had been in school together and she was one of the few people who helped me.'

'Betty?'

'I'll never forget her friendship,' said Mum. 'I'll never forget what she and her mother and father did for me. No questions, just a room in their house. Without them... well, it wouldn't have been easy.'

'But why didn't you tell me more about it – why didn't you tell me *all* about it?'

'I don't know. I just didn't want to think about it.'

'And Joseph Delaney? What happened?'

'I never saw him again.' She let go of my hand. 'I met someone years ago who told me he'd died. It was someone who'd worked with him in Dún Laoghaire and had joined the gang in Boston. Who knows what's true?'

It was too late, I thought. I'd waited all my life for this moment, and yet I didn't know what to feel. My father was suddenly real, with a name and a personality. She'd said he was funny. I thought I'd feel differently, this key unlocking my past, and opening into a brand new future. But I didn't know what I should do with this information. Mum was the person I loved and cared about. I realised that I cared far more about how she coped with it all above my feelings. I loved her. 'Why didn't you tell me before?' I said, gently.

'It was all so traumatic. Everything. Losing him. Being pregnant. Mam dying... Giving birth. Now, I think I must have had...' She gave a nervous laugh. 'I don't know... but Henry thinks it was a kind of PTSD... I thought you only got it after being in a warzone... but the more I've read about it, the more I've thought about it, I think he might be right.'

I put my hand against my locket. This Joe Delaney sounded

like the biggest idiot ever, to abandon Mum, to not acknowledge me. I felt ashamed of him, and I thought of Mum, my own mother, young, alone, devastated, going through all that.

'I remember I kept going to the post office,' went on Mum. 'Dad's sister Theresa was the postmistress there and one day I asked her if any letters had got lost and she was furious at me for even suggesting such a thing. "Do you think, Nell, that a single letter would be misplaced? Not when I am in charge!" I felt so awful to have even questioned her. She was one of the old-school, prim-and-proper types. There was nothing I could do. Mam was dying and my pregnancy was nearing the end, and I had to think of you. And me. The two of us. What kind of life were we going to have? I had to focus on that. My God... how on earth does the human spirit prevail?' She looked at me. 'I've often wondered that, how *do* we get through things?'

'We just do.'

She took my hand again. 'It takes a long time to shake off shame.' She paused. 'Oh God, the shame would eat away at you if you let it. I even...' She stopped. 'I even believed that Mam *died* because of the shame. I had caused her cancer.' She shook her head. 'Shame gets under your skin, it really does.'

'I'm so sorry,' I said, thinking of Mum being so young and vulnerable. And then I thought of something that seemed suddenly important. 'Did I ever meet my grandmother?' I needed to have met her. Please let me have her just a little bit, *please*.

'You did,' said Mum. 'She was in St Michael's Hospital in Dún Laoghaire and although I'd just given birth I was determined that she would see you and I would see her...' Mum had tears in her eyes. 'I took you on the bus to see Mam and refused to leave for four days. The three of us together. Of course, when Dad turned up, I had to pretend I wasn't around, and I walked you down by the seafront crying my eyes out. And then we'd go back as soon as the coast was clear.'

'Did he ever talk to you again?'

Mum shook her head. 'Never. He had no interest in seeing me, or you. That's what shame does to you. You put the parish, the community, your *standing*, above everything else. Shame clung to us. Actually, the only person who wasn't ashamed was Mam. The last thing she said to me was, "Look after Olivia, look after both of you".'

'And you did.'

She smiled at me. 'And I did. Well, as best I could.'

'And your dad?'

'He died an unhappy man,' she said. 'He missed out on you. And me. When he died the following year, his brother sold everything. All those things gone, all those lives dissipated, gone with the wind. But it's Mam I miss and I still think of her every day. If I was the person I am now, I could have helped her.' Mum still had hold of my hand. 'I'm sorry things were what they were,' she said. 'I'm sorry it wasn't perfect.'

'It was pretty perfect,' I said. 'I had you.'

Tears sprang into both of Mum's eyes. 'Oh, Olivia,' she said, her voice breaking. 'And I had you. I wouldn't have got through it without you.'

12

Roberto: Oxfam came up trumps, as per usual. Have found a perfect silver lamé jacket. Bit tight but worth it. Also a few interesting books including Elvis and Me by Priscilla Presley and Mary Berry's Complete Cakes and Bakes. Both page-turners.

Me: Glad you are keeping busy.

Roberto: Am practising eyeliner like Priscilla's and might even try some baking.

Me: Can't wait to try it when I get home.

Roberto: It all looks quite difficult. WTF is cream of tartar? Am going to see if our oven works.

Me: Of course it works!

Roberto: But I wouldn't know would I?!

Roberto: Just checked. It seems to work! I am already thinking I am going to be good at this. Maybe this is a new career? A little bakery of my own. Roberto's!

On Saturday morning, I woke early, my mind rolling through everything Mum had told me. The locket was on my bedside table and I opened the clasp and stared at the photographs. My poor mother. Whatever I'd been through in my life was nothing compared to her trauma.

I'd spent most of the hours I couldn't sleep googling Joseph Delaneys in Boston and obviously it was the proverbial long-lost father in a haystack. There possibly couldn't be a more popular name in Boston. I'd spent the rest of the night staring at the photograph of my grandmother. I couldn't quite believe that so much of my family had been revealed. But I didn't know how I felt about Joseph. He had abandoned my mother and he'd abandoned me. What kind of man does that? And yet...

I had to get out of the house, into the fresh air. I had to move.

I'd never run before. Well, never intentionally. But I wanted to now. I pulled on my trainers, leggings and a T-shirt, tied my hair up and set off, down our road and towards the village. There was a freshness to the day, a lightness and a brightness to the world, a cool in the breeze and blue of the sky that meant you knew it was going to be one of those golden days, the sun rising in the east, over Dublin Bay.

A man in a baseball cap overtook me, gliding past, his legs and arms pumping easily. I wished I could be that fast, I thought, looking at his legs in his shorts, long and muscular. There was a Yorkshire terrier running beside him. Dr Butler? But he was soon long gone, yards ahead of me, away into the distance.

I kept going. Down by the harbour, people were already swimming. I looked out for Bronagh as I ran past the Forty Foot, the sea shimmering and gleaming as the human heads bobbed in the water like seals.

My legs were starting to get tired, my whole body prickled with sweat, my clothes not remotely suitable to actual exercise... and yet I kept going. Back to the village, where things were slightly busier now. Anthony in the newsagents was opening up, hunks of newsprint being dropped off, the smells from Janet's bakery wafted into the air, and there was Mrs O'Keefe in the grocer's sweeping the floor. For a moment, I wasn't sure if my legs were going to manage to get me home, and slower now, I turned into our road, looking out increasingly desperately for the monkey tree. And there it was. Home. Thank God. I staggered home feeling brilliantly alive.

* * *

In the evening, it was Bronagh's parents' anniversary party. Her family home was at the top of Killiney Hill, a mile or so from the village, where the houses became increasingly bigger, the gardens more spacious, until it was mainly trees and driveways and too-big cars. The Kellys' was set in an exclusive estate of fifteen houses, centred around a green area with old street lamps and signs staked into the grass saying:

No Football. No Playing. No Dogs.

These days, Bronagh lived in her lovely cottage down by the harbour – beautifully extended and utterly tasteful, like something out of a magazine – but her formative years had been spent in this modern double-fronted white monstrosity, a little bit Georgian and a little bit Tara from *Gone With the Wind*.

Bronagh's parents, Audrey and Brian, were both vain, self-absorbed, small-minded and their only interests beyond their noses were their three sons and the latest gossip from the golf club. When Bronagh announced she was going to study architecture at college, Audrey had sighed. 'Why can't you do something normal, like everyone else's children?'

Brian, her father, rarely looked up from his newspaper. All anyone ever saw of him was the top of his head, which, over the years, went from brown to grey to receding to shiny. He was a man of so few words, you wondered if he could actually talk.

I rang the doorbell, clutching my bottle of champagne, happy to be able to give Bronagh some moral support while I was home.

A waitress dressed in a black dress, white apron and frilly cap, like something from a low-budget period drama, appeared. 'Good evening,' she said robotically, 'welcome to the Kelly residence.'

'Cara?' I peered at her. 'Is that you?'

'Oh God, Olivia,' she said, stepping to one side and allowing me to pass. 'Sorry I didn't recognise you. I'm half-asleep, and I've still got four hours to go.'

We stood in the hall, beside the teak bureau with multiple family photographs, mainly of Mark, Chris and Alan and only a few featuring Bronagh, and even in those she was invariably hidden by one of the boys' elbows.

'What about your revising? Why are you working?'

'I haven't done Posh Plates for a few months and I needed a night away from the desk,' she said. 'I've left Nan at home watching an old film and I'll be home by midnight. But I wouldn't have done it if I'd known they'd make me wear this ridiculous costume. It's all part of the longing of the middle classes to re-enact some kind of feudal fantasy. I have to play the poor girl, so they can feel like lords of the manor. Or dacha. Read Tolstoy. It's all in there.'

'I will when I retire.'

It was the first time I'd seen Cara smile. 'Why are *you* here?' she asked. 'Do you know these people?'

Now I laughed. 'Bronagh Kelly's my best friend, but I can't imagine she ordered the costumes. She doesn't go in for feudal role playing.'

'She didn't, and I heard her have a word with Simon who runs Posh Plates saying it was unnecessary, but people love it, according to him. Anyway...' She lowered her voice. 'I think Bronagh's on the verge of a nervous breakdown.'

'Really?'

'Her mother wasn't very nice to her, something about Bronagh's hair making her look like Angela Merkel. And something else about never wearing anything nice.'

'I'd better go in,' I said. 'And see if I can help.'

The living room, stretching the full length of the house, was full of the monied of Killiney Hill – the golfers and estate agents, the bankers and large-business owners – and Audrey Kelly was standing holding a glass of champagne, dressed in something frou-frou I'd seen in the window of Nouveau You.

'Happy anniversary,' I said, going over. 'Forty years! Congratulations.'

Audrey never smiled as she was convinced it gave you wrinkles and kept her face rigid and smooth and instead gave me a vague wave. She also hated touching other people, visibly cringing if anyone got too close. I made sure to keep a distance. 'Ah! Olivia,' she said. 'Bronagh did say you were coming.'

'I hope you don't mind,' I said, having forgotten just how miserable she was and how she made you feel as though everything was all wrong and it was your fault.

'We have enough food to feed the whole of South County Dublin,' she said. 'I *told* Bronagh she'd ordered too much. People will be sick, I said. We are a nation teetering on the precipice of dangerous obesity. But did she listen? Of course not. I mean, I don't eat a thing. I can't, not at my age. The boys will eat it, though, thankfully they have the metabolism of teenagers and Mark was thirty-nine last week! You must go and talk to them. Mark's hurt his back from his delivery business.'

Mark, according to Bronagh, had already been cautioned about using his rickshaw to deliver cannabis to parties.

'I will,' I promised. 'I'll go and say hello in a moment.'

'They are all doing so well. Of course, Chris has his music; tribute bands are so popular these days. And, apparently, they are in *communiqué* with various record companies, but none of them are quite right, according to Chris. Master of the fine detail. Always was. And Alan is perfecting his recipes at The Prickly Cactus. Who knew that he would become such a culinary success? Brian?' She called out to her husband who was walking past. 'We didn't, did we, Brian?'

'What are you talking about?' he said, irritated.

Audrey ignored his rudeness. 'We didn't think Alan would become such a culinary success, did we? Say hello to Olivia, Brian,' she commanded, as he squinted, as though trying to place me.

'Olivia?' I prompted. 'Friend of Bronagh's.'

'Yes, yes...' And he mumbled something as he disappeared back into the crowd, dodging out of the way, obviously wishing the party was over and he could return to his life behind a newspaper.

I spied Bronagh coming into the room from the kitchen.

'There's Bronagh!' I said to Audrey. 'Better see if she needs any help.'

Audrey waved me away, her face pained, her nose wrinkled, to go and find something else that was wrong.

'Thank God!' Bronagh said when she saw me. 'Someone normal!'

I laughed, as she took two glasses of wine from a crowd of them and handed one to me.

'Mum is worse than I thought she would be. She's spectacularly tense. So, to get myself through this family shitshow, I am

drinking alcohol and eating crisps, hoping both will have a tran-
quillising effect.' She held out a bowl of crisps. 'Take one. Salt and
vinegar. Your favourite.'

Home, I thought, is a place where people know the flavour of
your favourite crisp.

'Mum told me this dress looked like something a pregnant
Morticia Addams would wear to a funeral,' went on Bronagh,
'and that I should do something about my crooked tooth.'

'Which crooked tooth?' I asked.

'This one.' She pointed to her right canine.

'In all the years I have known you, I have never noticed that
tooth.'

'It does stick out a little,' she said. 'I mean, Mum is technically
right. I don't have *perfect* teeth. Or a perfect life. Or the perfect
husband and perfect children. And I am too tall, and my hair is
too straight and I am not charming enough or nice enough. And
yes, I like to wear black. I mean, God! What do I need to *do*?'
Bronagh glugged at her wine.

'You need to take a deep breath and remember that you are
charming and nice and good enough. And that your teeth are
amazing and I have always been jealous of your hair.'

'Oh God,' she said, when she resurfaced from her glass. 'I
need alcohol so badly. She drives me to drink. I just wish I could
stand up to her. In the rest of my life, I am perfectly confident. I
give speeches, I lecture at the university, I deal with builders every
day, which is frankly terrifying because every single time I speak
they look through me and I have to just keep going. And I regu-
larly chair meetings where I am the only woman. But here... in
this house, I am fifteen again, and scared of my own mother. She
has already asked me to make sure the boys have enough to eat
this evening. Look at them...' We had a clear view through the

open doors leading to the garden. The boys were sitting on the swing seat just outside. Three huge men with scraggly, overgrown facial hair and undersized T-shirts were guffawing about something. 'Do they look as though they *need* me to make sure they are eating well?' she said.

'They do look amply fed,' I agreed. 'No chance of wasting away.'

Mark blew a smoke ring towards the sky. On closer examination, it was no ordinary cigarette being passed around between the three of them, which explained the guffawing.

'I could kill them,' said Bronagh, putting her empty glass on the table. 'I really could. There was I thinking that they had made a real effort to do something nice. I actually thought that by coming they were supporting me, knowing how much bloody work I've put in. And then those three clowns smoke a spliff!'

'Just ignore them,' I said. 'And if your mother makes any more comments about anything, you are going to smile sweetly and let it all wash over you, yes?'

Grim-faced, she took another two wines from the table. 'Come on, we're going over.' She began walking away, giving me no choice but to follow.

'Yo, Olivia,' said Mark, peering out from under his knitted beanie. 'How's it going?'

The three of them sat in a row, like three overgrown children.

'Great,' I said. 'How are you getting on?'

'Still pulling rickshaws,' he said. 'Done my back in, so now I can only work if I've taken four Nurofen and a shot of whiskey.' And then he let out a huge burp which set the three of them off, whereupon Alan made a funny high-pitched sound, which made them laugh even harder.

Bronagh and I stood watching as the giggling got out of hand, tears rolling down their faces, forcing Chris to slip out of the seat, as though he was boneless, and dropping to the ground.

'Jesus Christ!' hissed Bronagh. 'I can't believe you have got yourselves stoned at Mum and Dad's bloody wedding anniversary!'

'It is pretty good stuff,' said Mark. 'Took delivery of it today. Delivered to myself on my rickshaw...' He giggled again. 'Would you two like some?'

'No, we would not!' Bronagh rolled her eyes, looking ready to punch one of them or all of them, and the boys, realising they had gone too far, immediately softened.

'Sorry, Bronagh,' Alan said.

'Cool party,' said Chris. But then he let out another giggle, which set them all off again.

'It's time for speeches,' said Bronagh. 'I thought we'd *all* say something.'

Alan then burped loudly, making some people standing close to us turn around. 'Apologies,' he said, in a loud voice, his hands up. 'Massive apologies to all concerned. I have a terrible problem with trapped wind.'

The other two could barely contain themselves.

'So, it's just me, is it?' said Bronagh. 'Yet fucking again?' She glared at them as they looked for a moment genuinely sorry, and she and I walked back into the house and over to where her parents were standing.

'Attention, please!' Her smile was plastered on. 'Just a few words about my wonderful parents, Audrey and Brian, on their fortieth wedding anniversary...' She stared expressionlessly at me for a moment. 'Thank you everyone for coming,' she carried on. 'Tonight is a moment where we celebrate forty years of married life. They met – so the legend goes...' She laughed weakly. 'On a train to Galway. St Patrick's weekend and they began talking to each other in Kildare and by the time they were passing through Ballinasloe, they knew they were right for each other…' She paused while there were 'ah's from the crowd. 'They were married twelve weeks later.' She turned around to her parents. 'I think that's right, isn't it, Mum?'

'Most of it,' said Audrey, elbowing Bronagh out of the way. 'Of course, we had a little resistance from our parents,' she said, addressing the audience. 'Brian's mother wanted him to marry someone else and I think after forty years, your mother has been proved wrong. As she was on so many things… too many to mention. Details in my autobiography…' She paused for laughter. 'But, of course, we went on to have our three wonderful boys, who have taken time out of their busy lives to raise a glass to their parents.'

The boys had shuffled into the room and seemed oblivious to the homily their mother was spouting at the expense of their sister.

'Thank you, boys,' Audrey continued. 'And thank you all for coming and, most of all, thank you to Brian for making the right choice!'

We all raised our glasses. 'To Audrey and Brian.'

Bronagh stood to one side, forgotten about and alone, and I slipped my arm through hers. 'Come on,' I said. 'Let's have more crisps and a glass of champagne.'

'It's the best offer I have had for a while,' she said, giving me a smile. 'Oh God. I don't know why I bother. I mean, I do know why I bother, because if I don't do it, then nothing will happen. The boys couldn't organise a game of noughts and crosses, Dad just wants to nap all the time, and Mum sulks if she isn't the centre of attention.'

Later, after we'd helped clean up and the waiting staff were finished and ready to go, their minibus outside, ready to drop them all home, I went to say goodbye to Cara, back in her jeans, the hat and pinny dispatched back into the dressing-up box.

'Bronagh gave me a tip,' she said. 'Fifty euros! How nice is she?'

'You deserve it,' I said, knowing Bronagh was the nicest person I had ever met. And far too nice to her awful family.

13

Roberto: How do you make your soda bread? Mary Berry says you need bicarbonate of soda? WTF is it?

Me: Go to supermarket and ask! They will assist!

Roberto: Easier if you just come home…

Me: I'll be home in three weeks… Go to baking aisle, ask nice person to help.

Roberto: There's a baking aisle? Why did no one tell me of this wonder? Love you Princess Liv xxx

Me: Love you Prince Roberto xxx

I did really miss Roberto. He was my friend, brother, confidant, spiritual healer, court jester, therapist and wise old man in one perfect human. He was the one person who'd kept me going over the last decade I'd been in London. Initially, I'd gone for a year. A change of scene, I had told everyone – trying to ignore the cloud of failure which hung over me – while I planned my next move. In fact, I had gone because I didn't know what else to do. After closing down Seasalt – and ignoring Mum's pleas to keep it going – I was at a loss. But in my very first week, after walking into a coffee shop in Hackney, I ended up with a job, a best friend and somewhere to live that wasn't the sofa of a friend's ex-boyfriend's sister. The job came about because of the handwritten sign on the door.

Barista needed. Must be FABULOUS.

Not, obviously, that I thought of myself as fabulous, but I liked its tone.

The café was a small room with a long plywood counter and a giant poster of Kylie Minogue on the wall, framed by a string of fairy lights. There was also an old Sacred Heart lamp, but instead of Our Lady, the icon was Kylie. Whoever worked here, I thought, had to be Irish. And there he was. A man, about my height, with thick black eyebrows and stubble, eyes rimmed in turquoise and wearing a top four sizes too small paired with a tiny pair of silver hot pants.

He caught me looking. 'They're new,' he said, in a Dublin accent.

'What are?'

'My hot pants.' He came round to my side of the counter. 'I saw you admiring them.' He grinned. 'Irish?'

'Dublin,' I said. 'You too?'

'Obviously. Ballymun-born and Ballymun-fled. You?'

'Sandycove.' I found myself smiling back. 'How long have you been in London?'

'Five years,' he said. 'Never going back. I wouldn't get away with wearing these where I grew up.' He held out his hand. 'Roberto. Formerly known as Robert. But I think Roberto sounds nicer, don't you? More me?'

'Much nicer,' I agreed, shaking his hand. 'Olivia.'

'Delighted to make your acquaintance, *Liv,*' he said and then strutted back behind the counter as though he was on a catwalk. 'Not everyone could get away with these,' he said. 'Only those with a tiny arse and great legs. Even if I do say so myself. So...' He leaned on the bar across from me. 'On a scale of one to ten, how *Kylie* am I?'

'Kylie?' I laughed again. 'Um... seven?'

'Seven?' He looked appalled, his eyebrows shooting up. 'Seven! Hey, Charlie,' he called to a man who was wiping down the long table. 'She says I am seven out of ten.'

'That's being generous,' said Charlie, without looking up.

Roberto ignored him. 'Kylie,' he went on to me, 'is, you see, my *muse*. My alter ego. By day I am but a humble and fabulous barista, by night I am Miss Minogue in Les Femmes Magnifique. You should come. You look like you could do with a bit of fun.'

'What is it?'

'A club. My God, you really are straight off the boat. I compère three nights a week – Thursdays, Fridays and Sundays. You've never heard of it? Or *me*?' He called over to the other man again. 'Charlie, we have a stranger in town. She doesn't know about the club... she's never seen Miss Minogue...'

Charlie shook his head. 'You're only a legend in your own little mind, Roberto. Have you made her a coffee?'

'Where are my manners?' said Roberto. 'Would you like a latte? Or a cappuccino? On the house. We like to welcome our compatriots when they are new in town. And I make the best coffees in East London. Right, Charlie?'

'Whatever you say, Roberto.'

'And you've got the job, by the way,' he said, grinning, fluttering those eyelashes. 'We need someone to corrupt, don't we, Charlie?'

'I didn't even...' I began.

'You didn't need to,' said Roberto. 'I read your aura. You need a job, right? And you need somewhere to stay. And you need a new best friend?'

I nodded.

'Well, then I'm your fairy godmother. Or your fairy disco queen.'

And that was it. We became inseparable, sharing life's adventures over ten years. He was the reason why I stayed so long, he made working for Maribelle bearable because I had someone to come home to, someone who made life better. But because of Maribelle's incarceration and my split with Jeremy, I had begun to question if I wanted to return to work with its long hours, stress and constant anxiety. There had to be more to life.

* * *

It was Sunday morning and I woke early again. Despite feeling the effects of the previous night's wine and champagne, I went for another run. The day was even more glorious, a beautiful sunrise, the sea like a diamanté cloak, the sky high and blue, with seagulls circling, the air so fresh and clear. I was wearing the locket. Just having it around my neck was giving me a feeling of strength. My runs were not so much rocket-propelled as locket-propelled, and I kept going, despite my legs aching slightly from the previous day, my mind going over everything, from work in London to Joseph Delaney to Seasalt to Roberto to Jeremy.

Mum was waiting for me when I got back home and handed me a cup of coffee.

'Go and have a shower,' she said. 'I want to take you somewhere.'

'Where?' I asked.

'I'll show you when we get there.'

She still wouldn't tell me when I came downstairs, freshly

washed and dressed, and we got into the car, Mum's crutches beside me, as she drove us back into the village, and up along Sandycove Avenue. She indicated and slowed down, and then neatly reverse-parked outside one of the houses I'd always noticed and loved. There was a small black wrought-iron gate and a terracotta, slightly cracked tiled path leading to a yellow door with large glass panels which were tinted pink.

I looked back at her. 'This was your house?'

Mum nodded. 'I like the yellow door,' she said, turning off the engine. 'Nice and bright. It used to be navy. Every time I drove past this house, I just felt so sad,' she said. 'I thought of Mam and... well, I just stopped coming down Sandycove Avenue.'

I looked at the house. 'But it's only a fifteen-minute walk from our house. You could have... just told me and...'

'I know,' she said.

'Because people need to know this kind of thing... I could have... I don't know... I would have liked to have known that this is the house my mother grew up in.'

'I know.'

We both looked back at the house again. So, this was Mum's home, this was *my* family's home, full of my history and stories and memories. These people, this house, these lives which were so connected to me were all here. I wished I'd always known it.

'It's a beautiful house,' I said. 'It looks friendly...'

She nodded. 'I always liked it. When Dad died, his brother was the executor and sold it and gave me a few bits and pieces. But Dad's will *did* leave me £5,000. He didn't leave me destitute. Although he never spoke to me again after Mam's funeral. He saw you and didn't say a word. But it was that money we lived on and, after moving out of Betty's house, we moved into the flat above the shop and then I took over the lease on it below.' Mum turned to me. 'I do wish I'd told you all this before. I should have done. I was just trying to move on, I suppose, and put it behind me. But the thing is, you bring your past with you. You can never escape. I couldn't put it into words. My great shame. My great undoing. The gossip in the village! And then losing Mam.' Her voice cracked a little. 'I felt as though I had brought this terrible thing on our nice family. For years I blamed myself when now all I want to do is go back in time and give me a hug and tell myself that eventually everything is going to be okay.' She smiled. 'And that the little baby is going to be the most wonderful thing that has ever happened.'

'I want to give your younger self a hug as well,' I said.

She smiled. 'Come here, sweetheart.' She hugged me. 'I love you.'

'I love you too. I think you're amazing.' I wished I had her strength.

We looked back at the house. 'Mam used to grow daffodils in the front, along the path,' went on Mum. 'And she'd pick them for the kitchen table and I'd look forward to them every spring. Every time I see one, or buy a bunch, I think of her and wonder if she'd been born twenty years later, how different her life would have been. She wouldn't have married Dad, that was for sure. He hadn't had a happy life.' She sighed and looked back at me. 'I never felt sorry for him until recently. And now, *all* I can do is feel sorry for him. He was trapped in that universe of shame and recrimination. Everyone must have been so scared to do the wrong thing.' Mum looked back at the house. 'Shall we go in?'

'We can't!'

'We can ask. Come on.' And she was already getting out of the car, leaning on her crutches. All I could do was follow her. There was no way she was facing this on her own.

'The knocker's the same,' said Mum, as we stood at the door. 'Mam used to Brasso it every Friday morning. At Christmas, she'd take it off the door and clean it at the kitchen table. That week, everything would be scrubbed to within an inch of its life.' She knocked on the door and immediately a dog began yapping. Then the door opened. 'Hello,' began Mum. 'We...' And then. 'Dr Butler!'

Pablo was furious at this interruption, still yapping madly, but Will, dressed in a pair of jogging bottoms and a T-shirt and holding a mug of coffee, just looked bemused. 'Is everything all right?' he said. 'I am just back from a run.' He glanced at me.

'We didn't know *you* lived here,' said Mum. 'I knew the house was on the market last year... but no one told me who had bought it.'

Will was looking increasingly puzzled, trying to make sense of what she was saying.

'We'll just leave you to it,' she said. 'Come on, Olivia.' She pulled on my sleeve. 'Sorry for bothering you. Thank you, Dr Butler, so sorry!' She yanked at me and began making her way down the path.

'What do you mean?' Will called us back. 'What's going on?'

'Mum grew up here,' I said, turning back. 'We didn't know you lived here.'

'Ah,' he said, slowly, thoughtfully. 'Well, then. That explains a lot. Would you...?' He pushed the door open more and stepped aside. 'Would you like to look around?'

It had been all right when we thought a stranger lived here, but asking for a house tour of someone we knew, however vaguely, wasn't right at all.

'We couldn't possibly,' said Mum.

'Absolutely not,' I said. 'But thank you anyway.'

'Again, so sorry to have bothered you...'

We turned around again.

'I really don't mind,' he said. 'Or come back for a cup of tea or a glass of wine later? I can imagine it must be lovely to see your old house. It hasn't changed much. I mean, there's no extensions, and there seem to be all or most of the original features. Fireplace, the coving... the windows.'

Mum stopped in her tracks. 'Oh, I'm so glad,' she said. 'The ceiling rose?'

Will nodded.

'The dado rail in the hall?'

He nodded again.

'The scullery with the little window?'

He smiled. 'I bought the house *because* of the scullery window.'

Mum beamed back. 'Well... if we *weren't* imposing. We could come back at a time that was more convenient.'

'What about an evening this week?'

'Lovely,' said Mum. 'If you're sure?'

'I'm sure,' he said.

'Goodbye, Dr Butler,' said Mum, almost swinging on her crutches, as though in training for an unofficial Olympic sport. Will must think we were utterly mad, I thought, as I raced after her. But I found myself smiling, thinking of him and Pablo in that lovely house. And the fact that he had invited us back.

14

Roberto: Am going to attempt a Victoria sponge. Mary Berry says it is 'entry-level'. Couldn't actually sleep with the anticipation. How are you?

Me: Lots going on! Busy!

Roberto: Good busy or bad busy?

Me: Not sure. Will let you know.

Roberto: Big hugs to my favourite girl. YOU, not Kylie (she's my second).

Jeremy: Hey Olivia. Hope all is well in the Emerald Aisle! Say hello to the leprechauns and Bono for me! By the way, I'm looking for my cuff-links. The ones with the Scottie dogs on them. You didn't take them, did you? TIA.

It was Monday morning and I was on my way to Nell's, texting Roberto, when I walked past James.

'Morning, Olivia,' he said, glancing up briefly. 'How's it going?'

'Morning, James,' I said, but something was wrong – there was no Sammy. James simply didn't look like James without old Sammy loping beside him. Every time I had passed him in the street, over the last week, or spotted him in the distance, or popped into the deli, Sammy had been there.

'Where's Sammy?' I asked. 'Having the day off? Still in bed?'

James stopped and turned around. 'It's not good news, Olivia,' he said. 'I mean... poor old Sammy... it's the end, really. He's twelve... and... that's old for a Labrador.' He stopped speaking and shrugged. 'I mean... it's best for him to just let go... the thing is, I think he's hanging on for me.' He gave a small laugh. 'It's the kind of thing he'd do, not wanting to upset me.'

'Oh God. Poor Sammy.'

'I've had him since he was seven weeks old. Tiny he was and the runt of the litter. His back legs weren't right. But I was going through a hard time, so was he, and we... we just understood each other.' His voice broke at the end. 'Sounds ridiculous, doesn't it? If you'd told me fifteen years ago that I would be crying over a dog, then I would have said you were mad.' He shook his head, pulling himself together. 'Anyway, I shouldn't be going on about it... you don't want to hear about Sammy.'

'I do,' I said.

James jammed his hands in his jeans pockets. 'I don't want him to go, but it's worse thinking that he might be in pain. And so, he's being put to sleep today.' He wiped his eyes with the back of his hand. 'What's wrong with me? I'm a state!' He tried to smile.

'James, I'm so sorry.'

'I don't think I can even say this without becoming a blubbering fool, but... last night, Sammy knew his time was up. At about 3 a.m., he tried to get onto my bed – he hasn't done that in years. He was struggling to get up, so I got out and helped him up. The poor fella. And so he crawled in beside me and kept staring at me, you know, his big brown eyes...'

'Everything all right, young James? Anything I can do?' shouted Bernard Murphy, looking over from across the street.

'You're grand, Bernard, but thank you...' said James, and then, back to me, 'I'm making a show of myself in the village...'

'Where's Sammy now?'

'He's at home. On his own... but I had to open the shop... I can't just close it for *a dog*...' His voice cracked. 'Alison had to get up early to go to Albatross. She's short-staffed this week. And so...'

'I'll look after the shop,' I said, immediately. 'Don't worry. You go home to Sammy.'

He wiped his eyes with the heel of his hand. 'I can't... I...'

'You can. Just give me the keys and I will look after everything. Okay?'

He looked at me. 'You're sure?'

I nodded. 'Totally.'

For a moment he didn't say anything. And then, 'Thank you.'

I told Jessica what had happened and she waved me away. 'I'll be fine,' she said. 'Poor James. I'll miss that lovely dog, I can tell you. Ellie-Mae and Frankie loved him. He let them sit on him and kiss his face all over and never pulled away.'

* * *

James's Deli was a small, square space, a counter running in a right angle around two sides. A row of low brass lights hung over the wooden counter, and one wall was painted a beautiful, dark glossy green, where long, open shelves displayed jars of peppers and artichokes and tomatoes and pickles shone like jewels. On one end of the counter was the fridge full of cheeses and meats and at the other end was the wine section. Tall shelves behind the counter contained everything you could think of – posh crackers, Belgian chocolates, tins of olives and anchovies.

With the lights on and blinds up, I prayed no one would ask

for some cheese that needed to be sliced or salami that needed weighing or anything difficult like that. But I started setting up the shop as best I could. In the storeroom, I found a navy canvas apron and tied it on and hovered for a moment, wondering what to do. James always stacked a pile of wooden crates with fresh vegetables and garlic cloves and tiny new potatoes and whatever fruit was in season just inside the front door, and I found them in the walk-in fridge and placed everything artfully.

The till looked a lot like the one in Nell's – which I had finally come to terms with – and after switching everything on and giving the floor a quick sweep, I propped the front door open. I carried in the delivery of fresh bread and milk which had been stacked outside, placing the bread in the baskets on the counter and the milk in the fridge beside the coffee machine.

Bernard Murphy poked his head in, eyes like saucers when he saw it was me behind the counter. 'I don't want to pry,' he said, 'but how is James? I sensed he was a little on the upset side this morning.'

'It's Sammy,' I said. 'He's being put to sleep today.'

Bernard Murphy put his two hands over his mouth. 'Oh, the poor man,' he said. 'I thought as much. I know what it's like to lose a best friend. I once had a spaniel called Daniel O'Connell. Lovely dog.' He stepped inside. 'He used to do this thing where he would rest his head on my foot while I was eating. And for years afterwards, I could still feel it, that warm head.'

Bernard seemed very moved by James's loss, gone was his usual puffed-up chest. He came over and stood at the counter, playing with bars of fudge which were stacked by the till.

'They ask nothing of you,' he said. 'No demands. Just give, give, give. Daniel O'Connell was a remarkable dog. Slept on my bed throughout my childhood. He died on the morning of my nineteenth birthday. I still remember it like yesterday. It was the end of innocence.' His voice cracked. 'Right!' He pushed the fudge back into a neat pile. 'We must get on with the day! I will return with an action plan to make sure James's Deli stays fully functioning. We will share this burden!'

He returned fifteen minutes later and placed a cup of tea from Albatross on the counter and a croissant.

'This will keep you going,' he said. 'Alison sent it over to say thank you. She and James have become very friendly lately.' He nodded at me, making sure I got the meaning. Gossip, I realised, could be imparted in a myriad ways. 'So, troops have been summoned, the cavalry assembled. We have organised a full schedule of reserve staff and you can stand down from your post at 11 a.m. Mrs O'Keefe will be preparing the lunch special.' He stood to attention, giving me a salute.

'Thank you, Bernard.'

For the next hour and a half, I wrestled with the slicer and the weighing scales and wrapped sourdough loaves in paper.

Henry, wearing cargo shorts and a checked shirt, open at the neck, sleeves rolled up, popped his head around the door. 'I heard you were in here,' he said. 'How are you getting on?'

'Do you have any idea how to use this coffee machine?' I asked. 'I just had to send someone across to Albatross because I had no idea how it works. This is quite different to any coffee machine I've ever used.'

'Hmm.' Henry came behind the counter and stared at the monstrous machine for a few minutes. 'Right,' he said, eventually, filling the spoon with coffee and clicking it in. 'I think, if we just press this, and then this, and do this...' Coffee poured into a small cup and he then poured milk into the silver jug. 'And then this.' He pressed another button while steam poured out, making that familiar frothing noise. 'And then this.' He swirled the milk into the coffee. 'There. Have a taste. See if it's okay.'

I took it and sipped it. 'It's perfect. Lovely and creamy. Have you ever made coffee in one of these things before?'

'Former engineer,' he said. 'Machines don't scare me. And then I did spend a year in Rome as a student, working for Fiat. I think I might have picked up a few things then while frequenting the cafés.' He smiled at me. 'Is there anything else I can help with?'

'I don't think so,' I said. 'Mrs O'Keefe is on her way.'

'Call if you have any more problems,' he said. 'I don't have many skills, but machines are my forte.'

'I will, thank you.'

He turned to go. 'Your mother is so delighted to have you home,' he said.

'She seems very happy,' I said. 'I don't think it's me necessarily.'

'Well, whatever it is, I am happy she's happy.' He smiled again. 'She's...' He stopped. 'She's not had an easy time of it.'

'No... she hasn't.' I wondered what exactly he was referring to.

Henry hovered for a moment as though he wanted to say more. 'She's a very special lady,' he said. 'And I will look after her, in case you are wondering.'

'I'm sure you will,' I said.

'Sometimes, something happens in your life and you need to notice it,' he said. 'You need to treasure it. And I intend to do so.' He smiled again. 'See you at the funeral,' he said, as he left.

Funeral? Whose did he mean? Mrs O'Keefe, when she turned up, was able to bring me up to speed. 'Sammy has now passed,' she said, reverently, tying an apron around her waist. 'There'll be a funeral this evening at 6 p.m. The doctor is with them now.'

'You mean vet?'

'No, *doctor*. Dr *Butler*. They're back from the vet's... and I was just passing James's cottage and saw Dr Butler knocking on the door. So kind of him, don't you think? "Dr Butler!" I shouted. "Finished your rounds?" "Not quite, Mrs O'Keefe," he shouted back. "A few more to go." "That's grand so, Dr Butler," I shouted again. "See you, Mrs O'Keefe!" "Yes, so long, Dr Butler!" I shouted again. And here I am.' She positioned herself behind the counter as though it was her shop. 'I've lost four of them in my life. Don't think I could go through it ever again.'

'Lost what?'

'Dogs! You take them as a puppy, full of jumping beans, eat everything, chew your skirting boards, get lost and found and lost again, get fleas and worms and everything else under the sun. My Dana had a three-hour operation once because she had eaten a sock. Lovely little girl that one.' Mrs O'Keefe's eyes were misty for a moment. 'There was Bosco as well, a large old dote of a yoke. He was able to sing the national anthem.'

'Sounds very talented.'

'Oh, he didn't do it *very well*... I mean, sometimes you couldn't make it out, but just every now and then it sounded just like it. But he was a little dote. A right character. Should have been on television.' She sighed at the memory. 'Now, where are we? I'm going to be making the lunch specials today. It's Monday, which is James's lasagne day, but lasagne isn't my strong point, so I'm going to make a quick Irish stew. Bernard has given me some lamb and I have brought some vegetables from the shop.'

The bell above the door rang, making us both look up. Dr Butler stepped into the shop, Pablo at his heels.

'Good morning again, Dr Butler,' Mrs O'Keefe said, smiling. 'How are you?'

'Fine,' he said. 'I just wanted to see if you were... okay?' He looked at me. 'I've finished all my house calls and I'm just on my way back to the surgery. James said you were working in the shop this morning. Can I help with anything?'

I opened my mouth to speak, but Mrs O'Keefe jumped straight in. 'Not at all!' she said. 'Not at all, doctor! Don't you be foostering and worrying about anything. We have this all organised and nothing should get in the way of a doctor and his doctoring. You carry on now with your good works. Never mind us here.'

'It's actually fine,' he said. 'My next appointment isn't for another hour.'

'No, Dr Butler, you go and rest. Have a cup of tea... or we can make you a nice cup of coffee... Olivia, can you use this infernal-looking machine?'

'I think so,' I said. 'Henry just showed me.'

'No, I'm grand,' said Dr Butler. 'I just wanted to help too.'

'You need to go and put your feet up,' insisted Mrs O'Keefe. 'Rest that brain of yours. You never know when you might be needed. There could be an emergency. And then Anthony Daly from the newsagents is going to do an hour, and then Janet from the bakery is going to send along one of her girls. Between us, we'll get to 6 p.m. for the send-off when Sammy joins the other dog angels in the sky. Like my Dana. And my Bosco.' She turned to me. 'Olivia, make Dr Butler a coffee... cup of chino okay for you?'

'No, I'm grand,' he said. 'I'll get on...'

'It's no trouble,' she said. 'Is it any trouble, Olivia? See! It's no trouble at all.'

'No, really,' he said. 'I'm fine.' Pablo scampered beside him as he opened the door.

I hadn't been able to get a word in edgeways but I also didn't want to say too much in front of Mrs O'Keefe, but when she headed to the back of the shop, I managed to blurt out, 'Thanks for yesterday.'

He stopped and came towards me again, this time smiling at me. 'My pleasure...'

'You must have thought it was strange us going round knocking on strangers' doors on a Sunday morning.'

'Not really,' he said. 'Nothing surprises me any more. And I sensed that it was really important to your mother.'

I nodded. 'She's only just talking about it... she is working through some things.'

'Ah... well, that can only be a good thing.' He smiled again at me, a big, handsome hug of a smile. 'Was that you I saw running this morning?' he asked. 'Down by the harbour?'

'I'm not very good,' I said. 'I am more a plodder.'

'I couldn't live without it,' he said. 'Sea swimming is something I am getting used to, but running is my drug of choice.'

'I still prefer chocolate and alcohol,' I replied. 'But I seem to have this compulsion to run these days. I can't work it out.'

'You see, you get addicted. Anyway, I'll see you later.' He smiled at me. 'I'll tell James that the shop is in good hands. And let me know when you want to come and look at the house.'

He was *nice*, I thought. More than nice. Maybe I'd been too quick to judge him.

15

Outside James's small cottage on Bird Road there was quite the buzz, the kind you find outside churches and crematoriums at human funerals; the chat, the catching up, the shaking hands, all done in the obligatory muted, reverential way.

Mum and Henry were chatting with Betty. Mum waved one of her crutches at Bronagh and I. 'Hello, you two,' she said. 'Lovely to see you, Bronagh.'

'Hi, Nell,' said Bronagh. 'How are you feeling? How is the hip?'

'Oh, let's not talk about the hip,' said Mum. 'I am missing doing everything I normally do. Going for walks, being able to get myself around the house. Working. I'm just lucky that I have Olivia.' Mum smiled at me. 'How was your day? All well in the shop?'

'I was only there for the afternoon as I helped out in James's in the morning,' I said. 'But it's all fine. Made a couple of sales. Feeling more confident about serving people.'

'Bronagh,' interrupted Betty, 'your mother was telling me about the anniversary party...' She laid a hand on Bronagh's arm.

'Such a pity it didn't go very well. These things happen, though, don't they? The best-laid parties go awry. Who said that? Shakespeare?'

I felt Bronagh bristle. 'What do you mean? What did Mum say?'

'Oh, I can't really remember now,' said Betty, casually. 'Something about the food which was meant to be cold was warm, and then food that was meant to be hot was frozen... and ditto with the wine. I was saying that you have to be so careful about who you get to do what, people cut corners, you see. No one bothers these days. You have to keep your eye on the ball... you have to! You can't outsource anything these days. Vigilance, always vigilance.'

'So, Mum said she didn't enjoy it, then?' persisted Bronagh.

'Well, not exactly,' said Betty. 'She was in the shop yesterday and we had a little catch-up. Having the boys there was such a treat, she said, but just that it could have been better. Such a shame I couldn't have gone, but we were having a little "do" to announce Jennifer-Louise's news.'

Bronagh seemed stunned.

'I thought it was beautiful,' I said. 'The food was delicious... and the wine...'

But Bronagh shook her head. 'Don't bother,' she said quietly. 'I am not rising to it...'

'Ah, I think it's time to go in,' said Betty. 'Shall we? Come on, Nell, we'll go in together.' She grabbed Mum's elbow as though she was trying to help her, but really it made it far more difficult for Mum to crutch herself in.

Henry, Bronagh and I trailed behind.

'How did you get on with the coffee machine?' said Henry. 'All well?'

'Totally fine,' I said. 'Thanks for your tutorial.'

'Any time.'

In the tiny living room, a queue had formed with people eager to give their condolences to James. 'I'm sorry for your loss,' I heard someone say.

'He was a gorgeous dog,' said the next person. 'The very best.'

'I'll always remember how he would wag his tail at me every morning.'

From the kitchen, Dr Butler appeared with a tray of mugs of tea and an open packet of biscuits. 'Anyone want a cup of tea? Alison's making sandwiches now and I'll bring those out in a moment.' He leaned down to some of the older guests who were sitting four-abreast on the sofa. At Will's feet was Pablo; he stared up at me, like a truculent teen.

'Thank you, Dr Butler,' said Mrs O'Keefe. 'Delicious tea. It's not easy making a good cup. People do get it wrong so often. And there was us trying to make you a cup of coffee earlier.' She laughed. 'Should have offered you tea. I'll know for next time.'

'Thank you, Mrs O'Keefe,' he said. 'I'll pass any tea-related compliments to Alison.' He turned to face Bronagh and me. 'Thanks for coming.'

'We're like a good local politician,' said Bronagh, 'because we never miss a good funeral. Even dog ones.'

Will laughed. 'Funerals are just another social occasion,' he said. 'Most people are here for the tea and sandwiches. When my dad died, I think I got repetitive strain injury from all the bread buttering I did.'

Now Bronagh and I laughed. Finding something amusing about a funeral is an Irish trait. It's all part of the grieving process. Every funeral has its moment, ranging from the priest's phone going off to the ultimate: the dangerous stagger at the edge of the grave.

'By the way,' said Bronagh. 'I've been wondering, what do you do with Pablo in the surgery? Are you *allowed* to have a dog with you?'

'He stays in the front office with my receptionist, Valerie,' Will said. 'He's become quite fond of her. And when I am out and about on my rounds, he comes with me.' He paused. 'Or, on serious cases, he just sleeps in the car. He loves being in Ireland. He found New York a bit noisy. Here, he gets to go on walks and even goes swimming.' We all looked down at Pablo, who wouldn't meet our gaze.

'What made you leave New York?' asked Bronagh.

'Well...' He kind of smiled. 'My wife decided she didn't really like being married – at least to me,' he said, shrugging. 'And so I'm newly divorced...'

'Will?' James called over. 'I'm going to get going, okay?'

'I'd better go,' said Will, smiling. 'Moral support. See you both later.'

James was clearing his throat and getting ready to speak. 'I just want to say a few words,' he said. 'First of all, thank you all for coming. It means everything to me to see you all here today. I am so honoured that you all know that Sammy wasn't just a dog – he was my friend. He got me up every morning and went to sleep with me every night.' He tried to laugh. 'And to all my friends here right now, I am beyond touched and feel so lucky to live and work alongside you all. And special thanks to Will for driving me and Sammy to the vets today. And I am sorry Pablo has lost his best friend.' He looked at Will. 'Thank you, from the bottom of my heart. Thank you. And, of course, to Olivia and Mrs O'Keefe and Janet and everyone else who helped out. I couldn't have done today without you. Thank you. And thank you to Alison for her sandwich making, her tea brewing. She's been incredible and such a great person in my life.'

I glanced up and found Will's eyes looking over at me and I

looked away. Since that moment on the street when I saw him kissing Pablo, I had kept thinking about him. But he must have got that all the time, women staring at him. And even though I had a feeling that my life was changing, I would have to keep my head down, do what I needed to do here in Sandycove and go back to London.

'I've never had a funeral for a dog before,' said James. 'And obviously it's a little self-indulgent, but I was thinking what do you do at a dog funeral? Should we read poems? Tell stories about Sammy running through the woods on Killiney Hill, the squirrels he terrorised, the flocks of seagulls he chased. Many of you here now were part of those walks. You'd stop and talk to us while we were out and about. Having a dog really brings you closer to your community, there's no way you can stay indoors with a dog. But what I thought I'd do is just play one of my favourite songs... as you know, I'm a Bruce Springsteen fan... and therefore so was Sammy.' He bent down to an ancient CD player and pressed play. 'This is "Dancing In The Dark" by the great Bruce Springsteen for the late, great Sammy.'

People began to join in, quietly at first, their voices slightly quavery. Bronagh and I looked at each other, as we sung the chorus. I would miss all this, I thought, when I returned to London.

Afterwards, when all the handshaking and hugging was done, we said goodbye to James.

'Will you be all right?' I asked.

'Yeah, course I will,' he said. 'Alison will be here. Thanks again for this morning, Olivia.'

'Any time.'

Outside, Bronagh and I said goodbye.

'I wish I hadn't agreed to go and see Paul,' she said, 'to watch the new *Star Wars* on the Disney Channel.'

'There's a *new* one?'

'Apparently.' She rolled her eyes. 'I mean, haven't they made enough? Aren't people satisfied with the amount of *Star Wars* in the world? And he's seen it a million times in the cinema, including IMAX, 3D, 4D and even the singalong version...'

'Singalong? It's a *musical*?'

She shrugged. 'Probably. I mean, if I have to look at Leonard Nimoy again and his preposterous elf ears, I am going to scream.'

'So, why do it?'

She shrugged. 'I've been single for five years,' she said. 'I got bored of not having anything romantic, not having any one of my own. Mum and Dad gave up on me ever finding someone they would approve of. I gave up on me finding anyone I would approve of. So I decided to go for a nice guy, someone I can drink wine with, and eat takeaway curries with. And he puts up with me wittering on about buildings and bridges, and I put up with him going on about *Star Wars* and the gossip from the sorting office.' She smiled. 'Not everything has to be the Great Romance. Sometimes nice enough is good enough.'

'But don't you want passion and excitement and everything else?'

'Of course I do! But in the absence of any of the above, I'll take this! I am going to think about it as a kind of noble and beautiful aloneness.'

We hugged goodbye.

'Love you, Liv,' she said.

'Love you, Bro.'

And I watched her walk away, wishing she knew quite how wonderful she was. And wishing her mother knew it as well.

* * *

Henry drove Mum and I home.

'I won't come in, Nell,' he said, giving her a look. 'But I will be round first thing. Maybe we could go for a drive in the morning, go to Wicklow, if that suits?'

She took his hand for a moment. 'I would love that very much, Henry.'

'The funeral was nice, wasn't it?' Mum said, as the two of us were walking into the house. 'Good turnout. He's scattering the ashes down by the harbour on Saturday. I think it's just him and Alison, though.' We went into the kitchen and she sat at the breakfast bar. 'Would you like to go to the house on Thursday? Dr Butler said it suits him. I could pick you up after work.'

I hadn't realised quite how ungrounded I had felt all my life, how my roots seemed too shallow to make me feel stable and secure. I thought of Joseph Delaney. And my grandmother and my grandfather and all the people who came before them. Suddenly, it struck me very clearly that I was connected to something much bigger than just me and Mum. For the first time in my life, Mum and I were part of a tribe, we were a branch on a family tree, we were part of a story which started long before us and which would go on long after we were gone. My hand went reflexively to the locket around my neck. It had taken on a greater meaning and was now a kind of talisman, as though I now had someone looking after me, as though it was telling part of my story.

'Yes, I'd love to go,' I said.

'I was wondering,' said Mum, looking at me sideways, 'about Seasalt.'

'What about it?'

'Well... I was wondering if you missed it? And if you had given any thought to perhaps bringing it back. A resurrection of some kind.'

For a moment I thought I was going to cry. It must have been the emotion of the funeral or just general tiredness from all the running I was doing. I managed to swallow it back. I did miss Seasalt and the thought of returning to Maribelle was increasingly horrifying. 'A bit,' I admitted.

She nodded, as though she guessed as much. 'We all get scared,' she said. 'All the time. The first five years of the shop, I don't think there was a moment I didn't feel sick with fear, with nerves, worrying about every bill that came in, or blouse we didn't sell, or the jacket which I'd decided would fly out but no one even looked at. Or if we had too much stock or too little. When I think back, I can't believe I kept going.'

'But you did,' I said.

'I didn't have a choice,' she said. 'I was in too deep. I think if I could have given it up, I would have done. But I'd signed a five-year lease on the building. And I had you to look after and I was too scared to change tack and do something else. I just kind of clung on.'

'It was all too much... I panicked. I didn't think I could do it. I couldn't sleep...'

Mum nodded. 'That's what business is like. It's part of you. I didn't always believe in myself. Which may explain some of the life decisions I made.' She pulled a face.

'Jeremy said that the world is divided into leaders and followers and that I am a follower,' I said. 'Do you think that is the reason why my business failed and yours succeeded?'

'What?'

'That you can't be a successful business owner if you are a follower.'

'A follower? What on earth does that mean?' Mum looked puzzled. 'This is nonsense. Claptrap. You can't define people like that. And, anyway, you *do* lead. And you also follow. And so do I,

as does anyone who interacts on a normal level in society. Take
Bronagh for example... she leads in her business, but what about
your festival meeting... who was leading that?'

'Me.'

'Right. Exactly. And was she happy to be led?'

I nodded.

'And the same with me,' Mum went on. 'You boss me around,
don't you? And then sometimes it's me. It's called normal human
interaction. And the reason why your business "failed", as you
put it, was a series of unfortunate events leading to a catastrophic
crisis of confidence. Exactly the kind of thing you can bounce
back from, and which leads to greater resilience and greater business success. There! That's my pitch for you! Now, would you like
to share one of my mini bottles?'

'Are you suggesting we go wild,' I said, 'and have a whole half
of a tiny bottle of wine each? You're the Keith Richards of Sandycove. I'll go and get it. You stay there. Crisps?'

'Go on so,' she called back. 'The nice ones!'

We sat side by side at the breakfast bar, our mini bottle in
front of us and a bowl of posh crisps between us.

Mum smiled at me. 'Not a bad life, is it?'

But she'd got me thinking. Yes, I wished I still had Seasalt, but
it was far too late for me. And I was far too old to make any
changes. I just had to keep going with this life I had made for
myself in London. There was no going back.

16

Me: I've taken up running.

Roberto: Away from what?

Me: Just for pleasure.

Roberto: Pleasure? Sitting down is a pleasure. Running is a skill you employ when a monster is chasing you. I see people in films doing it all the time.

Me: I'm quite enjoying it though.

Roberto: Is this something you will require me to share with you?

Me: If you want to?

Roberto: Did you hear that? It was the sound of me shuddering and hell freezing over.

Me: It's just so nice to be outside!

Roberto: Hmmm. I will allow it for now. But please stay away from big trucks and wear a high-viz vest. Not fetching but will keep you alive.

Me: How was the cake?

Roberto: A disaster. Thinking of writing to Mary B to tell her. Book is going back to charity shop.

Me: No. Try again. Go on.

Roberto: Maybe… Love you, Liv.

Me: Love you too.

On Wednesday morning, Jessica seemed slightly frazzled, her smile pasted on, her hair not quite its shiny, buoyant self. *And* she was drinking coffee. From a *mug*. Worse, a Kit Kat mug, the kind that comes free with an Easter egg. I'd noticed it before at the back of the cupboard in the small kitchen in the shop, dusty and unloved.

'Where's your lovely cup?'

'I'm on instant coffee today,' she said. 'The cheap stuff. You can't drink it from a china cup. It's just one of those days,' she said, putting the mug down, and reaching for the packet of own-brand custard creams. Her hand, I was sure of it, was trembling. But perhaps it was my eyesight. The kitchenette wasn't exactly over-endowed with natural light.

'Jess? Everything all right?'

'Grand, yes... grand.' Her smile again seemed overly stretched, as though she had coerced her muscles into movement. 'Just need some of these biscuits.' She wrestled them open with her teeth. 'You know what it's like when you need sugar.'

It probably was nothing, and here I was probing her and being intrusive. Except... except, I *did* have the distinct impression that something was wrong over the ordinary run-of-the-mill things that go wrong.

'Jess, are you sure you're all right?' I asked. 'You look really pale.'

'My alarm didn't go off,' she admitted, 'that's all. And it's just set me back a bit and explains why I need the coffee to wake me up. Normally I'm up at six, get myself a cup of tea, and then wake up Damien. And then the kids.' For a moment, she looked ready to cry. 'I have everything organised. The moment one thing goes wrong, so does everything else. I could kick myself. I mean, it's the same alarm every day and for some reason I forgot to set it. I'm so stupid!' She picked up a custard cream and pushed the whole thing in her mouth in one go.

'It's awful when you oversleep,' I said. 'In London, I start work at 7.30 a.m. and barely close my eyes at night because I'm so afraid of sleeping through the alarm, or not setting it.'

'It's such a little thing,' she agreed, 'but has huge consequences. Damien missed his session in the gym and it was all booked with this special boxing trainer and then Frankie decided to choose this morning to lose his tin whistle for school. And Ellie-Mae wouldn't let me plait her hair and wanted to wear her wellies to school.'

'Damien was probably glad not to have to go to the gym,' I said. 'He had the perfect excuse to stay in bed!'

'Yeah...' She gave a laugh, as she moved into the shop. 'He was really pleased.'

* * *

It was a quiet morning in the shop and we tidied up, rehanging clothes, checking sizes and labels, replacing accessories and making sure all the displays looked perfect.

'Jessica,' I said, slipping on one of the scarves and feeling ridiculous. 'How would you style me, if I was a customer?'

'You don't need my advice,' she replied. 'You look lovely.'

'No, but really,' I said. 'Please? As I'm working here, I would love some impartial critiquing. No offence taken. I'm feeling a little on the frumpy side. I've forgotten how to dress myself.'

Jessica put down the cashmere jumper she was rehanging.

'Well...' She came towards me. 'I would say that you dress like you are meant to dress for your job in London. You need to fit in, you're not allowed to be too fashionable, you can't stick out or be an individual and I think I am right in saying that there are very strict rules about heel height, make-up, tights and all that...'

I groaned. 'Yes, it's like being back in school and after a while you just forget what you like and who you are. Roberto is always saying that I should wear more colour, but what's the point when the weekend lasts about two seconds and my working week goes on forever.'

'So what are you looking for?'

'Just something that makes me feel like me.' I paused. 'The old me, the one I used to be before I was sucked into the corporate vortex.'

'Wear what you like,' she said. 'By which I mean, wear what you like, what you really like. Wear things that make you feel joyous and happy. It's actually much simpler than people think. Do you like it? Then wear it!'

I looked down at what I was wearing – a chambray shirt and dark denim jeans. 'I don't really like what I am wearing,' I admitted. 'I mean, it's fine... but it's not more than that.'

'What do you like in the shop? What is your eye drawn to?'

'That shirt, the one with the gold thread running through it,' I said, immediately. I had spotted the shirt ages ago but had dismissed it as not being 'me'.

'Great,' said Jessica, taking it out. 'What else?'

'The cashmere jumper, with the rainbow sequins on the wrists... the flowery blouse with the ruffles... the jeans... those trainers with the silver on the back...' I continued.

Jessica was collecting them all and hanging them outside a changing room. 'Try them on,' she ordered. 'The next stage is to see if the joy continues when you wear them.'

'Okay...'

I did as I was told. The jeans were tighter than the ones I had been wearing and paired with the gold shirt, it felt good, like a newer, improved version of me. And the same with the cashmere jumper and the ruffly blouse.

'What do you think?' I stood outside the dressing room, waiting for Jessica's verdict.

She shrugged. 'It doesn't matter what I think, what do you think?'

I looked at myself in the mirror. 'I like it,' I said. 'I really like it.'

Jessica was smiling. 'Well, there you go then, that's all you need. And I'd say you get a twenty per cent discount on them if you buy them.'

'Deal.' I put them up on the counter. 'I might buy some more things before I finish here.'

'You should,' she said. 'Go back to London a different person. And maybe see how you can bring a little joy to your work clothes, earrings, or a nice shirt, or something colourful.'

Maribelle had a succession of wildly expensive, beautifully cut suits which she wore on rotation. Mine were less well-cut and much less expensive suits which I wore with navy ballet flats. Just the thought of having to go back to squeezing myself into that uniform seemed horrifying.

I began piling everything I wanted on the counter. 'I'm buying them,' I said. 'I don't know why, but I just don't feel like I suit any of my old clothes.' It was as though, after the last ten days, I was already different to the person who had arrived.

Jessica picked up a top from the rails and held it against her. 'What do you think of this?' It was one-shouldered, shimmery, black. 'I think I might buy this for Barcelona,' she said. 'We're going on Friday for the weekend, just Damien and me. He's organised everything. Nice hotel, dinner, drinks... shopping. He wants to go to the Barça stadium tour, so we'll do that in the afternoon and then somewhere glamorous for dinner and I can wear the top.'

'Gorgeous,' I said. 'You'll look amazing.' I was swiping my debit card, after scanning my new clothes, excited to wear them.

'Really?' She looked worried for a moment and put the top back on the rail. 'Damien likes me to look nice but... you know... I don't want to be *over*dressed. Sometimes I get it wrong. Too sexy, too much, too low-cut... that kind of thing.'

'But does it bring you *joy*, Jessica?' I said.

She laughed. 'Totally, I love it. I've had my eye on it for ages. Barcelona is the perfect place to wear it.' But suddenly her face froze as a shadow fell on the room. I followed her gaze to see someone tall, extremely well built, a jaw like a JCB claw and a sprayed-on T-shirt revealing a chest like sand dunes.

'Ready, Jess?' he said, smiling. 'I've been waiting in the car.'

Jessica glanced up at the clock. 'I'm so sorry, Damien,' she replied. 'We were... just... I lost track of...'

'Don't worry, princess,' he said, smiling, 'you take your time. You're obviously enjoying yourself.' He turned to me and held out his hand. 'Damien Ward. Jess's other half. Now, you must be Olivia? Jess has told me so much about you.' He grasped my hand with both of his. 'Seriously, thanks for looking after her. You and your mam have been so good to her. Jess means the world to me and to find a workplace where she is valued and respected makes everything easier.'

'Well, yes, of course... she's wonderful.'

Jessica was standing to one side, her coat over her arm, her red Gucci bag across her body, smiling the same forced smile she'd worn this morning. My hand, when Damien released it, felt crushed like a bag of broken biscuits.

'No matter how many times I tell Jess to take it easy, put her feet up at home,' Damien went on, 'she still wants to work. I tell her I can do all the breadwinning and salary-earning and all that. She can have an easy life. But she keeps insisting...' He smiled over at her. 'She's too beautiful to be working, wouldn't you say? Luckiest man in the world to have married my princess.' He turned to her. 'Right, Jess? Ready?'

'See you tomorrow,' she said, not looking at me. 'See you...'

'Take your time, sweetheart,' said Damien. 'We're in no rush, are we?' He walked slowly out as Jessica seemed desperate to be gone, straining like a stallion at the start line. She looked back at him, as he sauntered out. 'Bye, Olivia,' he said. 'Good to meet you.'

'See you in the morning, Jessica,' I said, as the door closed and their two bodies faded from the glass in the door, disappearing to the giant Range Rover double-parked outside.

* * *

In the evening, Bronagh and I went for a walk along the seafront, past the Forty Foot swimming place, around the Martello Tower and back along the seafront. We headed towards Dún Laoghaire to the pier. We were discussing the midsummer festival.

'I think all meetings should be walking meetings,' said Bronagh. 'Get your steps in and get things organised.'

'We could eat our lunch as we walk and talk,' I said. 'Be even more productive. Or do our hair. I am sure you can buy solar-powered hairdryers. Or read a book...'

She laughed. 'They've already invented that,' she said. 'It's called the audiobook.'

'You see? There is no such thing as just a walk these days. Anyway, just to let you know that trying to organise fireworks at short notice is impossible. I rang at least twenty-five places today. Every one saying it's not going to happen.'

Bronagh looked disappointed. 'But they are practically the only thing I'm looking forward to. Them and the alcohol, obviously.'

'I'm going to keep trying. There's a guy in Bray. He's in his eighties and someone said today that he might have some.'

'I'm going to say a prayer to the saint of fireworks...'

'Saint Elmo?'

She laughed again. 'We have to have them!'

'I have everything crossed,' I said. 'Fingers, eyes... the lot.'

'By the way,' Bronagh said, 'love the blouse. Do I suspect a little of Jessica's influence?'

'You might do,' I said. 'She's brilliant. I feel like setting fire to everything I own and just asking her to tell me what to wear.'

'She is fab,' agreed Bronagh. 'I mean, as an architect I am contractually not allowed to wear anything but black. Maybe dark grey if I am feeling outrageous. But even I can see how good she is. I saw her earlier walking through the village with a pink jacket and red shirt. She looked great.'

'Black is cool, though,' I said. 'I love what you wear.'

'I think I could be confused with a local parish priest,' said Bronagh. 'Either that or an undertaker. It's part of the job description. Must dress in black.'

'Well, I think you look gorgeous,' I said. 'This is my running route,' I noted, as we headed around the Forty Foot. 'Every morning at 6 a.m.' I was actually quite proud of myself because it was a long time since I had stuck to a habit for longer than one session. Roberto wasn't going to recognise me when I went back to London.

'I still can't believe you've taken up running,' Bronagh replied. 'Next, you'll be entering a triathlon like most of my colleagues. They are all obsessed with PBs, protein bars and something called "moisture-wicking". Which has to be the *worst* phrase ever invented.'

I laughed.

A man was walking towards us. 'Hi, Bronagh!' he called.

'Hi... Ferg...' She stopped. 'Fergus... Fergal... Fergie...'

He was tall, with a bushy red beard and wild red hair. 'Did you go in today?'

'Yes, yes!' she said, not stopping. 'Keep walking!' she hissed to me under her breath.

'Not too cold for you?' he said, eagerly.

'No, not remotely!' She didn't break a stride. 'Come on.' She pulled me along.

'Okay, then, see you in the sea soon!' he said, giving her a wave.

'Who was that gorgeous hunk?'

She rolled her eyes. 'Fergus, I think. Or Fergal something. He's on the lifeboat crew, so he's a do-gooder. He's always trying to talk to me,' she said. 'He's one of those nice men, the kind who are nice to people, talk to all the older swimmers and the kids...'

'And your problem is?'

'Nothing,' she said. 'I should talk to him. I just have to work on being nicer.'

'You are nice.'

She pulled a face. 'Not nice-nice. Not generally nice.'

'I didn't think we had to be nice any more,' I said. 'I thought feminism had rid us of all that.'

'It has,' she replied. 'And so has work. Sometimes I forget how to be when I'm not working. How the real Bronagh Kelly is, not Bronagh Kelly the architect.'

'You need to have more fun,' I said.

'I don't know how,' she said. 'Not really.'

'Well, let's make the midsummer festival as fun as we can make it.'

She nodded. 'Anyway, I have a little bit more time on my hands now I don't have to endure conversations about some kind of film franchise which takes place in space.'

'You mean?'

She nodded. 'Yup. Paul finished with me,' she said. 'After Sammy's funeral. As if my life can't get any more ridiculous. I just happened to fall asleep in front of that infernal film and he shook me awake to say he said didn't want to be with someone who he couldn't share in all her life... that he knew I was faking it...'

'Faking it? You mean your...?'

'My interest in *Star Wars*, yes. And apparently, it's Star *Trek*. Did you know they were two *completely different* things?'

'I think so,' I said. 'I mean, I am sure they are. I've never given it too much thought.'

'Nor had I,' she replied. 'I had no idea I was watching an entirely different franchise to the one I thought I was watching. Sorry, not franchise. Universe. Although I have probably got that wrong as well.'

'Galaxy?' I suggested.

She shrugged. 'So, I'm back to square one, just me. A little bit lonely...'

'Oh, Bronagh...'

'At least I have my perfect cat Mies van der Rohe.'

'And me,' I said. 'You've got me.'

'Thanks, Liv,' she said. 'But don't let me feel sorry for myself. I am so lucky, I have so much in my life. I didn't want to go out with Paul, not really. We had nothing in common. And being alone is empowering and self-sufficient.' She paused. 'Isn't it?' She tried to smile and she suddenly looked so sad, and so defeated. It was so wrong that someone so ridiculously successful, so clever and talented and such a wonderful person could feel lonely.

'It totally is,' I said. 'I like being single. And we've got each other.'

'I just want someone on my side,' she said. 'I mean, I know I can do my work, and I live a great life. I have my cottage and Mies and my business is going well.' She shrugged. 'I need a little bit of love. And okay, so Paul wasn't perfect... but it was *something*... Am I asking for too much if I say I want someone on my level, who is interested in what I am interested in and also likes cats?'

'No, you're definitely not asking for too much,' I said. 'But it sometimes feels like we are. If you're not prepared to settle.' I thought of Jeremy and again silently thanked Cassandra for calling me. Without her, how long would that relationship have lurched on for?

'So are you going to try and track down your father?' said Bronagh.

'Maybe,' I said. 'One day. It's not my priority. Mum is. I'm just glad I came home.' And then I thought of Mum... but really I had thought of little else. The idea of her being so alone made me feel so protective of her. And I felt guilty about being so annoyed with her for so long.

Bronagh nodded. 'I bet she is too.'

I had also been thinking about Joseph Delaney. I had an image in my head of him, a man with long hair and leather jacket. I looked a lot like Mum, but there were other things – my wide mouth and big hands and feet – that I had thought were just mine. Perhaps I shared those with someone? I'd never thought about this before and I liked the idea that somewhere out there, there was someone a little or a lot like me.

And I still hadn't answered Jeremy's misspelled text from earlier, he was already feeling so long ago, so far away, and yet he

was intruding on my thoughts and my time here in Ireland.
'Jeremy messaged me this morning,' I told Bronagh. 'I could have
him reported to the Irish bureau of cultural insensitivity. He said
to say hello to leprechauns.'

'Oh dear.'

'I know.'

We both looked at each other for a moment.

'And he can't spell "isle" and he accused me of stealing his
cufflinks. I spent six months of my life with him and I wonder
what the hell I was doing. Sometimes you try and convince yourself that someone is better than no one.'

'I called Mum today after Paul's phone call,' said Bronagh,
'because I thought that she might just say something nice to me...
I don't know why I don't ever learn.'

'What did she say?'

'I did tell her about the fact I've been nominated for the
Arbroath Prize... I suppose I was looking for her to say she was
proud of me, or that she and Dad would come to the fecking ceremony... I don't know why I went to *her* for a little bolstering. But
she said she and Dad were too busy and that Mark is moving
home because he has lost his flat *again*, and she has to get his
room ready... and... well, the usual excuses...'

'I'm sorry.'

'Don't be.'

'I'll come with you,' I said. 'For the ceremony. When is it?'

'But you'll be in London.'

'*I'm coming*,' I said. 'I'll be there. Just put me down as your
plus-one. Okay?'

'Okay. Right! And it's in September.' She was smiling.

'I can't wait.'

17

Jeremy: Are you there? Or have you been stolen by leprechauns? Haha! Just to say the cufflinks turned up! Just one more thing, my umbrella... I know I lent it to you... but I don't think you returned it??????

Roberto: What are you doing?

Me: Walking home. You?

Roberto: Thought you'd never ask. Trying a new recipe. Actually.

Me: What is it?

Roberto: A Swiss roll. Used to be my favourite. Have bought jar of posh strawberry jam. Will send photographs.

Me: I am so impressed!

Roberto: So am I! How is the running going?

Me: Still doing it! Loving it more and more. Have bought some nice new leggings and top.

Roberto: Sorry, have I been texting the same Liv O'Neill I used to know? Hates exercise?

Me: Haha. Love you Prince Roberto.

Roberto: Love you Princess Liv xxx

It was Thursday evening and Mum and I were on our way to the house on Sandycove Avenue.

'How are you feeling?' I said to Mum, getting into the car beside her.

'Nervous,' she replied. 'What about you?'

'Same.' I was excited about seeing the house and knowing that the woman whose photograph I was wearing around my neck had lived there. I could imagine them in the kitchen or walking up the path; my grandmother was becoming real in a way she never had before.

And... I was excited to see Will. I'd seen him a few times while running and he'd waved at me, but to invite Mum to look at the house was so unnecessarily kind. He didn't have to, he could have politely sent us on our way, but he obviously understood how much it meant to Mum, sensing the house was more than bricks and mortar, that those bricks were steeped in memories and feelings.

'I'm a little worried, actually,' said Mum, as we waited for the traffic lights to turn green at the end of Bird Road, 'that I will feel the ghosts of Mam and Dad. He *died* in that house. She was *dying* in it.'

'Do you think they are going to jump out at you and shout "boo"?'

She laughed. 'No, of course not...' She paused as we started driving and turned into Sandycove Avenue. 'Well... actually, *that's* exactly what I'm worried about.'

We parked and we walked across the road – Mum was only using one crutch these days – and through the small wrought-iron gate, up the path, and stood in front of the yellow door.

'Ready for the ghosts?'

She nodded. 'I think so.'

'Now, you know they are ready to jump out...'

'Olivia, *please!*'

And then Will suddenly pulled open the door, making us both jump and scream at the same time.

'I saw you parking,' he said, beginning to laugh. Pablo was at his heels, glaring at yet another intrusion. 'Would you like to come in?' he said, still seeming amused, as we stepped inside the house.

'We're so sorry. It was Olivia's fault,' said Mum. 'She was putting all sorts of notions in my head, about ghosts...'

'Ghosts, is it?' Will said, closing the door behind us. 'Well... I may have a few stories...'

Mum looked at him, panicked. 'In this house?'

'No, no, nothing here,' he said, smiling. 'It's such a quiet house. There's actually a calm energy and after being in Brooklyn for eight years, it's like a retreat. It's so peaceful. I can hear the birds from my kitchen table. The odd lawnmower in summer. I love it. And Pablo snuffling about, playing with a bone or going upstairs to take a nap on my bed.'

But Mum wasn't listening, she was staring around the hall, from the skirting boards to the coving, her eyes taking everything in. 'I like the wallpaper,' she said, feeling it. 'It really suits the house. And the ceiling rose looks as good as new. And the bannisters...' She traced the wood carving with her finger and then she put her palm flat on the ball of the finial. 'I used to do this every morning. I had to do it or I wouldn't get good luck.' She beamed at us briefly, her eyes far away, before continuing to sweep her gaze all around, like a lighthouse. 'And the little door beneath the stairs is still here.'

'It's a bathroom now,' said Will. 'I put one in.'

'Is it?' Mum went over. 'May I...?'

'Of course.'

Mum went inside. 'It's lovely,' she echoed from within. '*Such a* good idea. We used to keep all the cleaning supplies there and Dad's shoe-shining box, the Christmas decorations, Mum's sewing machine... that kind of thing.' She reappeared again.

'Where would you like to go first? Upstairs or down?' asked Will.

'Up, I think... if you don't mind?'

'Not at all. Lead the way.'

Mum went first, then Will and Pablo, then me. Will was right about the energy in the house, it felt like somewhere you were safe. I thought of Mum growing up here, running up and down the stairs, coming in and out of the front door, playing hopscotch on the tiled path.

At the top of the landing, Mum stepped into the front bedroom. 'Do you mind?' she said.

'Please... go right ahead.' Will turned to me. 'All right?' he said, smiling.

'Yes, thank you,' I said. 'It's so nice of you to let us come. And it's a gorgeous house. You've done a lovely job.' And it was. Three bedrooms and a nice bathroom. Walls painted white, some lovely art on the wall.

'Thank you,' he said. 'It's my first house of my own and I just feel so lucky. The moment I walked in, I loved it. It was the pink glass in the front door and then all the things your mother loves... the ceiling rose and the coving. And I was so ready just to have my own house, somewhere for me and Pablo to just... to just stop.'

We all needed that one place, I thought, where we could stop. That's what a true home was, when you closed the door behind you, you were safe and you could take a break from the world.

There was a large black-and-white photograph of a housing project in Brooklyn hanging at the top of the stairs and another of a New York bodega.

'These are good,' I said, peering at them. 'I like the man in the hat.'

Will laughed. 'I used to buy my coffee from him every morning on my way to work,' he said. 'He was Spanish, he'd escaped Franco. He'd been in New York for half a century and yet his accent was still so strong.'

'You took these?' I asked.

He nodded. 'They're just snaps,' he said, 'but I really liked this one so I had it enlarged. It's not very good, but it reminds me of New York energy. Whenever I might think that Sandycove is small, I can look at this and remember the sheer size of New York, the immensity of it all. I joined a photography club while I was there... just as a break from the hospital and everything else that was going on. Taking photographs means you can focus on things outside of your own little world.'

'Literally,' I said.

'And metaphorically.' He pointed at a tiny Yorkshire terrier in the photograph who was at the heels of the man in the hat. 'See the dog.'

'Pablo?'

'Pablo's mother,' he said. 'She had puppies and I couldn't resist taking one. Alexei gave me Pablo as a present, and he was just another reason to come back to Ireland. It's a good place for a dog to grow up.'

'You wanted him to have an Irish accent, do his Holy Communion, put on the green jersey on match days?'

He laughed. 'Yes, he even barks with an Irish accent. But he didn't like the trip home as he had to be put in the hold of the airplane and still hasn't forgiven me.' He looked down at Pablo, who was looking up at him. 'Have you, fella?'

'He does look as though he is still holding some residual anger,' I said. 'He'll need therapy.'

Will laughed again. 'He's always looked like that, though,' he said. 'He just has one of those faces.'

On the wall at the top of the stairs was a huge photograph of the sea in close-up, and within the ripple, at the top of the frame, was a blurred figure swimming. It was the kind of picture that made you feel as though you were in it, swimming or drowning or doggy-paddling or whatever, but the water was visceral, the ripples, the reflecting light, you could feel the cold shooting through your body.

'Is that one of yours as well?'

He nodded. 'It's Sandycove,' he said. 'Closer to home. I took it last summer.'

'It's beautiful.' We stood looking at it for a moment.

'Do you swim?' he asked.

'Never,' I said. 'Not here, anyway. Way too cold.'

'It *is* far too cold,' he agreed. 'But I've been doing it since I've come back. My brother Dermot goes and brings my nephew down.'

'Why do you go if you hate it?'

'Because it's good for me,' he said, grinning. 'It's like eating muesli or not getting *too* drunk... you have got to stay on the right side of everything. And then, once you've eaten the muesli or not drunk a whole bottle of gin and gone for your arctic swim, you don't feel too guilty when you do indulge and have a bar of Fruit and Nut...'

We both looked back at the photograph. 'I've been thinking a lot about seaweed lately,' I said. *Why did I say that?* I thought. *What kind of weirdo says they have been thinking about seaweed?*

But if Will thought it was a strange, he actually looked interested. 'Really?'

I nodded. 'I mean, I do think of other things, but it's just that I've had an idea... well... it's an old idea... I used to make beauty products and sell them...' I glanced at him, briefly, feeling a little embarrassed. 'And I always wanted to do something with seaweed...'

But he was nodding, listening intently.

'It's so good for you, you see,' I said. 'Seawater, seaweed. It's all those minerals. I used to use flowers oils but I've always wondered about seaweed. It's so full of good things.'

'John B. Keane's *The Field*,' he said. 'The greenest field in Kerry because of the seaweed.'

'I just never thought people would put it on their faces. Fields, yes, but faces? I always thought people would be disgusted by it.'

'Disgusted?'

'Repulsed.'

He laughed. 'People are repulsed by seaweed?'

'You know when you are at the beach and you have to walk through seaweed and it's the most horrible thing, all wet and slimy...'

He nodded. 'You never know what's lurking underneath, some monster that could grab your ankles.' He paused. 'That at least was what was going on in the very strange mind of the young William Butler.'

'I used to take it and tear some of it open and rub the... whatever it is, the gel on my hands.'

'You should meet my nephew, Jake,' Will said. 'He is one of those kids who is utterly obsessed with things and becomes an expert in a matter of weeks. We've been through dinosaurs, the night sky, a cordon bleu phase where he spent four weeks making cheese soufflés, and there was his poetry phase. Anyway, to cut a long story short, he's in his seaweed phase now. Knows all the names of them... there are hundreds, apparently. Draws them, colours them in, collects them and dries them on his bedroom windowsill. Dermot and Catherine have had to buy him a special table for his collection.'

'How old is he?'

'Nine, nearly ten. He's a really great kid. We all love him to bits.'

'So you grew up in Sandycove?'

'Yeah,' he said. 'Went to St Jarleth's. Which school did you go to?'

'The Abbey.'

'It's funny we never met before.'

'I think I know your brother,' I said. 'He was the year above me.'

'I never went out,' he conceded. 'That might have something to do with it. I was a little too studious.'

'I was the opposite,' I said. 'I had a hobby which took all my spare time.'

'A hobby?'

'My own market stall,' I said, just as Mum appeared from the back bedroom.

'I used to love the view of the trees at the bottom of the garden,' she said. 'That's the thing with nature, it doesn't change.'

'Ready to go back downstairs?' asked Will.

Mum led the way again, down the stairs, through the hall and into the front room.

'This was my dad's domain,' she said. 'I think, Dr Butler, he was a little depressed. But we didn't know it at the time. He was a bit of a difficult man...'

'I used to have one of those,' said Will. 'And call me Will.'

'And I'm Nell.'

They smiled at each other.

'I knew your father a little,' said Mum. 'He always struck me as a man who liked his own way.'

Will laughed. 'That is a very nice way of putting it.'

Mum gazed around the room. 'The tiles around the fireplace are so beautiful. I'd forgotten quite how yellow the flowers were. I always thought they must be daffodils, don't you? My mother used to grow them in the front.'

'They still come up,' said Will. 'I had lots of daffodils this year.'

'Really?' Mum looked delighted. 'Could they be my mother's daffodils? They could be, couldn't they?' She beamed at us, and I thought that ghosts can be wonderful things, that they can appear in a little daffodil. 'I will walk past the house next spring,' she said. 'Just to see them.'

'And you have to promise to knock on the door,' said Will, 'and come in for a cup of tea.'

'I would love that.'

'And I could dig them up for you? Put them in a pot?'

'Well, just one or two would be lovely.'

'It would be my pleasure,' he said. 'They belong to you, anyway, don't they? Shall we go to the kitchen?'

She nodded, and then, when his back was turned, she poked me. 'He's gorgeous,' she mouthed, as I frowned at her to shut up, but she smiled happily to herself, as we went into the kitchen.

'The range!' she said. 'I would have thought this would have been thrown out years ago!' She laid her hands on it. 'It's lovely and warm. My mother and I would stand against this during the winter.'

'It hadn't been used for years when I moved in,' said Will. 'But I found this company that refurbishes them, takes them apart, cleans every piece and puts them all back together again.'

'Well, you've done a beautiful job,' said Mum. 'The double doors out to the garden are lovely, what a great idea... and may I see the scullery?'

'Of course,' he said. 'You know where it is. I'll make the tea or pour the wine. Which would you like?'

'Well, we'd love a cup of tea,' Mum said. 'If it isn't too much trouble.'

'None at all.'

* * *

We sat at the kitchen table – Pablo on Will's lap – as Mum talked about growing up in the house, and not at any moment did Will appear bored or impatient for us to leave. In fact, he seemed the opposite, as though he was enjoying himself too.

'So you and your mother hung that wallpaper?' he said, pointing to old Anaglypta on one wall of the kitchen. 'I thought it was too nice to remove. It was hidden behind an old dresser. The rest was a little dirty to keep, but that was perfect.'

'Mam was the paster and the cutter,' said Mum. 'I was the hanger. Had to stand on the kitchen table and try and keep it from sticking together or sticking to me.' She laughed. 'We weren't the best at it, I can tell you.'

'Well, it's still here. Can't have been too bad a job.'

'No,' said Mum, her voice wavering. 'It wasn't. I remember the two of us laughing a lot that afternoon.' I reached over and held her hand. 'Ah, I'm all right,' she said. 'It's just so lovely to be here. I feel a little overwhelmed. But very happy.' She smiled at Will. 'Thank you.'

'It's a real pleasure,' he said, smiling back. Pablo had been asleep but woke up and started barking as a motorbike roared past the house. 'He may be a tiny Yorkshire terrier,' said Will, 'but he thinks he's a Rottweiler.'

'Well, I think he's a very lovely dog,' said Mum, taking a bit of biscuit and holding it out for Pablo. He nibbled it, and then gave her hand a lick, before taking the whole biscuit, hopping down onto the ground and snaffling it whole. He then came over to me and sniffed at my ankles and looked up at me, and then gave me the tiniest lick. Our relationship was definitely improving.

At the door as we left, Mum turned to Dr Butler. 'Thank you for such a lovely visit... it brought back lots of memories... good ones. Thank you.'

'You are so welcome. Both of you,' he said, smiling at us as we trotted down the path, all nerves gone as we happily rushed to the car, Mum slinging her crutch onto the back seat like an old hand.

'How was that?' I said, when we were inside. 'What did you think? Was it nice to be back?'

She nodded. 'I can't really express how nice it was,' she said. 'It's as though the ghosts have been put to rest.'

'It's really lovely to think of you there. You and... Gran.'

She smiled. '*Gran*.' She lingered on the word. 'She would have made a lovely grandmother.'

'She *is* a grandmother,' I said, holding the locket.

'Yes,' she said. 'Yes, she is.' She put the key in the ignition. 'And what did you think of *Dr Butler*?'

'You mean *Will*?'

'I think it's a long time since I have met a young man as nice as him,' she said.

I glanced back at the house. 'Oh my God!' I said. 'He's still standing there, waiting to wave us off!'

'I like him even more,' she said, giving a regal wave. 'A man who waits to wave you off is a true gentleman.'

And we pulled away, both of us giving Will – with Pablo in his arms – another wave goodbye, as he turned and closed the yellow door behind them.

Something has happened, I thought. Except I wasn't sure

what that something was. But there was a feeling that I was slowly moving towards something, like a liner making a painfully slow turn in the ocean. As though everything was falling into position. But that was silly. How could it be? I just hadn't been at home for this amount of time in so long. But I felt lighter and happier and more joyful than I could remember.

And then there was Will. I couldn't stop thinking of him waving Pablo's paw goodbye. And how lovely he was to Mum... and to *me*.

Stop it, Olivia, I ordered myself. *Stop dreaming. You're going back to London in two weeks and that's it. You have a life there, which you have built up over ten years. And a proper job. And a flat to live in. It's more than you have here. Except...*

No exceptions, I told myself. *Dreams are for those who don't have plans. Dreams get you nowhere.*

18

Jeremy: Have I done something wrong? Why are you not responding? I thought you were going to be resting and yet you seem too 'busy' to text me back.

Jeremy: When are you coming back to London?

Jeremy: Olivia? Are you there?

Jeremy: Olivia!

Jeremy: I have said I am sorry. What ELSE DO I NEED TO DO?

Me: Hi Jeremy, I am really busy working at the shop and I am also organising a festival.

Jeremy: WHY DO YOU NEED TO BE SO HOSTILE?

Roberto: Someone knocked on the door last night. I had just made a caramel chai (OBSESSED!) and I heard a knock…

Me: Who was it?

Roberto: Someone who isn't my friend any more. Someone who doesn't deserve to be in my life.

Me: Felipe?

Roberto: Might be.

Me: And?

Roberto: I told him I'd think about it. Will call later. Off to make a
treacle pudding. Love you Princess Liv. Miss you.
Me: Miss you too.

'Mam's taking the kids and the flight's at 6 p.m.,' Jessica said on
Friday morning as we were unpacking new stock. 'As soon as I
finish, we're going straight to the airport. We'll have a glass of
bubbles in the bar because Damien always says you have to start
the holiday before you get on the plane...'

'He's got the right idea,' I said, unfurling some long silk
dresses in beautiful, bright colours and hanging them on the rail.
I'd be going back to London with a brand new wardrobe... not to
be worn to the office, obviously, but at least on my time off I'd
look a bit more like me. I laid one of the long silk dresses against
me. 'What do you think? I might wear this to the midsummer
festival...'

'It'll be gorgeous on you,' said Jessica. 'I've got the one-shouldered top ready for Saturday night.' She looked excited. 'I'm
keeping it as a surprise from Damien. I'm going to wear it with
my jeans and heels. I hope he likes it.'

'He'll love it,' I said. 'You'll look amazing. He's a very lucky
man.' I walked across the shop to the back of the window. 'We
should change this for midsummer,' I said. 'Maybe some of these
lovely dresses... a midsummer theme? What about flowers?
Bunches of wild flowers in little vases, as though they've been
picked from the fields. Daisy chains... what else? A shrine to
some pagan goddess!'

Jessica looked unconvinced. 'Not very fashiony,' she said,
wrinkling her nose. 'A bit arty.'

'Yes...' But the more I thought of it, the more I liked it. 'I'll go
down to the flower shop and see what they have. I promise
nothing too ridiculous.'

My phone rang and I went into the back to answer it. 'Hello?'

'My granddaughter says you need fireworks for the twenty-first. Midsummer,' said the voice. 'Is that right?'

I'd been leaving messages for Harry Daly for the last couple of days and finally he'd called me back.

'Is this Harry Daly?' I said.

'It is the very one,' he said. 'Now, you do know you're asking for the impossible. All our fireworks were booked months ago.'

'I know,' I said. 'I'm sorry...' We'd have to forget about the fireworks, I thought. 'It's very last minute...'

'Tis,' he said. 'Tis indeed. But apparently this is for Sandycove...'

'That's right...'

'I grew up in Sandycove,' he said. 'I was born in the little blue house down by the harbour. Grew up with seals swimming in front of the house. Used to have my own lobster pot from about five years old. But moved to Bray when I got married... that was some time ago now... I'd say sixty years now. So, it's for a festival, is it?'

I nodded. 'Midsummer...'

'When the fairies come and play, is it? When they steal babies if you don't keep an eye on them, when they put stones in your boots and will turn your hair white overnight, is it?'

'Well, just music and food,' I said. 'And fireworks... but...'

'Well, fireworks – good ones, mind – are getting harder and harder to find these days. You can get the cheap ones easy as rain on a holy day. The cheap ones make more of a noise but less of a display. But the ones I sell are special. Mine come from a man in China. Fifth-generation firework master. End of a line, like me. No sons, no grandsons, no one to teach and no one to learn. Now, his fireworks, though, they'd make the hair on your neck stand to attention, they would. His fireworks dance with the stars.'

'They sound wonderful,' I said. 'But...'

'Every time I set one off,' he said, 'I feel like I'm seeing a firework for the very first time. Suddenly the whole world is magic.'

I wondered why he was torturing me with stories of these fabulous fireworks which were unavailable. 'So you don't have any...' Bronagh would have to be disappointed, I thought. *I* was disappointed.

'Now, I didn't say *that*,' said Harry. 'It just so happens that I have a few in the back of my shed. I thought to meself, I did, if Sandycove needs fireworks, then I will have a small dig around and see what I can find. And I found quite nice ones, so I did. Left over from the display at the Phoenix Park on New Year's Eve. Now, that was quite a night, even if I say so myself. I will see you on midsummer's eve. I'll be there early evening to set up.'

'That's brilliant! It's the church car park, Sandycove,' I said. 'We'll see you then!'

I put the phone down, delighted. Another thing to tick off the list.

In the shop, Cara was sitting on the chaise longue, looking pale. Jessica was leaning on the arm, beside her.

'Just wondering if you needed a spare pair of hands,' she said. 'I just can't look at my books again. I think I'm going mad.'

'How are the exams going?' I asked.

'It's all a bit stressful,' replied Cara. 'I just needed to get out for a while. I don't have another exam until Monday. And then it's all over on Friday.'

'I remember doing mine,' I said. 'It's not an easy time.'

'No,' said Cara, quietly. 'It's not.'

'I'm going to make you a cup of tea,' said Jessica. 'You sit there on the chaise longue and put your feet up.'

'Let me help you sort out the shoes,' Cara said. 'It's just nice not to be revising.' She sat down beside me and quickly and efficiently began sorting everything into sizes and pairs.

'So how are you getting on?' I asked.

She pulled a face. 'It's just weird to think that once these exams are over, my life is decided,' she said. 'I can't get my head around it, like why do these choices or decisions or moments in your life define *everything*? It seems wrong, somehow.'

'But they don't define *everything*,' I said. 'You think they do, but you can change your mind, make U-turns, and head off in a totally different direction. Life is not mapped out.'

'Yeah… perhaps.'

Jessica returned with two mugs and one cup of tea. 'Here we go,' she said, smiling, handing them out.

'How are Ellie-Mae and Frankie?' asked Cara, taking a mug and perching on the edge of the chaise longue.

'Fine,' said Jessica. 'Frankie is all excited about the midsummer festival that Olivia is organising. He's hoping Miss Rachel will give him a more prominent role because last year he was at the back, behind the girls. And Ellie-Mae has decided she doesn't want to be a ballet dancer any more. But she says she will only go on stage if she can wear her scientist outfit that my brother made for her. It's this little white coat made from his old shirt and a pair of goggles.'

'She sounds adorable,' I said.

'Damien isn't so into the idea,' said Jessica. 'He told her that scientists are boring and they develop squints from looking down a microscope. Honestly, you'd think he was born in the 1800s!'

'Tell him that you can be whatever you want these days,' Cara said. 'You certainly don't need your father's permission.'

'Oh, he's only joking,' said Jessica, quickly. 'You know how he is. He'd do anything for Ellie-Mae.' She paused and she caught my eye and quickly looked away. 'Anyway, so we're off to

Barcelona tonight, did I tell you, Cara? It's always been one of my fantasy places to go to.'

'Moscow's mine,' said Cara, without hesitating. 'But one hundred years ago. I want to live the life of a member of the aristocracy. Obviously, before they were all murdered. I would like to travel around in horse-drawn carriages, through snow, wrapped in furs.'

'And go to balls and things,' said Jessica.

'I'd even wear a dress,' said Cara. 'Although I know aristocratic Russia is obviously *ideologically* everything I stand against, but... it's just nice to think about.'

'When did you first fall in love with pre-revolution Russia?' I asked.

'Nan and I watched *Doctor Zhivago* when I was eight. And she was all about Omar Sharif, and I was all about the snow and the costumes and the accents. It kind of changed my life. We had it taped on an old VHS and I wore it out.' She stopped. 'The course in NYU has six months in Moscow. In the winter.'

'There you go!' said Jessica. 'It's made for you.'

'It's Moscow *now*... not one hundred years ago. And anyway, I really would prefer to stay in Dublin. What about you, Olivia?'

'Um...' I thought for a moment. 'A beach in Kerry,' I said. 'On a hot summer's day. And there's no one around, except you and the white sand and the cold sea... and you are paddling in a rock pool and there are little fish swimming about and crabs, and seaweed...' Mum and I had gone to Ballybunion on one of our rare holidays. We never went away as Mum was always working, but one year, she actually closed the shop for a week and away we went, staying in a little B & B close to the beach.

Since talking to Will yesterday, I couldn't get the idea of seaweed out of my head. Local seaweed, cleaned and all the oils extracted, salt from evaporated seawater. I could feel it now on my skin, that silkiness. Would it work? If people loved sea swimming, wouldn't they love to feel all that goodness on their skin?

Stop it, Olivia, I told myself. *People dream all the time and that's all they are, dreams.*

Being back in Sandycove was making me see London afresh. I felt lost in the city and I wanted to visit London as a tourist but then be able to live my *real* life somewhere with soul. And Sandycove had soul in spades. When I'd left, ten years earlier, I couldn't wait to leave, but either it or I had changed. There was real quality of life here, I thought. A community. And I loved all the talking... here, you really took the time of day with people. You wanted to know how they were, what they'd been up to. In London, you never even made eye contact.

'And you, Jessica?' I said. 'Where would you like to be right now?'

'At my mam's,' she said. 'With my sister and brother, and we're all little and it's Christmas Eve. Nothing has ever topped that feeling. You know, when life is so simple and Santa is on his way.'

Cara and I nodded, remembering what Christmas Eves used to be like.

'We'd decorate the house,' Jessica continued. 'The whole place would be done. Tinsel, that silver stuff that hangs off the tree like icicles, the cake would be cut on Christmas Eve. And, most important of all, the crib. Ready to put Jesus into his bed the next morning.'

I thought of Mum as a little girl with her mother – Gran – and had a vision of them listening and singing along to Christmas music, getting everything ready for the next day. My locket was still there, around my neck.

'How is Shirley?' said Jessica to Cara. 'Is she still remembering to take her tablets?'

'I think forgetting on purpose,' said Cara. 'She still thinks she's twenty-five in her head. Doesn't need Dr Butler nagging her on the phone to ask how she is. She just doesn't realise she's getting older.' She rolled her eyes. 'I mean, who's going to remind her to take her tablets? I can't rely on Dr Butler to keep calling her.' She stood up to go, just as a customer came in.

'See you, Cara,' I said. 'Let me know if we can do anything. Good luck with the rest of the exams.'

She nodded. 'Thanks, Olivia. Have a great time in Barcelona, Jessica,' she said, standing back for the customer. 'Oh, hi, Catherine. How's it going?'

The woman had long brown hair and a thick fringe, eyes outlined in smudgy black and she wore a long cotton scarf around her neck and an Indian-print jacket. She smiled at us. 'I'm just looking for something new,' she said. 'Something nice.'

'Well, we have some lovely new things in,' said Jessica. 'Let me show you.' She turned to me. 'By the way, have you met Olivia? Olivia, this is Catherine who owns the flower shop. You know you were saying about the window display?'

Catherine held out her hand, looking at me curiously.

'Good to meet you,' I said.

'You too.' She was smiling at me as though she knew something I didn't. 'What kind of flowers are you looking for?'

'I was thinking of small bunches in old jars, the kind of things you might have picked in a field or at the side of the road and put in a vase... I just thought it would be nice for our midsummer window, it's the thirteenth of June now, so next weekend.'

'That sounds beautiful,' said Catherine. 'I love it! Of course we can help. Free flowers in return for a sign saying where they came from? Could that be a deal?'

'Definitely,' I said. 'And would you be able to do wild flowers?'

'Of course,' she said. 'All our flowers are Irish-grown and

totally natural, none of those hothouse, air-mile flowers. Corn-flowers, grasses, poppies... that kind of thing?'

'And Olivia wants daisy chains,' said Jessica. 'But I told her that they die too quickly. I'll just go and have a look for some clothes for you... we have a few nice pieces in.'

'Thank you, Jessica.' Catherine turned to me. 'Daisy chains?' She paused for a moment. 'Would you consider daisies made out of silver?' she asked. 'Or wire... I am sure I could make something.'

'Make something? I wouldn't want you to go to any trouble.'

'I used to be a jewellery designer,' she explained. 'I could make something that could trail along the front of the window. I need a project at the moment. I would love to do it. And it won't take me long... I'm thinking maybe around fifteen small daisies... it could look really lovely.'

'It sounds beautiful,' I said, 'but making something would be too much. I don't think...'

'But I would *love* the excuse,' said Catherine. 'You've given me an idea and I am desperate for a commission. My company was called Drithle. I gave it up when my son was born and it had all become too much. I thought I'd be able to pick it up again, but it just got further and further away from me. I've been looking for something to do.'

'Drithle?' I'd heard the name before.

She nodded. 'The Irish for "sparkle".'

'I have one of your bracelets,' I said. 'My friend Bronagh bought it me for Christmas years ago. It's really delicate, silver with a few tiny beads... that's you?'

She laughed. 'Sounds like one of mine,' she said, looking pleased.

'It must have been hard to give it up.'

'I had to,' she said. 'We'd just had our son, Jake, and I couldn't think straight. Dermot already had his plant business and opening up a flower shop in the village just seemed so much more manageable. Whereas, before, I felt totally on my own.'

'I know the feeling.' I then remembered my conversation with Will from the day before. Hadn't he mentioned his nephew called Jake? 'Is your son obsessed with seaweed by any chance?'

She laughed, nodding. 'Will told you about him?'

'Yesterday...' By the way she was looking at me, I also had the feeling Will had told her about me. 'He showed my Mum and me around his house. Mum grew...'

'...Up there,' she finished. 'Yes, he was delighted that you both seemed to like the house so much.' She smiled at me.

Jessica came back over to us. 'I have a few things here,' she said, holding up a dress. 'What do you think?'

'It's nice...' Catherine put it against her and looked in the mirror. 'It's just a bit... I don't know... too *nice* for me? *Nothing* feels right any more. Like I just don't know what to wear these days. When I was at art college, I never gave clothes a second thought, but now... I just feel and look awful in everything.' She sighed. 'I just want to feel like me again, you know?'

'Olivia was saying the same thing recently,' said Jessica.

I nodded. 'I am going for joy these days. Colour, sparkle... a bit of lurex...'

'Exactly!' said Catherine. 'There's no joy in anything I wear... this jacket is the only thing left over from the old days, but everything else is just practical. I want something that reflects who I am, something that makes me feel like I am not quite so far from the overalls-wearing, paint-spattered girl I used to be.'

And then I had a thought. We had a really cool jumpsuit on the rails. Navy, with a belt and puffed sleeves, but still boiler-suity enough that it might work for a frustrated ex-art student.

'What about this?' I said, pulling it off the rack.

Jessica nodded at me, impressed, as Catherine gazed at it for a moment.

'Wouldn't I just look like I was trying to be the *old* me?' she said.

'Isn't that what you want?'

She laughed. 'Okay. I'll try it on.'

'It has to bring you joy, though,' I called as she disappeared into the dressing room. Emboldened, while she tried it on, I had a look around for what else we might have. Arty but not art school. Not boring but not wacky. I found a sweatshirt with a tiger's head on which I'd been admiring. On Catherine, it might look cool. 'Try this,' I said, poking it through the curtain, along with a striped top and a pair of jeans.

When Catherine emerged in the boiler suit, she was smiling. 'I like it,' she said, gazing at herself in the mirror. 'No, I love it!'

'Me too,' I agreed, feeling a leap of pride. The boiler suit was a perfect fit, she looked super-cool but also arty and not remotely boring.

'You don't think it's too much of a pastiche of the old me?'

'It's an homage to the old you,' I said. 'Do you feel joyful?'

'You know,' she said, studying herself, 'I think I do.'

As she tried on everything else, I waited slightly nervously on the other side of the curtain. Was the tiger thing cool, or had I lost the plot entirely? But when Catherine came out of the dressing room, she was grinning.

'I love them all!' she said.

'Really?' I tried not to look too surprised as Jessica gave me a thumbs up behind her back.

Catherine handed everything to Jessica to pack up. 'And I'll start thinking about the flowers and the little silver daisy chains. I'll make them in aluminium, so it won't be expensive. Why don't you come for a walk to the beach after work? We can chat more about it then?' She looked delighted. 'I am so excited to have a project again! I'd forgotten how much I love it!'

I remembered it too, that glorious feeling of anticipation. 'I used to have a skincare range,' I explained. 'Years and years ago. Soaps and body oils, that kind of thing. It wasn't much, just my own stall in Dún Laoghaire market. I thought about seaweed... if I could extract the oils and then perhaps combine it with other oils... make an emulsion, and then a scrub using salt from the sea... and a body oil...'

Catherine suddenly smiled. 'Seasalt! I knew I recognised you! I used to buy from the stall all the time. I was in college and I used to find your hand cream the only thing that worked... and that soap... what was it? Rose and something?'

'Calendula. It was so popular. I couldn't make enough of it.'

'And there was a gorgeous face oil... raspberry and rose hip?'

'Yes...' I could smell them now, suddenly I was back in Mum's house mixing my oils, writing my notes, measuring and pouring and funnelling. The whole house smelled so gorgeous, infused with the scents of Irish flowers and herbs.

'Why did you give it up?' Catherine asked.

'I don't know,' I said. 'I just felt too young for it all, I wasn't able to handle it.'

'You didn't believe in yourself.'

I nodded. 'That's putting it mildly. I just ran out of confidence,' I said. 'I think I developed a kind of stage fright. Is that possible?'

She nodded, totally understanding. 'It's not easy to run a business. But there's no feeling like it when all is going well. It's just that you have to deal with the downtimes as well.' She picked up her shopping bags. 'I'll see you at the harbour, okay? I'll be there with Jake; he paddles while I sit on the bench. We could have a coffee?' But before she left, she said. 'By the way, Will said you were lovely and he was right.'

When the door closed behind her, Jessica gave me a look.

'What?' I said.

'Dr Butler said you were *lovely*,' she replied, smiling.

'I don't know what she meant,' I said, feeling my cheeks go red. Why would he call me lovely? Perhaps he meant lovely *enough*. Or maybe he said lonely? But there was that glow spreading through my body and I felt myself smiling. Jeremy didn't believe in compliments. 'Only needy people need to be told nice things,' he'd said. 'Nice people don't need things.'

But then, Jessica looked at the clock. 'Time to go!' And she grabbed her bag and jacket.

'Have a wonderful time!' I shouted, but she was gone, just as the black Range Rover loomed outside.

19

The sea was a million crystals dancing on the waves. It was Friday evening and teenagers were jumping off the harbour wall, dive-bombing into the sea, while those of a more nervous disposition and lower adrenaline threshold lowered themselves down the steps, stepping gingerly into the water, the day's work done, a summer evening stretching ahead. The harbour was a small sandy beach and a harbour wall, creating a lagoon at high tide.

I slipped off my sandals and walked along the shore, over the coarse rocks and the smooth pebbles, across the ripples of sand and through puddles of water and then to the sea itself, letting it run over my feet and through my toes, the seaweed licking at my feet. I thought of everything I now knew about Mum. Why did Joseph Delaney just abandon her? Why didn't he respond to the letter about Mum being pregnant? I wondered if he ever thought about her and me, and did he ever come back to Sandycove? Maybe he'd seen us and didn't feel able to come over after treating us so badly. Whatever it was, there was no excuse. It was a shame that, after all this time, my father turned out to be a total waste of space. I preferred imagining that he was Keanu. *He* would never have treated us like that. I found myself laughing a little at the thought of it all. Joseph Delaney didn't matter, I realised.

Leaning down, I scooped up some green, frilly, silky fronds, and studied them. There was something so elemental and so pure about them, not beautiful but magnificent. I picked up a stray piece of bladderwrack which floated past my feet and pressed open one of its pods, releasing its gel, along with the mineral scent of the sea. This, I knew, would make a wonderful body oil. The smell was incredible... only in Ireland did seaweed smell so gorgeous, so fresh and clean, like an oyster.

'Bladderwrack,' said a boy who was paddling nearby. He was around ten, wearing a red hoodie and shorts. 'Fucus vesiculosus, red fucus, dyers fucus, rock wrack, black tang, and bladder fucus.'

I laughed. 'You must be Jake.'

He nodded, not remotely surprised that a complete stranger would know his name.

'Do you like seaweed too?' he asked. 'I thought you did because of the way you were looking at it. Not many people like to touch it and no one stares at it the way you were. Or smells it.'

'I do like seaweed. I always wanted to use it in my...' I stopped, realising I was envious of Catherine and how she had the opportunity to reignite a part of her old life. 'I think it's so interesting,' I said, instead. 'Don't you?'

He nodded. 'Mum says it looks like mermaid's hair, but I like the way it holds on all day waiting for the sea to come back.'

'Hello!' It was Catherine, walking across the rocks towards us. 'So you've met my Jake.' She put her two arms around him and pulled him towards her, kissing the top of his head. He allowed it briefly before pulling away.

'We were just talking about seaweed,' I said.

'Of course you were,' said Catherine, smiling. 'I've been sitting on the bench sketching. I think I know how I can make the daisy chain work.'

We sat on a large boulder looking out to sea, while Jake continued his paddling.

'I couldn't live anywhere else other than Sandycove, now,' said Catherine. 'When I met Dermot, I was living in the city centre, near Temple Bar, and thought I'd be bored senseless here. I love the sea and the village and the fact that there's always something going on.'

'Well, I live in London,' I said. 'There's always something going on there too, except I never had much of a chance to do anything. I used to finish work too late.'

'I thought you'd moved back?'

'No... I'm only here for a couple more weeks,' I said. 'But *maybe* I will come home in a couple of years, once I've had enough of London. I moved there looking for a bit of fun and excitement and...'

'You got it?'

I thought of Maribelle and the time we were flying home from New York and she was nearly forcibly ejected from the plane because she was drunk. I had to reassure the stewards I would take complete responsibility for her, but, when they wouldn't serve her alcohol, Maribelle kept starting arguments. Luckily, she had a couple of Xanax and when they finally kicked in, she fell asleep all the way to Heathrow.

'Yeah... in a way...'

'I'll show you the daisy chain sketches.' Catherine took out a notebook from her bag. 'Wire and then small aluminium petals, and I could thread them through each other. It could be beautiful. What do you think?'

Her sketches were works of art in themselves, so delicate and perfect. 'They look beautiful,' I said, amazed. 'Are you sure you will have time to do it?'

'Absolutely. I'm going to make thirty of them, which I think would be enough to stretch across the window. And they will all be different.' She looked back at the sketch. 'I had a look at flowers and I can order some lovely wild and garden flowers. And I thought even a few thistles or dandelions, just to mix in and give them that hedgerow look. And what about a flower crown for you to wear for the festival?'

It all sounded magical and lovely. 'If you're sure?'

'It's a pleasure. It's our way of being involved in the festival. And Jake is in the tin whistle orchestra, so we're delighted.'

Jake wandered over, bored. 'Mum, come *on*!' he said. 'Daddy and Will said they would buy me an ice cream. They're coming over now.'

Will? There was that fairy-dust feeling, and I realised how much I wanted to see him.

'You can't have an ice cream,' said Catherine. 'We'll buy some and have it after dinner.' She looked up. 'Oh, here they are!' Catherine had turned around and lifted her hand to wave to two figures walking out of the sea towards us, a small dog running beside them to keep up. 'They are such good friends, the two of them. When Will said he was coming home, Dermot was so happy. He'd really missed Will when he was so far away.'

And there, in his swimming trunks, was Will, his shoulders still wet with seawater, his hair soaking. I had to force myself to look away because he would have caught me staring.

Beside him was a slightly less good-looking, shorter version of himself – Dermot. He put his arm around Jake. 'You should have come in with us,' he said. 'There were jellyfish, you would have loved them.'

'Dermot, this is Olivia,' said Catherine. 'This is Nell's daughter and she's working in the shop.'

'Yes, of course!' He held out a wet hand, smiling. 'Great to meet you. Will was telling me all about you...'

Will looked embarrassed. 'I was just saying about your mother and her house...' he explained, Pablo sniffing at some seaweed beside him.

'*Your* house,' I said.

'It's both of ours,' he said, smiling almost shyly, 'in a way.'

'I really need to start bringing my dressing gown here,' said Dermot. 'That's what all the old guys do. We stand out as newbies because we don't have a frayed, faded dressing gown and a towel under our arms.'

'Yes, but when do we get to join their ranks?' said Will. 'How many years do you need to have been swimming for?'

'Fifteen,' replied Catherine. 'At least. You don't become a veteran overnight. I bet they don't even talk to you.'

'They nod,' said Dermot. 'Nothing more. They save their chat for the insiders.'

'Right,' said Catherine. 'Who's hungry? Olivia, would you like to join us?'

'I can show you my seaweed collection,' said Jake.

'Now, *there's* an offer you can't refuse,' said Dermot.

'Um, well... I don't know...'

'Come on,' said Catherine. 'We're getting bored of each other... we need someone new to talk to.'

'Well, I'm not bored of you,' said Dermot.

'So, it's me then,' said Will, laughing.

'I think Catherine just needs us to up our conversational game,' replied Dermot. 'But until we do that, we need Olivia to come and stop us from boring each other.'

They all looked at me.

'Okay,' I found myself saying, thinking how simple, friendly and straightforward life was here. And, if only I wasn't going back to London in a few weeks, then we could be real friends.

* * *

At their flat, above the flower shop, Jake insisted on taking me straight to his bedroom to show me his seaweed collection consisting of hundreds of books, seaweed samples in jam jars, dried seaweed stuck into scrapbooks and posters on the wall of finely drawn botanical pictures. It was like Darwin's study. Jake spoke incessantly and breathlessly about it all, like a pocket seaweed encyclopaedia, so I decided to use him as research.

'So, what's in seaweed?' I asked.

'Lots of good things,' he said. 'But I don't know what your level of understanding is...' He looked back at me, waiting for an answer. 'Do you want the big version or the small version?'

'Somewhere in the middle?' I said. 'I mean, I won't ever understand it like you do, but I want to know more.'

'Minerals,' he said. 'Heard of them?'

I nodded.

'Seaweed absorbs them from the sea. Some brown seaweed like Ascophyllum nodosum or knotted wrack or fucus vesiculosus or bladderwrack contain all the minerals on the planet.'

I could feel myself smiling as Jake went on, delighted to have a brand new and receptive audience. When I first began Seasalt and started making my own infused oils, I would borrow Mum's car and drive off to flower growers around the county, collecting armloads of rose hips and lavender. There was that feeling of connection pulling me in, that glow, as though I was doing exactly what I was meant to be doing. And now, that lovely feeling seemed to be hovering around me more and more and especially earlier when I was standing with my feet in the sea and absorbing the heady scent of seaweed.

Catherine poked her head around the door. 'Dinner's ready, come on, you two. I am sure Olivia could do with a break from hearing about seaweed.'

'No, not at all,' I said, as we followed her out. 'It's giving me some ideas.'

'Really?' She glanced behind at me. 'What do you mean?'

'Oh, nothing...'

If only, I thought. If only I could pick it up again. A million questions without answers tumbled into my head. What about London? How would I make money? Who would buy from me? How could I compete with all the billions of products out there? How on earth would I finance it? Where would I live?

There was no sign of Will in the kitchen, which was probably a good thing as I was starting to think about him too much, especially him coming out of the sea like some kind of Poseidon. That is, if Poseidon wore Hawaiian trunks and a towel around his neck, the water droplets hovering on his smooth skin.

'*I* want to sit next to Olivia,' said Jake. 'She wants to know about my collection.'

'I do,' I said. 'It's very interesting.'

Catherine moved up a seat to let Jake in, while he slipped a book on the table in front of me.

'You can borrow this,' he said. 'I learned a lot from it.'

'Thank you,' I said. 'If you're sure? I promise I will look after it and bring it back.'

The book reminded me of the one I had from the library all those years ago which had old remedies and recipes for making medicines and creams from plants. There was a recipe for a seaweed soak, where you washed the seaweed and added it to salted bathwater. Or another where you extract the oils from bladderwrack and combine with other oils as a base for a body moisturiser. I even had a vision of me on the market stall again, freezing in the winter, hands around a mug of coffee, talking to customers and even hardier stallholders.

Dermot began serving out the stew, handing the bowls down the table.

'Will is looking so much healthier,' said Catherine, turning to me. 'He arrived back in Ireland a bit of a wreck. Thin, unhealthy, unhappy...'

'It's the sea swimming,' said Dermot. 'The old ancient cure.'

'You say that as though it didn't take a team of horses to get you in that first day,' said Catherine.

Dermot looked at me. 'I have never been renowned for my bravery,' he said. 'I would quite happily never take a risk in my life. But Cath here... well, she doesn't stop. And now you're back. Drithle is making a return! Did she tell you about it?'

'Olivia knows all about it,' said Catherine. 'She's getting my first commission, the daisy chain. And I was thinking I could remake them in silver, and make bracelets and necklaces. And I was on to the council and there are a couple of free stalls for the Sunday market, starting in September, that would give me enough time to prepare. And, of course, we can sell some of the jewellery in the shop, can't we?'

Dermot nodded. 'We may have to take on another staff member, someone to do the daily running of the shop, the arranging and all that, and I will focus on the ordering and the weddings.'

'I haven't felt like this for years.' Catherine grinned at us. 'Something for me.'

'I have my seaweed,' said Jake. 'You have your jewellery and Daddy has his plants and flowers and Will has his bottles,' said Jake.

'Bottles?' Was Will an alcoholic?

'You know the surgery is the old pharmacy?' said Dermot. 'Well, when the building came up for lease, no one wanted it because there's a preservation order on the outside and the internal building and there was an old glass-blowing factory at the back. The shelves are all made of teak and there were cabinets and mirrors and all these hundreds of...'

'Millions,' said Jake. 'Trillions.'

'...bottles.'

'I work there,' said Jake. 'He's given me a job. I sweep the floor and I have to wash the bottles. I've done twenty-five so far. I hose them down and leave them to dry outside.'

'There are even more bottles in the old glass-blowing factory behind it,' said Dermot. 'And huge ones with glass lids.'

'A world before plastic,' said Catherine. 'Everything handmade and reusable.'

'So it's been quite a project for him. Therapy,' said Dermot. 'He came home a bit battered, slept on our sofa for two months and got himself sorted. There's great healing to be done in Ireland,' he went on. 'You forget when you're living abroad what actually being in Ireland means, how you're treated, how people are actually interested in you.'

'I always thought it was nosiness,' I said.

'Oh, there's that,' laughed Dermot. 'But there's the other kind as well.'

I put my hand on my locket and thought of Mum walking up the main street of Sandycove knowing that people were gossiping about her and that they knew everything that had happened. I don't know how she faced them all down and built her business. She'd weathered her storm for the both of us.

There were footsteps on the stairs. 'Ah, talk of the devil.'

And there he was, dressed, hair still damp, face still glowing from the swim. 'Hello, everyone.' He smiled at everyone, his eyes falling upon me. 'Olivia, hello.' Pablo was at his heels.

'Hello.'

'Stew, Will?' said Dermot, standing up. 'You sit beside Olivia there.'

'So, what were you all talking about?' asked Will, sitting down and reaching up to take the bowl passed over by Dermot. I could feel Pablo settle down beside Will's shoes.

'Olivia is thinking of resurrecting her business again,' said Catherine. 'Do you remember that stall, years ago, in Dún Laoghaire market... the one that used to sell lovely soaps and creams? I used to get a rose and... What was it again, Olivia?'

'Calendula.'

'Calendula! That's it, why do I keep forgetting? It was so soothing, I can feel it now. And my hands would be so cracked and sore and aching I couldn't hold a paintbrush and then I used this cream and it was miraculous. And then you were gone...'

'I think I remember,' Dermot said. 'But I was too interested in the vinyl stall and the guy who made these amazing sausage rolls.'

'You're such a philistine,' said Catherine, shaking her head.

'Fred had the record stall,' I said. 'And it was Werner who made those sausage rolls. They were both so nice. On really cold days, Fred would make us all have a disco before we were open to warm us all up and Werner would give every stallholder a sausage roll. The camaraderie was amazing.'

I could still taste those sausage rolls, drinking tea from Margaret's tea and cake stall, the anticipation of another day's selling in front of us.

'Why did you give it up?'

'It fell apart,' I said, feeling foolish as I spoke, my cheeks going redder, but for the first time I felt protective over the younger me.

'I wanted to just be invisible for a while. I took a break and then never went back. I've been working in London ever since.'

'Everyone runs out of confidence in their twenties,' Will said. 'It's normal.'

Catherine and Dermot were nodding. 'Totally normal.'

'We all do things at that age that looking back aren't *quite* in our best interests.'

'You got married,' said Dermot to him. 'I gave up law in college. Which was actually a good decision. But at the time, I was having a massive life wobble. My girlfriend at the time told me she didn't want to end up with someone who wasn't going to be earning more than 100K a year and basically left me for a man who is now a QC. And so I got a job in the Craft's Council on reception, answering phones... which is where I met the beautiful Catherine Duffy.'

Catherine smiled. 'And the rest is history.'

'And then I got a job for this amazing florist in town, and I learned the business that way,' said Dermot. 'Even did the flowers for my ex-girlfriend's wedding.' He rolled his eyes. 'She wanted me to give them a reduction in costs, but... Catherine wouldn't let me.'

They laughed as Catherine shrugged. 'Cheek of her!'

'So, do you think you will bring your business back then?' asked Will.

'I was only saying it would be *nice*,' I said. 'But I can't afford it. I mean, I would need to rent a place to make everything, a distilling machine and then bottling... I used to do it at my mum's kitchen table but now... it would be impossible.' I sounded like Cara, batting away everyone's ideas for how she should live her life.

'I have a place at the back of the surgery,' said Will. 'It's a small outhouse that used to be a glass-blower's years ago. I found so many bottles there when I was clearing it out. But it's clean, and warm and right in the village.'

Dermot was nodding. 'I was telling her about it.'

'No,' I said firmly. 'I couldn't afford to do anything at the moment.' That glow in my stomach was for dreaming, not for real life. 'I was only thinking out loud.'

'But you must,' said Dermot. 'Dream-following should be mandatory. Never give up on dreams.' All eyes turned to me.

The glow was completely gone. What had I been thinking? I was a follower, not a leader. I was just me. And *just me* wasn't good enough. I was going back to London, and that was that.

20

Jeremy: Why are you not responding to my texts? I thought we were going to be friends?

Jeremy: FFS Olivia! Come on!

Jeremy: It's very rude to ignore people you know.

Me: I'm really busy. Sorry.

Jeremy: You can tell you went to a State School. Rude.

Roberto: Hello Princess Liv… Just sending hearts across the Irish Sea! Love is in the air! Tra-la-la!

Me: Have you been drinking?

Roberto: Only a love potion!

Me: Tell me EVERYTHING!

Roberto: All in good time. Will tell you all the juicy gossip when you make your triumphant return. LOVE YOU COMPLETELY! PS Have just made an apple crumble. Prouder than anything I have ever done. Bought the custard though.

Me: Really?!?!

Roberto: Is it possible to be in love with an apple crumble? Because I am. OB-sessed.

I spent the weekend making lists for the midsummer festival with Bronagh, reading Jake's book and dreaming of seaweed, and in constant argument with myself about what to do with my life. Why was I feeling the pull of Sandycove? I tried to remind myself why I had left Sandycove in the first place, but when I thought of Mum and what she'd been through, I felt like a wimp.

The seaweed book was proving fascinating. Who knew that seaweed was so incredibly good for your skin, all those amino acids and vitamins and minerals? I was learning a great deal. But this was all just fantasy, I couldn't afford to start up all over again. In London, I was on a trajectory... to God knows where, but it was at least a trajectory. You couldn't just get off one at the age of thirty-two... could you?

And I also kept thinking of Will. And it wasn't *just* the handsome face or the way his shoulders had glistened with seawater... but I liked everything I had seen so far about him. His kindness to Mum, his lovely brother and sister-in-law and nephew... I wanted to know more.

Monday morning and Jessica was back from Barcelona. '*Buenos dias*!' She handed me a paper bag, with a gold ribbon tied on the handle. 'Just a little present,' she said. 'It's not much.'

'Jess... you shouldn't have.' I untied the ribbon and pulled out the tissue-wrapped present inside.

'It's only small,' she said.

It was a tiny, swirly blue jug with the word '*alegría*' painted on the outside.

'It means "joy",' she said. 'I thought of you.'

For a moment I thought I was going to cry. 'Oh, Jessica! It's beautiful.'

She shrugged. 'I'm glad you like it,' she said. She was smiling, pleased at my reaction.

'So how was the weekend?'

'Oh...' Her smile faded a level, like turning the sound down. 'We had the *best* time.' Her enthusiasm seemed forced.

'Why don't we have our drinks and you can tell me all about it?' I placed the little jug on the counter by the till. 'I'll put some flowers in it,' I said. 'Brighten up the shop.'

'Barcelona is beautiful,' said Jessica, when we sat at the little table in the kitchen. 'We wandered around, went to the football museum...'

'Oh yes?'

She rolled her eyes. 'Boys will be boys, and I didn't mind. I was thinking how much Ellie-Mae and Frankie would have loved it. And it was quite interesting, all those cups they've won, the history of the club. And then we drank cava and ate lots of tapas.'

'How did Ellie-Mae and Frankie get on without you?'

'They had a lovely time! Spent the weekend being spoilt rotten and eating sweets and sleeping in a tent in the garden which my brother had put up for them.' Why was I under the impression that the kids had a better time than Jessica on her romantic weekend away? But I couldn't pry because I was probably wrong and looking for trouble where there wasn't any.

'How was dinner?' I said to Jessica, as she sipped her matcha. 'Remember you were going to wear that top?'

'Oh yes!' Another almost-imperceptible shadow flickered across her face. 'I just wore one of my old tops. The one-shouldered one felt a bit... *sexy*... I don't know... I felt a bit silly. I'm just getting too old for that kind of thing.'

'*Really*?' I was confused and couldn't imagine Jessica looking anything but incredible in that top. 'I bet you looked amazing. And you're never too old to wear anything... isn't that our philosophy in Nell's? Don't we laugh in the face of ageism? I've seen you style our older customers in jeans and trainers, and didn't you dress that woman who was on her fourth wedding in a silver jumpsuit? And didn't she look great?'

Jessica nodded. 'She did, but... oh, you know...' She smiled again. 'I'm just going through a crisis of confidence. Like the one Catherine went through, except mine is taking longer to get over... Anyway, it's nice to be back home, that's all. You know what it's like. Nice to go away, nicer to come home. And work! My haven.'

'Your haven?' However much you loved your work, I had very rarely heard it described as someone's haven. And mine, with Maribelle, was the very opposite of haven, it was the source of a gnawing ulcer. No wonder Maribelle drank too much. Working with her was bad enough, *being* her must be truly terrible.

'Work *is* my haven,' said Jessica. 'Isn't it everyone's? You *choose* where you work. It should be a good thing, right?' She gave a laugh. 'It sounds silly when I have a lovely home and two beautiful kids... but it's nice to come to work and feel happy.'

'It's really hard to be happy in work when you have a boss who'd rather undergo a smear test on a bed of nails than be nice,' I said. 'If her tea did not match her Pantone colour card exactly or if her phone ran out of battery, then she would release all kinds of hell. And it was almost always Maribelle's fault – timekeeping or forgetting things, or losing a charger – but she would blame me. I just had to keep one step ahead, have copies of all her papers, always have a spare battery pack, double-check times of meetings and tell her that it was a half-hour earlier than it actually was.'

Jessica pulled a face. 'Okay, so not a haven then,' she said.

'And there was the time she had forgotten to order some kind of PlayStation thing for Sasha – her son – and she sent me out to get one. On December the *twenty-third*. Obviously I failed. I had to endure forty-three minutes of shouting, while I cowered in the office counting down the minutes until she ran out of steam.'

'She sounds like a nightmare.'

'She's struggling with a few things,' I said. 'Which is why I am here while she sorts herself out.'

But it wasn't Maribelle I was thinking about, it was Jessica. Something was wrong, I was increasingly sure of it. Was it Damien? Could it be something else?

'Jess...' I began, but there was a knock on the window and a woman was waving in.

Jessica went over to unlock the door.

'It's Mary Talbot,' she said. 'Everyone was talking about the argument at the golf club. It was the talk of the village. There was this special golf dinner and everyone was dressed up to the nines, all Nouveau You dresses, that kind of thing, and she discovers her husband had been sleeping with her best friend for the last fifteen years. Threw a golf trophy at him. A big one apparently, with a lid and handles, and everything.'

'Wow.'

'And she's loaded. Owns her own estate agency.'

Mary Talbot emerged, sunglasses on and dressed in a collarless black leather jacket.

'Oh my God,' I breathed. 'It's Arnold Schwarzenegger.'

'Good morning, Mary,' said Jessica, 'how's everything with you?'

'I was lost but now I'm found!' Mary announced, slipping off her sunglasses. 'And I need clothes to tell the world who I now am. I have survived hell and my life is not what it was, and nor am I. No longer the beige and peach woman I once was. I am woman scorned. Hear me roar!'

'Roar away,' said Jessica. 'Sometimes you have to just let it out.'

Mary nodded. 'Tell me about it. But I've been through the crying, the disbelief, the anger... I am now at the transition stage, ready to step into my new existence. I need clothes that make me look ten years younger and as though I am at the top of my game.'

'Any particular occasion?' I ventured.

'Yes, the occasion called LIFE!' Mary threw herself down on the chaise longue. 'And Revenge,' she said. 'Empowerment. I will not be erased! I will not be scorned!'

Jessica nodded, 'I think I know exactly what you need. First of all, a cup of camomile tea.'

This was Jessica's realm and although I may have had a fleeting success with Catherine's boiler suit, when it came to a life overhaul, Jessica's expertise was what was required. I became the assistant, making the tea, running to get a cashmere jumper, a pair of ecru jeans, a lovely shirt... and whatever else was decreed as Mary hopped in and out of the dressing room, staring at herself in the mirror, seeing if the image matched the fire inside. The pile of tried-on clothes grew higher as I raced to rehang everything. Finally – miraculously – Mary reappeared smiling.

'This,' she said, pointing to her all-black trouser suit, studded ankle boots and a low-cut black silk shirt. 'And that, and that, and those...' She pointed to all the other items she wanted.

Jessica gave me a quick wink.

'How do you feel now?' said Jessica.

'How do I feel? How do I *feel*?' Mary strutted around for a while. 'I feel incredible. And what's more? I look incredible.'

There was a face at the window, the nose squashed against the glass.

'Who is it?' I said.

Jessica squinted. 'It's Betty!' She went to the door. 'Come in, Betty,' she said. 'Is everything all right?'

'Yes, yes, of course!' Betty followed Jessica into the shop. 'I was just walking past and I noticed Mary Talbot in with you.' She turned to Mary, her face liked a sucked lemon. 'Mary, I thought you were one of my ladies.' She paused. 'I thought you were a Nouveau You woman. Not a Nell's... client.'

Mary turned to face Betty. 'Ah, Betty,' she said, imperiously. 'I was once a patron of Nouveau You but no longer.' She turned back to Jessica. 'Will you wrap all of these up for me? Thank you!'

'But, Mary,' stuttered Betty, 'I've been dressing you for years! We have a rapport, an understanding. I know your colours. I have two beautiful dresses laid aside for you. Would you like to come and try them on? This place...' she waved her hand around, 'is fine... I love Nell, as you know, but Nouveau You is for a different type of lady. A cut-above kind of lady. Like you, Mary.'

Mary stood there, not really looking at or listening to Betty. Jessica was scanning each item, and I was wrapping each in tissue paper and sliding them into the bags.

'Betty, did you know about my husband and Monica?'

'No! Of course I did not!'

'But you and Monica are in the same book group. The very same book group which I have it on very good authority has never in its history ever read an actual book. Instead, this book group is a viper's nest of white wine and gossip. And I have heard that on every first Thursday of every month, each of you has to be poured into a taxi at the end of the book group.'

'That's a scandalous thing to say!' spluttered Betty.

'And I also know that it was at this book group that Monica confessed to you all that she had been sleeping with my husband.'

'Who told you this? It's an outrageous slur!'

'Monica told me everything. She came to my house three nights ago, drunk and disorderly, begging my forgiveness. I asked who in the village knew and she confessed to wine loosening her tongue at your illiterate book group!'

Betty looked like a chipmunk who had just been slapped. 'But...'

'So, in conclusion, I will not be frequenting your establishment ever again.' She turned to us at the till, handing over her card. 'Thank you, ladies. And it's a lovely shop. Much nicer than the overpriced and unfashionable Nouveau You. I will be making sure that my friends – my real friends – hear my thoughts.'

We handed over the five paper bags full of her new clothes.

'Goodbye, ladies, thank you,' Mary said to us, and then stood for a moment while Betty blocked her way. Eventually, Betty moved to one side and Mary was gone, into her Mercedes outside the door.

'Betty,' I began, but she held up her hand.

'I don't want to talk about it!' she said, and stalked off.

'Oh my God,' I said, to Jessica.

'I know,' she said. 'It's suddenly so hot in here!' She was slipping off her jacket. At the top of her arm was something strange. A bruise. A big one, which stretched from the front of her arm and reached up her sleeve to God knows where. It looked like someone had grabbed her. Hard.

'Jess...'

She looked up and saw my face and quickly moved away, reaching for her jacket. 'Mary really looked great, didn't she?' she said, her big smile back on, swiftly covering up again and tossing her hair back as though nothing had happened.

'Jess...' I tried again.

'It's nothing,' she said, looking me straight in the eye. 'Absolutely nothing.' And for a moment, I thought I had imagined it, my eyes playing tricks, or the light in the shop, a shadow, a blink of the eye.

21

After work, I called for Bronagh. It was only five days to the festival and I was already feeling a little anxious. Going through everything with Bronagh was the only way to double-check everything. The weather had been fine for weeks... would it rain by Saturday? I was wearing out the weather app on my phone, and so far it kept predicting 'fine and sunny'.

Bronagh's secretary waved me through and I waited for Bronagh on a small sofa inside her large open-plan office.

'There in a moment!' Bronagh mouthed, before returning to her phone call. *'Danke sehr... ja, ja...'* She laughed. *'Ja, ich stimme dir zu.'* She laughed again. *'Ja, ja... sehr gut... ja... okay, tschüss, auf wiedersehen!'* She put the phone down and smiled at me. 'Berlin,' she explained. 'The library. I'll have to go over soon, to sign off on it.' It always impressed me quite how successful Bronagh was. She made it all look so easy and yet I knew how hard she'd worked over the years. My phone rang.

'Olivia O'Neill? It's Sandra from Party People.' She had the kind of voice that was more nose than mouth. 'We can't do the chairs you ordered. So sorry...' She didn't sound very sorry. 'Turns out,' she went on, 'Bono is having an impromptu family celebration and we can't let Bono down, can we?' She gave a giggle which incensed me. The blood rose to my face. 'Bono is an international rock star... and well... when I think about what he's done for the country.'

'But this is a community gathering,' I said. 'Far more important than a family party. Even if he is famous.'

'But Bono is a very important client of ours,' she said. 'We never let repeat clients down. It's the DNA of the business. So...'

I was under the impression that she was about to end the conversation, leaving the festival chair-less. I thought of Shirley just out of hospital and all our other attendees. They weren't going to be able to stand all evening. I summoned everything I had ever learned from Maribelle.

'Excuse me,' I said, in my most calm voice, 'I am quite happy to ring Bono myself and tell him what you are doing. Bono and I are friends from the old days. It was my grandfather actually who gave Bono his very first guitar and told him he didn't have a bad voice.'

I might as well invent members of my tribe, I thought. These ghosts in my family may as well come in useful.

'In fact, it was my father Joseph Delaney who gave Bono his first leather jacket. Before, he was a denim-jacket kind of man, and once he put on the leather one, he was transformed.'

It *could* be true, I thought. It wasn't *totally* beyond the realms.

'He won't be pleased to hear that you are denying the community of Sandycove their festival because you don't have enough chairs. I'm going to have to call him straight away.'

Sandra paused. 'Deckchairs,' she said, quietly. 'Would you be happy with deckchairs?'

'What kind?'

'Wooden sling ones,' she said. 'They are very nice, actually.'

Her laugh had a slightly nervous quality to it. 'We were holding them for a garden party but I can move a few things around and have them with you on the Saturday afternoon. We'll collect first thing Sunday.'

'Okay.' Maribelle, I knew, wouldn't settle for anything until she was happy she had won everything possible. 'Anything else? It would be good to have a choice of seating.'

'Benches,' she said. 'Log benches. We have some we use for barn dances, country weddings and festivals. They're very nice and surprisingly comfortable.'

'Perfect,' I said. 'Thank you, Sandra. And I'll be letting Bono know how helpful you have been to an old friend.'

'You're very welcome,' she said. 'Good to be doing business with you.'

I felt bad when I put down the phone, but organising a whole festival with a minimum amount of time was obviously going to take a little bit of Machiavellian trickery, learned from the mistress of them, Maribelle. She would look you straight in the eye and lie about the colour of the sky.

'Ready now!' called Bronagh.

'Fancy a drink?' I asked. 'Or a walk? Or an ice cream? But preferably a drink.'

'I want a drink too,' she replied. 'Even if it is Monday. Actually, *especially* because it is Monday.'

'Come on then,' I said. 'Nice German, by the way.'

'I thought it was Spanish,' she smirked. 'Must have a word with my teacher. Anyway...' She stood up and took her jacket from the rack. 'I've been thinking that, despite my humiliating experience of being dumped by Paul, I'm not going to feel sorry for myself. In fact, I will celebrate never having to watch another film with Dr Spock or the other one, whatever his name is...'

'Obi-Wan Kenobi?' I suggested, having searched in the

recesses of my brain. 'Or is that the other film? Who's the little one?'

'George Takei?' Bronagh suggested, just as I said 'Yoda?'

'We're both as bad as each other,' she said, as we walked onto the street. 'But we've come this far without having seen *Star Wars*, so I think we'll survive.'

I was thinking of Jessica and that bruise and the look on her face. Could she have just got it from the kids? Weren't children pretty full on with their pulling and tugging? Or could she have got it from... *What, Olivia,* I asked myself, *walking into a door?*

'So, regarding the festival, I've made my calls, you've made yours,' said Bronagh. 'The Mexican food truck is booked...'

'The DJ is available,' I said, 'as is the ballet troupe who are only too delighted to dress up as midsummer fairies...'

'And the tin whistle orchestra, the ukulele orchestra and the ice cream van are all available.'

'And James says he will have a wine stall,' I added. 'He and Alison are going to be serving tapas.'

'Poor James,' said Bronagh. 'I met him earlier. He was telling me he has phantom dog syndrome...'

'Is that a real thing?'

Bronagh nodded. 'It's when you imagine your dog is still alive. You can hear it breathing and panting and you can sense it's there, but when you reach down to pat it, there's nothing. I don't know what I'm going to do when Mies dies... I'll have phantom cat syndrome and I'll think the pile of clothes at the end of my bed is him.' She had tears in her eyes. 'You see,' she said, 'I am far more upset at the thought of Mies dying than Paul breaking up with me. I can't bear to think about it. Can we talk about the festival again?'

'So, James and his phantom dog are all set,' I said. 'He's going to serve Irish wine. Apparently, one is from the Blackwater

Valley Vineyard and another from Lusk and something from Kinsale.'

She shrugged. 'Patriotic wine. Why not?'

'And Matt from The Island is setting up a cocktail bar. Says it's a chance to practise some of his bottle-tossing skills. He's also going to design a special midsummer mocktail for the kids, something with strawberries.'

'Do you think everyone is going to just get really, really drunk?' asked Bronagh.

'Of course not,' I said. 'It's a family event. We've got a bouncy castle and face-painting, but a bit of alcohol will just lubricate the wheels of social interaction.'

'And maybe a small amount of alcohol will make people a little more appreciative of the tin whistle orchestra.'

'Exactly,' I said. 'Anyway, don't worry, the kids will be long gone before the serious drinkers arrive.'

'By the way,' said Bronagh. 'I need another favour. Would you mind coming with me to collect my mother from her Botox appointment on Wednesday evening?'

'Botox?'

'No one must know, though. But I can't go on my own because she's particularly sensitive after each appointment – emotionally and mentally. Feels very vulnerable and tends to take it out on me. So I need you there to make sure she behaves herself.'

'Of course I'll come,' I said. 'But won't she be annoyed if I am there and no one is meant to know?'

'I'll make something up and I'll say you won't say a word.' She seemed relieved. 'I've been dreading it,' she said. 'Last time, she alternately shouted and cried all the way home and told me that I'd always been difficult to get on with.'

'Bronagh...'

She shrugged. 'I know, I know... but she's my mother. I just want everything to be nice between us, like you and your mum. You're so lucky.'

'But she can't talk to you like that,' I said.

'I know. I really want to get better at standing up to her. But Mark has moved back home and she's spending all her time looking after him. She's been making him all his favourite meals, which turn out to be quite complicated roast dinners. I called in the other night and she was in the kitchen with five pans boiling away and an entire pig in the oven. He has been smoking in his bedroom and set fire to one of his curtains so she had to go and buy a new set, plus a flouncy pelmet, and the state he leaves the bathroom in is unspeakable. Yesterday, I found her on her hands and knees scrubbing the toilet wearing rubber gloves and an old shirt of Dad's and my old science goggles. She said she couldn't let the cleaner deal with it.'

'Oh dear...'

'I know. She's pretending she loves having him home, but I know that she's doing it all through gritted teeth. I think she knows that he's useless but can't admit it because she'd have to accept her share of the blame for his general fecklessness. So she's more on edge than normal, and I have to be extra nice to her when I collect her from her Botox appointment.'

'I'll be there,' I said.

'Thank you.' She gave me a grateful smile.

Across the road, a crowd had gathered outside Bernard Murphy's butcher's shop, his boomy voice floating on the air and then the thwacking sound as though someone was chopping down a tree.

'He's giving one of his meat masterclasses,' said Bronagh. 'Showing off his butchering skills. They've become quite popular with women of a certain age.'

'Meat is an essential part of Irish life,' Bernard was saying.

'Show me an Irish vegetarian and I will show you either a liar or someone in need of a good feed!'

His all-female audience seemed to be something of a fan club and everything he said was received with a titter of appreciation. Bernard was clearly enjoying himself.

'Dinner is simply not dinner without a good piece of meat,' he proclaimed. 'Now, I am a nose-to-tail man.' There was another titter. 'Ladies, *please*!' said Bernard. 'I know some men are breast men, or leg men...' He held up a hand to stop the chuckling. 'I am talking meat.' He winked. '*Obviously*. But! If you *were* to ask my preference, then it's rump all the way!' Again, he held up his hand as the laughter threatened to boil over into hysteria. 'I like something to get my teeth into!'

One woman was wiping her eyes, another was gasping for breath, and a third was sinking to her knees.

'I need a volunteer,' Bernard shouted. 'Anyone like to come and have a go at my haunch?'

Cue more tittering and laughing, as Mrs O'Keefe elbowed her way to the front.

'Now, I don't always get such a gaggle in the shop,' said Bernard, his straw boater pushed back off his head, 'but I feel a little like a gander with my geese!' There was more laughing as he turned around to waggle his backside at the increasingly appreciative crowd. 'Right, Mrs O'Keefe,' he said, his face redder than normal as he passed her a meat mallet. 'You are going to tenderise my rump!' He paused as the tittering reached fever pitch. 'Ladies! Please!'

'Oh God,' said Bronagh. 'I can't stand any more. Come on, I need a drink.'

* * *

'I think I might be experiencing abandonment issues,' said Bronagh, when Matt placed the drinks in front of us. 'My lodger Susie decided to hand in her notice. Not that she was ever around, but still... she's moving in with her boyfriend. Hopes I don't mind... et cetera...'

'*Do* you mind?'

'No, not at all. Glad she's happy. Mies is delighted. She has a very loud voice and I think it hurt his ears. He's a sensitive little chap. And she had a tendency to dry her huge grey bras in the bathroom. Every time I brushed my teeth, I came face to face with them. It was traumatising.'

Bronagh waved at someone behind me. 'Hello!' she said, cheerily. 'Yes, just a quick drink! Lovely!'

She looked back at me with a funny expression on her face. 'There's *your* Dr Butler,' she said. 'Looking particularly handsome this evening.'

'He's not *my* Dr Butler.' But I felt my stomach swoop suddenly and I forced myself to stay facing Bronagh.

'Well, you've been to his house. Which is more than anyone else in the village has done. What's he doing in a pub on a *Monday* night? I thought only ne'er-do-wells like us did that.' She kept her eye over my shoulder. 'It's okay, Matt's giving him a coffee... now, they're chatting. Dr Butler is laughing... oh, look, Matt's giving him one of his special biscuits... he must *like* Dr Butler.' She looked back at me. 'But then again, who doesn't?' She glanced up and dropped her voice. 'Oh God, it's that guy from swimming. The lifeboat crew member!'

I looked up and recognised him as that nice beardy man from our walk last week.

'But he looks so nice,' I said. 'Like a sexy teddy bear.'

Bronagh groaned. 'God, he's insufferable. Always in the sea, swimming around, showing off his big arms. And there's me, just wanting to do my own thing. And he always wants to chat. Like chatting is what I go to the Forty Foot for! He's always asking about the weather, how cold the sea is, remarking on the rainbow or clouds or whatever. He's like a cross between a Connemara mountain man and David Hasselhoff. He keeps trying to organise dinners in the Sea Shack, so we can all get to know each other better.' She looked horrified. 'Like, being sociable! The very idea!'

I laughed. 'Maybe he likes you.'

She shook her head. 'The only people who like me are pasty types, the kind that don't see much daylight, who consider speaking and eating as complicated multitasking and think ordering chips with curry sauce counts as being exotic. Anyway, as you know, I am off men and glorying in my wonderful aloneness!'

'He's coming over!'

'Oh God.'

The mountainy man stood at our table, looking down at us, smiling, torso and chest and shoulders like Croagh Patrick on a sunny day. He had red hair and a huge matching beard, his T-shirt looked two sizes too small, probably because it was impossible to buy something to sheathe that rippling body.

'Hey, Bronagh,' he said. 'Good to see you.' He smiled down from his great height. 'Is this the first time with clothes on? I mean...' He'd gone as red as his beard, hair and T-shirt. 'You know, I mean... usually we are swimming...'

Bronagh laughed. 'I know what you meant. Fergal, this is my friend Olivia O'Neill, Liv, this is Fergal...' She looked up at him.

'Ferguson,' he said, holding out his hand to me. 'Fergal Ferguson.'

'Wait,' said Bronagh. 'You're Fergal Ferguson, the architect? I just finished your book... I had no idea.' She looked utterly puzzled. 'I thought you were the lifeboat crew.'

'Only part-time,' he said. 'I've just moved back from Los Angeles...'

'Yes, I was reading about what you did there... that house in Laurel Canyon... oh my God.'

'You liked it?' He blushed again.

'I loved it. The way every room was facing the courtyard and how you used the trees outside... it was beautiful.'

'Thank you,' he said. 'I've been trying to introduce myself for ages now, because I saw your library in Cork... I think I spent an hour in it, just walking around and sitting down... it was like being in a church.'

'That's what I wanted,' said Bronagh, 'this feeling of worshipping books. And a feeling of peace. I wasn't sure if I had quite achieved it, but I am so glad you liked it.'

He nodded, enthusiastically. 'I didn't like it,' he said. 'I loved it.' And they both laughed.

'Wow, I can't believe it's you.' She turned to me. 'Fergal's book is called *A Place Called Home* – modernism and domesticity and putting the life into real life. I haven't been able to put it down. I've been marking it and underlining bits. You don't look like the photograph in the book.'

'It's my beard,' he said. 'As soon as I left LA, I just went wild. I mean, not that kind of wild, the drinking kind, but I've just kind of rewilded myself. Grew the beard, ditched the suits and just found myself again. LA was quite restrictive, dealing with rich clients, having to deliver ahead of time... I'm trying to find what I want to do here. So, I'm teaching in UCD, volunteering with the lifeboats. My friend George is part of the lifeboat crew and I'd grown up surfing and swimming so joining them was a no-brainer.'

Bronagh was nodding along. 'I still can't believe it's you,' she said. 'Small world.'

'Yeah... well, it's Dublin, isn't it?' He hovered for a moment and then said, 'I'll let you get back to your drinks. Lovely to finally meet you properly, Bronagh. Good to meet you, Olivia.' He turned to go and then at the last moment, said, 'Maybe we could meet sometime? Discuss buildings, or is that too nerdy? You probably hate talking buildings outside of work?'

She shook her head and tried to speak. 'No,' she said, after clearing her throat. 'No, I love talking about buildings. It's my favourite subject.'

He grinned. 'Mine too,' he replied. 'Well, that and cats. I'm afraid I'm a crazy cat man. I just love cats. All my Instagram is either buildings or cats.'

'Mine too,' croaked Bronagh. I thought she was going to faint.

22

I looked across to the bar and realised that Will was looking back at me. His face softened and he smiled. I smiled back.

'How are you?' he mouthed.

'Fine. You?'

'Not bad.'

'What?'

'Not bad...' He was still smiling, when I saw him gather up his jacket and bag and he and Pablo came over.

'May I join you? Hi Bronagh, hi Fergal.'

'Hi Will,' said Fergal. 'How were the waves today?'

'Bracing,' said Will. His hair was still wet. 'How's the running going? Still enjoying it?'

'Weirdly, yes,' I said. 'Still aching, still questioning why I am getting out of bed at 6.30 a.m. and plodding around the seafront, but there is something strangely nice about it.'

He nodded, understanding. 'You feel more alive,' he said. 'And you can really enjoy your breakfast.'

Fergal and Bronagh had resumed their conversation, Fergal was now sitting on a stool beside Bronagh, who was laughing at something he had said. I thought of Mum and Joseph Delaney meeting in this very bar all those years ago. Pity he had turned out to be so useless.

'How's Jake's seaweed book?' said Will. 'Is it actually interesting?'

'It's fascinating. Did you know seaweed is like this magical substance that absorbs all the goodness of seawater and then it's all there, ready to be used?'

He smiled. 'I hope you do something with it or set up your business again, it's obviously what you're passionate about.'

'I think it's the kind of weird passion that will have to go nowhere,' I replied.

'I had a few of those when I was a teenager,' he said, making me laugh.

'Anyway,' I said, 'I have to go back to London. My boss is very needy.'

'Is she a *child*?'

'In many ways she is,' I said. 'She has meltdowns if she doesn't have a soy-milk latte by 8.30 a.m. The only way I got her to sleep on a long-haul flight once when she was so wired she paced up and down the gangway for an hour was by downloading *Harry Potter and the Deathly Hallows* and giving her my headphones.'

He looked confused. 'And you *like* this job?' Will was stroking Pablo as he talked.

I shook my head. 'I wake up every morning dreading the whole day. I go to sleep with my phone under my pillow just in case Maribelle calls. I'm only home because she is in rehab. I live in fear of her getting better and being given her phone back.' I'd be back in London in two weeks and I hadn't realised quite how much I was already dreading it.

Will's mobile rang. 'I'd better take this. I'm so sorry. It's one of my patients.' He lifted it to his ear. 'Everything all right?' His face was serious as he stood up. 'No? Okay, I'll be right over. Stay calm, okay? We'll get her better.' He looked back at us. 'I've got to go. I'm so sorry.' Pablo had already sprung to his side. But at the last moment, he turned to me. 'Olivia, would you mind coming as well? You might be able to help? It's Cara. Her nan has collapsed,' he said. 'I presume it's a hyperglycaemic attack. The ambulance is on the way, but Cara's on her own.'

And, without thinking, I was running behind him and Pablo, down the street to his car.

* * *

At her front door, Cara was distraught. 'The ambulance!' she said. 'It's not here! Where is it? I called half an hour ago!'

'Where's Shirley?' said Will, urgently pushing past her.

'She's through there.' Cara pointed down the hall into the back room.

'It's on its way,' I said, more confidently than I felt. 'It'll be here.' I put my arm around her. 'Please don't worry.' Her whole body was shaking.

'She was making dinner and I was reading upstairs and...' Cara began to cry, as we followed Will into the sitting room where he was kneeling on the floor next to Cara's nan, his doctor's bag wide open.

'Hello, Shirley,' he was saying. 'It's Dr Butler here. Can you hear me? Shirley?'

We stood at the door – Cara clutching my arm – as Will placed a vial on a needle and injected it. He held her hand, patting it.

'Shirley, will you open your eyes for me? We're all here, Cara's here... I'm here, Will from the surgery... Shirley?' But she lay motionless on the floor.

Cara went over to kneel beside her. Panic floated into the air and hovered above us all. 'Come on, Nan,' she was saying. 'It's me, Cara.'

And then, suddenly, Shirley's eyes opened, and she tried to sit up.

'Stay there, Shirley,' said Will, grabbing a cushion from a chair for the back of her head. 'A blanket?'

'I'll get one,' I said, seeing a tartan picnic rug on the back of the sofa.

Cara laid it over Shirley, pulling her skirt down and then holding her hand. 'Nan? Nan? It's me!'

'Will you make a cup of tea, Olivia?' Will said. 'Lots of sugar, please?'

'Of course!'

In the kitchen, I flicked on the kettle and found mugs and teabags and milk, and once the water was boiled, I spooned six sugars into both, carried them back into the living room where Shirley was now sitting up, with her back against the sofa.

'Here, Shirley,' I said. 'Some sweet tea.'

Will poured the tea into the saucer and then held it to Shirley's lips. 'Here we go, Shirley.'

'You might need some too,' I said to Cara, handing her the other mug.

She looked at me. 'She didn't take her tablets. She said she was feeling better... and I told her...' She stopped, listening to something. 'Is that them?'

From far away, there was the sound of an ambulance.

'I'll let them in,' I said, rushing into the hall, and as soon I opened the front door, the whole street, including the worried faces of the neighbours, was illuminated by the sweeping blue light. In seconds, the ambulance crew were already unloading the stretcher and heading straight for me.

'She's in the back!' I shouted, my voice shaking.

'How is she?' one of the neighbours called.

'Not sure,' I said.

'She hasn't been looking well for a few days,' I heard another woman, who then crossed herself and muttered under her breath, while I thought about how I could be most useful. Should I pack a bag for Shirley? Her things and some of Cara's?

Upstairs in the front bedroom – Shirley's room – I packed a pair of glasses from the bedside table, a holy-water bottle, Shirley's nightdress under the pillow and an old shawl which was folded neatly on the end of the bed. I opened the top drawer of the old dressing table and found a pair of warm socks. What else? Her toothbrush from the bathroom, along with a clean flannel and towel. In Cara's room, I found her copy of *The Brothers Karamazov*, the spine broken in a hundred places, her notebook beside it, full of tiny scribbles. I put both of them in the bag. And I found her long brown cardigan, the one I'd seen her wear before.

Back downstairs, Shirley had been placed on a stretcher and was being manoeuvred though the narrow house and outside, the crowd stepping back reverently, as she was placed in the ambulance. Cara jumped up behind her. There were calls of: 'See you soon, Shirl,' and 'God be with you!'

Cara's eyes were filled with tears. She looked absolutely terrified.

'Would you like me to come with you?' I asked.

She nodded. 'Would you?'

I looked back at Will. 'I'll see you there,' he said.

* * *

We sat in the waiting room for hours until, finally, a doctor came to find us.

'The family of Shirley O'Donnell?'

Cara looked up from under her hair.

'Here!' Will said.

'She's doing well,' said the doctor. 'Asleep now. You can go in and see her. She was asking for Cara.' She turned to Cara. 'That's you?'

Cara nodded.

'I'm Shirley's GP,' said Will to the doctor, reeling off a list of what she had been taking.

'But she didn't take it yesterday,' said Cara. 'I remember. She said she was feeling a bit sick in the morning and that the medication was making it worse.'

'Well,' said the doctor. 'She's all right now. Lucky you were there.'

I waited while Will and Cara went in to see Shirley, and after a few minutes, he came back out.

'Cara's going to sleep here tonight,' he said. 'We can go home.'

We walked out of the hospital, in the dark, to an empty car park and when we opened the car, Pablo was overjoyed to see Will, insisting on sitting on his lap all the way home.

'Do you always go to hospital with your patients?'

'Not always,' he said. 'But I've been keeping a special eye on those two. I don't want anything to happen to Shirley for Cara's sake...'

'She doesn't want to go to college in New York because she doesn't want to leave Shirley,' I said.

'I know,' he replied. 'They've both told me all about it, separately. Shirley thinks she should go and Cara is adamant she won't.' He shrugged. 'They are lucky to have each other. Love. You know? Someone to take care of.' His hand was on the gearstick as we pulled away from the lights and Pablo lifted his head and rested it on Will's arm. 'We all need it.'

As we got closer to home, there was a fox standing in a puddle of moonlight, staying absolutely still, his eyes gleaming, his nostrils quivering in the night air. And then in a moment, he was gone again, his tail curling upwards as he disappeared into the night.

'I love urban foxes,' I said. 'They always look like they need a friend.'

Will laughed. 'I've never thought about them like that. But I suppose they do. They are not dogs who are universally loved. Or cats who have warm homes to go back to. No one touches them or feeds them...'

'They're on their own,' I said.

'Not like Pablo here,' he replied, 'treated like a little prince.'

I laughed. 'He looks very happy,' I said. 'You don't need much to make a family.'

'Even just a tiny Yorkshire terrier,' he said.

Was it my imagination or was Pablo warming to me? The expression on his face was softening. Perhaps one day he might actually let me stroke him?

'Thanks again for showing us around your house,' I said. 'Mum never spoke about her childhood much and I think she found it really...' I searched for the word. '...healing. She had to leave home because she was pregnant. And unmarried.'

He shook his head. 'The poor thing,' he said. 'But she was lucky.'

'Lucky?'

'She got to keep you. So many weren't allowed.' And then he brightened, as though he'd had an idea. 'You know,' he said. 'There are boxes up in the attic. I found them when I first moved in and there was a problem with the water tank. There are some letters and things... I remember seeing it but not doing anything about it. I was going to, but I've been so busy but... you never know. It might belong to your family?'

'I doubt it,' I said. 'There were people there before you...'

'But it looked completely untouched, hidden behind the tank?' He looked so desperate to be right.

We pulled up outside Mum's house. 'Mum gave me this last week.' I opened the locket and showed it to him. 'It's a photograph of my grandmother. I hadn't seen her before. That's her there with Mum.'

He studied it. 'She looks like you.'

'Really?' I peered closely at it.

'Yes,' he said. 'She's beautiful.'

I don't know how I managed to get out of the car.

'Thank you, Will,' I said.

'See you, Olivia.' And he pulled away, Pablo still looking out from Will's lap.

23

Roberto: Am currently in bed with Mary Berry.

Me: Lucky Mary.

Roberto: She's an excellent read. Who knew that Battenberg was so simple? Mary says it's 'an exceedingly easy teatime treat'. That's been said about me from time to time.

Me: Teatime?

Roberto: Anytime. Love you Liv.

Me: Love you Miss Minogue.

I hadn't slept well, my mind sorting through everything that had happened. I kept thinking of Cara and how young and alone she had looked when we turned up. I hoped fervently that Shirley would be all right. She looked the same age as Mum, so far too young and far too important to Cara to die. And then there was Jessica, and the bruises on her arm. There were all the pieces to a jigsaw but I couldn't get any of them to fit and maybe I was jumping to conclusions, looking for drama where there was none. I didn't want to leave Sandycove, I realised. I really didn't want to go. There was too much I was now invested in, too much I cared about to just go again.

And then there was Will. Did I just imagine that he called me beautiful? Is that how he got people to like him, by complimenting them?

'Morning, Olivia,' said James, stopping in front of me. 'How's it going?'

'Fine, how are you?'

'Ah, you know...'

'It must be hard without Sammy.'

'You could say that,' he said. 'But he had a good life and was a happy dog. I'm trying to tell myself how lucky I was to have him. The thing about dogs is they are not here for a long time, they are here for a good time. And he certainly had a good time.'

'Have you thought about perhaps... you know...' I didn't want to be insensitive. 'Getting a new one?'

'Maybe. I was saying to Alison the other night that I might think about one later in the year. She's moving into my house this weekend and so I'm busy trying to declutter and make some room for her. Anyway...' he gave me a wave, 'see you soon, Olivia.'

'See you, James.'

Outside Albatross in the early-morning sunshine were Catherine and Jake.

'Hello, you two,' I said. 'On your way to school?'

'We have a dental appointment,' said Catherine, 'so we have a little time to waste.'

'We're going for breakfast,' said Jake.

'Why don't you join us?' suggested Catherine. 'I've made some little daisies for the chain. I'd love to see what you think. I think they have turned out really well.'

'Mummy's wearing her tiger top,' said Jake. 'She said you gave it to her.'

'Well, *give* isn't quite the right word,' I said, laughing. 'I *sold* it to your mummy.'

'Well, I want one too!' he said.

'I've told you, Jakey,' said Catherine. 'They don't come in your size. Just Mummy's big size!' She turned to me. 'He's desperate for one,' she said.

'I just want to be like a twin,' he said, 'with Mummy.'

'I will go and check,' I promised him. 'Keep your fingers crossed.'

He crossed his fingers on both hands. 'I won't uncross them until Mummy and I are twins,' he said, solemnly.

Catherine, Jake and I sat in the window of Albatross with our hot chocolates and coffees. 'Try and draw something that isn't seaweed,' Catherine said, taking out a sketch pad and handing it to Jake and then she unwrapped a small tissue parcel; a dainty silver daisy rolled out. 'There's a little hole in the stem,' she said, 'so I will be able to make a chain of them.'

'It's perfect,' I breathed, amazed at her talent.

Catherine smiled. 'I haven't done anything like this in so long... but it kind of came back to me.'

'I can't believe you made each petal!'

'It was fiddly,' she said. 'But that's jewellery for you.' She shrugged but still looked pleased at my reaction. 'I enjoyed it. I've already made twenty others. I've set up a space in the upstairs office for now, dug out my old welding equipment.'

'So Drithle is back!'

She grinned. 'Drithle is back. Now what about Seasalt? I know you want to!'

'I wish I could...' I said.

'So...?'

'I need to earn money. I have some savings, but I would need more. And anyway, I have a job...' I stopped, suddenly feeling ill at the thought of going back, back to being in the office for 7.30 a.m., working twelve-hour days, spending my life surrounded by concrete and leaving the sea behind.

'Ah...' Catherine looked almost as downhearted as I felt. 'That's a real shame. I thought I had you convinced.'

'It's just that *practically...*'

She looked up at someone over my shoulder. 'Good morning, Will!'

'Good morning! I thought it was you!'

I looked back to see Will was standing behind me, Pablo at his feet.

'Uncle Will!' Jake shot up to hug him.

'How are you all this morning? Recovered from last night?' he said to me, smiling.

Catherine glanced at me and then back to Will. 'Why, what happened last night?'

'Medical emergency,' he said. 'Olivia very kindly stepped in as...'

'His assistant,' I said. 'I made tea and got in everyone's way.'

'And everything's all right? Everyone okay?' said Catherine.

'Is it?' I looked at Will.

'I've rung the hospital,' he said. 'And all is well. I'll pop in later. Maybe you'd like to come with me?'

'Okay.'

Catherine stood up. 'We'd better go,' she said. 'Come on, Jake, say goodbye. I'll have the finished daisy chain ready for Friday. And the flowers and the flower crowns on Saturday morning.' She smiled at the two of us for a moment.

'What?' said Will.

'Oh, nothing,' she said. 'Nothing at all.'

Jake bent down and kissed Pablo goodbye, before he and Catherine left me and Will on our own.

'Catherine is going to be moving into the bottle factory as her new studio...'

'Oh yes?' How lovely, I thought. A workshop. It had always been my dream to have a space of my own. Lucky Catherine.

'I thought of asking other artists or business owners if they would like to take part of the space...'

'Like an artists' colony?'

He laughed. 'Yes, why not? So if you...' He stopped.

I wished I could ask him for a share of the space. The thought of being in the old glass-blower's, making up my lotions and my potions, was such a faraway dream that it was pointless and indulgent to even think about.

I looked at the clock on the wall above Alison behind the counter. 'I'd better go. Jessica will be wondering where I've got to.'

'I'll walk you.'

We began walking to Nell's, the June morning bright and blue and glorious. 'So, what's your day looking like? Busy?'

He nodded. 'The surgery is opening at 9.30 a.m. And then house calls this afternoon. And then a swim. And then visit Shirley. Shall I meet you at the hospital or do you need a lift?'

'I'll see you there,' I said. 'I don't know what time I'll finish here.'

He smiled. 'Okay, well, see you...' He paused.

'Around.'

He laughed. 'See you around.'

I waited for him to turn and go, but he hesitated. Maybe he was waiting for me to go first. Did he want to wave me off?

'Well, thanks again for last night,' he said. 'It was nice to have the company.'

'I enjoyed it,' I said. 'I mean, obviously, I didn't enjoy the fact that a woman collapsed and was rushed to hospital. I don't take pleasure in that... in fact, there was nothing about the evening I enjoyed but...'

He was laughing. 'No, there was nothing to enjoy at all.' He smiled at me again.

'So,' I said. 'I'd better go.'

'Yes, okay, have a good day.' He really was waiting to wave me off.

'Bye, Will.'

Finally, he walked off, towards the surgery, and I went to push open the door of Nell's, but at the very last moment, I looked back at him just as he turned round and smiled and raised his hand.

I began changing the window display at Nell's that morning. Greens and yellows and bright shots of colours, I was thinking, for midsummer. I wanted it to look like a summer garden – the yellow sandals, the red straw beach bag, the cobalt silk dress... and then the vases of flowers and the silver daisy chains... it was going to be beautiful.

I stood back to admire it when a customer came in. It was Janet from the bakery.

'I have an emergency,' she announced. 'I'm off to the Riviera for a week and I need to look the part.'

Jessica was on a phone call in the back of the shop so it was up to me to take charge. 'The part of what?'

'The part of a woman on holiday,' she said. 'Like everyone else on the Riviera.'

'Glitzy?' I suggested. 'If Liz Hurley was going on holiday... That kind of thing?'

'Exactly!'

As I chose a few pieces – I was becoming more confident at

picking shapes and colours and working out what customers were looking for – I could hear Jessica on the phone sounding increasingly upset.

'You try these on,' I said to Janet, 'and see what you think. Now, they have to make you feel the joy.'

The woman laughed. 'That would be nice,' she said, 'but it might be asking too much of clothes. Cakes make me feel the joy. And bread.'

'Me too,' I agreed. 'But I am starting to see the appeal of clothes. Jessica has me in training.' Today I was wearing another new outfit that Jessica had made me buy and I was feeling far more confident that I had in years. I had caught the sun and I could feel my freckles reappearing like they used to and I was feeling fit and healthy.

Jessica stepped back into the shop. Fleetingly, she looked utterly defeated, her eyes red and so sad, but in a second it was gone, as she arranged her face into her smile.

'Everything all right?' I said, casually, as I hovered outside the dressing room.

'Yes!' Jessica said. 'Everything's fine!'

'What do you think?' Janet had emerged, resplendent in white jeans and gold blouse, unbuttoned to reveal her impressive cleavage. 'Liz Hurley enough?'

'Definitely,' I said. 'What do you think, Jess?'

There was silence for a second too long and when I looked back at her, tears were rolling down her face. 'Yes,' she said, swallowing, pretending that she wasn't actually crying. 'Glamorous but understated. Off on holiday?' Her voice was shaking.

'Cannes,' said Janet, looking at herself in the mirror. 'I am agoraphobic, claustrophobic and aerophobic so obviously I wasn't going to go. But last night I was saying to Hubby how much I missed out on all the girls' trips and he said to me, you can do anything, Janet. Anything you want. I am behind you all the way.'

'That's so nice,' said Jessica, her voice wobbling.

'Next thing I knew, he'd booked me on the flight and waved me off!'

'So lovely,' said Jessica.

'Hubby is my rock,' replied Janet, still admiring herself. 'Without him I wouldn't have got through my cancer last year. He was there every step of the way. "Janet," he said, "we're doing this." Not you. *We*.' She fiddled with her buttons. 'Should I open another or is that too much?'

Jessica began to openly cry. 'I'm so sorry,' she said. 'I'm just having a bad day. You are so lucky to have each other. So lucky, so, so lucky... I wish... I just wish I had a hubby like yours...'

'Have you got a rotten apple?' said Janet.

Jessica was nodding.

'You do? I used to have one of those years ago, before Hubby. Wasted eight years with him and then walked out. Thankfully found Hubby a year later.'

'I thought it was me,' Jessica was saying, 'that I was the bad one, that I was ruining everything but... I don't think so any more. I've tried to be the best wife and mother so Damien had nothing to blame me for, but he always manages to find something. Just this morning, he kicked off again because Frankie backchatted him. So, he started shouting, saying the kids are only good with me and that they are ganging up on him and they have no respect for him. And it's all my fault because I have taught them to have no respect for him, and Ellie-Mae is a little madam, according to him. Which she isn't. They are both so sweet. I think he's jealous of them. It's mad, isn't it? Who could be jealous of children? He thinks I spend too much time with them and not enough with him. It's exhausting. They have to be in bed by 6.30 p.m. and the house all tidy and no noise from either of them just so we can have an evening together. The thing is, I don't want an evening with him.' She wiped her eyes and tried to steady her voice. 'He criticises them all the time,' she went on. 'I mean, I don't mind when he goes on about me, because I probably deserve it. But them! My mam says she's never seen such good children. Ellie-Mae tried to make me a cup of tea this morning after Damien had been...' She stopped.

'Damien had been what?' I said, everything falling into place. My instincts had been right. The bruises, the controlling behaviour, the charm, and Jessica trying to cover over the cracks and be the perfect family.

'He loses control,' she said. 'He gets angry and we have to wait until he calms down. And he always does. Always. It's just the waiting. I mean, I know he will be fine tonight at dinner. He sometimes buys me something, like flowers or whatever, and he is nice to the kids, letting them watch cartoons. But it...'

We waited for her to find the word.

'It lingers. All day. His voice in my head. It's like my whole body is reverberating from what he's said. My teeth are shaking, my brain rattling. Like he's *inside* me.'

Janet had Jessica in her arms as she began to sob, her tears soaking the Liz Hurley gold blouse. 'There, there,' Janet patted her better. 'You let it out, that's it.'

Eventually, Jessica managed to stop crying. 'I'm so sorry,' she whispered, using one end of the scarf which had been tied around her neck to wipe her mascara. 'I'm so embarrassed.'

'No need to be embarrassed,' said Janet. 'And now your scarf is getting all wet. Let's untie it.'

Jessica grabbed at it, trying to tie it back on, but it was already too loose and her neck was exposed. It didn't look right, something was wrong with her neck, the colour of her skin. And then

Jessica let her arms fall limply to her sides, as though she was giving up and the game was over, tears once more pouring down her face as Janet exposed Jessica's neck. It was red and purple, as though she'd been strangled.

The world stopped. Silence. Neither of us dared to breathe.

'So it's not just shouting then?' said Janet, quietly.

Jessica shook her head.

'How long for?' I said. 'How long has he been... doing this?'

Jessica's eyes filled with tears again. 'Since before the kids. When I was pregnant with Ellie-Mae.' Her voice was flat. 'He's nice most of the time. Really protective, loves us so much. Too much, really. Hates anything that doesn't involve the family. I can work, but have to be home. I have no friends, they all gave up on me when I couldn't go out...'

'And your mam?' I asked. 'Does she know?'

'I'm not sure, I mean, I think so. But I haven't told her. He would kill me.' She looked at us, frightened. 'You're not going to say anything, are you? You can't...'

Janet shook her head. 'I won't,' she said.

I shook my head. 'We'll support you.'

'He doesn't mean to be like it,' she said. 'And if I tell anyone then it's over. Once you start talking, it's over.'

We nodded, understanding her impossible position where leaving seemed scarier than staying.

'I still love him,' she said. 'And I want a family for Ellie-Mae and Frankie. I don't want to be a single mother. And Damien is a great dad... he is... I promise you. Ellie-Mae sits on his lap to watch *Strictly*. And Frankie... well, he's a little mammy's boy and a bit scared of Damien.'

I didn't blame Frankie one bit, I thought. Seeing your mother being hit or shouted at would terrify any child.

'When he does calm down, Damien is so sorry,' said Jessica.

'Cries, calls himself terrible names. And he's lost, I know that. That's why he goes to the gym so much to work out. Helps with his self-esteem.' She took in a deep breath. 'I'm fine now,' she said. 'I promise. And it will get better. I know it will. He doesn't mean it, and he's really trying to be better. And I love him.'

Janet looked at her. 'I think you should leave,' she said.

'So do I,' I agreed. 'What he does to you is wrong. It's abuse.'

But Jessica was shaking her head. 'It's fine, really. People go through bad patches, and he's not a bad man. I have to give him this chance to be better. I couldn't live with myself if I didn't. I have to do this for Ellie-Mae and Frankie.'

Janet hugged Jessica. 'You look after yourself,' she said. 'I feel guilty now going off to France when you are going through this.'

'I'll be all right,' said Jessica. 'I always am. And I'm not always this unprofessional, crying in the shop. Am I, Olivia?'

'I'll be thinking of you,' said Janet as she paid for her blouse and jeans and then turned to Jessica and hugged her again, tighter this time. 'If you were my daughter,' she said, 'I would want to know. And I would do everything in my power to keep you and those children safe. You need to know that life doesn't have to be like this, okay?'

Jessica nodded and I walked Janet to the door.

'Have a good time,' I said.

'That girl,' she said to me, 'needs minding, okay? You look after her. All right?'

'I will,' I promised.

'I'll be in next week to see how you all are, okay?'

* * *

When she'd left, Jessica was determined not to talk about Damien or think about what had happened.

'It's best if I just have a normal day,' she said. 'Get everything back to normal again. By tonight Damien will have calmed down and so I'll get dinner on and we'll watch TV and the kids will be so relieved...' She started crying again and spent the whole day sobbing on and off as though a dam of emotion had been breached and, as she desperately managed to stem one flow, another hole formed.

By 5.30 p.m., when the big black car pulled up outside, she was recovered enough to go home, her make-up redone. I wanted to stop her from going, to go and pick up Ellie-Mae and Frankie and... I don't know, find somewhere safe for them to live.

'Will you call me, at any time, if you need anything? Promise?'

'I'll be fine!' Jessica's big smile was back, like an actress transforming before going on stage.

I watched as she ran out of the door and into the car, and I couldn't shake this feeling that something was going to happen and that it wouldn't end well.

24

That evening, I took the bus to the hospital in Dún Laoghaire, thinking about Jessica and the children. I kept taking out my phone to see if she had texted – which of course she hadn't – or to attempt to send a text myself, just hoping she was okay, but I kept deleting everything. Should I never mention it again and wait for Jessica to bring it up? Or maybe everything would be all right and Damien would change?

At the hospital, I found my way to Shirley's room. I knocked on the door and peeked in. 'Hello?'

Cara was sitting on the chair, her feet pulled up and resting on the bed, her copy of *The Brothers Karamazov* open beside her. Shirley, meanwhile, was sitting up in bed, propped up by about eight pillows, her shawl over her shoulders. She looked up and smiled.

'I just came to see how you were,' I said. 'I'm Olivia... I was...'

'Oh, I know who you are,' she said. 'My Cara has been telling me all about last night... I can't remember too much about it...'

'I've been filling her in,' Cara said. 'Telling her about what happens when she *doesn't* take her tablets. And reminding her that invincibility is not one of her superpowers.'

Shirley looked apologetically at Cara. 'I thought I was doing so much better,' she said, 'thought I didn't need those silly pills... you know how it is...'

'I've bought you two cups of tea,' I said, putting them down on the table over the bed. 'And some fruit cake from the shop downstairs.'

'That looks lovely,' said Shirley. 'Thank you. Cara needs building up after the exams, I think she needs a little bit of TLC.'

I moved the table closer so she could drink her tea.

'I certainly don't need my grandmother not taking her tablets which causes her to *black out*,' said Cara. 'This was all a very nice end-of-exams surprise. Thanks, Nan.'

'The doctors are finding the right dose for me, and I'll be in for another couple of days. And then, right as rain...'

'As long as you take your tablets *every day*,' said Cara. 'And don't miss one.'

'I won't! Better do as she tells me because she's such a clever girl,' said Shirley. 'Brains to burn this one. Born clever. She's got a place in New York University. Did you know that? Refusing to go, however, despite the *scholarship*. How many people get a scholarship to college?'

'It's incredible news,' I said.

But Cara was busy studying her hands. 'It would be,' she mumbled, '*if* I was going. Which I'm *not*.'

'I've told her to go,' said Shirley to me. 'It's not like New York is Mars.'

'But it's a six-hour, three-hundred-euro flight away. It's not like popping into town.' Cara paused. 'And then there's *you* who doesn't take her tablets when she's been told to.'

Shirley looked at me and then back to Cara. 'I was foolish,' she said. 'But I've learned my lesson. And we have Dr Butler close by and he has told you he'll keep an eye on me. He said he'll come and make sure I take them. Not that he will need to because I am not going to allow yesterday to happen again.'

'But Dr Butler isn't going to come in every day, is he?' Cara said, getting upset. 'That's not practical. I'm the only one who can do that. I can't trust you to stay well!'

Shirley sighed. 'It used to be me who was overprotective of this one,' she said to me, 'and now it's the other way round. We look after each other, both worry about each other.' She smiled. 'It's just the two of us, you see. My daughter... well, she didn't make it through the birth...' She stopped for a moment and Cara was looking at Shirley, listening intently. 'My Sarah was just like Cara, bright as a pair of patent shoes. Sparkled, she did. Wouldn't stop talking, ideas flying around like birds. She had wanted to go to college, you see. But then she fell pregnant. And we were going to make it work. Stay here, I told her. I'll mind the baby. You do your study. And it will be the three of us in our house.'

Shirley looked back at me, her eyes full of sorrow. I wished Mum had had the same loving support that Sarah had had, but then for Sarah not to have made it was such an insurmountable loss. Mum and I were lucky.

'I am so sorry to hear about Sarah,' I said, sitting down at the very end of the bed.

Shirley shook her head. 'Do you know, I have struggled to come to terms with it, to understand why God took my Sarah, and it was a test, I know that, and, at times, one I didn't think I would pass. I'm no scholarship girl!' She gave a little laugh but tears were in her eyes. 'But each morning I kept waking up. And each day, I had *this* lovely girl here to look after. And once Cara started talking, she didn't stop, just like Sarah. And there was no way I could spend all that time missing what I lost, I kept being faced

with all I had gained. So, God, they say, works in mysterious
ways.'

I noticed that Cara didn't try to change the subject, as she did
when Shirley was complimenting her, she was just listening.
Every word was a new brushstroke in the portrait of her mother.
She leaned over and pulled the shawl over one of Shirley's shoulders where it had slipped a bit, as though Shirley was the most
precious thing in the world to her.

'I was at home when they called with the news,' went on
Shirley. 'We didn't have a phone back in those days, so Sarah's
emergency number was the neighbours'. I remember Mrs O'Brolchain running over, crying. She didn't speak for a moment and
then she just blurted it out. "She's gone. Your Sarah's gone."'

Shirley stopped. She turned her head to look out of the
window. In the background was the sound of the hospital –
voices, rattling trolleys, someone laughing. Cara was fiddling with
the buttons on her brown cardigan.

Shirley continued, 'I said, "Gone where?" I must have
sounded like I'd lost my marbles and poor Mrs O'Brolchain had
to say it again. "Gone. She…" She was trying to remember the
word. "She haemorrhaged." And I was looking at her as though
she was speaking a foreign language. And then other neighbours
began to arrive. Mrs O'Brolchain's husband had been knocking
on the doors, lovely man, telling them, and they were all
suddenly there, all these women in the kitchen, leading me to a
chair, kettle on, hushed voices, and I sat there with my heart fully
stopped.'

Cara had her head down.

'And then,' Shirley went on, 'it was about an hour later when I
thought to ask about the baby. "Mrs O'Brolchain?" I said. "What
about the baby? Where's the *baby*?" I was suddenly so worried
that there *wasn't* a baby. That the baby was gone too. And

everyone turned to Mrs O'Brolchain and she went bright red. "I forgot to tell you about the baby!" she said. "It's a girl. And they said she was doing fine." Well, I stood up then, my heart pumping away again, because it had to. I couldn't sit there for any longer, despite losing my Sarah. I said, "I am going to the hospital to see my daughter and to collect my granddaughter." And I put on my coat and six of us went in on the bus to town.' She took Cara's hand in hers and patted it. 'And when we got here, I kissed my Sarah goodbye, told her I'd see her again – I am certain of that – and then we all went to the nursery where there were all these cots. In one was this little baby, the smallest, who looked just like Sarah, same tiny nose and the same way of scrunching up her face. On her wrist was a little label, "Baby Sarah", and that just broke my heart because I'd had a baby Sarah, I'd taken her home all those years earlier. And here was another one except this one was Baby Cara. I had her in my arms and inside my coat all the way on the bus.' Her hand squeezed Cara's. 'This one's just like her mother, just as clever, just as kind...'

There was a knock on the door of the room. The three of us looked up to see Will standing there.

'Hello,' he said. 'And how is the patient doing?' He smiled at Shirley and then Cara... and then me. 'Now, Shirley, I have bought some crossword books for you. The only ones they had in the shop. Hope they aren't too easy for you. I know you like the impossible kind.'

'Thank you, Dr Butler,' said Shirley. 'And thank you again for last night.'

'It very much was a joint effort,' he said. 'Cara was amazing. Calling the ambulance, looking after you. Staying with you the whole time. And Olivia, of course.'

Shirley nodded. 'Olivia is a Sandycove girl,' she said. 'She's part of the village where people look out for each other. I thought it was only in the old days. Someone would keep an eye on your children. Clothes cleaned and everything. I thought things would change, that once new people started moving in, that it wouldn't be the same. But it is. People are just as kind as they always were... it's... what's the word I'm looking for, Cara?'

'Community.'

'That's the one, community. Except you two are Sandycove born and bred. It's nice when people come home again. You in New York, wasn't it, Doctor? Olivia, where were you?'

'London,' I said.

'And now you're back,' went on Shirley. 'Ready to put down roots?'

'Maybe...' I said.

'I'm looking forward to going home,' said Shirley. 'You know what film Cara has lined up for us? She can do that, you see, any film I say I have a fancy for, she can find it. I don't know how. Well, we have *Casablanca* next, don't we, Cara?' And she began singing. *'A kiss is just a kiss, a sigh is just a sigh...'* She nudged Cara. 'Come on, Cara, love. You know this one.' And Cara suddenly wasn't the slightly moody, highly intellectual teen she normally was, she was a loving granddaughter, who'd do anything for Shirley, even sing.

'The fundamental things apply... as time goes by.'

'Will, Olivia, join in,' ordered Shirley.

And so we had to, a little awkwardly and quietly.

'And when two lovers woo,' the four of us sang, gaining a little more confidence. From the bed, Shirley held Cara's hand on one side, mine on the other, as we swayed from side to side. Shirley's voice was slightly quavery, Will's deep and quite impressive, Cara's sweet and high and mine pretty rubbish. *'They still say I love you...'*

'Will, take Olivia's hand,' Shirley quickly shouted before the next line and Will had no choice but to take my hand.

'On that you can rely. No matter what the future brings...'

I caught Will's eye and he grinned.

'As time goes by...' Shirley went high on the last note, and Will went low, making us all laugh.

For a moment, I felt so happy, bathing in this simple moment with these lovely people. And I knew I would miss Will when I went back to London. I would miss everyone, from Jessica to Cara, to Shirley, to Catherine and Dermot and Jake, and all these lovely people. And I would miss Sandycove and, most of all, I would miss Mum. I wanted to be around for her and support her in all her new adventures, not hundreds of miles away, the two of us not involved in each other's lives. She was too important.

* * *

When Shirley's dinner arrived, Will and I took it as our cue to leave

'I'll stay here this evening,' said Cara. 'Get the TV to work. We could watch *Coronation Street* together.'

And then I realised Will was still holding my hand.

'Do you need a lift home?' he said, releasing me.

'That would be great, if it's not too much trouble.'

He shook his head. 'None at all.'

'By the way,' he said, as we walked through the hospital towards the main doors. 'Remember those boxes I told you about, the ones I found in the attic? I went up this morning and I found an envelope, tucked in beside the water tank. It had a name on the outside. Thomas O'Neill. Inside, there are letters. Lots of letters.'

They were probably nothing: bills, receipts. Just something

left up there by mistake. Except... they'd been hidden. By some-one. Who would have done that? Hidden, and then forgotten about them. We'd reached Will's car, where Pablo sat in the driver's seat waiting impatiently for Will.

'Would you like to come and see them?' he said. 'When suits you?'

'Tomorrow?' I said. 'I'll bring Mum... I have to do something with Bronagh first... we're collecting her mother from... from somewhere... but I should be back by 7 p.m., would that work?' It was probably nothing, I thought. Definitely not lost treasure or anything worthwhile. But still. We were O'Neills, so even if they were only bills, they still belonged to us.

'Yes,' he said, 'that sounds perfect.' And he smiled at me before opening my side and then getting in the driver's side, to the delight of Pablo.

And then the thought ran through my head that maybe it would be okay to allow myself to think nice things about Dr Will Butler, that I wouldn't be hurting anyone if I did join the swarms of his fans. When you find yourself singing and holding hands with someone, it turns out there's no going back.

* * *

Mum seemed cautiously pleased when I told her about the letters. She and Henry were sitting in the garden having a cup of tea, the evening still warm, when I got home.

'I don't know what they could be,' she said. 'Dad's brother threw everything out. He employed this crowd of house clearers to come in and take everything. I had Mam's locket and that was all I wanted. What do you think, Henry?'

'There's only one way to find out.' He shrugged. 'I think it sounds intriguing.'

'Could Gran have put it in the attic herself,' I said, 'without telling anyone?'

'It's a possibility,' Mum conceded. 'It would be nice... and it's very kind of Dr Butler to even try and make the connection. But I imagine they have little value to us. I wouldn't hold out too much hope.'

'You're right,' I said. 'But it's worth a try.' And, I thought, it was another excuse to see Will.

'By the way, Olivia,' Mum went on, 'you will come to Henry's birthday party on Friday, won't you?'

I nodded. 'Of course.' I was fiddling with my handbag strap. The leather had come loose and it was about to snap off.

'I'm going to buy some champagne,' said Henry. 'Treat it as a celebration for all of us. A welcome-home-Olivia party, a nearly-off-the-crutches-Nell party and a happy-birthday-Henry party.'

'Sounds fab,' I said, still fiddling.

'What's wrong with your bag?' asked Henry.

'It's the strap,' I said. 'It's about to snap off, the leather is all worn away.'

'May I have a look? Hmmm.' He looked at it. 'Nell, may I borrow your hammer? Failing that, a large stone.'

'My toolbox is under the sink,' said Mum, as Henry disappeared inside. And within a moment, we heard a giant thwack and another and he was back.

'There we go,' he said. 'Good as new.'

And it was. 'What did you do? It's amazing,' I said, marvelling at it.

'Just made another hole,' he said. 'It will be strong enough, but it's ten centimetres shorter...'

'I can't notice a difference, and anyway, I always found it a bit too long.' I smiled at him. 'Thank you, Henry.'

'My pleasure.'

'I'm going to miss you when you go back, Olivia,' said Mum.

'I'm going to miss you,' I said. 'I'm going to really miss everyone, actually. And Jessica…' I stopped. 'You see…'

'What?'

'Damien…' I began, and stopped again. I had promised I wouldn't say anything but I hadn't stopped thinking and worrying about her.

Mum gazed at me, her face serious. 'So you know then?'

'You know?'

She nodded. 'Of course. It doesn't take a genius to work out what's going on.'

'I saw this bruise and this red mark on her neck. And then she told us about it, but she won't leave, because she loves him and he's always sorry.'

'She's stuck. It's an impossible situation. Sometimes people don't ever make the jump. Sometimes you are doing all you can to survive.'

'What can we do?'

Mum shook her head. 'I don't know. I've lain awake worrying about her. I've kept the flat above the shop empty… it sounds silly now, but it's been in the back of my mind that one day she and the children might need somewhere to go. Every time I think I should rent it out, I just can't. Just in case.' Mum shrugged. 'It's such a hard place to be, because you can only act when you are asked to. As a friend, you've got to be ready for when she does.'

Henry was looking grave. 'Men like that don't deserve a lovely family.' He shook his head. 'He's a disgrace.'

25

Roberto: Finished Call My Agent last night.

Me: WHAT?

Roberto: Sorry. Just thought I would tell you so you could go ahead if you wanted to. Just box-set courtesy.

Me: But I didn't think you liked watching on your own?

Roberto: Who said I was alone?

Me: Ah… the plot thickens.

Roberto: Did you get the photograph of the pineapple upside-down cake. Are you impressed?

Me: I nearly fainted.

Roberto: My thoughts exactly. Love you for ever.

Me: Love you for ever.

Roberto: Can't wait to see you soon.

'Thanks for coming to the Botox clinic,' said Bronagh when she collected me after work.

'My pleasure,' I said. 'It's nice just to spend time with you.'

She looked at me. 'It's been really lovely to have you home.'

I would miss Bronagh and our margaritas in The Island, or meeting up for an evening walk and even organising the festival.

'How's your mum?' I asked.

'She's on the edge, but then she always is. Mark is still at home and is not only not lifting a finger to do anything, but he's taken over the living room. Dad's in the TV room, and so Mum has had to set up in the kitchen and is watching TV on her phone at the kitchen table every evening, sitting on those pine chairs. And Mark yells from the living room whenever he wants anything. Last night, I called in with this special moisturiser that she asked me to buy online – something with retinol and snake oil – and Mark shouted, "MUM! ANOTHER BEER!"' Bronagh's impression was uncanny. 'So she brought him his beer and he looked up from the match he was watching and instead of saying thank you, the loudest and longest burp came out of his mouth and straight into Mum's face.'

'Oh my God.'

'I know. It was almost impressive in its obnoxiousness. And Mark laughed and then tried to be serious and apologise, but Mum looked so appalled... my heart went out to her.'

'Did you say anything?'

'No, because we went back into the kitchen and she went on and on about how she was old and haggard. And then when I told her she wasn't, she said that I am patronising and that I'd always acted superior to her...' Bronagh stopped, her voice beginning to wobble.

'You should have agreed,' I said.

Bronagh nearly laughed. 'I know. I walked into it. It was as though she had been waiting all day to have an argument with someone and Mark's burp was the last straw.' We stopped at some traffic lights, and Bronagh looked at me. 'I've got to get better at this. I mean, in other areas, I'm not doing too badly.' Her voice was shaking. 'My career is going well. I live in a lovely house. I have a beautiful cat. But I am thirty-two years old and Mum can still cut me down to size. Okay, so we're never going to be close, not like you and *your* mum. We're never going to have that going for afternoon tea or a glass of Prosecco, or whatever it is everyone else does with their mums...'

'For the record,' I said, 'Mum and I have never had afternoon tea or shared a glass of Prosecco. A mini bottle of mediocre wine, yes. But Prosecco, no.'

Bronagh sighed. 'And the irony is, I'm the only one who knows about the Botox.'

'And me,' I said, 'although obviously my lips are sealed.'

'And therefore I am the only one who can collect her because she can't drive because the needles she paid to have stuck in her face could affect her eyesight. But I googled it and apparently, after Botox, you can drive, operate heavy machinery and be a perfect bitch to your only daughter.'

I laughed.

'She just likes playing the poorly invalid, the highly sensitive woman who needs taking care of.'

Bronagh flicked the indicator angrily, as we turned a corner into the long, leafy avenue, where houses had their own grounds and cars so huge, they came with their own steps.

'Let's change the subject, shall we?' she said. 'What do you think of Fergal?'

'Fergal? Why?'

'Because he asked me out. As in a date. Restaurant. Some-where nice.'

'Really? Well, I think he seems lovely. Handsome.'

'He called in earlier with a custard slice from Janet's.'

'How did he know you liked them?'

'I made a vague reference to one, using Janet's famous custard slice as a metaphor for the perfect house. Not that I thought anything about it, until he returned with one in a paper bag.' She smiled at me. 'I was quite touched.'

'How incredibly sweet,' I said.

'Him or the cake?'

'Both.'

'Do you like him?'

'I am not sure,' she said. 'I mean, after being dumped by Postman Paul, I was rather enjoying my single status, my *beautiful aloneness* and feeling rather empowered. And then someone gives me a custard slice.'

'Who says romance is dead?'

Bronagh laughed. 'I mean, I like my Saturday yoga class and going for a gluten-free, chocolate-free chocolate bar in Albatross afterwards. So, I am not sure if I want to go out with someone, even if he does appreciate a fine building.'

'Could you go out with someone who didn't own a pair of jeans?'

'Hmm.' She thought about it. 'I don't know if I could. I mean, I would like to think I could, but in reality, no, I couldn't.' She looked at me. 'And you went out with this man.' She shook her head. 'Thankfully you saw sense and ended it.'

'I'm an idiot.'

'No!' Bronagh practically shouted. 'NO! He's the idiot. Don't you see? He was never good enough for you, and not just because he's a denim-eschewing, clay-pigeon-shooting fool, but because you are you!' Bronagh was on a roll. 'You have to change your mindset. Feeling lucky is a state of mind. Everyone has not-so-wonderful things happen to them. I struggle every day with the fact my mother and father aren't that bothered about me. But it doesn't stop me from getting on with my life for me. You can't let anything stop you. You can't let *anything* drag you down. And certainly not losers who sleep with ex-girlfriends and don't wear *jeans*, for God's sake!'

'But your mother drags you down…'

'But she's my mother!' she said. 'I can't *choose* her! She will be dragging me for the rest of my life. But you get to choose people like Jeremy!'

'You're right.' I looked out of the window, feeling pathetic. I hadn't been outraged enough with Jeremy. 'Roberto says I've got to wear my crown,' I said.

'Exactly!' Bronagh agreed. 'Get out your phone and text that pillock that from now on you will be wearing your crown and he is not fit to even touch the hem of your queenly robe.'

I laughed.

'Is his number still in your phone?'

'Yes…'

'Delete it after you send the text.'

'But…'

'Now. No, wait. Block it then delete it.'

'You sound well-practised.'

'It's what any self-respecting woman should do,' she said. 'Move on. And never look back. Do it.'

I took out my phone and wrote a message.

'Yo Jezza,' I read it out loud. 'You are not fit to touch the hem of my robe. Signed Queen Liv.'

Bronagh laughed. 'No, seriously. Say what you feel.'

I tried again. 'Hi Jeremy, I think I was too understanding about you sleeping with Cassandra. What I do understand now is that only immature and not very nice people do things like that. Just thought I'd share my feelings. And goodbye forever! Please don't contact me again.' I looked at Bronagh. 'Too much?'

'Perfect!'

I scrolled and found Jeremy's number, sent the text and then blocked and deleted his number. And that was it. He no longer existed in my life.

'Expunge and delete!' said Bronagh.

'I needed that,' I said. 'I needed an intervention.'

'Good. Isn't that what friends are for?' She indicated and turned sharply into one of those sandstone mansions. 'Here we are!' said Bronagh. 'REVisage, where any signs of a life well-lived are erased with the prick of a needle. Now, come on, queen! Let's go and release the dragon!'

* * *

Inside, REVisage was a vision of white floors, ceilings, white flowers and white people in white clothes with terrifying white teeth. 'It's like a nightmare,' I whispered.

Bronagh nodded and we took a seat in the waiting area. 'A horror film. I've never been so unsettled in all my life.'

After a few minutes, Audrey emerged in sunglasses, doggy-paddling in the air, as though afraid of falling over, a nurse walking slowly beside her.

Bronagh looked up. 'Mum?' She got to her feet. 'Are you all right? Are you blind?'

'Bronagh?' Audrey turned her head around, as though trying to hear where the voice was coming from. 'Is that you?' Her voice was weak.

'Yes, Mum,' said Bronagh. 'It's me.'

Audrey clawed at the air uselessly until she found Bronagh's body and then clung on. 'Thank you,' she said imperiously to the nurse. 'My daughter will take it from here.'

The nurse dashed off.

Bronagh rolled her eyes. 'Come on, Mum,' she said. 'Let's get you out of here. Olivia is here also,' she said. 'She... she needed a lift somewhere. And she's sworn to secrecy.'

'Hello, Mrs Kelly,' I said, as Audrey just nodded vaguely in my direction before stepping gingerly forward, clinging to Bronagh for dear life. She shuffled out of the doors and down the steps to the car and waited as Bronagh opened the door and helped her inside.

'Mum, seriously,' said Bronagh, as we started our journey home, me sitting behind them. 'Open your eyes. You have not had your eyeballs removed. You have only had Botox!'

'SHHHHHH!' Bronagh's mother whipped off her sunglasses and glared at Bronagh. 'SHHHH! How dare you say that! No one must know! Both of you must promise me!'

'I promise not to tell anyone,' I said, more than a little scared. 'Not a soul.'

'You cannot,' said Bronagh's mother. 'This is a secret we all must take to our graves.'

I nodded. 'Of course.'

'But, Mum,' said Bronagh, 'it's only Botox. Lots of people have it every day, sometimes people pop out at lunchtime and instead of buying a prawn sandwich they get injected with botulism...'

'Don't get smart with me, Bronagh Kelly,' said her mother. 'Don't give me all that kind of cheek. It's a very painful process... well, it is for me who has a phobia of needles. I was shaking in there, you have no idea. I had to be talked down from walking out. But if I don't do this, then I wake up one morning and my whole face has collapsed and I look like...'

'You look like your age,' said Bronagh, 'that's what you look like.'

Bronagh's mother stared at her. 'What has got into you today? What's given you this kind of cheek? Are you performing for Olivia here, trying to make her laugh...?'

'No, Mum,' said Bronagh, sucking in air, her eyes resolutely staring ahead. 'I suppose... I suppose I am just trying to draw attention to the fact that you are making a huge fuss over a procedure which is entirely unnecessary. You chose to do it, it is a non-invasive, very simple process that just does not warrant this level of hysteria.'

'Hysteria?' Audrey's mouth dropped open. And then, 'I am so glad I only had one daughter,' she said. 'One is more than enough. My *boys* would never speak to me like that.'

'That's because your boys don't give enough of a shit to bother speaking to you at all!' said Bronagh.

Audrey looked as though she was about to cry.

'Look,' said Bronagh, softening. 'I am sorry if I was rude and I know I should have not said a word and been a good girl and all that, but I'm probably pre-menstrual...'

Bronagh's mother gasped. 'Keep your voice down!'

'It's only the three of us in the car!' said Bronagh. 'But, Mum, I'm tired of being the one person you can treat badly and yet you treat the boys as though they are little princes. Mark burped in your face last night! And I am tired of you not thinking I am worth being nice to. But I am worth being nice to, and worthy of respect and kind words and... love. And until you realise this, I won't be at your beck and call any longer!'

But Audrey had her hands over her ears and every time Bronagh said something, she looked out of the window, as though she hadn't spoken. I was feeling more than a little awkward sitting in the back of the car, a silent witness to this mother-daughter aggro, but nevertheless very proud of Bronagh, as well as glad my own mother wasn't anything like Audrey.

We arrived at the mock-Georgian monstrosity. 'Okay, Mum,' said Bronagh. 'Here we are. Say hi to Mark and Dad for me.'

'Thank you, Bronagh,' said Audrey stiffly, who seemed

suddenly cured and was able to get out of the car unaided. 'I am sorry that you think I treat you badly,' she said, through the window. 'And you're right about Mark and that... wind. It wasn't pleasant. And nor is living with him. I am going to ask him to move in with his brother. I have had enough of running after him. And besides, I need the living room back.'

'Well, that's a start,' said Bronagh.

'And I do appreciate you,' went on Audrey. 'Very much. But I'm not very good at showing it.'

'Well, get better at it!' shouted Bronagh.

'I will try,' said Audrey in a quiet voice. 'And thank you for collecting me. And I would very much like to come to the award ceremony.'

'So you *were* listening!'

'If you would like me to accompany you, then I would like that too.'

'I'm going as well,' I piped up.

'Well, we can all go, can't we?' said Audrey.

'Yes, Mum, we can.'

'Good evening, girls,' said Audrey, and walked into the house, as I scrambled into the front seat.

Bronagh turned to me. 'I'm so sorry you had to observe family dysfunction at its best.'

'Are you okay?'

Bronagh held up her hand for me to see. 'I'm shaking,' she said. 'I've never spoken to her like that before.'

'I'm glad you did.'

'I've wanted to say it for years.' We started driving. 'I've tried to be a good person all my life and the one person I wanted to love me, to like me, to think I was wonderful, was the one person who refused. And I used to try and tell myself that deep down she loves me, or deep down she cares, she just can't show it.'

'She does love you, though,' I said. 'And I do. I think you are wonderful.'

'Thank you.'

'You were amazing, so empowered! You wore your crown.'

'Yes, I did.' She grinned at me. 'I had to, didn't I, after all my lecturing! But the thing is, Liv, I don't think I would have done it if you hadn't been here.' She smiled at me. 'Mum and I are going to have a find a way to be better at being mother and daughter. She needs to get out more and do her own thing, away from Dad and the boys,' said Bronagh. 'Who knows, maybe she will. But I can't force her. All we can control is us and we've both got to wear our crowns, okay? Crowns are for every day, not just parties and coronations.'

And so are friends, I thought. God, I would miss her when I went back to London.

26

At Will's house, we stared at the large brown envelope on the kitchen table. Mum gave me a hopeful, worried smile and grabbed my hand. It was nothing, I was telling myself: the kind of thing that people hold on to needlessly such as tickets for a show or a restaurant menu or a clipping from a newspaper that meant something to someone once, long ago.

'It's my father's name,' said Mum, hopefully. 'Thomas O'Neill.'

'But what would it be?' I said, thinking that if this man – my grandfather – had sent her away, pregnant, refusing to acknowledge her, or me, ever again, then we didn't want anything from him.

'Wait,' said Will. 'There's a stamp on the back.' He peered at it. An old, inky stamp, skew-whiff, as though someone was trying it out before stamping something else properly. 'Sandycove PO,' he read. 'Church Street, Sandycove.'

'PO?' I said. 'Post Office?'

Mum nodded. 'Has to be...' But she was frowning now, as though something wasn't quite right. She picked up the envelope and drew out a package of letters, held together with elastic bands, the rubber dry and cracked and ready to snap. She turned them over and read the address on the top one, the colour drained from her face. 'Joseph Delaney...' She looked at me and cleared her throat. 'Joseph Delaney. 225 Salem Street, Beacon Hill. It's my writing. It's my letter to him.' She moved to the next letter, and the next, and the next. '*All* my letters to Joe.'

It was like someone had pressed pause on the world and, for a moment, the two of us didn't move, both looking at each other. Beside us, Will was totally still, watching us, and even little Pablo, who had been asleep on the faded green velvet armchair, lifted his head to watch us.

'But how...' I began. Had he sent them back? Is that what happened, they were sent back to Mum and her father had got his hands on them and hid them, so she wouldn't be upset?

Mum put her hand into the large brown envelope again and drew out another pile of envelopes, also wrapped in elastic bands. 'Nell O'Neill, 25 Sandycove Avenue,' she said, moving to the next one. 'Nell O'Neill...'

'Are these all your letters to Joseph... and his to you?'

'Who is...?' asked Will, gently, obviously desperate to know.

'Joseph Delaney is my father,' I said. 'He went to Boston and didn't know Mum was pregnant. He never answered her letters...'

He nodded, taking it in.

'I don't remember how many I wrote,' said Mum. 'But this looks like it could be all of them... what are there? Twenty? I never received a single one from him.' She picked up one. The top had been neatly slit open. 'It's been read,' she said. 'Someone read my letter.'

'He did, Mum,' I said. 'He sent them back.'

She shook her head. 'No, they weren't sent. Look, they weren't stamped. They didn't leave the post office.' She gently pulled out the paper inside another envelope. 'My darling Nell... I haven't

heard anything from you so I will just tell you my news anyway...'
she read. 'It's him.' She looked like she had seen a ghost. Or was
hearing a ghost. 'It's your father.' Tears were in her eyes, her voice
was shaking.

'Oh my God.' That was Will, not me. I was too shocked to
speak. 'You mean, someone took your letters? And was able to
intercept...' He shook his head. 'But who?'

'My Aunt Theresa,' said Mum. 'Dad's older sister. Of course it
was. She was the postmistress. The most upstanding woman you
could ever meet. Only ever wore navy and would frequently
quote from the Bible. I was terrified of her. She did it for Dad and
he put all this in the attic, away from Mam. Oh sweet mother of
divine Jesus, I can't believe it.'

'Can you be sure?' I said, finally finding my voice.

'Yes,' she said, her voice flat. 'Yes, I can. And I went to her
funeral, like a good niece! Yet she was the one who decided to
change the course of my life. The year she died, I think I had
some kind of breakdown. Well, not breakdown, that's too strong,
more like... I'd had enough. I knew something was wrong, some
wrong had been done, but of course I had no idea what it was and
it was driving me mad, the not knowing, my sixth sense scream-
ing. At Theresa's funeral, people were talking about me and I
didn't know why. Dad's brother was there as well, and he gave me
such a look which I couldn't read at the time, but now I know it
was triumph. I came home and closed the shop for a week. We
went to Ballybunion... do you remember?'

'The beach in Kerry. We had two ice creams every day.'

Mum laughed. 'And you built the world's biggest sandcastle.
Or one that we thought could easily be the world's biggest sandcastle.' She sat heavily in the chair. 'I think I'm in shock.'

'I'll get you something,' said Will, he and Pablo disappearing
into the kitchen.

'What are you going to do?' I asked.

'Read them, I suppose. His letters to me. It changes every-thing. All these years, I was heartbroken over him. And I should have been heartbroken over my own father and what he and his sister did to me. How could they?' She met my gaze, her clear blue eyes hurt and confused. 'I know it was a different time. I know fathers thought they could control their daughters and so many succeeded, but to do this?' She shook her head again.

'And it's illegal,' I said. 'Tampering with the mail.'

'And I had gone to see Theresa,' said Mum. 'Remember? Begged her to tell me if any letters had got lost and she rose to her feet – and she wasn't tall, but she had a rather powerful energy. Everyone in the village was scared of her. But she rose to her feet and glared at me, breathing fire. "How dare you insinuate such a thing, Nell O'Neill!"'

'What a total witch.'

Mum nodded. 'That's a good way of putting it.'

Will came back into the room with two glasses of brandy. 'Here we go, Nell,' he said. 'A nice glass of Hennessy if you want one.'

'Thank you, Will,' she said, taking it and throwing it back like someone doing shots at Mahiki. She closed her eyes for a moment. 'Thank you. Exactly what I needed,' she rasped. She took the second glass and sipped it. 'I don't know where to start or what to think.'

'Take your time,' I said. 'You don't have to sort it all out now.'

She nodded. 'You can read the letters too,' she offered.

'Maybe.' I wasn't sure if I wanted to. They were Mum's letters to the man she loved. Her privacy had already been so egre-giously invaded so shouldn't they just be hers, and no one else's? I looked at Will. 'I can't believe we've brought this family drama to your door.'

'I think the family drama was already here,' he said. 'In the attic. I'm just glad the letters have been returned to their owner.' He smiled at me and I smiled back. He was a tremendously reassuring presence.

'We should go,' said Mum. 'We've taken up more than enough of your time.' At the door, she hugged Will. 'Thank you,' she said. 'You don't know what you've given me.'

'I'm so glad,' he said, making sure she had her crutch and she was steady on her feet before letting go again. 'If you need to come back, let me know. Or for a chat. Or anything.'

Pablo was standing at Will's feet and suddenly came up to me and licked my ankle. 'Pablo?' I said, as he looked up at me. 'I think you might have the wrong person.' But in answer, he just licked me again, as though to prove that he did have the right person. My heart melted.

'Thank you again,' Mum said. The envelope under one arm, she began to crutch down the path. 'You'd better drive, Olivia,' she said to me.

In the car, as I pulled out of the parking space, giving Will and Pablo a final wave goodbye, she said, 'I like that young man more and more.' And then she gave me a look. 'I'm becoming very fond of him. Very fond indeed.' But she was crying, as though the shock was passing and now only the hurt remained.

Now I knew about my father and that he hadn't abandoned me, I also knew that one day I would try and find out what happened to him. God knows how, though. But he wasn't actually my priority at the moment. Mum was. Now I realised what she'd been through and how badly she'd been treated.

'Would you like to see him again?' Mum and I were eating

tinned tomato soup and cheese on toast, the kind of meal Mum
used to make when she was too tired to cook. It was the ultimate
comfort food, but she was barely eating. 'If he was alive?'

'I don't think so,' she said, slowly, pushing her spoon around
in the bowl. 'I've had a whole life since then. I was so young. It's
so hard thinking of me, that young girl, and how these grown-ups
thought they knew better! And now I'm old... older... and it all
seems just so wrong.'

'How could they have done it?'

Mum shrugged. 'Easily. People thought nothing of interfering
in the lives of others in those days. The whole place was policed
by villagers commenting on anyone who seemingly put a foot
wrong.'

'But why did you stay in Sandycove?' I said. 'Why didn't you
leave... go elsewhere?'

'Ultimately, I didn't want to live anywhere else. I suppose I
was stubborn. And I couldn't imagine not being by the sea. After
Dad died, a year after Mam, and when I moved out of Betty's
parents' house, I found a flat in the village. I had to walk down
the street, knowing everyone knew everything. But I kept walking,
you in the pushchair, head held high, and once you do it the first
time, you can do it again. And again. And again. And then I was
used to it. One day, the landlord – a lovely man – told me that the
shop below the flat was for lease and would I consider taking it
on. Oh my God.' Mum's face lit up for the first time. 'A clothes
shop! I knew exactly what I wanted to do. And we'd shaken on it
before I'd thought it through properly, but by that point, I felt
kind of bulletproof.' She smiled at me. 'I'm so glad I stayed and
faced them down.'

'I'm glad too. I love the village as well.' I paused. 'When are
you going to read the letters?'

'I'll take my time... one by one, see how I feel. I won't rush it.

My God, it's like it happened in another world or to someone else.' She shook her head. 'It was such a cruel thing to do.' Mum looked up at me, putting down her soup spoon. 'I can't tell you how much I have loved having you home and...' She paused. 'Look, correct me if I am wrong, but maybe it's time to come home, for good? If I am being interfering, just say it.'

I didn't say anything.

'It's just...' Mum continued, '...you don't look very happy to be returning to London. And life is long and complicated, but it's never set. Plans change, you can take charge at any moment, you can change at any moment, nothing is ever written in stone, *nothing*... it's just...' She hesitated. 'You either continue living your life for other people or start living your life for you. I think you might have forgotten that you deserve more. I mean, Jeremy wasn't *quite* good enough, if you don't mind me saying, your *job* doesn't seem quite good enough. Is it what you really want...?'

I didn't say anything for a moment, Mum looked worried that she'd said too much.

'It's just that I think you are marvellous,' she said. 'I want you to realise it too.'

'Yes, but it's not that easy,' I replied. 'I'm scared.'

'Of what?'

'The *unknown*.'

'But every single person who has ever lived is scared of the unknown,' said Mum. 'You've got to get comfortable with the feeling of fear. What do you think makes for a more interesting and a more satisfying life? It's the things that go wrong, it's the taking a chance, it's the unknown.'

'But I had my chance,' I said. 'And I blew it. I failed and shut it all down. Looking back now, I should have persevered, but I was too young to really manage it all. Too inexperienced.'

'I could have helped,' Mum said. 'I could have given you

advice. We could have done it together.'

'Yes, but...' I looked away. 'I wanted to do it on my own. And...'

'And what?'

'And I always felt a little annoyed that you hadn't told me about... Joseph Delaney.' I could feel the locket against my throat, the reassuring presence of my grandmother. 'It was stupid of me.'

'Not stupid,' said Mum. 'Understandable.'

'Now I know, though.'

'Now you know.' She reached for my hand and squeezed it. 'Sorry again.'

'Me too.'

'But mistakes can be rectified. You can learn from them. It's like cutting all your hair off...'

'I was sixteen!'

'And you cried for four days. But it grew back... and what did you learn?'

'Never trust people who say short hair would suit my face? It doesn't.'

'Exactly. Lesson learned and you moved on...'

'And grew my hair. Is this analogy really working?'

Mum laughed. 'My point is, mistakes happen, but they shouldn't make us scared. They should be empowering.'

'I know what you mean. I'll bear it in mind.'

When I was clearing away our plates, Mum picked up her phone. 'I have to call Henry,' she said. 'He'll be dying to know what happened. He won't believe it.'

'You don't wish that things had been different?' I said. 'That Joseph had got your letters and you had got his...?'

Mum shook her head. 'No, not really. Because my life is this one, everything that happened. I kind of like the way my life turned out in the end. You, the shop, my friends, living in Sandy-cove... Henry. I wouldn't change a thing.'

27

Roberto: Am attempting a tagline today.

Me: TAGLINE?

Roberto: Stupid eejit autocorrect! I mean TAGINE! Lamb and apricot. Doing meringue for dessert. Strawberries and cream topping.

Me: OMG. Sounds incredible. Is this still Mary Berry's influence?

Roberto: Absolutely. She's my new muse. Maybe I could be Miss Berry? Do you think that might be good?

Me: Stick to Miss Minogue. Let me know how the hotpot and dumplings go.

Roberto: Love you Liv.

Me: Love you Miss Berry.

The next morning, I didn't go on my run, because instead, Mum and I went to visit Gran's grave. She heard me moving around in my room and knocked on my door. 'I think we should go,' she said. 'Tell her we love her and that we know none of this is her fault.'

I drove Mum's car to the cemetery. It was only 8 a.m. and yet there were other people, just like us, walking along the central path, beside the yew trees, to find the resting place of the person they loved.

Gran's grave was towards the back of the plot. A rectangle of earth, a headstone. 'In loving memory,' I read. 'Eleanor O'Neill, much loved.'

Below her was:

Thomas O'Neill, beloved husband and father

Mum was on her knees with the trowel, digging up the primulas which were dead and quickly planting some lobelia. 'I try to ring the changes, florally,' said Mum. 'In the spring, it's always daffodils. Summer... whatever looks nice.'

'Do you feel anything?' I asked. 'Her ghost?'

'If I felt anything, I felt it in the house,' she said. 'But not here. I just come here to make it look nice.' She stood beside me. 'Oh, Mam,' she said. 'Mam, I love you. I miss you. I wish you were with us now. We'd have a laugh, the three of us.'

'You could give her a mini bottle of wine.'

'I could,' she said. 'And we could listen to Frankie Valli and sing along. She was a lovely woman, was Mam. Too good for this world. When I think of Auntie Theresa living until she was ninety-two, it makes me furious.'

'Where is Auntie Theresa buried?'

'Oh, over there somewhere. She's got her own angel statue. All paid for by the General Post Office.' She nudged me. 'Go on, say something.'

I didn't know what to say. 'Like what?'

'Like hello or something. You can't come to a grave without saying something. That's the whole point.'

'Hello, Gran,' I said. 'I wish you were still around. I wish you were around for me, but more than anything I wish you were around for Mum. She really, really loves you. I think you made a great team, the two of you. We miss you.'

Mum nodded. 'We would have made a great team,' she said, 'the three of us. We would all have got on well. Same sense of humour.'

I held my locket. 'I'll come back and see you again,' I said. 'And I'll bring some flowers. I am thinking of roses and dahlias and peonies.'

'She'd love that,' said Mum. 'Mam always did have notions.' She linked her arm in mine. 'Shall we go back? I'll drop you at the shop. And you must be busy with the festival? Only two days to go?'

'I'm feeling nervous now,' I said. 'Just praying for no rain.'

*　*　*

All week, Jessica had acted as though nothing had happened. I had hoped she might see me as someone to confide in, and then, perhaps, she might take action. Now I knew a little, I didn't want to be shut out. Was Damien managing to control himself? Was Jessica safe? Had anything else happened? But I didn't like to bring it up, I just hoped that she might talk to me if she needed to. But by Thursday, I cracked.

'So, everything all right at home?' I asked.

'Fine!' Jessica replied, her eyes slightly glazed, her smile wide, as though there was nothing that could possibly be wrong.

'How are the kids?' I kept going.

'They are great,' she said. 'Both practising for the festival. It's only two sleeps. Frankie has asked Mam to make him his fairy costume for his ballet performance. Miss Rachel said he could be a wood nymph and he wasn't having any of it. "But I'm a fairy!" he said.' Jessica laughed. 'He was so cross at the thought of being a wood nymph. He said, "What's a nymph? It doesn't sound like a real word!" I've told him it's more like a forest ninja and he seemed happy with that. And good news, Shirley's out of hospital. I met Cara yesterday and she says she's finished her exams and is ready to work in the shop whenever your mum needs her.'

'That's great,' I said, but tried again. 'And how's Damien?' I asked. 'Is he... is he well?'

'Never better,' she said, still smiling. 'He's cranked up the whole health regime another notch. Not only are his gym sessions longer, but he's also taken up boxing and is even eating egg-white omelettes for breakfast. There's me and the kids with our Rice Crispies, and he's whipping up egg whites.'

I wasn't quite sure what to say in response. 'Jess...' I began.

She sighed, as though giving in. 'He's trying to be better,' she said, quietly. 'Says he's going to try anger management.' Her shrug was so helpless, as though she didn't know what to believe any more. 'But thanks for asking,' she said. 'I appreciate it. I really do.' She held my gaze for a moment too long and I thought she was going to say something else. But she didn't.

* * *

After lunch, my phone rang. It was a London number.

'Is that Olivia O'Neill? Valerie here, HR Manager. I'm calling about a few things at the office.'

My heart sank. Oh God, I thought. They needed me back sooner than I had planned. And I *really* wasn't ready. The thought of being back in London, working in that job, commuting on the Tube, dreading bumping into Jeremy in one of the million Starbucks. I knew I wanted to stay here for as long as I could.

'I presume you've heard,' she went on. 'Did the ex-husband call you?'

What was she talking about?

'Valerie,' I said. 'Do you have the right number? This is Olivia O'Neill. I'm in *Ireland*.'

'Yes, Olivia,' she said. 'I'm calling about Maribelle.' She paused. 'So, you haven't heard?'

'Heard what?'

'She's left the company. Resigned. And she's left the UK. We only found out last night. She called from Athens and left a message on Mr Cox's private phone. A rather rambling message to all accounts. And expletive-laden. Apparently, and I hope I am not breaking confidentiality agreements, she wants to live in Cornwall and grow vegetables. Don't we all? Anyway, Maribelle told Mr Cox that he could... I can't use the language exactly, but she told him he could "eff" his company and she was "effing off" to St Austell.'

'Wow.' *Good for her*, I thought, feeling strangely proud. She had escaped, maybe the good life in Cornwall was exactly what she needed.

'It's one way to resign, I suppose,' said Valerie. 'And we do receive quite the variety. I once had a man who put all his furniture in a pile, the sofa on the table, the filing cabinet, the chair, a bad reproduction of Monet's *Water Lilies* and even the wastepaper basket all on top of each other and walked out. Another man wrote his resignation letter in crayon. And someone else employed a mime artist to mime how he felt about the company. Corporate life does tend to take a mental toll and people do like to make an exit that reflects their emotional state. It's almost like performance art.'

'Was Maribelle okay?' I asked. 'Did rehab work?'

'We didn't ascertain that,' said Valerie. 'All we do know is that she says that she has discovered a certain kind of peace and contentment. I am paraphrasing, of course. Her language was a little more colourful. But suffice to say we are satisfied that she will be happier in Cornwall.'

'What about Sasha?'

'Who?'

'Her son, Sasha.'

'As far as I know, he's with his father at the moment, but apparently he's quite keen on growing vegetables as well. He won BBC Young Gardener last year. Did you know?'

Know? I filled in the application form and videoed him in the garden.

'If you talk to Maribelle again,' I said, 'will you send her my best wishes?'

'Will do. Anyway,' went on Valerie, 'we've been clearing out the office. She's left something for you.'

'Me?' What on earth could Maribelle have left me?

'A pair of shoes,' she said. 'Navy Manolo Blahniks. You are lucky. Are you the same size?'

I actually laughed. Those were the shoes that she would take off and aim at my head. And now she had given them to me, maybe as a reminder of the eight years I spent learning how to duck. 'Would you do me a favour?' I asked. 'Would you drop them off at a charity shop for me?'

'Of course. Any particular charity shop? I like Cancer Research myself.'

'Women's Aid?' I said. 'Is there one near you? I would really appreciate it.'

'Yes, I pass one every day on Upper Street. Consider it done. Anyway, back to your employment. We are pleased to offer you a new position in the company,' went on Valerie. 'We have a wonderful new equity strategist starting in two weeks, and we look forward to you starting with him.'

Oh God, no way. I just couldn't. This was my moment, this

was my chance to make a choice between living a life for me or living a life for other people.

'Your salary will be in line with your previous salary...' went on Valerie. 'Terms and conditions, holidays, et cetera, benefits in continuation. Or...'

Or? There was an *or*? 'Or what?' I could barely breathe. There was no way I was going back. Over the last few weeks, I had rediscovered that there was life outside of that toxic bubble.

'Or we could offer you redundancy. Now, I know this isn't what you might want. Not in this economic climate. And having to go back out there and do the whole job search again. I know I couldn't...'

I could have danced. I did dance. Yes, please!

'I'll take it,' I said, quickly. 'I am formally announcing my resignation and acceptance of the redundancy.'

'But you don't want to hear the terms? It's not the most generous of redundancy packages... I mean, the statutory pay is something we could negotiate.'

'I don't care,' I said. 'I'll take it.'

'Okay, Olivia,' she said, 'I suppose we could add another £10,000.'

'I don't care,' I said. 'You have just given me my freedom. I feel like I just might have a life to live.'

'You are a very tough negotiator,' she went on. 'We might be able to stretch to another £15,000. Would that satisfy you?'

'I don't mind,' I said, elated. 'I used to have a life, Valerie. I used to be excited and passionate about what I did all day. Working with Maribelle nearly crushed me. But now I am free!'

'You really do drive a hard bargain,' said Valerie. 'If pushed, we could add another £10,000 to the package. Will you accept?'

'Yes, please!'

'Well, we'll start the paperwork straight away and get back to you. And I'll drop the shoes to Women's Aid this evening.'

'Thank you, Valerie,' I said. 'Thanks for everything.'

'Olivia,' she said, 'you drive a very hard bargain.' I wondered, was she saying this for the benefit of someone else? 'And best of British to you. Or should I say *Irish*.' She gave a little laugh. 'Top o' the mornin' to ya!'

'And to you, Valerie! Goodbye!' I put the phone down, thinking I could forgive her terrible stage-Irish because I was now in delighted receipt of a very nice redundancy package. This changed everything... this meant I would be able... But from outside, down the street, there was a scream. Jessica and I looked at each other.

'It sounds like Betty,' said Jessica, as we both ran to the door.

The woman was now screeching at the top of her lungs and we both tried to make out what she was saying.

'Did she say a fire?' I said.

The two of us stared at each other in horror.

'Nouveau You's on fire!' Jessica yelled, and we immediately began running down the road, to the soundtrack of Betty's increasingly blood-curdling screams.

'FIRE! JENNIFER-LOUISE IS IN THERE! MY SHOP! FIIIIIIRE!'

The world seemed to tremble as Betty's ululations shook the very foundations of the village. People appeared out of doorways, heads were poked out of windows, villagers began a stampede as, en masse, we moved up the main street shouting random unhelpful things. We panicked as one.

Smoke was billowing out of the flat above Nouveau You. Jennifer-Louise and Graham lived there and Betty was standing on the street below shouting up, 'Jennifer-Louise! Jennifer-

Louise! My baby! YOUR BABY! Oh my God! Oh My GOOOOOOOOOOODDDDD!'

And then we saw flames licking at the window, the black smoke appeared darker and more malevolent as it plumed heavenward, the whole sky like a shadow above us.

Alison from Albatross was on her mobile. 'Fire engine is on its way!' she shouted, as we all looked desperately to the window upstairs.

Mrs O'Keefe tried to put her arms around Betty. 'We'll get her out,' she said, 'you don't worry yourself about it now. It's not like it's *The Towering Inferno*. Now, that was some fire. We'll get it before it gets to the rafters... that's when it really burns.'

Betty shook her off, eyes pinned to the windows up above. 'Jennifer-Louise!' she shouted. 'JENNIFER-LOUISE!'

I rattled the door of the flat uselessly.

'I've phoned a fella who has a skeleton key,' said Bernard Murphy, his face flame-red with excitement. 'He could get into the Central Bank. Not,' he added, 'that he's tried. Not recently anyway. Those days are past him now. He says.'

'Couldn't we break it down?' I suggested, desperately wishing that there was something we could do.

'We could,' said Bernard Murphy, 'but my hips are not what they were.'

Everyone began to gather – Catherine and Jake, Mum and Henry, the whole team from Janet's cake shop, Matt from The Island. Anthony from the newsagents. Bronagh and her team. Soon, the whole village was staring up at the window, shouting for Jennifer-Louise.

Finally, in the far distance was the sound of a siren.

'Here they are now,' someone said.

'Thanks be to God,' said another.

And then a silence, where there was no crackle, no shouting, no panicking, not even any breathing, and then BOOM! The front windows of the flat exploded, glass fell like hailstones and we screamed as one.

Poor Jennifer-Louise! We all began shouting her name as the sirens got louder and for a moment none of us knew what to do. Did we just wait for them to arrive or should we try and get her?

I kept my eyes on the window, hoping she would appear. We could catch her, I was thinking. We could stand with our arms out and catch her...

But someone was pushing his way through the crowd and headed straight for the door of the flat, his foot raised, and with one heavy, hard thump, he booted in the door and disappeared inside. On the ground was a tiny Yorkshire terrier, his face one of terror as his owner disappeared inside, suddenly consumed by the thick black smoke. It was Will.

'Go on, Dr Butler!' someone shouted.

'Jaysis!' shouted someone else. 'Be careful in there!'

Catherine clutched my arm. 'Oh my God,' she breathed. 'Please let them be all right.'

Jake stood beside her, watching, eyes wide.

Bernard announced, 'Right, if he's going in, so am I!'

And just as he took a deep breath, ready to plunge inside, Mrs O'Keefe screamed. 'Bernard! Don't! You'll get yourself killed!'

But emerging from the smoke was Will again, this time carrying Jennifer-Louise in his arms.

'I'm all right!' she shouted. 'I'm all right!'

Betty fell onto the two of them, sobbing. 'Thank God,' she said. 'My babies, my babies.'

Pablo began yapping at Will, looking to be picked up. 'Come here,' said Will, scooping him up. 'You didn't need to worry.'

Two fire engines and an ambulance pulled up and, in

moments, hoses were rolled out and attached to faucets and water was being directed at the top window.

Jennifer-Louise was sitting in a wheelchair stretcher being examined and Will was also being checked out by one of the paramedics but was soon submerged by the crowd.

'It wasn't too bad,' I heard him say. 'She was on her way down, and just fell at the end. I think the fire is in the front of the flat, and she was in the back... No, no, I'm fine... I didn't think, really, just had to go in... No, I'm grand, thank you... Cup of tea would be nice...' He caught me looking over and he smiled, but then he was suddenly swept up by the crowd again, backslapping, arm-rubbing, excited chatter. There was the sound of steam hissing from the flat as the water extinguished the flames. There was a shout behind us, as Graham, Jennifer-Louise's husband, raced towards her, his briefcase abandoned mid-road, his face a vision of blind panic. The rest of us stood back to give the crew and Jennifer-Louise space and we crowded around Will, eager to hear his side of the story.

'I once forced my way into a house,' Bernard was saying. 'The lock was broken and...'

But no one was listening as everyone was far too busy marvelling at Will's heroics.

'Like Superman,' I heard someone say.

'No, Superman would have *flown* in,' someone answered. 'This was more like the Hulk.'

Jake had both arms wrapped around Will's waist as Will nodded and tried to play it down. 'It was nothing,' he kept saying. 'I was lucky, honestly. I didn't do anything. I would have had to have turned back if it was any worse.'

Jennifer-Louise's chair was being lifted onto the back of the ambulance just as Betty was trying to scramble on board, sobbing, 'I'm here, Jennifer-Louise, Mummy's here!' But Graham had jumped on board before Betty could grab hold of the rail.

'Sorry, Mum,' said Jennifer-Louise, removing her oxygen mask to speak. 'It's only one person allowed. It has to be *Graham*.'

'But... but...' Betty tried to speak. 'I can be there as well,' she said, in a small voice. 'You won't even know I'm there.'

'Sorry, Mrs Boyle,' said Graham.

'I'll call you from the hospital!' shouted Jennifer-Louise just as the doors were closed.

'Here, Betty.' Mum held out her hand to her, as Betty, shoulders slumped, turned away from Jennifer-Louise, defeated. 'Come on, we'll get everything sorted. Okay?'

'Everyone come to Albatross,' shouted Alison to the crowd. 'Tea and cake on the house!'

28

In the café, Alison went round handing out cups of tea and large slices of various cakes, James was behind the counter expertly frothing milk for the coffees.

'I'll try the chocolate cake *and* the lemon drizzle,' Bernard said.

'You could never make up your mind, could you?' said Mrs O'Keefe, giving him a look.

Jessica had gone back to the shop to close up, not wanting to be late for her pickup by Damien. 'Will you be all right?' I asked, meaningfully... hopefully.

'Of course I will!' She gave me her beautiful big smile. 'Remember, *alegría*!'

'*Alegría*,' I echoed, and then hugged her. I wasn't quite sure why, but suddenly I felt I needed to. 'Take care, Jess,' I said. 'Okay?'

I watched her walk back up the street to the shop, looking small and dainty, the kind of woman that, if you saw her in the street, you would think she had everything. You might even feel envious of her, a woman who had it all.

In the café, I stood with Mum and Henry, who were talking to Betty.

'It was a scented candle,' Betty was saying. 'Tuberose. Set fire to the curtain. I knew there was polyester in them! I was told they were one hundred per cent cotton, but you can always tell. And we'd know, wouldn't we, Nell, being in the business we're in? We know our polycottons from our natural fibres. I knew I was right.'

'Of course, Betty,' soothed Mum.

'And I always say to my customers a scented candle is the most relaxing thing you can have.' She shook her head. 'I was wrong. To think that one could have killed my precious daughter and my as-yet-unborn grandchild. You don't sell them, do you, Nell? I think I am going to start a campaign to ban them... we can't have innocent families going through this! I'll write to *The Irish Times...*'

'You do that,' said Mum. 'But first we're going to have a nice cup of tea and then we can go and have a look at the damage so you know what you're dealing with and then you can get your insurance claim in.'

Betty nodded, meekly. 'Thank you, Nell.'

'I'll go and get a cup from Alison,' said Henry, disappearing.

'Extra sugar!' shouted Betty at him. 'I shouldn't for my gut biome,' she said to Mum and me, 'but I think today calls for it.'

'At least it didn't touch the shop,' went on Mum to Betty. 'You'll be open for business in the morning! Ah, here he is, the man of the moment. The hero of Sandycove.' She and Will exchanged special smiles.

'How are you feeling today, Nell?'

'Wonderful,' she said. 'I can't express...'

'Oh, Dr Butler,' muscled in Betty, back to her full self. 'How can I ever thank you? As Nell was just saying, we are so, *so* grateful for your heroics. Like Rhett Butler when Atlanta was burning, I was thinking. The way you braved those flames! I don't know how you did it. But the most important lesson to be learned is the perils of the scented candle.'

Will looked confused. 'Scented candles?'

'Yes! Do you like them?'

'Um...' Will had obviously not given the subject a lot of thought. 'Well, I am not *against* them...'

'But you *must* be!' she said. 'You *must* be against them!'

'Okay...' He nodded at her, making an allowance for Betty's trauma. 'I will be against them then...'

'Good, good, because it would be a great irony if you, of all people, were for them.'

Will turned to me for some kind of explanation. 'Betty believes it was a scented candle...' I began.

'*Tuberose*,' Betty reminded me.

'That it was a tuberose scented candle which started the fire.'

'Ah,' said Will, it all making sense. 'Then I am definitely against any fire-starting tuberose candles.'

Mum and Henry were, I noticed, holding hands. They looked good together, just happy and comfortable in each other's company. That's what relationships were meant to be, someone who made your life better simply by being who they were. It didn't have to be complicated or a constant negotiation or anything that wasn't easy. It should be easy. Mum was right, I had been living life for other people, putting their needs first. And it would be good if I could think about mine. But I didn't even know what they were. And now with the redundancy, this was perhaps my chance to make a change. Maybe I could...

Will turned to me.

'Olivia,' he said, 'I was wondering if you might like to join me for a drink?'

'Just Olivia?' said Betty, looking put out. 'Because I could...'

'Just Olivia,' said Will, firmly.

He was still smiling at me, while Mum made wild and enthusiastic facial expressions at me from behind Will's back. Even Henry gave me the thumbs up.

'That would be lovely,' I said, relieved I was wearing my new top and jeans and that my frumpy clothes were destined for the charity shop. And now I was no longer a corporate slave, all those skirt suits and shirts and low-heeled shoes would be gone. I couldn't believe how much had changed in the last three weeks. I felt like me, but improved. Me, but a little bit more like me, if that made sense.

* * *

'Well, *that* was exciting.' Will and I walked, side by side, along Church Street towards The Island, Pablo trotting along between us.

'Oh God,' he groaned. 'I feel something of a charlatan. It wasn't as if I *saved* her life. It was only a small fire. And the door opened embarrassingly easy. I think the lock was loose. I mean, *Jake* could have kicked it open.'

'You may as well enjoy it,' I said. 'How often do you get to play hero?'

'I should take out an advert in the *Sandycove Newsletter*, explaining how easy it was. How the lock was loose and Jennifer-Louise was already down the stairs, and how she only fainted when I arrived.'

We sat in the courtyard garden of the pub, on an old park bench surrounded by pots of red-flowered geraniums, their scent hovering around us as the sky above was like a canopy of deep blue.

'Why do things happen here?' I asked. 'In London, nothing

happens. It's just me and my friend Roberto living our lives. Here, it's been a rollercoaster.'

'I think that when you live in a small place, you get caught up in things,' Will replied. He looked up as Matt delivered our drinks. 'Thanks, Matt. Anyway,' he said to me, 'here, you're really part of things so life seems more dramatic, but it's really second-hand drama.'

'I thought I would really miss London,' I said, 'but a month back home has been more exhausting than a month in London.' Pablo had crept up on the bench and was resting his head on my leg. He was warming to me, as much as I was to him.

'So...' Will spoke exaggeratedly casually, 'tell me about your boyfriend?' He gave me a look which made me feel as though the universe liked me.

'I don't have one... I mean, I did. But I don't now. Anyway, how do you know that I had a boyfriend.'

'Someone mentioned it.'

'Who?'

'Betty. She took great pains to tell me that you were not available. But you never mentioned him. And I couldn't work out what was going on.'

'Well, nothing's going on. There is no boyfriend,' I said. 'There was, but the aforementioned boyfriend no longer exists.'

'You *killed* him?'

I laughed. 'No, he's very much alive. Probably clay-pigeon shooting. I didn't quite fit in. And he slept with his ex-girlfriend.'

He rolled his eyes, shaking his head. 'Why are people such idiots?'

'We all are at various points,' I said. 'It's just some people are more idiotic more often.'

'My ex-wife had an affair with a friend of mine...'

'No!'

He nodded. 'It was a bit of a shock, but once I'd got over that, I was able to move on and realise that she and him weren't the kind of people I wanted in my life.'

'What happened?'

'Married after eight months, both of us aged twenty-four. She was a doctor – *is* a doctor – and we met volunteering in Yemen. She's Irish, from Kerry. And that's what brought us together. Two Irish people abroad. But when she got a job in New York, it just seemed easier to get married, and then we could go together. We were in love – or so I thought – and I wanted to do it properly. My parents' marriage wasn't exactly textbook, but I wanted mine to be. So, we get to New York, rent a pretty horrible apartment – cockroaches, bedbugs and these ants that used to fly around.' He shuddered. 'She's working at the hospital. So am I. But I joined this photography club, as you know, and it was nice, just a break from work. I'm not a big drinker...' He smiled at me and for a moment I found myself bathing, basking in, delighting in, *loving,* adoring, ecstatically enjoying his beautiful smile. I could love this person, I thought. I could actually *love* him. 'Anyway, so I was out of the flat a lot – and so was she. Both working long hours and I got friendly with one of the other doctors on my team. He was this super-cool guy... Zachary. Hair like a 1970s woodsman, hand-knitted jumpers... from – get this – Donegal...'

'Oh my God.'

'I know.'

'I hate him.'

He smiled. 'The jumpers did irritate me. A bit of a try-hard. But at the time, I liked him, and so I invited him over for dinner with me and Liza.'

'He didn't...'

'He did. And she did.' He rolled his eyes. 'They were sleeping together for nine whole months. Who's the idiot now?'

'I'm sorry.'

'I'm well over it,' he said, 'and I wish her well.'

'Probably wearing a shawl and playing the mandolin somewhere.'

He laughed. 'Probably. But it was all a such a mess. I moved out to an even worse apartment – bigger cockroaches, bigger bedbugs and even bigger flying things.'

'And rats,' I said. 'I bet there were rats.'

He laughed again. 'So, Liza and Zach were together, and she would ring me up and cry and say that things weren't working out or that they'd had a huge argument. And then I wouldn't hear anything and then she'd call again. And this went on for a year. And I was like... enough. I need peace. I'm going home.'

I nodded. 'I can see why you would need that,' I said.

'Obviously, I had to work out what I could do back home. I had to apply to get onto the Medical Council here and then there was other paperwork such as bringing this little fella home.' He gave Pablo a little scratch on the head. 'But we did it... and meanwhile Dermot and Catherine found the old pharmacy for me and I had to get that certified and, by the time I was on the flight home, I was ready to hit the auld sod running.' He smiled. 'I have a confession.'

'What is it?'

'Adele got me through.'

'Adele the singer Adele?'

He nodded. 'I have never told a single person this, but her songs were a deeply cathartic wallowing place... She got me through the end of my marriage and the omnishambles of my life in New York. It was quite remarkable. I played the album one day, listened to it from beginning to end, put it on repeat and it was hugely therapeutic. Every time I needed a wallow, I would listen to the album. It was like she was able to get into my mind while my subconscious sorted out my thoughts.'

'Remarkable,' I said. 'I also have someone. Kylie. She's my happy place. She's got me through some of the bad times and also given me some of the best. My friend Roberto and I were in the front row last time she played Wembley. She just makes you feel amazing. Even when you don't.'

He lifted up his glass and clinked mine. 'Here's to pop music. Better than antidepressants.'

'Here's to Kylie and Adele,' I said. 'For the healing powers of their music.'

He laughed again, as though he was really enjoying himself. Nearly as much as I was. We looked at each other, both smiling.

'You know,' he said, 'with you, it was intrigue at first sight.'

'Intrigue?' I laughed, loving this compliment. 'No one has ever called me intriguing before. I didn't even know I possessed such powers.'

'Well,' he said, 'take it from me, you do. Special powers... the kind that make someone... me, for example... think about you and wonder about you.'

My throat was dry. 'I... well... I...'

He shrugged. 'You exude a rather fascinating aura... you're fun and thoughtful and kind and intelligent and you want the very best for people. More than you want it for yourself.'

I swallowed. 'Sometimes,' I said. 'It feels greedy to want it for yourself.'

'I think that you can want it for yourself and others. And know that sometimes it's their turn and then sometimes it's yours.'

I nodded, getting it. 'Everyone is telling me to wear my crown.'

'Maybe it's your turn now?' he said. 'Take it from me, believe in yourself. Like *truly* believe in yourself.' He smiled. 'It took me a bit of time to realise that if I wasn't going to believe in myself, then no one else would. And that if no one else did, at least I still had me.'

I nodded. 'It's hard to believe in yourself sometimes, though.' I thought of the business and that run of bad luck I had. And now, I realised, what I should have done was not panic, but taken time to think and recalibrate.

My phone buzzed. Text from Mum. 'Jennifer-Louise and the baby are absolutely fine,' I read out loud. 'Thank God for that.'

Will nodded. 'She didn't look like she had breathed in anything or done any damage, but it's good to know. What about some dinner?' he said. 'The Sea Shack? I pass it every day after my swim, and I've been studying the menu. Lobster and chips. Followed by a banana split. I've become slightly obsessed by the thought of it.'

'A banana split?'

He nodded. 'I last had one when I was eleven. It was practically one of the only times we ever went out to eat and I've been haunted by banana splits ever since.' He paused. 'In a good way.'

'Well, then,' I said, 'we'd better go and get one.'

* * *

We were given a small table at the back of the restaurant, a tea light flickered between us, and we ate lobster and licked our fingers and dipped chips into mayonnaise... and talked incessantly. Pablo looked in, enviously, from his place on the bench outside. The owner laid down a rug for him and sent out some lemon sole goujons that were left over.

'Ready for the banana split?' I asked Will.

He nodded. 'As ready as I'll ever be.'

'I hope there are sparklers in it,' I said. 'We should say it's your eleventh birthday.'

When it arrived – with two spoons – he said it was better than he remembered. 'What do you think?'

'I think it's literally the best thing I've ever eaten,' I said. 'From now on, I am only eating banana splits. Three times a day.'

Afterwards, we began walking back to the village, the sky pink and gold, the world bathing in this magical glow. Will took my hand. 'It's nearly midsummer,' he said.

'You're going to have to dress Pablo in girls' clothes or the fairies will steal him.'

He laughed. 'What?'

'Folklore,' I explained. 'That's what people did in the old days. It was the night that the fairies would come out and steal little boys. So, they used to dress little boys in girls' clothing so they wouldn't be stolen. You'll have to be careful.'

'I will.' He was still laughing. 'So, how's the festival going?'

'Fine,' I said. 'All sorted. I'll close the shop early on Saturday and help with all the setting up. We have these bonfire people coming, they are called the Firestarters...' I told him what else we had planned.

'And then you're going back to London?' he asked.

I was just going to answer when my phone rang. 'It's Jessica...' I said, puzzled. 'I hope she's...' I answered the call. 'Jessica?'

All I could hear was her sobbing and gasping for breath.

'Jessica? Where are you?'

'Home.' Her voice was barely audible.

'Are you okay? What's happened?'

'I can't take it any more,' she stammered. 'I've had enough... the kids... Mam's in Galway... I don't know who to ask. No one knows... just you... please!'

'Jess, don't worry,' I said. 'I'm coming now.' I ended the call, barely breathing. I tried to remember where she lived... what was the address again? And then I remembered, the cul-de-sac on Seapoint Crescent.

Will was staring at me. 'What's wrong?'

'It's Jessica... it's her husband, she's... he's... she needs to get out of there with the kids...'

'My car is at the back of the surgery,' he said, as we began to run.

29

'Damien is incredibly charming,' I told Will as we drove along by the harbour into Church Street and out of the village.

Will pulled a face. 'I've seen this so many times. In New York, you would see women covered with bruises, not able to see out their eyes, broken bones and still they would go back.'

'She was always saying how amazing he was, but there was something strange about it, like she was overcompensating. And then last week, I saw a bruise on her arm and then on her neck... and... well, she couldn't hide it any more. The poor thing.'

Will just shook his head silently as pulled into Jessica's cul-de-sac. The whole road was some kind of suburban dream, the waft of barbecue, children riding their bikes, someone clipping their hedge and the ubiquitous female power-walking duo.

'Number twenty-five...' I peered out, looking for Damien's blacked-out Range Rover.

And there it was, parked on the driveway of a double-fronted newish-build. It looked like the perfect house, mown lawn, cobble-lock driveway. But there was something eerie about it because, even though it was still bright out, every single window was lit up, no curtains or blinds were drawn. We stared at the house.

'What do you think is happening?' I asked.

'I don't know,' said Will. 'Can you hear anything?'

'No,' I said, getting out. 'You stay here, and I'll knock on the door.'

'No, I'm coming,' he said. 'I'll stay behind their car.'

I nodded, reminding myself to breathe as I walked up the path. What must have happened for Jessica to phone me? She must have been desperate. At the front door, I put my finger on the doorbell as the noise reverberated into the evening sky, disturbing the whole street. My heart thumped in my chest.

From behind the car, Will nodded encouragingly as I turned to stare through the opaque glass of the front door. Just as I was about to ring the bell again, a man's shape appeared on the other side. Big shoulders, tight black T-shirt stretched across the chest while I focused on arranging my face into something neutral. What was I going to say? That I needed Jessica earlier in the morning and I couldn't get through on my phone? That there had been a break-in at the shop, and she was the only one with the codes? Or that...?

I should have thought of this before. All I knew was that I had to get her and the children out.

The door opened. 'Hello, Damien!' I smiled.

'Olivia...?' His eyes were glittering and spaced. Drunk, I realised, but he had smoothly moved from surprise to smile; charming men can reconfigure in nanoseconds. 'Everything all right?' I hadn't noticed his tiny mouth before, disproportionate to his huge jaw.

'Yes, fine,' I said. 'I mean, well, not really. There's been a fire in the shop and I need Jessica because she knows the combination to the safe...'

'A fire?' He shook his head as though it didn't make sense, deliberating, like he was playing a game. 'Shouldn't you...?'

'Could she come to the door?' I asked. 'May I speak to her?'

He hesitated and then, without saying anything, left me standing there and, beyond, I heard the sound of voices and then Jessica came to the door, Ellie-Mae and Frankie clinging to her legs, both in their pyjamas. All three had been crying.

Jessica locked eyes with me and almost imperceptibly shook her head. Did she mean me to go?

'Olivia,' she said, trying to sound surprised, 'what brings you here?'

'There's been a fire,' I said, 'in the shop. Could you come and open the safe? I am so sorry it's late...' I kept my eyes on hers, trying to work out what she wanted from me. But she looked apologetic, as though she regretted making that phone call.

'I can't,' she said, quickly shaking her head, 'not now, I'll do it in the morning.'

'Jessica,' I said. 'I need your help.'

Damien stepped into the frame beside her, his bulbous muscles like a terrible tropical disease, his tiny mouth like a whelk's.

'What are you doing here, Olivia?' he said, sharply. 'What do you want?'

'I just want to...' I looked at Jessica. 'I want to see if Jessica is all right.'

'Of course she's all right,' said Damien, a puzzled smile on his face. 'Why wouldn't she be?'

'Are you?' I said to her. 'It's just that I...'

'Just that you are a nosy bitch, getting involved in other people's business? Yeah?' He stared at me.

'No, I just...' I said. 'I heard some arguing.'

Pablo must have managed to get out of the car window

because suddenly he was beside me and began yapping loudly at Damien.

'Shut that mutt up!' shouted Damien. 'Shut him up or I will drop kick him over the fucking estate!'

Pablo kept barking and growling and I quickly grabbed him and held him tight. 'Shush, Pablo,' I begged. The poor little dote was like a tiny lion, and I felt so touched that he was trying to protect me. I kissed his head. 'Don't worry, Pablo,' I whispered.

Damien had turned to Jessica. 'Did you call her? Did you? Because you tell her everything is all right, okay? Because it is, isn't it, Jess?' He stared at me, his eyes on fire.

Jessica shook her head at me, the two children clinging like limpets, as though terrified they were about to be pulled off their mother.

'Tell her, Jess,' Damien commanded.

'Everything's fine,' said Jessica. 'Thank you for coming, but everything's fine.'

Sneering, Damien began to close the door, but at the last moment I put my foot in it. I thought of my conversation with Bronagh. Jessica deserved better. She needed to wear her crown too.

'Jessica,' I shouted. 'Jessica, you deserve better than this, you deserve more. You and the children...'

Damien, the bodybuilder, pushed the door closed, trapping my arm against the door frame, my scream alerting the neighbours who had not already gathered. *It's going to be severed off*, I thought. *I will be leaving this place armless.* But suddenly Will was beside me pushing on the door, Pablo growling furiously, and I managed to wriggle my arm free and the door was slammed in our faces.

And that was it, we had lost. Jessica was stuck with this monster for the rest of her life. I thought of every brilliant woman

I knew – all of them, every single one of them, even my grand-mother hidden in my locket around my neck

'Believe in yourself, Jessica,' I suddenly shouted. And then, rather desperately, 'Wear your crown! Put it on!'

Neighbours were standing on the street open-mouthed, curtains twitching, and Jessica, who had suddenly pulled the door as hard as she could, launched herself at the outside world, the two children still attached, and we all began running for the front lawn, just as a Garda car pulled up and Jessica fell to her knees, hugging her children, the three of them sobbing.

Damien came out and walked over to us, like a man walking along a beach on holiday, relaxed and casual.

'There's nothing wrong, Garda,' he said. 'Nothing at all. We were just watching television. Jess?'

She looked up.

'Come over here, Jess,' he said, his voice like a drink of hot whiskey. 'Come on, love. What's got into you? Tell them there's nothing wrong.'

Will and I looked at each other, wondering what Jessica would do.

'Jess?' Damien was still smiling at her. 'Are you all right? Are you feeling okay? Listen, everyone understands what you're going through.' He looked at the police officers. 'Postnatal depression,' he said. 'Terrible thing. She had it with Ellie-Mae and with Frankie... it's still going on.' He turned back to Jessica, calling over to her, 'Jess, please. Just tell them you're fine, and we'll get you back in the house. I'll get the kids to bed and you could have a nice bath, or something, whatever you girls like to do? Yes? A bit of pampering?' He turned back to the male police officer. 'We were only in Barcelona a week ago,' he said. 'That was to cheer her up. No expense spared, nothing but the best for my girl.'

The officer gazed at him, expressionless.

'We just had a normal argument,' he went on. 'You must have them. We all do... it's normal. Especially when Jess is so run-down, working, looking after the kids... I've told her to take it easy, put her feet up, but it's too much for her sometimes and...'

'Damien...' Jessica stared at him. 'Just stop...'

'Jess, come on, baby, please?' Damien tried again. 'I love you, you know I do.' He held out his hand, 'Come on, princess?'

And then Jessica spoke. 'I love you too.'

'That's right, course you do.' Damien smiled, smelling victory. 'Come on, come inside and everyone can go back to their lives and we'll just get on with ours.' He smiled. 'Thank you, Garda,' he said. 'But there's nothing...'

The children were peering out from behind Jessica's legs, as Jessica pushed herself upwards, eyes blinking at the sky, as though trying to make herself physically bigger.

'I love you, Damien,' she said, fixing him with a steely gaze. 'I love you. But I love you less and less every day. And one day, I won't love you at all...'

'Jess... what are...?'

'Damien, I don't *like* living with you,' she said. 'You scare me, you scare our children. We never know how you're going to be, whether you will be nice or if something – even someone not letting you out of a junction – anything! – will set you off.'

He looked at us all, pulling a face, as though he couldn't believe what he was hearing. 'Jesus! Honestly...' he laughed, 'you have no idea what she puts me through, crying and hysterics... and always going to see her mother!' He turned back to Jessica. 'Baby, I love you,' he said. 'Neither of us is perfect, but we're good together. Didn't we have a nice time in Barcelona? Jess, please.'

Jessica began to take off her cardigan. She undid the top button, then the next...

One of the officers spoke, 'We are not leaving until it is

confirmed that no charges will be pressed. Madam, do you want us to go? We are here because of an allegation of domestic violence...'

'Domestic violence?' shouted Damien, his voice breaking. 'The only crime being committed here is a man loving his wife too much!'

Jessica had now slipped off her cardigan, revealing her vest top underneath, her white skin gleaming under the street light. There, at the top of her arm was the blackest bruise I'd ever seen, far, *far* worse than the previous one.

'*This*,' she said, 'was for not getting out of bed the other night when he got home late to make him a hot drink and to ask him about his day.' She turned around and on her right shoulder blade was a red mark, the size of Damien's hand. 'And this was... this was *just because*.'

The police officers stepped forward. 'Do you want to press charges?' said the officer. 'Do you want this man arrested?'

'I want him gone,' said Jessica. 'I want a life of peace and quiet and calm for my children. I want him away from us.'

The Garda nodded and turned to Damien. 'We will be taking you into custody and it is entirely up to you to come quietly or not. Which is it to be?' Damien opened his mouth to speak but the officer continued. 'We are arresting you for the violence perpetrated against the accuser. You will have access to a solicitor in the morning, but in the meantime, you are being taken to Dún Laoghaire Garda Station. You have the right to remain silent but anything you do say may be used in evidence against you.'

'What the fuck?' shouted Damien. 'What the fuck, Jessica?' He began to laugh, shaking his head. 'Are you serious, all of you? You should be catching criminals, not arresting hard-working, law-abiding citizens like myself. The law's a joke. It hates men and fathers and people like me who work hard and just want the best for their families. That you would believe the word of a woman who is obviously mentally unstable? Didn't I tell you she was depressed! She hits *me*! *I'm* the victim!'

We watched as he was manoeuvred into the police car. Will had Pablo in his arms. Jessica knelt down with Ellie-Mae and Frankie, holding their small hands.

'I'm sorry,' she said. 'I should have done this better. For you.'

'Is Daddy going to prison?' said Ellie-Mae.

Jessica shook her head. 'Only bad people go to prison. Daddy is just going away to...' She glanced up at me. 'He's just going away to have a rest. And get better. He's been under pressure and it's made him angry. Hopefully, he'll be feeling a lot better soon. Okay?'

'Okay.' They seemed to accept it, Ellie-Mae holding Frankie's hand, the two still pressed against Jessica.

'I don't like Daddy,' said Frankie. 'He gets angry.'

'I don't want him to live with us,' said Ellie-Mae. 'I think he should live with someone else. Maybe Nanna?'

The police officer was asking where Jessica wanted to go. 'We can get you a place in a refuge now, but we'll keep him in with us tonight for breach of peace, tomorrow we can make sure there is a barring order so he can't come back to the house. Where will you be?'

'I want to stay in the house,' Jessica said, as she tried to put her cardigan back on, but she was shaking so much she couldn't quite do it, her teeth chattering so loudly as though they were loose inside her head.

'What kind of family support do you have?' said the Garda, notebook out, pen at the ready.

'My mam,' said Jessica, 'but she's in Galway. I'll call her.'

'Is she aware of your situation?'

'I don't know. I think she suspects.' Jessica's shaking became more violent, the two children clung to her even more, the three trembling as one.

'Would you like to come to Mum's house, just until your mam is home?' I said.

Jessica shook her head. 'I want the kids to be in their own beds, I want them to know they can be safe here.' She began crying again and crouched down to Ellie-Mae and Frankie. 'We're going to be fine,' she said as they both looked at her with their eyes wide.

'A liaison officer will be with you in the morning,' said the Garda.

Jessica nodded, still shivering, as the officer put her arm around Jessica. 'You are doing the right thing,' she said. 'The worst thing you can do is go back now. This is your chance of a new future.'

* * *

When the police had gone and the neighbours had retreated, we went into the house.

'Who would like hot chocolate?' said Will to Ellie-Mae and Frankie, and then to Jessica, 'I can go to the shop and get what we need?'

'No, we have everything.' She smiled at him. 'Thank you, Dr Butler.'

'Call me Will,' he said. 'I am sorry you've gone through this. It's so hard to get away from abusive people. You spend so long trying to change them.'

While he was warming the milk and spooning the drinking chocolate into mugs, I went into every room turning off the lights. Upstairs, I switched off the central lights and turned on the bedside lamps in the children's rooms and in the main bedroom, hoping they looked warm and cosy. And safe.

Downstairs again, the children were drinking their hot chocolate silently, both squashed up against Jessica. Will put Pablo beside them and Ellie-Mae stroked his head.

'We're just going to be as normal as possible,' Jessica said. 'And Daddy's going to get better, isn't he? Now, you two, time for bed!'

Will and I tidied the kitchen while Jessica was upstairs.

'Do you think she will press charges?' I said, picking up toys from the floor and putting them into a plastic crate.

'I don't know,' said Will, turning around from the sink where he was washing the cups. 'I hope she does. My mother should have...' He looked over at me, an expression on his face I couldn't quite decipher. 'My Dad was a bully,' he went on, after a pause. 'Mr Butler... scion of the community, great man around town. A teacher, no less! But at home he was an angry little man. He used to bully all of us, put us down, shout, ignore us. He would walk past me in the street and act like I didn't exist. Or other times when I was reading a book or doing something really quietly, he'd come up to me and swipe me across the side of my head. And he was awful to Mum. He used to treat her so badly, but Dermot and I couldn't ever protect her. He would find exactly the right word or thing to put you in your place. He always found a way to get under your skin that would leave you helpless...' He looked at me and shrugged. 'I just wish Mum had left him. He had a heart attack when I was nineteen. My God, that was a relief. I remember thinking I can *now* get on with my life...'

'I'm sorry,' I said, my fingers touching Mum's locket, feeling so lucky to have Mum and for her to have had Gran.

'It's a long time ago,' he said. 'I've done a lot of work on myself since then, but I was just telling you because I know what it's like to live with someone who bullies you. I have spent my life trying not to be someone like him. Who knows what was wrong with him, what feelings of insecurity and jealousy he had or what his demons were? But I'm more concerned with my life and... finding contentment.' Will was leaning against the side of the counter. 'I'm lucky. I like my life and I wouldn't change a thing.'

Jessica came back into the kitchen and immediately burst into tears, her hands up to show she was all right. 'I'm fine, I'm fine... just scared and worried but also happy. I'm going to call Mam and Kat, my sister, now and let them know what's going on and I can decide what to do.'

'Will you be all right?'

'I will have to be,' she said. 'I've no choice.'

On the doorstep, I hugged her goodbye. 'You're not coming to work tomorrow, okay? But I'll call you in the morning to see how you are.'

'Thank you,' she said. 'Thanks for coming. I just needed it to end. It was just going on and on and on...' She was still shaking. 'It was you saying wear your crown,' she said. 'I didn't know what you meant at first, and then it suddenly made sense. I want to wear my crown. I want Ellie-Mae and Frankie to know their worth,' she said. 'And it comes from me.'

And then it was Will's turn to hug her. 'I've written my number down on the pad on the kitchen table,' he said. 'Call me any time.'

Jessica nodded. 'It's time I changed my story,' she said, 'and not go round and round in circles.'

* * *

Will drove me home, holding my hand all the way and, when he said goodbye, he kissed me – softly, lingeringly.

'I'm really happy,' he said, looking at me.

'Me too,' I said, feeling a wonderful sensation that all was well with the world.

'I'll call you first thing,' he said, smiling. 'Goodbye, intriguing Olivia.'

He smiled and I stood on the road for a moment, wondering how on earth my life had changed so much and so quickly. So, I was moving back to Sandycove? Could I do it?

Kylie went through my head. *And everything went from wrong to right... then there was you.*

30

———

Roberto: OMG. The meringue was a disaster. It exploded in the oven. Still cleaning the kitchen. Am finding meringue particles everywhere, including parts of my body. Think St Mary of Berry made a mistake in recipe. Going back to check.

Roberto: No, not Mary's mistake. I used too much vinegar. She said teaspoon and I used a tablespoon and I put in bicarb and not corn-flour. Made for a science experiment. All is forgiven Mary!

Roberto: Going to try again. Love you Princess Liv!

Roberto: Liv? Are you there?

Roberto: Liv?

Me: I'm here! Will tell you everything later.

Roberto: Are you OKAY? Do you need rescuing? I will come to Ireland for you. IF YOU NEED ME?!

Me: No! I'm fine. I'm more than fine... will explain. Love you!

Roberto: Call me when you can. Love you too!

The next morning, I knew I couldn't go a step further with my plans without letting Roberto know. He was the only thing I was going to miss about my old life, and I was already feeling disloyal. He answered after the first ring, even though it was only 8 a.m.

'Liv? What's happened? You're running off with Bono? You've just won Best Soda Bread in the Irish Countrywoman's Annual Show? You've discovered you're the only heir left to the Guinness fortune and you are retiring to Maui?'

I laughed. 'None of the above,' I said. 'Sadly. But I am about to do something radical and I need to know what you think. You give the best advice of anyone I know.'

'Better than Bronagh?'

'*Different* to Bronagh. You don't worry about my feelings, you give it to me straight... and sometimes that's exactly what I need.'

'Are you dying?' he said. 'Just tell me it's not that and I can breathe and make myself a cup of tea and dispense my bounteous wisdom.'

'I'm not dying...'

'Good. What time's it with you?'

'8.03 a.m... the same time as you.'

'Ah...' I could hear him getting out of bed, and his voice muffled. 'But London time is different to Dublin time. Faster? I think we might be a few light-seconds ahead... right, dressing gown on. Lovely new Balinese slippers gifted by *Felipe*.'

'*Felipe*? So he *is* back?' I hoped he was. Roberto had never been happier than when he and Felipe were together.

'Who do you think I have been doing all this cooking for? Well, he is worming his way – very successfully, I might add – into my affections. Apparently, he's very sorry and should never have left in the first place. Hated every moment of travelling. And missed me. Apparently. And so I've decided to give him another chance. We will see how he gets on. He's got a lot of making up to do.' I could hear Felipe's voice in the background. 'Yes, Felipe,' he said. 'I'm talking about you to my *real* friend Olivia. No, she hasn't forgiven you, Felipe. And she never will. Now, Liv, tell me, how are you? I am going into the kitchen to make a cup of Earl Grey...'

'I'm going to stay,' I said.

'Stay where?'

'In Ireland!' I said. 'In Sandycove! I am going to start up my business again... so much has happened. Maribelle has resigned and I've been given redundancy and I have met *someone*. We went out last night after the fire in Nouveau You and we had banana splits and then we went to Jessica's and Damien was arrested!'

'Hold it! Hold it! Whoa! Right. Deep breath. First of all, what the hell? Secondly, who the hell? And thirdly, when the hell? You've been gone for three weeks and there have been fires and arrests and banana splits?'

I laughed.

'I want to stay,' I said, 'except I'll miss you too much. You've been the most fun and best friend ever. I wouldn't have stayed in London without you, but I want to stay and start up Seasalt again.'

There was silence on the end of the line.

'I just think it's the best thing for me...' I said. 'Please say something.'

'I'll miss you, sugar cane,' he said.

'And I'll miss you, Miss Minogue.'

'I suppose I will *have* to come over to Dublin from time to time now.'

'Will you? Because I don't want to not see you all the time. And we can FaceTime and we can still talk to each other.'

'It's not the same, though,' he said.

'No.'

We were silent again.

'But I think you're doing the right thing,' he said. 'You have my blessing and my complete and utter support and love, and I throw confetti and stardust on you from afar.'

'Really?'

'Really. You don't know how amazing you are. I wouldn't have survived London without you either.'

'And you're happy with Felipe?'

'I think so,' he said. 'He's making it up to me.'

'Because I need to know that there is someone to take care of you.'

'And I need to know someone is taking care of you. Tell me about this man. Does he deserve you?'

'I think so,' I said. 'He's the kind of person who makes you feel as though you are important, as though everyone is important. I've never felt so comfortable with someone... so happy. And he has big shoulders and he likes dogs. You will love him. And he'll love you.'

'But the big question is, does he like Kylie? Or is he into Cold-play or Mumford & Sons?'

I laughed. 'He likes Adele. She got him through his divorce.'

'I like him,' Roberto said. 'I think a man who cries along to Adele is someone I could respect.'

'I think so too.' I paused. 'I love you, Prince Roberto.'

'Love you too, Queen Olivia.'

My next job was to call the council to be put on the list for the new stalls in the Sunday market. Seasalt was a go.

The man on the phone remembered me from ten years earlier. 'We'll put you down for September, all right with you?'

'Yes...' I felt excitement bubbling in my veins, my brain working overtime... there was so much to do. I'd need to register the business, start buying bottles, packaging and labels and sourcing my ingredients, all the lavender and rose petals and orange oil and calendula. And I needed to start collecting seaweed.

'And, Olivia?' he said. 'Welcome home.'

* * *

'Remember, it's Henry's party tonight,' said Mum. 'He's sixty-five today. We're going into town for the day… and I am going crutch-free!'

'Take it easy, okay?'

'I will,' she said. 'We're going to park on St Stephen's Green and wander up to the National Gallery.'

'Are you sure you can do all that walking?'

'I feel better,' she said. 'I really do. They said three weeks and I feel like I could walk for miles. I might even go back to Pilates next week.'

'Steady on,' I said.

'We're going to have a lovely lunch in Chapter One and then party at 6 p.m. Bring Will.'

'I might.' I'd ask Will and Bronagh. Maybe Bronagh might like to bring Fergal?

'How did it go last night?' said Mum.

'I don't know how to describe it. We had a lovely evening. Will was great, as you know. We talked and talked and had nice food and all that, but then Jessica called me…'

I filled Mum in on what had happened. 'I'll give her a call,' she said. 'See if she's all right. And also remind her that the flat above the shop is ready to move in to. She and the kids could stay there.'

There was the beep of a horn from outside.

'Henry's here!' she said. 'I feel like dancing, I really do!' She attempted some kind of soft-shoe shuffle. 'I don't know why, but I feel like a huge weight has been lifted off me. I feel free.'

'Me too,' I said. 'Me too.'

Mum grabbed my hand. 'Come on, Olivia, let's dance.'

The two of us staggered around for a moment kicking out our legs.

'You'd see better in an old-people's-home Christmas party.'

Mum laughed. 'We could go for line-dancing lessons,' she said.

'I hope you're joking...'

'Well, we could if you weren't going back to London.'

'I'm going to stay in Ireland. I don't want to go back to London. I've been offered redundancy...' For the first time, it was starting to sink in. This was the opportunity that I had been waiting for.

'Oh, Olivia!' Mum had tears in her eyes. 'Now that is the best news ever!'

There was another gentle beep from outside.

'You'd better go,' I said, pushing her to the door. 'We can talk later.'

Mum hugged me tightly. 'The best news ever. I love you, Olivia.'

Outside, Henry was sitting in a rather beautiful green vintage Morris Minor, the roof down.

'Everything all right?' he called, as we walked over.

'Everything's wonderful!' said Mum. 'We were just testing my hip!' She winked at me, as she opened the passenger door and slid in.

'Happy birthday, Henry,' I said.

'Thank you,' he replied. 'June the twentieth... the sun always shines. I feel very lucky.' He leaned over to give Mum a kiss and they gave each other the sweetest and dopiest smiles. Just seeing them together made me feel better about the world.

31

The morning was quiet in the shop and I managed to finish off the midsummer window display, transforming it into something bold and bright. Each of the three mannequins was clothed in long silk, ethereal dresses – one grass-green, one pale pink and one orange – and just before opening, Catherine and Jake dropped over the wild flowers which were in jam jars. Catherine helped me dot them around the window.

'And the daisies,' she said. 'Jake, will you pass me my bag?'

Wrapped in tissue was a trail of tiny flowers, each silver centre framed by a corona of silvery petals, and each long, spindly stem was slit to slip the next flower through.

'They are a bit delicate,' said Catherine as she pulled them out, each flower following the next, like a magician pulling out handkerchiefs.

We coiled them around the flower jam jars, threading their way around the feet of the mannequins, glittering and shining in the morning sunlight through the window. I placed a sign:

Midsummer flowers donated by The Garden, jewellery by Drithle

'I love it,' I said. 'I absolutely love it.'

'Do you?' Catherine looked pleased. 'They have come out really well, actually,' she said. 'Better than I had thought. What do you think, Jake?'

He shrugged. 'They would have been nicer if they'd been seaweed. No one likes daisies. People always mow their grass, so seaweed would have been better because no one mows seaweed.'

'That's true,' said Catherine. 'Maybe next time I will do seaweed.'

He nodded, satisfied.

'My new collection is going to feature daisies,' said Catherine. 'I have to have it ready for September for the relaunch.'

'I'll be joining you,' I said. 'I'm going to get my stall back. I've already applied to the council for a new stall in the Sunday market. They have some available from September.'

Catherine gave me a huge hug. 'Congratulations,' she said, 'that's wonderful news! We can be moral supports for each other, our artists' collective. I'll bring the flask of coffee every Sunday morning.'

'Deal.' We grinned at each other.

'Jake,' I said. 'Would you be able to help me collect some seaweed next week? I am going to begin experimenting and I need your brainpower to help me.'

He nodded, excited. 'Is it a project?'

'Yes, and I will be relying on your expertise.'

Jake saluted me. 'At your service,' he said.

'I'd better get him to school,' Catherine said, giving me a kiss goodbye. 'I'll drop down the flower crowns for you and Bronagh in the morning, okay?'

* * *

My phone rang. *There he is*, I thought, excitedly, grabbing it from the counter.

'Hello?'

'Olivia? It's Jess.'

'Jess!' I was so relieved to hear her. 'How are you? Are you okay? Did you sleep at all?'

'Not too bad,' she said. 'I think I finally dropped off at around 3 a.m. But I knew Mam was on her way home because I called her before I went to bed, after you and Dr Butler left... but I just wanted to say thank you for being there. I could have been going round and round in circles all my life and there's no going back now. But I keep thinking I hear the front door, Damien roaring and shouting outside.' She paused. 'And the kids? What if I have scarred them for life? I got their father arrested. In front of them...'

'It's the first step in giving them a better life,' I said. 'At least you've got him out.'

'He's in court this morning,' she said. 'I wonder what they will do to him. The Garda liaison officer said they will be looking for a barring order. Not allowed to come near me or the kids and then we'll have to look into separation and... Oh God. I was thinking that it's easier just to keep going, keep the head down and no one knows what's going on. The whole street was out last night, having a good old gawp. But I found flowers on the doorstep this morning – from Mr O'Shea's garden. He's so sweet. And Sarah from across the road sent over brownies...' she swallowed. 'And Kate next door gave me a huge hug. I do feel a little better now I'm wearing my crown.'

'You should always wear yours. Don't ever take it off again.'

'Well, you made me do it,' she said. 'I just thought that I could almost sacrifice my life so I could keep the marriage going. I was resigned to it being like this for ever, or at least until the kids were eighteen. I didn't matter, because it was terrifying the thought o what I needed to do to even stop any of it. Because he could be nice – so lovely. But you never knew when he wouldn't be. And last night, he was kicking off about dinner being scrambled eggs because I didn't have anything else in. And he got his fork and he…' She paused. 'He stuck it in my hand. Not hard. I mean, he didn't *stab* me, but I shouted at him, and he stood up and…' She stopped again. 'Sorry.' She began to cry. 'Normally, he bars my way, or if I manage to run into another room, he'll follow me and will shout at me until I am crying and he's kind of got me where he wants me, pathetic and desperate. But last night, I saw Ellie Mae's face and she looked… not just terrified, but it was like all her innocence was being ripped from her. All her little-girlness her Ellie-Maeness. It was horrible and I felt as though I'd been given a shot of adrenaline and I grabbed her and Frankie and ran to the bathroom, and I called you.'

'I'm so glad you did.'

'Dr Butler was the one who called the police,' she said. ' think if he hadn't, then Damien would still be here. I've got my crown on now,' she said, 'and I'm not taking it off. It's like hair extensions. It looks amazing and it's not coming off unless you cut it off!'

* * *

I still hadn't heard anything from Will by lunchtime and on my trip to pick up a sandwich at James's, I had to stop myself from taking a detour to the surgery to peer pathetically through the glass. I was beginning to wonder if something was wrong.

'Olivia! Yoo-hoo, Olivia!' It was Betty.

'Hi, Betty, how are you?'

'Devastated,' she said. 'A shell of my former ebullient self. This morning I had to force myself to put on my make-up. *Put on your face, Betty*, I ordered myself. *People expect you to look the way you do, the village looks up to you.* And so here I am. I was saying to Dermot Butler how much I owed his brother and wanted to call around with a little thank-you present – not a scented candle, obviously – but apparently he's gone back to his wife.'

'His wife?'

'She arrived in on the red-eye. And our handsome doctor rushed to her side. So...' she was looking carefully at me again, 'he's off the market again. They always go back to their wives. There's no point in thinking that they won't. Ex-wives have a power, a draw... like a moth to the flame.'

I felt like an old football that had been kicked around too many times and I was worried that all my energy and enthusiasm for moving back to Sandycove had been totally wrapped up in Will. Was I about to rearrange my whole life for him? I'd even resigned from my job, I'd told Roberto that I didn't need my room and I was all set to come home. For good. Was I really going to do all that because of the promise of romance? There was no way I was ever going to be the kind of person who would upend her life because someone dangles love like a carrot. And anyway, was my London life so bad that I had to leave it? There was so much I loved about London – the city itself, obviously, the fact I had a well-ish paid job, and there was Roberto and the flat and the laughs we had. Being back in Ireland had been like a holiday romance, as though I'd drunk too many pina coladas and wasn't thinking straight. And the weather wouldn't always be this good. What about Sandycove in the winter, when the rain doesn't stop and the wind whistles and the waves wash over your car as you drive along the seafront? Actually, forget that, because those days were arguably even better than a summer's day, when you nip into The Island for a hot port and warm your hands on the fire.

But still... it was time to go home, to London. The holiday romance was over. I would ring Valerie and explain I'd changed my mind and could I instead take up one of the other personal assistant jobs? Who said you had to have an incredibly brilliant life, anyway? What was wrong with a perfectly fine, not-going-to-kill-me life?

* * *

The bell rang and a man came into the shop. I looked up, but my smile froze on my face. It was Damien. The charm had all gone, his whole body exuded a kind of barely suppressed fury, his eyes glittered with anger, his tiny mouth gripped and his jaw clenched, his shoulders braced for a prize fight.

'I'm not allowed to go near my wife and my kids because of you,' he said. 'I was trying to be a good husband and you go and fucking destroy people's lives.'

'Damien...' He was walking towards me. 'Don't...'

'None of it was your fucking business... and yet people like you...' he spat, 'people like you think you fucking know everything, with your shop, and your fucking love-yourself and everything about you.'

'Damien...'

'You make me sick... you really do.' He stepped closer and I could smell him, a mix of sweat and something else... something acrid, something *mean*. 'Oh, don't worry,' he said, 'I'm not going to hurt you, I'm not stupid, whatever you think of me. Much as I would take great pleasure in hurting you, I am not going to give you that. But you haven't won.'

I was standing against the counter, trying to plan what to do if he lunged at me. Which was closer, the front door or the back?

'I just want you to know what you have done, what your actions mean for my family. My fucking family, my wife, my kids. My two kids. If I go to my house, I am taken into custody again. If I go near my children, or try to talk to Jess or anything, I can be arrested. My family has been taken away from me and that's on you. You and the fucking system that is rigged against men like me.'

'Damien... I think that...'

Someone walked outside the shop window. *Please look in*, I thought. Or I could call for help?

'They were going to keep me in custody until I appear in court,' he continued. 'But if I agree not to contact my own kids, or not to make any contact with my own wife... then I will not have to stay in custody. In fucking custody? Like I am a criminal? Me? An innocent man!'

'I just think...' I started, not really knowing where I was going with it. Should I say I was sorry and try and be nice and understanding or should I stand my ground? All I knew was that I was scared.

His eyes, which had been focused on mine, suddenly moved to the till. He jerked forwards and I nearly screamed. He moved quickly towards me, but instead of hitting me, he picked up the little *alegría* jug which I had filled with some of the wild flowers. 'She gave you that, didn't she? From our trip to Barcelona?' But before I could do anything, he had taken it, holding it in the air for a few seconds before dropping it. We both watched as it bounced and smashed all over the floor, its handle knocked off. And then he smiled, and he sauntered out.

For a moment, I stood stock-still, too shocked and too scared to move. There were sounds from outside, normal life in the village on Friday afternoon continuing. My hands were trembling as I kneeled down to pick up the broken pieces of the jug. The handle had come off relatively cleanly, a bit of superglue and it would be fine. Broken... but not destroyed. And Jess need never know. What was that Japanese notion of *wabi-sabi*, where there is beauty in the imperfect, the perfectly imperfect life? Broken pottery took on a new meaning when it was mended. And that was us, all of us, scarred and yet still here.

And suddenly I knew I was going to stay in Sandycove. This hadn't been a fleeting flirtation, this was where I wanted my life to be. Will had been a welcome and undoubtedly handsome distraction, and maybe he had even helped me think that coming home was the right move. But I was staying for me. After all, this was where I was from, this was where the ghosts of my family were... and this was where my heart was.

But first, Damien. Who else was he going to call in on during his wanderings? Jessica's mam? Her sister? Her friends? I called the guards.

'Thank you for reporting,' said the officer. 'We'll take a drive around and see if we can see him. We'll have a chat and see if we need to take him in again.'

Whoever said that nothing happens in Sandycove?

I locked up and began to walk home, winding my way along the main street, past The Island and Janet's bakery, and Albatross, and there was James himself sitting inside Albatross. I looked up at Nouveau You with the blackened windows of the flat above, and, in the shop, Betty was sticking up a poster to the inside of her front window.

Ban deathtrap scented candles!

Next door, in the butchers, Bernard was scrubbing his great

wooden block, and next door was Catherine and Dermot's flower shop.

I loved this village, I thought, I wanted to be here for the next chapter in everyone's lives. I needed to be around for Jessica, if she wanted support, and I wanted to see if Cara went to New York and if she needed me to call in on Shirley. And would James get a new dog, and would Alison ever sell that vegan tofu cake that no one ever seemed to order? And I wanted to go to the market and buy some of Catherine's jewellery. And actually, more than that, I wanted my own stall with a passion that I could feel. And I wanted to see Bronagh all the time, and be around for Mum. I was ready to come home, where my family and friends were.

I had liked Will. But, as Roberto would say, *his* loss. And with my crown on my head, I started walking home.

I called Bronagh. 'Are you still coming to Henry's party? I've got some news and I need to celebrate! Bring Fergal!'

'He's on call for the lifeboat crew,' she said. 'He's swapped shifts around so he can come to the midsummer festival. But what's the news?'

'I'll tell you later!'

* * *

All of Mum and Henry's social whirl were drinking sparkling wine and eating crisps, the house filled with neighbours, friends, villagers, everyone who knew and loved Mum.

Henry came up to top up my glass.

'I would really like the benefit of your wisdom,' he said, quietly, in my ear. 'I really love your mother. And, with your permission, I am planning on proposing to her when we go to Rome next weekend.'

I laughed, delighted. 'I give you my permission,' I said. 'But think she'll say yes.'

'Thank you.' He beamed at me. 'I'm thinking Trevi Fountain down on one knee, ring proffered expectantly.' He looked worried for a moment. 'Do you think that acceptable or tacky? You know your mother best, would that suit a woman of her sophisticated taste?'

I looked at this lovely man, who obviously made Mum so happy and who had brought all this adventure into her life. 'I think it's perfect,' I said.

He looked thrilled. 'I won't be able to sleep until it's all over. It's quite the turmoil.'

I raised my glass. 'Bring on turmoil.'

'To turmoil!' Henry squeezed my arm, before moving on with his bottle of fizz, and I saw Bronagh coming through the door into the kitchen and she spotted me and waved.

'Thank you for coming,' I said, handing her a glass of champagne.

'Wouldn't miss it for the world,' she said. 'Isn't that what friends are for, to go to their parents' parties? By the way, the window of Nell's looks beautiful... I just walked past on my way here. The colours, the flowers, the daisy chain. It's like a gorgeous midsummer night's dream.'

'That's the idea,' I said, realising that creativity was something I had been longing for, for so long.

'Hello, girls,' Mum said, coming over to us. 'Lovely to see you Bronagh.'

'You're looking so well, Nell,' replied Bronagh. 'Radiant...'

'Well, I have had a few weeks off,' said Mum, 'thanks to Olivia... and it's worked, as my hip has totally healed.'

Bronagh was right. Mum looked incredible. She was off the

crutches and wearing a slinky mink-coloured top and a pair of white jeans. Maybe that's what being at peace looked like.

Mum put her arm around me. 'And I've had my wonderful daughter home all this time. Now, that's what has put a smile on my face.'

'Which brings me to my news,' I said. 'I've decided to stay. I've been given redundancy and I am going to start up Seasalt again.'

'You're *staying*?' said Bronagh. 'You mean, *permanently*?'

I nodded. 'I want to stay here... at home. But I'll find somewhere to rent.'

Bronagh had already let out a shriek and grabbed me. 'This is the best news ever!' she shouted, squashing me against her. 'And you can move in with me. Susie is moving out this weekend so it's just me and Mies.'

'I'd love to.' We grinned at each other.

'And you can join my yoga class,' Bronagh said. 'Saturday mornings. You will love everyone there. And you'll have to come sea swimming...'

'Can't I just wave you off in the morning with my dressing gown on?' I said. 'While eating a croissant?'

She laughed. 'I suppose...' I grinned at both of them.

'Girls, if you don't mind,' said Mum, 'I need your advice. Henry and I are going away next weekend and Cara's going to look after the shop on the Friday and Saturday. But for some reason, I've got it into my head to propose to Henry. Do you think it's a good idea? I know people do it these days, the woman asks the man, and I just know I would like to spend the rest of my life with him.'

'I think it's a brilliant idea,' I said. 'I think he's going to love it.'

'What do you think about the Trevi Fountain?' she asked. 'It's such a beautiful place, but is it too much of a cliché?'

'Clichés are only clichés because they are the best ideas,' said Bronagh.

Mum beamed. 'That's exactly what I was thinking. And we can go for an ice cream afterwards to celebrate.'

And as I stood there with my wonderful mother and my gorgeous best friend, I felt really and truly and deeply happy. For the first time in my life, I knew without a shadow of a doubt I was making the right decision. I wasn't remotely scared of what lay ahead.

Bronagh raised her glass. 'To you, Nell, and your continued adventures. To me and Liv in ours.'

'But most of all to Mum and Henry,' I said. And there was one more person I was thinking of. 'Here's to Joseph Delaney,' I said, holding up my glass. 'Wherever he is. I hope he's doing well. I hope he's happy.'

Bronagh touched her glass to mine. 'Me too,' she said. 'To Joseph Delaney. Wherever he is.'

We smiled at each other. Wherever he is. I hoped he was at least *somewhere*, but even if not, I was determined to try and do what I could to find another few pieces in my jigsaw.

And as for Will... I remembered last night, and him kissing me, and how I'd felt... I couldn't let disappointment stop me from moving on. I hoped he was happy too, he deserved it, he really did.

32

Roberto: Good luck today. Sorry to miss the fun.

Me: I'll see you soon. I'll be back in London soon to pack up.

Roberto: My heart is broken.

Me: At least you have Mary Berry.

Roberto: And Kylie. Always Kylie. Kylie 4ever.

Me: And us. Roberto and Liv 4ever.

Roberto: <sobbing>

The village car park was normally a grey and unprepossessing place but on midsummer afternoon, it was slowly being turned into something of a wonderland. Strings of multicoloured lights criss-crossed overhead, the ground was strewn with heavily scented lavender flowers, at the far end the bonfire was set, ready to be lit later, and the food trucks were waiting, awnings pulled out, generators rumbling. Over at the far corner of the car park, an old man in a threadbare brown suit and pale orange shirt and purple-patterned tie was rifling through a huge black box.

'Harry Daly? The firework man?'

'Tis the very one,' he said, standing to his not very full height, and shaking my hand. His was slightly blackened. 'I have my box of magic, just setting a few things up. I managed to find a few specially special specials as well. We'll have them dancing with the stars later, so we will. Magic guaranteed.'

'I can't wait,' I said. 'Thank you, Harry.'

'I'll make sure to book you in for next year,' he said. 'So you don't have to rely on luck.'

'That would be great.'

'And good news,' he said. 'My friend in China, the firework master? The family were very worried because he didn't have a son or a grandson to take over the family expertise. But they've had a family conference and his granddaughter is now his apprentice.'

'I am so glad to hear it,' I said.

'Now, that's progress,' he said. 'An ancient art is modernised. My own daughter does all my accounts and my granddaughter says she'll do one of those website things for me.'

I left him kneeling beside his box of magic. Over by the stage, Miss Rachel's fairies were excitedly dashing around, a blur of sequins and wings, and I spotted Frankie dressed as a forest ninja with twigs in his hair and a camouflage T-shirt practising his pointed toes. Under the oak tree, the tin whistle orchestra were rehearsing a slightly screechy version of 'Down By The Salley Gardens'. James was rolling a large oak red-wine barrel over to his open-air bar, where he had unfolded chairs and tables and had unfurled large garden umbrellas. Matt was standing inside a converted ice cream van, ready with his cocktail shakers. He'd pulled some of the benches close to the bonfire. Alison was wrapping potatoes in tin foil and placing them at the bottom of the fire.

Bronagh looked at me. 'What do you think?'

'It looks beautiful,' I said. 'I am particularly looking forward to a margarita from Matt.'

Bernard Murphy was carrying sacks of charcoal on his shoulders. 'I'll put my barbecue beside James!' he called over. 'Got myself some lovely flanks of steak!'

'Did you know he was doing a barbecue?' I said to Bronagh.

'He must have just decided that there wasn't enough meat in the world,' she said. 'Thankfully, he is not setting up next to Alison and her vegetarian zone. You don't think we have too much food, do you? I don't want Mum worrying about the village's obesity levels.'

'Is she coming?'

'Yes, she's trying to make an effort and being a more supportive mother. And I am trying to be a nicer and more supportive daughter. We're a work in progress. What about alcohol... too much?'

'I doubt it. I mean, it's a family festival, not Woodstock. The parents of the tin-whistlers and the fairies will probably just stay for a while for the face-painting, a baked potato and one of Alison's smores, and then leave...'

Bronagh nodded. 'And then the disco and the fireworks... it's going to be lovely and civilised.'

Fergal and another mountainous man were setting up some of the deckchairs.

Bronagh waved to him. 'I've decided that I will accept any more custard slices he wants to throw in my direction,' she said.

'Is that a double entendre?'

'It might be.' She winked at me.

At 5 p.m. we both went back to Mum's to change into something midsummery. I had bought one of the full-length silk dresses from Nell's and gold flat sandals, Bronagh a black cotton

strapless midi dress with black sandals, and we both wore flowe
crowns made by Catherine.

'Do we look ridiculous?' I said, as we both looked at ourselve
in the full-length mirror in my bedroom.

'Yes, but does it matter? We're wearing our crowns!'

We walked back to the car park, talking all the way. I told he
about my plans for Seasalt and seaweed and she told me abou
how her mum had evicted Mark and had reclaimed the livin
room and had refused to cook for anyone, even Brian. 'She
commandeered the big armchair and is sitting with her feet u
watching all the soaps,' said Bronagh. 'I think she's really happ
for the first time in her life.'

I thought of Will for a moment and felt a little foolish. You'
have thought he would have just texted to say that he and his wif
were giving it another go. But nothing... it just seemed rude. An
disappointing. But with my slightly silly but lovely flower crow
on my head, I was determined not to let anything spoil my fun.

* * *

By 6 p.m., the car park was full and I stood up onstage, lookin
out at everyone. Behind me, the tin whistle orchestra were read
to start – their tiny instruments in their tiny hands. At the othe
side of the stage, Miss Rachel and her troupe of fairies and woo
nymphs were gathered, all tutus and wings and twigs. Behin
them was Henry and a group of bespectacled, hand-knitte
cardigan wearers clutching their ukuleles, and beyond, th
Mexican food stall was serving tacos and sloshing out margarit
from big jugs. Less adventurous villagers were sticking rather rel
giously to James's offerings of Irish wine, while others tried Matt
cocktails.

I saw all the faces of people I knew. Betty and Jennifer-Louis and Graham were together, Betty with a large glass of wine. Dermot and Catherine were right in front of the stage, ready to watch Jake in the tin whistle orchestra. Mum was there with a group of her friends. Bernard Murphy was flipping burgers on his barbecue, while next to him Mrs O'Keefe sliced bread rolls and squirted ketchup on them. Audrey Kelly was sitting on a deckchair, a large pina colada in her hand. Jessica and her mother were both clutching another of Matt's cocktails – his tequila sunset. I gave them a wave, before clearing my throat and speaking into the microphone.

'Hello, everyone,' I said. 'It is midsummer's eve and we are here on this great pagan festival...' I gave Jessica a look and she winked back, '...to celebrate the most magical night of the year. Tonight we celebrate life in our wonderful village, we are raising a glass to all of us Sandycovers.'

Everyone cheered and raised their glasses.

'And according to folklore, tonight is when the fairies slip from their world to ours, and so it is with great pleasure that I present Miss Rachel's Midsummer Night's Fairies, to be followed by the tin whistle orchestra from St Joseph's National school!'

And I left the stage to more cheering, which seemed a little too excitable, a little too loud.

'You don't think everyone seems a little drunk already?' I said to Bronagh, who had been waiting for me at the bottom of the steps.

'They do definitely seem drunk,' she said, 'as though they have taken some magic potion. Bernard Murphy just downed a margarita as though it was lemonade and Betty's already got her shoes off.'

I looked over, as Betty, heels in one hand, swayed along to the plink-plonk of Miss Rachel's keyboard. But Bronagh was right, there *was* something in the air which seemed to give a slightly heady, heavy atmosphere, as though it *was* Woodstock, and not some local community festival, as though for this night only, we were one ancient tribe.

When the children were finished performing, the audience cheered them as though it was nothing they had ever seen or heard before. Feet were stamped, arms clapped, throats sore from cheering. Miss Rachel, a little bemused, ushered her fairies offstage, followed by the tin whistlers, each child flying into the arms of their proud and delighted parents. Jake was lifted onto Dermot's shoulder, his tin whistle held aloft as though it was the Liam MacCarthy Cup. And he was wearing the tiger jumper I had given him, exactly the same as Catherine's. I'd found an extra-small in the shop and had given it in exchange for the flower crowns. Jake couldn't have looked happier.

By the time the Sandycove Ukulele Orchestra took to the stage, the audience were as excited as if it was Live Aid.

'One, two, three...' The ukulele players counted themselves in, and then they began... with... It took me a while to realise what they were playing, and then, in all its brilliance, I realised it was 'I Should Be So Lucky' by Kylie. If only Roberto was here, I thought. Standing here in a church car park, surrounded by lovely people and feeling so completely and happily at home, it wasn't very often that you catch up with the universe and you are exactly where you are meant to be. When it does happen, it's the most wonderful feeling.

Dusk was creeping into the village, the longest day of the year was slowly coming to an end.

Bronagh handed me a margarita. 'Here's to us, best friend and lodger,' she said.

'Here's to us.' We clinked and grinned at each other.

'I'm so glad you're staying,' she said.

'So am I.'

A man tapped her on the shoulder and she turned round. 'Paul!' said Bronagh. 'What are you doing here?' He was dressed in navy blue shorts and a light-blue shirt, with the badge of the Irish postal service on the pocket.

'To say sorry,' Postman Paul said. 'To say that you are the best thing that has ever happened to me.'

'That's not what you said two weeks ago,' said Bronagh.

'I love you, and I don't care if your parents don't like me...'

'Paul, I don't care if they don't like you either,' said Bronagh. 'I don't care what they think of anything...'

'And I don't care if you don't know the difference between *Star Wars* and *Star Trek*.' He had dropped to one knee. 'Bronagh Kelly, will you marry me?'

'Paul, please!'

'Bronagh, I'm sorry. Will you do me the honour of being my wife?'

'Paul, don't! Stand up!' She tried to pull on his T-shirt, but he remained kneeling.

'Bronagh... please.'

'Paul... it's a no. I suggest you find someone who does like *Star Trek*.'

'But I said I didn't mind.'

'But *I do!*'

'You do?' He looked delighted.

'No! I don't! I definitely don't. I meant that I did mind, not I do!' She looked at me, desperately. 'Paul, come on!'

I spotted Fergal, craning his neck, creeping closer to hear what was going on as Paul got to his feet and hung his head. 'Okay, I accept your negative response.'

'Thank you, Paul, for your apology and I am sorry too. And I really hope you find someone really nice, someone you deserve.'

He nodded, dejected, and then held up his hand in a strange shape. 'That's Vulcan for goodbye,' he said, and walked away.

Fergal went straight up to Bronagh. 'Listen, Bronagh,' he said. 'I just want to say before any other man proposes to you that I am a major fan of you, your work and your aura.'

'Okay...' Bronagh was starting to smile.

'And I may as well tell you that I would like to buy you more cakes... for as long as you would allow me to and I would like to entice you to come to London with me... there's an open house at the Barbican next weekend... would you come with me?'

'Yes,' she said. 'Yes, I would! The feeling's mutual, by the way. That stuff about being a fan of you and your work and your aura. Yours is pretty cool as well.'

They grinned at each other, as though they couldn't believe they had found each other, and I slipped away, leaving my beautiful and brilliant friend to enjoy her new romance.

Margarita in my hand, I wandered around the crowd, stopping to speak to people, waving to others. Cara and Shirley were sitting on the deckchairs in front of the stage. 'Hello, you two,' I said, kneeling down beside them. 'How are you feeling, Shirley?'

'Never better,' she said. 'Back to normal. Cara's set me up with two alarms in the kitchen – one at 8 a.m. and the other at 8 p.m. so I remember to take my tablets. I'll be relying on them when she goes to New York.'

'You're *going*?' I said to Cara.

She nodded. 'It's only three years and I'll be home for Christmas and summer. And Nan and I can Zoom every day – we've already practised it. And she has every single neighbour in our street looking out for her...'

'Not that I need it,' said Shirley.

'And I'll be around,' I said. 'I'm not going back to London now.

I can call in and see you, Shirley, if that's okay?' I turned back to Cara. 'What made you change your mind?'

'Anna Karenina,' she said. 'I thought about what she would do. What is the difference between an interesting life and an uninteresting life? Living the most exciting life you can. Leaving Nan, going somewhere so far away... it's... terrifying. But...' She pushed her long hair out of her eyes and blinked at me from behind her glasses. 'My mum didn't get a chance to go to New York.'

Shirley was nodding away, agreeing.

'I know she is looking down on us and she won't let anything happen to Nan.'

'She won't,' I agreed. 'And I think you are really brave.'

I spotted Jessica and Ellie-Mae and Frankie eating baked potatoes beside the bonfire. 'I'll just go and say hello to Jessica,' I said. 'Bye Shirley, have a lovely evening, bye Cara.'

I gave Jessica a big hug. 'How are you doing?'

'Fine,' she said. 'We're having a lovely time. Olivia, this is my mam, Pauline,' said Jessica. 'Mam, this is Olivia, you know who...'

Pauline nodded. 'Thanks for taking care of our Jess,' she said, in a quiet voice. 'Wish I'd been there. Of all the weekends I chose to go to Galway! But anyway, things always come to a head, and it's always for the best. Right, Ellie-Mae and Frankie, who's for some of those smore things?'

'Your mum's asked me to be manager of the shop,' said Jessica. 'Starting Monday. Can you believe it?'

'I can. And you're going to be brilliant.'

'I hope so.' She smiled at me. 'Me! Manager of a boutique!'

'And how is everything with Damien? Have you heard anything?'

'He's back in custody,' she said. 'And the hearing is on

Monday morning. And then it's the first day of the rest of my life.
A new start.'

I hugged her. 'It's exciting, it really is.'

'I may lose the house, but we'll be all right. I'm determined
we'll be all right. And your Mum has offered us the flat above the
shop if we need it.'

I hugged her again. 'And I'm around to help and do whatever I
can.'

'Thanks, Olivia,' she said.

'Ah, Olivia!' Betty came over to us, still barefoot, and Jennifer
Louise and Graham were behind her, holding hands. 'I must
congratulate you on this evening. It is a very commendable
effort,' said Betty, slurring her words slightly.

'It's more than commendable,' said Jennifer-Louise. 'Graham
and I were just saying that you and Bronagh have done a brilliant
job. There is such a lovely atmosphere and the food is to die for.'

'I am going to put you down for next year, yes?' said Betty.
'Jennifer-Louise will be far too busy with the baby. And anyway,
now you are staying...'

I actually couldn't wait to organise it next year. Flamethrow
ers, I was thinking, Oberon and Titania moving through the
crowd, greenery, as though we were in a forest... and then there
was a shout from the street at the end of the car park.

'YOU FILTHY ANIMAL! YOU DISGUSTING MAN!'

Everyone looked up to see Bernard Murphy running down
the road, his face a vision of pure panic, naked (it looked like
anyway) except for his butcher's coat, his white hairy legs sticking
out. Mrs Murphy, Bernard's wife, a meat mallet in her hand
sprinted after him. And out of the corner of my eye, I saw some
thing move at the back of the church – it was Mrs O'Keefe
running through the graveyard, Bernard's straw boater on her
head.

33

On stage, Bronagh had taken the microphone. 'And now in a slight change to the programme...' She was smiling right down at me. 'This next act has flown in all the way from London. I think you're all going to enjoy... our very special guest... he hasn't been back in Ireland for fifteen years... but he's made the extra-special effort for the midsummer festival... for one night only!'

The music began... the unmistakeable sound of 'Spinning Around' by Kylie. No. It couldn't be. I looked over at Mum, who winked.

'Get your dancing shoes on,' shouted Bronagh, 'put your hands together for MISSSSSSSSS MINOGUE!'

And there on stage was Roberto, in his Miss Minogue costume of hot pants, blonde wig and full make-up and looking fabulous as per usual. At that moment, I felt my heart might over-flow with love. My friends, my family, everything I needed in life was right here at this moment. I was completely and utterly blessed and so incredibly lucky. I should be so lucky? I *was* so lucky.

'How did this happen?' I shouted over to Mum. 'Did you know?'

'He called me yesterday,' she said, grinning. 'He wanted to surprise you!'

I'd seen his act a hundred times before but the reaction of the Sandycove crowd was phenomenal, the whole car park shaking as people danced their hearts out and their feet off. Every word to the songs was shouted, as people hung off each other, eyes closed, arms outstretched, as though we all were high on life, intoxicated by this great collective experience.

I was dancing, singing harder than anyone, but as I swung around, I crashed straight into someone tall, someone who was putting two hands on my arms and someone who was calling my name. 'Olivia!'

Will. My flower crown nearly fell off. I stopped dancing and stared up at him. Where was his *wife*? It felt like weeks since I'd seen him, not a matter of hours. He was smiling as though nothing had happened. But everything had changed. *Everything* was different. Even Pablo was different. He ran straight up to my ankles and licked them, as though he was pleased to see me.

'It's okay,' I said to Will. 'I understand.' I wanted to explain that it was okay, I was okay, and he didn't need to feel bad about anything. It didn't matter because I was staying here and I couldn't wait to get started on my next adventure.

'Understand what?' He shouted above the music. 'I couldn't get mobile reception... I tried to call from the service station, but we had to get there so quickly...'

'Where? What service station?' I shouted into his ear above the sing-shouting of everyone in the car park.

'I've only just got back from Listowel,' he said, 'six hours in the car, I kept my foot down all the way. Pablo was carsick... but...' He was still smiling as though he was pleased to see me, as though it was still Thursday night and he hadn't left me for his ex-wife. But then again, where was she? And what were they doing in Listowel? No one went to Kerry on an overnight trip.

'Elizabeth – my *ex*-wife – flew in on Thursday morning...'

I smiled at him. 'I don't need any...'

He shook his head, as though I didn't understand, pulling me to one side, away from the noise. 'Her father was dying,' he said. 'She flew in on Friday morning on the red-eye from New York, but then there was a problem with her car hire. She was desperate to see her father and so she called me.' He shrugged. 'I had no choice but to go and pick her up. And we drove all the way down, and I kept thinking I should phone you, but then something else would happen. We were at the hospital for the whole of yesterday.' He shrugged. 'Poor Elizabeth. I did feel sorry for her, but... well, I left her there. I told her I had someone to see. I left as early as I could and drove straight back. There was no way I wanted to miss the festival.' He smiled again. 'And I was missing you!'

I nodded, not knowing how to respond. I was trying to take it all in.

'I can't tell you how happy I was to get in the car again,' he said, still smiling, 'knowing I would see you again.'

I was still confused. 'But why didn't you call?'

'I kept trying, but it wasn't working, and then by the time I was on the road again, I knew I'd see you soon.' He smiled at me. 'And here I am.' His hand was holding mine, the fairy lights twinkled above us, the sky was the colour of a golden apple as the sun set, and everywhere were the faces of the villagers smiling and laughing and dancing. 'I am really, really pleased to see you,' he said.

On stage, Miss Minogue was speaking into the microphone, the music playing underneath her. 'And now,' she was saying, 'a song for all the lovers out there... the Australian lovers...' The audience cheered. '...And the Irish lovers...' There was a bigger cheer. '...And, most fabulously, the best lovers in the world, this is for the SANDYCOVE LOVERS!' The crowd went ballistic as she began singing 'Love At First Sight'.

I looked at Will and realised that I was really, really pleased to see him too. Perhaps he was going to be part of my new adventure, after all. It might be nice to take someone along with me for the ride and, if I was going to have a sidekick, then the only person I wanted it to be was Will.

'I'm really pleased to see you too,' I said.

And then... he kissed me.

'I told Elizabeth about this dark-haired girl who has me bewitched,' he said, when he pulled back a little. 'Captivated. *Intrigued*. I have done *nothing* but think of you. Your beautiful face, the way your hair kinks at the side. Those three freckles beside your ear, like stepping stones.'

Joy and love and happiness spread through me like a hot bath on a cold night. Over his shoulder, Mum gave me a thumbs up.

'I'm staying, by the way,' I shouted again into his ear. 'I'm not going to London.'

'Now that,' he said, putting his arms around me and pulling me into his jacket, 'is the best news I have heard in a very long time. All the way up I was trying to work out how I might persuade you to stay. But then I was telling myself that that was unfair, and... I don't know. I just knew I wanted to get back home to you.'

Roberto was standing on stage, basking in the applause. 'And now, this is for Queen Olivia,' he said, 'the queen of Sandycove.' Betty pulled a face, aghast. 'Love you, Liv!' shouted Miss Minogue. 'This is "On A Night Like This"!'

And with Will's hand holding mine we joined in as the whole

illage danced midsummer away. And right on cue there was a huge bang and then a long whiiiiiizzzz as the first firework burst open in the sky. Harry had been right, it was just like dancing with the stars. *Remember this moment, Olivia*, I said. *Because they don't happen every day. Remember this time in your life when you, the stars and the universe are perfectly aligned.*

EPILOGUE

Roberto: Felipe and I were talking about what to wear to the wedding. He thinks hot pants are not suitable.

Me: Maybe just hot pants, nothing else?

Roberto: I like it! He's wearing a suit. He wants me to wear one as well.

Me: Hot pants under suit? Too itchy?

Roberto: Nice compromise! Which is the basis of marriage, apparently. Have you got your dress sorted yet?

Me: Jessica has a few ideas for me. She's suggested a gold dress with a cape!

Roberto: Wear it. You're my superhero Best Woman. Have you spoken to the florist? And the cake lady?

Me: Catherine and Dermot are doing the flowers. All sorted and will be beautiful. And Janet is making the giant cake. She's calling it a Queen Victoria Sponge. Seven layers, buttercream, strawberries and cream. Okay with you?

Roberto: Sounds FABULOUS. As are you.

Me: I learned it all from you.

Roberto: Au contraire. My dear Liv, the original fabulista.

It was a Saturday in April and that evening we'd been invited to a wine-tasting in James's Deli. He and Alison had had a little girl, Flora, the month before.

'How is Alison doing?' I asked James, when I popped into the Deli at lunchtime.

Will, Pablo and I had gone for a chilly morning run, our breath blown in front of us, a sliver of sun peeking out from the horizon. I was getting faster and stronger these days, able to keep up with Will and Pablo as we ran through the village to home. And then I'd spent the morning in the glass-blower's factory packing up my crates for the next day's market. I loved my little workshop, with my old cooker where I stirred and melted my beeswax and added my oils. There was a huge old seamstress' table where I weighed out and mixed all my precious oils and where my soaps would harden into bars and I would wrap and label and pour. I had retrieved my old saucepan and every time I used it, I thought of Mum and her mother in their kitchen and now me in my workshop.

Will said it was like being in some old French perfume laboratory, he reckoned he could tell if I was making my lavender body oil or if it was a rose-hip day. 'My nose is becoming quite expert.' He'd come in and make tea for us both and we'd sit on the old sofa, my feet on his lap, and chat about how my seaweed experiments were going. And tomorrow I was introducing a new product – my silky seaweed body oil. The feedback from all my testers had been hugely positive; everyone from Mum to Catherine to Bronagh all loved it. I'd even made a seaweed bubble bath especially for children, perfect for sensitive skins, and had called it Professor Jake's Bubble Cave. He loved it more than anyone.

In the Deli, James was packing up my sandwiches. 'Alison's doing brilliantly,' he said. 'It's honestly the best thing that has happened to either of us. Alison's doing the days, I am on nights. Means I'm a bit tired during the day but nothing that strong coffee and a few vertical catnaps can't sort out.'

'Are you sure you're able to do tonight?' I asked.

'Totally,' he said. 'I've done it every year since I've opened. I'm not going to miss a year. Flora will be with us, though, in her sling. And neither Alison nor I will be drinking very much. We'll actually just be tasting. By the way,' he said, 'there's someone I would like you to meet.'

I followed him behind the counter and into the back office – I hadn't been this side of the counter since that day last June when he'd lost poor Sammy. The office was dark, with just a low light. 'I don't want him to have too many bright lights,' he said.

'Who?' But then I saw a large, old cardboard vegetable box, which had a folded blanket inside, and on top of that was a golden Labrador puppy. 'Oh, my God...' I breathed.

'I know,' said James. 'He's nine weeks old... Alison loves him as much as me.' He scooped the puppy up, holding him close to his chest and kissing his head. 'Would you like to hold him?'

'I would love to...' He put the warm, velvet bundle into my arms. 'He's gorgeous,' I breathed. 'What's his name?'

'Bruce. As in... Springsteen.'

'It's perfect. *He's* perfect.'

He nodded, agreeing. 'He really is.'

I handed Bruce back to James. 'A new best friend for Flora.'

After saying goodbye to James, I walked home. It still seemed a little strange that the house on Sandycove Avenue was now my house. I'd stayed with Bronagh until the end of September and then moved in here in October, nervous about living in the house and taking on a step-dog.

'It was yours before it was mine,' Will kept saying, and I always thought of Mum every time I walked up the path, and of my grandmother. I don't know if ghosts exist but every time I stepped into the house I had a feeling in my stomach that I was exactly where I was meant to be. The universe had brought me here. I'd worn my locket every day since Mum had first given it to me, and every morning as I put it on, I would say in my head to my grandmother, 'We miss you and wish you were here, with us.'

I'd even forgiven Mum's dad and Aunt Theresa, as much as I could, telling myself that they were a product of their time and were doing what they thought was right. And anyway, Mum and I had been happy, so old resentments needn't be nursed. We could let it go. And as for Joseph Delaney? I had started trying to find him, but it was going to take some time. Will and I were planning to go to Boston next summer and see what kind of research we could do. 'We'll be Miss Marple and Hercule Poirot,' said Will. 'We'll find him.'

But I didn't hold out much hope. I'd read Mum's letters from him and I really liked the sound of him. He was funny and intelligent and kind. At least I had those.

I stepped into Will's – our – house. 'Lunch!' I called and stood in the hall, the afternoon sun streaming through the stained glass, Pablo bounding down the stairs – he spent most afternoons sleeping on our bed – to greet me. Every time he raced down the stairs, I held my breath, waiting for him to tumble down, the stairs were too big and he was too small. But yet again, he survived and came over and licked me hello. It hadn't taken him very long to accept me as part of the family.

Will came out of the kitchen, wrapping his arms around me. 'I've missed you,' he said. 'How was your morning? Did you get much done?'

'All packed up and ready for the market.'

He and Pablo had taken to coming to my stall every Sunday and it turned out Will was even better than me at all the selling and chatting. He sold far more than me every week. Who wouldn't want to buy from a charming, handsome man? Catherine's stall was right next to mine and sometimes Dermot and Jake came down to help out.

In the evening, the whole village had turned out for the wine-tasting. Bernard and his wife were there – him a shadow of his former avuncular self. And there was Betty and her husband, Jennifer-Louise and Graham with their little baby, Brian, in a sling.

I waved to Jessica and her mam. I saw Jessica most days when I popped into the shop to say hello. The divorce was proceeding, and although, in the end, she didn't press charges, Damien had been ordered to stay away from her and the children. He was undergoing anger-management classes and was claiming to have found Buddhism. None of us believed any of this. But Jessica was doing well and every day was stronger than the day before.

I joined Bronagh and Fergal.

'Oh, there's Mum,' said Bronagh, giving Audrey a wave. 'I told her that we'd be here and she would enjoy the film. And now Dad is golf club chairman which means he's barely at home, she's really making an effort to do her own thing.'

Audrey joined us. 'Glass of wine, Mrs Kelly?' said Fergal.

'Yes, thank you, Fergal,' she said. 'Ask James if he has a nice Syrah... I find it's the only one that doesn't give me a terrible head. Fergal, you know what I like. You're always so good at choosing wine.' Fergal disappeared to the trestle-table bar. 'He's such a nice man, Bronagh,' she said. 'But, Bronagh, your dress...'

Beside me, I could feel Bronagh bracing herself.

'...your dress is very nice,' ended Audrey.

'Thank you, Mum, yours is too.'

Last year, Will and I, Fergal and Audrey had all gone to Edinburgh and clapped furiously when Bronagh had gone up on stage collect the award. Afterwards, we'd had a long, boozy dinner where Audrey had got quite drunk and quite tearful and told ronagh that she was proud of her. It had had a hugely positive ffect on their relationship. Since then, Audrey hadn't got quite so loppy or affectionate but she was really making a big effort.

'And how are the plans for your mother's wedding, Olivia?' sked Audrey.

The double proposal had gone brilliantly, by all accounts. Just s Mum was about to say her piece, she looked at Henry who had ung himself to one knee and they both said 'Yes!' in unison. And pparently, the ice cream was to die for, as only ice cream eaten in ront of the Trevi Fountain, surrounded by the chaos and the fun f tourists of every nationality and basking in the glow of love, an taste.

'It's only two weeks' away now,' I said. 'And it's going to be very mall... a few of their friends and me... and Will.'

'Her family,' said Will, his arm around my shoulders. '*Our* amily.'

'And we have another wedding coming up,' I said. 'My friend Roberto and his boyfriend Felipe. They live in London but are oming to Ireland to get married in Dublin City Hall. I think half f Ballymun has been invited.'

'And then there's ours,' said Will, kissing me on the side of the ead. 'I can't wait for midsummer's eve.'

He'd proposed one cold February evening after I'd spent the vhole day in the glass-blowing factory and had come home to nd Will insisting that we were going to the Sea Shack for lobster nd chips. He waited until the banana split arrived to ask me to narry him. There was a note tucked under the banana. 'Oh, vhat's this?' he said, opening it. 'It's from Pablo.' He turned to ablo who was on the bench next to him. 'I didn't know you could vrite,' he said. 'Well, you're a clever dog. Right, let's read it. Okay.

It says, "Dear Liv, I am writing this on behalf of Will. He is in lov
with you and loves everything about you. And so do I. We wou
like you to do us the great honour of marrying us. And we w
love and treasure you forever."' Will had one eyebrow raised
his eyes met mine. '"Lots and lots of love, Pablo",' he'd said.

'Oh my God.'

'Will you?'

I nodded, my heart soaring, thinking how happy I wa
Another moment to file away, another time in your life which yo
should treasure and draw upon. Love was something wor
waiting for. 'Of course I will.'

He grinned. 'Pablo!' he said. 'She said yes!' He stood up an
hugged me, kissing my tears away. 'Oh, I do love you, Liv O'Neil
he said. 'I love everything you are, everything you've been an
everything to come.'

So that was us, a little instant family – me, Will and Pabl
The date was set for midsummer's eve... the very thought of th
night was magical to me now. It would always remind me of th
summer my life changed and the summer I came home to Sand
cove, the place I loved and the place where I was loved and whe
I belonged.

ACKNOWLEDGMENTS

Thank you to Caroline Ridding and her amazing team at Boldwood Books – I am delighted to be part of the family. My clever and brilliant agent Ger Nichol is always so kind and encouraging and I'm happy to be tucked under her wing. All my impressive and gorgeous friends are a constant source of joy for me – but thank you especially to Jenny and Arantza who made lockdown walks fun.

And, of course, most of all to the best person I know, Ruby.

MORE FROM SIÂN O'GORMAN

We hope you enjoyed reading *Life's What You Make It*. If you did, please leave a review.

If you'd like to gift a copy, this book is also available as an ebook, digital audio download and audiobook CD.

Sign up to Siân O'Gorman's mailing list for news, competitions and updates on future books.

https://bit.ly/SianOGormannewsletter

ABOUT THE AUTHOR

Sian O'Gorman was born in Galway on the West Coast of Ireland, grew up in the lovely city of Cardiff, and has found her way back to Ireland and now lives on the east of the country, in the village of Dalkey, just along the coast from Dublin. She works as a radio producer for RTE.

Follow Sian on social media:

facebook.com/sian.ogorman.7
twitter.com/msogorman
instagram.com/msogorman
bookbub.com/authors/sian-o-gorman

ABOUT BOLDWOOD BOOKS

Boldwood Books is a fiction publishing company seeking out the best stories from around the world.

Find out more at www.boldwoodbooks.com

Sign up to the Book and Tonic newsletter for news, offers and competitions from Boldwood Books!

http://www.bit.ly/bookandtonic

We'd love to hear from you, follow us on social media:

facebook.com/BookandTonic
twitter.com/BoldwoodBooks
instagram.com/BookandTonic

Printed in Great Britain
by Amazon